VANESSA'S DAY

There was a woman named Vanessa, and nobody around her knew what she was or who she was; every single one of them saw her in a different light, and they all hated her because they could not break her down and make her into something they could understand. But she didn't care, she hardly knew they existed. She was waiting for The Day.

The Seasons Hereafter

Elisabeth Ogilvie

AVON
PUBLISHERS OF BARD, CAMELOT, DISCUS, EQUINOX AND FLARE BOOKS

AVON BOOKS
A division of
The Hearst Corporation
959 Eighth Avenue
New York, New York 10019

First Avon Printing, December, 1969
Third Printing, November, 1972

The Seasons
Hereafter

CHAPTER ONE

On an afternoon in April, when rags of dirty snow twisted about the blackened tree trunks and the wind off the wrinkled gunmetal harbor blew in chilly puffs between the buildings, Vanessa walked home from the public library with five books in each arm. She passed among the smuts and dreariness as if none of it existed, or as if she herself were invisible; by the grimy variety store on the corner, the service station, the Harborview Hotel (two rooms to let over a bar); through the children, including the retarded one who was fastened on a long chain let out of a ground-floor window. He sat all day on a box digging in the mud with a spoon, while the others swirled shrieking around him in a vortex of vituperative energy.

She crossed General Mattox Square, a sad triangle of wiry barberry and turfless soil tramped stone-hard. In a puff of wind her open raincoat flew out, and one hem brushed the granite shaft with the bronze plaque that no one had read since the Mayor did, aloud, on the day it was dedicated in 1880. On the other side of the barberries she was on Water Street, and she drew a long breath and lifted her sleepwalker's face to the dense black tangle of elm boughs that arched the street. The elms had been set out when the shipyard and limestone gentry inhabited Water Street, before the days when General Mattox Square was dedicated, with the Grand Army Veterans all out and the town band playing "The Battle Hymn of the Republic."

Gulls flew over the elms then as now, slanting white against the dark clouds, their voices lost in the noise rising up from the city. Vanessa's eyes, yellow-gray under the thick ginger bang and the strong eyebrows, contemplated the gulls and not the sordid destiny of Water Street a hundred years after the planting of the elms. As if by extrasensory perception, she avoided holes in the pavement, other walkers, and trash spilled across uneven bricks. She walked on with her gaze uplifted, the end of

7

her pony tail bouncing lightly between her shoulder blades. The man's black raincoat was too large and blew out around her like a cloak, her white sneakers were wet and dirty, and the edges of the narrow-legged jeans rubbed harshly against her bare ankles.

As if she had been secretly counting her steps, she came to a stop by a lamp post, lowered her chin, and looked straight ahead. At that instant a mass of slate-colored cloud opened to let the sun shed a sudden pale light on Vanessa's house, turning its dampness into a luminous mist that obscured the scars and stains of the façade; for this moment the house stood in stately radiance behind the elms. The sight warmed her even down to her chilled feet and into the numbed fingers cramped around the books. The jungle dooryard beyond the broken iron palings took on an artful confusion, as if it had been landscaped, and the fanlit door and long front windows displayed their perfection with no suggestion of what lay behind them.

The door under the fanlight was scaly and pitted, but she kept the hinges oiled so that it moved with a rich ease she enjoyed. In the hall she ignored the smell of old plumbing, and moved lightly past closed doors and the staircase to the kitchen at the back of the house. She shifted her books again, dredged the key out of her hip pocket with two fingers, and unlocked the door. Inside, she kicked the door shut behind her, and she was home.

She dropped the books to the square table, flexed her arms, and looked about her with a small indulgent smile at the exposed pipes, the soapstone sink and set tubs, the pine wainscotting nearly black with varnish and dirt, and the massive black range, behind which an oil jug gulped noisily at regular intervals. Against an outside wall were a primitive gas stove and an early Frigidaire. The walls and ceiling were darkened by years of smoke and cooking, and the thick screen of overgrown shrubbery outside the windows shadowed the room into early dusk. Dirty dishes were piled on the drainboard and in the sink, and there were little heaps of cigarette ashes here and there on the top of the stove.

Still smiling, Vanessa pushed a dented and grease-filmed teakettle over the burner flame and took a mug from the cupboard over the sink. She turned on the pin-up lamp hung between the windows and over the table, took a teaspoon from the cluster standing in an old pressed-glass cream pitcher, and measured out instant coffee from the jar always kept there along with sugar, canned milk, vinegar, pencils, and nonfunctioning ballpoint pens. Several crushed cigarette packages containing one or two cigarettes lay beside empty match-folders, the last electric-light bill, a small gray egg-shaped rock, a twig of forsythia she'd brought in from the back yard to force and had forgotten. It had been lying there for a week. The rock had been there longer. She didn't know why that was there.

Vanessa was thirty, and tall. The thick hair, ginger brown, brushed tightly back over her skull and fastened into a pony tail, would have seemed an affectation except that she was unaware of it. She hadn't cut her hair for a long time, and simply hauled it back hard to get it out of the way. She had worn it like that for fifteen years, as she had lived in jeans, sneakers, and men's shirts except for the period when her foster mother made her wear dresses and proper shoes to school. At this moment, as she drifted about the gloomy kitchen, she could have been still the tall bony fifteen-year-old. The poor light softened her features, her long mouth was young with pleasure, the cat-colored eyes above the sharp cheekbones were mysterious with the luminosity of quiet water.

Whenever she came near the table she touched the books with nervous, sinewy hands. Suddenly she seized one and opened it and became instantly hypnotized by the print. She stood entranced until she was freed by the noise of the kettle boiling. Hurriedly she took a thick heel of bread from the box, spread it with margarine and jam, and poured hot water over the coffee in the mug.

She dragged a chair across the aged linoleum and settled herself, the books about her plate and mug like ramparts. There was the long ineffable moment of delicious indecision, fingers hovering over one binding and then another. She finally opened one book and propped it against the others. As definitely as if a soundproof door had swung shut behind her and locked, she had left this world.

CHAPTER TWO

"I'm glad she's a bookish young one," her foster mother used to say. "Rather a book than a boy any time, that one, and Lordie, I'm some thankful! It's books or being down at the shore with Ralph, and let me tell you, I don't say a word when she comes in stinking with bait."

She never said much anyway. The Bearses were sparse with words, middle-aged when they took her at a bony long-legged twelve. She had never been a cuddly, confiding child; she had never learned to be in her long hegira from one foster home to another. The Bearses were not demonstrative, but neither were they naggers, and after her first meal at their table and her first night in the neat plain room that was not shared with anyone else, she made up her mind she wasn't going to be moved from this place.

There was a wary respect on all sides. She knew what the general opinion was of state wards, and though she watched the boys at school she had nothing to do with them. If one approached her, she ignored him, suspecting that he thought she was loose because she was somebody's mistake.

Sometimes a girl was genuinely friendly, and she was invited to come to Sunday School, and join the Girl Scouts or the 4-H. Mrs. Bearse insisted on Sunday School, but said she could suit herself about the others. Vanessa hadn't ever wanted to be a Scout or a 4-H member. She felt that she had nothing in common with those girls; besides, if you were a state ward it was better to start early being a loner. She went to Sunday School by herself, decently dressed even to gloves, and read "The Song of Solomon" behind her quarterly. *Behold, thou art fair, my love. . . .*

"Are you happy here, Anna?" Miss Foster asked.

"Yes, Miss Foster."

"Mrs. Bearse seems satisfied too."

Vanessa knew Miss Foster was always glad to get this visit over with. Vanessa wasn't one of her problems, but neither was she one of the easy ones. Some perversity always took hold of her whenever anyone turned full attention on her, and she became blank and wooden. Dismissed, she sped to the shore, and as she ran, her thoughts followed a familiar pattern. *There was this girl . . . Vanessa . . . and she was fourteen, and everyone thought she was a state ward. Even Miss Foster thought she was, because everyone had to believe it; positively everyone, so nobody could give away the secret. It was absolutely important that nobody should know who she really was. Even she couldn't know, until The Day.*

What had been the dining room in the old glory of the house on Water Street was Vanessa's and Barry's bedroom. She rented out the front and back parlors, and it was from the back parlor that the shuddering crash came. Brutally it knocked her out of the clear icy air around the convent in the Himalayas where the eagles flew level with the lawn. She sat staring across the kitchen until there was a thump and a yelp. Then she got up and went to the back-parlor door, where she beat her fist against the panels. Nothing moved inside, so she opened the door. The smell of cheap gin, stale cigarette smoke, a kerosene heater, sweat, and dirty clothes, was thick as a wall. She said coldly through it, "What's going on?"

"Oh-oh!" The woman giggled through her fingers splayed across her lips. She was dumpy and frowzy, her housewifely print ripped on one shoulder. She rolled her eyes foolishly at Van and kept giggling. Van pushed her hands into her hip pockets and sighed. "Where's Brig?"

"What do you think he tried?" asked the woman, suddenly prudish. "And him old enough to be my father!"

"I doubt that," said Van. "Brig!" He rose from the floor on the other side of the bed and hauled himself up by the ornate headboard. He was bald and stubby, chinless, wet-eyed, his belly sagging out in the grimy undershirt over unbelted pants. He looked pitifully at Vanessa.

"It's not what you think. We was just having a sociable little drink."

"I know your sociable little drinks. Remember what I told you the last time. And there's not a place in town that'd rent you a room."

Brig hung miserably to the headboard. "White slaver!" the woman spat at him and began looking around for her

11

coat. "Honest," she appealed to Van. "I never *dreamed* when I come in with him. He seemed a real nice gentlemanly fellow, the kind a girl could feel safe with."

"Oh, rats," said Vanessa. She stood aside and the woman minced out, giving her head a haughty toss as she passed Van. On the way through the hall she stopped outside the front-parlor door, then looked back and saw Van watching her. She tossed her head again and went out.

Brig snuffled wretchedly. "If you throw me out where'll I sleep tonight?"

"I'm not throwing you out tonight. But you've got no more chances, you understand?"

"Yeah, yeah." He began to weep. Vanessa thought with a keen pain of the thin pure air and the eagles, Kanchenjunga's snows rosy with sunrise. She slammed the door on Brig and started back to the kitchen, just as the big front door swung open and one of her upstairs lodgers came in.

"Hi, Van." The woman leaned on the newel post and looked tiredly up the stairs. She worked at the Harborview Bar; she was in her late forties and had a bleached, prim prettiness, but there were lines in her face from bad hours and tired feet. "You talked Mooney into swapping rooms with me yet?" she asked, with a longing glance back toward the front-parlor door. Television began to blare behind it.

"Mooney and I don't talk." Vanessa gave her a small smile and went back to the kitchen as Brenda began wearily to climb the stairs.

Outside the kitchen, the dusk thickened. The back yard became a jungle, dense and impenetrable except for cats. Vanessa read on in the island of light from the pin-up lamp. The oil bottle gurgled, the ancient refrigerator heaved into asthmatic life, there was a persistent drip in the black sink, and faint scratchings and rustlings inside the cupboards. She heard, yet did not. In the three years that they had lived here, rent-free because their presence kept the house from being ripped to pieces or burned down by vandals, she had grown used to the house's sounds. She didn't stir until the back door was flung open and Barry came into the kitchen in his work clothes and rubber boots, his oilclothes over his arm.

She saw him as if from a great distance, blinking

dreamily. He put a newspaper-wrapped package on the dresser. "Caught a big haddock in one of my traps today," he said. He kicked off his rubber boots and stood them beside the stove. He contemplated the emptiness of the stove and then the alarm clock on the mantel shelf. It had stopped. He grunted something and went in his stocking feet to the sink to wash. Vanessa returned to her book, and instantly his motions and noises became as insignificant to her as the others had been.

When he pulled out a chair opposite her and dropped into it, she saw him as if he had just come in. "Oh. What time is it?"

"Suppertime. Not that it means anything to you." He said it without malice. "Did you hear about the haddock?"

"What haddock?"

He laughed outright. There was a boyish delight in it, as if he'd caught her with an April Fool joke. In fact, as he sat opposite her, in the softening meld of shadows and yellow light he could have been a high school boy—snub-nosed, twinkling-eyed, square-chinned, his fair hair cut short as it had always been since she first knew him in grade school. Her gaze dropped back to her book, and the arrival of the General, riding up to the door of the convent with a hawk on his wrist.

A hand reached across the table and snapped the book shut. Rigidly she faced Barry, but before she could speak he leaned toward her and his smile had changed. "I've got something to tell you. You want to start supper while I talk, or will you sit right there?"

"You'd better get it over with. I don't know if I'll get supper or not."

"All right, we'll go over to the Harborview and celebrate."

"With what and for what?" Why couldn't he come and go and leave her alone? A new thought stabbed her. "Did you tramp across the lilies of the valley when you came in?"

"No, I did not. Come on, loosen up, honey, you're stiff as a cat in a pan of ashes." He laughed at that, and when she didn't move he sat back and took out cigarettes. "I've got a job. *The* job. No more fubbing around with a leaky boat and a handful of traps where everybody and his brother's got traps. God, how I hate this place and always did." He sprawled back luxuriously and blew smoke at the ceiling. "This waterfront, this stinking old tomb of a house—"

"You agreed when I got the place that it was better than those two rooms over the garage."

"Anything would be better than that. And I told you before, honey," he said winningly, "you did a good job talking Burrage into letting us move in here. Not many women could walk cold into a lawyer's office and put up a deal like that, and carry it through. But we've been here three years, and you ought to be as sick of it as I am." He leaned toward her, his eyes bright as sunlit water in his red-brown face. "And this time *I've* done it, the way it should be. We're going to be all right, Van. For the first time since we left home we're going to be all right."

"Mooney's got you that job on the dragger." Her heart began to beat faster, she came wonderfully alive. Ten days out and ten days home. Every other ten days she wouldn't have to get meals, think of his clothes, listen to him talk. "Listen," she said fervently, "if you haven't enough cash to join the union I've got some of the rent money saved up. I can let you have that."

He was shaking his head, a child bursting with a secret. "This is better than the dragger could ever be! This is a whole new start in a new place. You ever hear of Bennett's Island? Sure you have. Remember back home, some Bennett's Island boats used to tie up in the harbor when they came to the mainland?"

She remembered, but not willingly—not with an eagerness to flesh out the memory. When she married Barry, after the Bearses moved to Florida, it had been in the belief that Seal Point would be home forever. Neither of them had anticipated his family's fury; and Van hadn't realized that Barry didn't even own his boat and gear, so that when his father put him out he had nothing. One thing to which she hadn't become indifferent in twelve years was Barry's use of the word *home*. As always when she felt threatened her fingers twitched toward a book, but Barry had drawn it away from her, so she folded her hands tightly and waited with resignation for this to be over with.

"Almost unlimited fishing grounds, if you can imagine such a thing. When you see 'em sometimes on Main Street, it's like looking at Rockefellers. At least it is for somebody like me, the way I've been living from hand to mouth for so long." He was all ablaze, even his voice sent off sparks. "Well, I was over at the factory dock today, trying to get some bream cuttings for bait, and Simmy introduced me to this big guy standing around with a pipe in his mouth and his hands in his pockets. Turns out he's Philip Bennett from Bennett's Island."

"Did you kneel and bang your head on the wharf three times?" She hated Barry's capacity for admiration.

Barry grinned. "Nope, but I felt like it after he said he was looking for a man to work for him, and Simmy recommended me."

"Work doing what? Chore boy? Baiting up?"

"Fish for twenty per cent! My God, girl, they each run eight hundred, a thousand traps out there!" He sprang out of his chair and walked rapidly around the kitchen, waving his arms. "Do you *realize*—right out of a clear sky like that too—why, half these ginks fubbing around the waterfront would give their eyes for a chance like that!"

She kept her eyes on her laced fingers. "When do you go?"

"I can go out on the next boat. You come as soon as you can talk to Burrage and get packed."

"Are you *crazy?* I'm not going anywhere! I'm settled here."

"Honey, there's a nice house out there for us, away from this stink and these—these—" He ran out of words, but his gestures took in the house and its tenants. "It's clean out there, lots of green grass and woods, a place for a garden—it's like home, Van," he pleaded.

"If you're so homesick you could've gone back anytime. They'd have been delighted. Angela's married now, but they'd have picked out someone else for you."

He sagged onto the edge of the table. "I thought you'd be tickled foolish. Do you know what I can make out there?"

"Well, go on out and make it. I'm not stopping you. I've never stopped you."

"No, that's right," he said. "That's the truth. You've never stopped me. If you saw me about to take poison by mistake, you wouldn't stop me either, would you? It's a funny thing, Van. I always admired you. Back in school before you'd give me a look, I liked the way you walked and held your head and stuck out your chin, as if you

15

didn't give a damn." He spoke with a kind of reverence. "Even when all hell broke loose when we got married, I was proud because of the way you went ahead and took what you wanted. And even the way we've lived since— even if I couldn't be too proud of myself—when I see you coming along the street I'm still proud of you. You read highbrow stuff and understand it. You *think* different from other women. Fancy houses and new clothes don't matter to you, you still don't give a damn. But Van," he said, and his voice cracked. "I'd like you to give one little damn for me."

They looked at each other silently. Then she said "Damn," and they both grinned. He reached out and took hold of her pony tail. "Come on, Van," he whispered. "Let's go away. We could start all over again. We could think about kids, we—"

"I don't have to start all over again. This is my home and my life." At the thought of being uprooted she was physically ill, her stomach roiling. But nobody could uproot her, least of all Barry. She didn't ever have to be afraid of anything Barry could do.

He was halfway across the kitchen, grabbing up his cap and jacket on the way. He slammed the back door behind him. She thought of the new green spears under the dining-room window. If he tramps on them, she thought, if he does . . . But already she was reaching for her book. In a few moments she would forget that he had been there.

CHAPTER THREE

Mooney thrust into the kitchen without knocking and pulled on the overhead light. Dazed, she swung in an abyss between Kanchenjunga and Water Street, staring at first without recognition at the grinning mask in the white glare from above.

"The Sleeping Beauty," he said. "What do you find in those pages that's better than life?"

"Something that's better than life," she said. "Put off

16

that light." He did, and came to the table looking more human, a broad-shouldered stocky man with a strong freckled face and thick hands. He took hold of her chin and wagged her head back and forth. Stony, she didn't please him by resisting. He let her go and sat on the edge of the table.

"Where's your other half?"

She shrugged.

"You mean he's not in yet? God, it's after eight and blowing like a man out there. You can't hear anything in this morgue, but it's keening around my window like a banshee."

"Oh, he's been in," she said vaguely. "After eight, you said?" She leaned past him to see the clock.

"It's a wonder you saw him."

She got up and went to push the teakettle forward on the stove. She was ravenous now. She saw the fish on the dresser and remembered Barry's voice saying something about a haddock. She put it in the refrigerator and looked to see what she could eat right away. There was not much there besides eggs. Sometimes she had an urge to cook, to make hearty stews and meatloaves, and bake sweet things, but she hadn't had such an urge for a long time. Behind her Mooney said, "I suppose a bookworm's better than a rummy wife or a nympho. What's the matter, isn't he man enough for you, kid? You too scared to step out?"

He was close behind her and she hadn't heard him coming. She stood with the frying pan in one hand and two eggs in the other, tensed for the hand on hip or arm, but it didn't come.

"I thought you were getting him a job on a dragger," she said quite naturally.

"I did. Didn't he tell you? No, he turned it down today. If that ain't some notional son of a bitch."

"He turned it down?" She slammed the frying pan onto the stove. "Are you lying to me?"

"I am not." He laughed and spread out his arms in a gesture of surrender. "So don't I get A for effort? A reward for my good intentions?"

"Sure," she said with a cold little smile. "Brenda was looking hungrily at your room this afternoon. Next time I'll let her have it."

"What've you got to be so snotty about?"

17

"Oh, get out," she said in a bored one.

He swung his arm up as if to strike her with the back of his hand, then called her a bloody bitch and went out of the kitchen. She locked the door behind him. Then she fried the eggs and ate them with bread and butter and coffee. She wanted to go on reading *Black Narcissus,* but she had been reached from the outside—the wound was too deep. Mooney had got the job for Barry, and Barry had slyly refused. If she'd known, when he came in with his eyes lit up as if he were a five-year-old just given a ride on a fire engine ... Let him go, she thought in a fury. Straight out to the Promised Land and lick the Bennett boots, gurry and all. I don't need him. If I ever thought I did, I got over the notion within six months.

Now she abhorred the kitchen and took her book into the bedroom. The room smelled fresh and clean because she kept the windows open most of the day, but it was a jumble of everything—clothes heaped on chairs, the bureau top a solid clutter, candy papers and ashtrays everywhere, the floor littered with objects dropped and never picked up again. At Vanessa's side of the bed a chair was loaded with books and magazines. One day she would clean the room with such a passionate loathing of untidiness that even a wrinkle in the quilt could cause her acute pain, but until then she would be oblivious of the mess and move through it without seeing or disturbing it, like a cat.

She settled in bed to finish her book and start a new one. In June she would smell the lilies of the valley when she went to bed. She would begin to spend her days in the yard then, in the undersea light of the green grotto she'd made under the immense old trees and among the thick lilacs and syringas. Neither Barry nor Mooney existed in this leafy world, no one but Vanessa.... *There was a woman named Vanessa, and nobody around her knew what she was or who she was; every single one of them saw her in a different light, and they all hated her because they could not break her down and make her into something they could understand. But she didn't care, she hardly knew they existed. She was waiting for The Day.*

Vanessa never let herself go any farther than this. It was a condition imposed upon herself at the age of twelve, when she had first realized that The Day was to come. She had made the rule then that she should never

18

try to imagine what. The Day would bring—she must never wonder or guess. She would recognize it when it came, or when she came to it.

Barry was sitting on the edge of the bed, heavy against her legs, and she was trying to hold up her eyelids and focus on him. In the lamplight she began to see that his face was red and he had been drinking. She was befuddled herself from deep sleep. His voice came fuzzily as if through layers of cloth over her ears.

"Listen," he said. "We're going out there, you hear me? I've been thinking all night."

"Drinking and thinking," she said. "That's a rhyme if you take it in time. Who do you think you're sweeping off their feet?"

"Don't like it, do ye?" he jeered. "You're supposed to do all the sweeping. Like when you told me we better get married quick. My mother wanted tests made but you convinced me that was an insult. No, it had to be done *your* way, because you knew damn' well there wasn't any baby, didn't you? And when I found that out, you went on with your little sweeping jobs so I wouldn't have time to think. Everybody told me you'd ruin me and I told 'em to go fly a kite, but now by God I believe 'em!"

"They threw you out, I didn't." She yawned. "You could have gone back any time you wanted, as long as you left me behind. Why didn't you?"

"Because you were my wife. Because I still thought I was a goddam lucky bastard to get somebody with so much class." He laughed and shook his head. "Goddam *foolish* bastard, some folks said. But I believe a man has a duty to his wife."

"Consisting of what? Parking her in shacks while he digs clams or cuts pulpwood? We never had any real home till I got this place for us."

Suddenly the fury went out of him and he became small and crumpled. "It's like I told you before," he pleaded. "I know I haven't been much, I guess I wasn't much to begin with even if you thought so, and it knocked the guts out of me when the old man turned me out. But I've got this chance to take care of you the way I should've been doing all along, and make up to you for all the hard times."

"Look," she said patiently. "You go. I'm not stopping you. You start your new life, but I'm staying here."

"How'll you live?"

"I've got my rents and I can get a job."

He hooted. "Think you can hold it any longer than you held the others? You were always too damn good, remember? Low company in the sardine factory, stupid company in the stores, and a bunch of lechers in all the restaurants. Shorthand and typing bored hell out of you in high school, and I thought that showed how much spirit you had. I still like your spirit, Van," he said desperately. "Don't get me wrong! But it doesn't seem to do much for us, does it?"

"I suit me," she said. "Go to bed, Barry. Or go somewhere. Just stop trying to change my mind."

"You can knit twine like hell," he argued, "and there's not many women want to do that nowadays. Out there you'd have all the trapheads and baitbags you could handle, and make yourself a damn good penny."

"Out there, out there," she mocked him.

He leaned over her suddenly and tried to kiss here, and she drove him off with her hands against his chest. He held her wrists, but she turned her face away when he tried to rub his against it. "It's been like this for too long," he muttered. "And it's been plain hell for me, but I never thought you were saving it for somebody else. If you don't go with me now, that's what I'll think. You asked Mooney to get me that job, didn't you? What'd you promise him?"

"I promised him nothing! I wouldn't have his paws on me, or anybody else's! Now get out and leave me alone."

He released her and stood up. For a moment he looked down at her, and then went around the foot of the bed and out of the room, closing the door very quietly. She was surprised to find herself shaking. It had been a long time since anything so violent had arisen between them. She felt like shouting after him, I *will* get a job! I'll show you! But as she reached for her book she was able to comfort and calm herself by thinking, But I won't need to go to work and mix with those people, because he'll never go away from here without me. That was just the cheap liquor talking. Barry'd be afraid to do anything without me. He doesn't hate me; he just hates his dependence on me.

Pleased by her logic, she could almost believe that the violence had never occurred, and she read until she fell asleep again.

CHAPTER FOUR

She knew when she woke up that Barry hadn't been in bed all night. It wasn't the first time that he'd slept in damp blankets in the little cuddy of his boat; he'd come home with a streaming cold, and be sheepish and sorry. The sun was shining, and a strong wind tore at the tree tops and sent the slaty clouds bellying along. The restless brilliance of the day penetrated the house, and Vanessa was affected as cats and children are. Stimulated by the prospect of Barry's repentance, she felt a powerful urge to clean and cook. When he showed up she would have a proper meal ready, hot water for a bath, clean clothes. The Bennett's Island myth would have dissolved overnight, and would never be mentioned again.

She made a chowder with the haddock, and baked a custard pie. Then she began to tidy the bedroom. Its shabbiness offended her today, and she decided to take some of the saved-up rent money and buy paint and new curtains. As she filled a box with rubbish, the old-fashioned doorbell jangled in the kitchen, and she left off with annoyance; she wanted to work fast and hard until she was finished, she couldn't bear to be interrupted. In a rage she ran through the front hall and pulled open the front door. Mr. Burrage was on the doorstep.

Her rage went as they smiled at one another and exclaimed "Good morning!" Mentally she reviewed the house behind her; silence from Mooney's room, Brig long since stumbled out in search of breakfast, the roomers quiet upstairs. "Come into the kitchen," she invited. "You're just in time for a cup of coffee." She hoped Barry wouldn't show up in the middle of the visit, looking as if he'd been dragged through a knothole.

"No coffee," Mrs. Barton," the lawyer said as he fol-

lowed her down the hall. "I can't stay long enough. . . .
These old places smell, no matter how well you take care
of them, don't they? But this was a great house in its
day."

"It still is for me," said Vanessa. "It's still the most
elegant house in Limerock. Won't you sit down?"

"Only for a moment." He was graying and soldierly,
with a shrewd youthful eye and a taste in clothes that
always gave her pleasure and a sense of luxury. "Good
Lord," he exclaimed, "how do you stand this kitchen?"

She laughed. "I'm very fond of it. It has real charm. I
was never in love with these modern kitchens, they look
too cold and heartless."

He seemed preoccupied as he offered her a cigarette
and lit it. "How's your husband doing?"

"Pretty well. The lobsters are starting to come now. But
better than that, he's got a chance to go out on one of the
Universal Seafoods draggers."

"Fine, fine! Nice chap, Barry."

"How about a piece of fresh custard pie?" she asked.

"No, no, I couldn't." With an air of having suddenly
come to a decision, he crushed out his cigarette. "Mrs.
Barton, I don't like the news I'm bringing, because I know
how much you love this house. But change comes to all of
us, and you're young, so it's good for you, and necessary."

She felt a sick shivering in her and couldn't control her
facial muscles; she felt that her chin was shaking and her
mouth loose as she faced him. "It's about the huh—huh—"
She could not say *house*. She could only try, and hate him
for his obvious pity as he took the word away from her.

"Yes, the house. The estate has sold this land and the
parcel across the street. The house will be torn down, and
new buildings put up, four-apartment houses. If you'd
like, I'll give your name to the new owner so you can get
one of the flats—they'll be moderate in rent."

The kitchen was quiet, and yet his words seemed to
come through a great deal of interference. "You have two
weeks' notice," he went on. "I wish it could be longer, but
I heard about this only yesterday. The heirs conducted the
business in Boston," he said dryly. He stood up. "If I were
you I'd waste no time getting settled somewhere else, at
least until the new places are ready. It's not pleasant to
see anything old knocked down—a tree, a house, or a

22

man." He touched her arm lightly. "I'll let myself out, and you'd better have that coffee."

She was humiliated to think that she looked upset. "Oh, I was just thinking of my lodgers," she said airily. She walked down the hall with him. "They'll survive, I imagine. They were getting to be a bother, anyway."

She said goodbye like a hostess and went back to sit by the kitchen table, her knees drawn up and her body hunched over them as if to shelter a deep pain. She tried to think, but she could not. Wherever she looked she saw something to push her mind further into chaos. She was aware of a great formless fury, like a black cloud mass blotting out light and landscape, directed against the company of destroyers and murderers. Distantly she heard someone rap at the kitchen door. She didn't move, and heard footsteps going away, and a mutter of voices; Brenda going to work had just encountered Mooney on the way out, and they would walk up Water Street together, unaware.

She was still sitting there when Barry came in. He stood by the table looking down at her. "You sick?" he said finally.

"Cramps."

"Oh." He waited, and she gazed at his rubber boots. Now she felt neither kindness nor hatred for him. After a moment of silence he said politely, "Well, I don't like to bother you when you don't feel good, but I'm going to Bennett's Island on the mailboat tomorrow. If you want to come along with me or on the next boat, I'll be pleased to have you. If you don't want to, I'm going anyway."

"All right," she murmured. The boots moved away from the table toward the sink, and she knew by the sounds that he was stripping to the waist to wash and shave. This calm and positive Barry wasn't the man she'd expected home, but by now she was too numb to be affronted. Let him go, she thought, let him go, and for an instant she was dazzled by the old vision of all the hours in the day completely hers. Then she remembered that the house was dying, and she had nowhere to go. She stared at Barry's back as he leaned over the sink, splashing cold water onto his skin. She wouldn't even have the rents now. She swallowed and swallowed, trying to raise enough saliva to wet her throat, so that her voice would not break rustily.

"I've been thinking all night, Barry. I think I'd like to go out there." Any faint quaver could have been caused by the cramps.

He stopped splashing and was motionless, still bent over the sink. "Change comes to all of us," she said. "Sometimes it's good for us, and necessary." Her long mouth twisted. "I've got lazy, that's all."

He straightened up, reaching for the towel, and dried his head. His face was flushed and happy. "You won't be sorry, Van, I promise you! Kee-rist! I haven't been this happy since I was ten years old and got my first skiff!"

And you look about ten, she thought in contempt. She shut her eyes and he said penitently, "Hey, I forgot about your guts-ache. I'll fix you a good hot cup of tea. Want something in it? Mooney's always got a bottle—"

"He's gone out. No tea, Barry, thanks. I guess I'll go lie down a while and plan out what I have to do."

CHAPTER FIVE

She was relieved because the house was the last one around on the far side of the harbor, with a high point of yellow rock and spruces rising up beyond the northwest windows. It could have been one of the cluster near the store, where you couldn't even cross the yard to the toilet without being observed. The nearest neighbors over here were some fifty yards away, but she was still angrily conscious of them, as burnt flesh is conscious of heat; the girl was forever running out onto her husband's wharf for something, or into her windy dooryard to hang up clothes, or sitting on the front steps reading while her children played. She had a short yellow haircut like a dandelion head, and her children were miniatures of herself.

In the house there was too much light, waves of light lapping across walls and ceilings so that even if you lay down and refused to look out, the harbor was with you just the same, glimpsed past the corner of your book, seen from the side of your eye, washing over your head. The windows were full of sky and clouds, gulls, and sometimes a black spatter of crows. The wind blew, and the sound of water was as unrelenting as the light; surf splashed on the rocks at the foot of the lawn and swashed around the spilings of the wharf. From the back windows upstairs she could look across swale and cranberry swamp to a long barrier beach where the seas rolled in and broke with a constant booming. The long dull thunder oppressed her. Back at Seal Point there had always been more calm days than wild ones, and then she'd loved rough weather, ranging the shores just out of reach of the surf like a sandpiper, greedily salvaging lumber, pot buoys, spare oars, fancy liquor bottles.

But this was different; here she was a prisoner. She could hardly bring herself to speak to Barry, who was too happy and too tired to notice. She loathed to the point of nausea the sound of his voice running on and on about new wonders. It seemed to her that one reason for his exhilaration was the belief that she couldn't live without him after all. If she could have trusted herself to speak composedly about it, she would have told him that she'd come only because the house was to be torn down; but that too would have been a triumph for him, because he knew how she felt about the house.

Now she hated Mr. Burrage, and saw his regret as false, put on to hide the fact that he was probably one of the investors in the new project. He was one of the destroyers. They were all trying to destroy her. . . . The cardboard cartons with their few belongings still stood in the kitchen. She had opened only the one holding her books. She had spoken to no one but Barry except at the time of her arrival, if you could call "speaking" the stiff nods and the barely audible murmurs to the people on the wharf and in the store. She had seen in their broad smiles and outstretched hands a mockery of her as a captive, and she had armored herself in proud silence.

"Where is the house?" she asked Barry. He pointed it out to her, directly across the harbor. She picked up the box of books by its string, but Barry caught up with her as she left the wharf. "Hey! Mrs. Phil wants us to come up there to dinner, she's got it all ready."

"You can go." The wind sliced through her raincoat,

sweaters, and slacks; it whipped her pony tail around past one cheek. "You can tell them I was seasick."

"You were never seasick in your life."

"There's always a first time." She started on. "Unless you want me to throw up in my plate and I promise you, Barry, I *will*."

"Oh, goddam," he growled, and then grabbed the box of books from her and put it under his arm. He walked behind her around the shore, past the fishhouses and wharves on one side and the village on the other. The road then passed along the brow of a pebbly beach where skiffs were drawn up, and where a man was coppering the bottom of a keeled-over boat. Across the road a marshy field began, bounded on the far side by a sea wall crawling along against the peculiar luminosity of the eastern sky. Gulls were rising and falling in slow high circles over the unseen water beyond the wall. The rough wind, pushing and slapping from every direction, was at once mild and chill and carried the wild acrid tang of open ocean and the birthplace of the long deep seas.

The man working on his boat waved his paint brush, and Barry shouted, "Hi there, Cap'n Foss. . . . Foss Campion," he explained importantly to Vanessa. "Hell of a nice guy. Awful moderate, though. He lives on our side too. Next is Terence Campion, he's his nephew." Not needing any response from her he led the way along a plank walk laid over the rolling beach stones past two low-roofed houses whose front yards were mostly granite ledge; yet they looked as settled and at ease as cats. Each was faced across the walk by a wharf and fishhouse. Vanessa saw no one—the women were at the store and the men all busy—but her skin prickled and the back of her neck seemed to feel the stare of curious eyes. And there was nowhere to hide.

When she saw children's toys outside the second house, her stomach twisted. She did not like to be close to children. But she needn't look at them. There was the point beyond the house, and twenty-five miles of ocean to be seen from the sunporch windows.

She stood in the kitchen, her ears ringing in the sudden relief from the noise outside. "All papered and painted new," Barry gloated. "Ain't this some bright after that smelly dark hole?"

She wanted to cover her eyes against the blaze of

yellow and white. "You can go back after the other stuff. I'll look around."

"The stove and refrigerator run on bottled gas," he said. "Later on we can have a generator if we want, and buy a television set. Hey, how about *that*, honey? The cistern's full for dishes and washing, and I lugged in fresh drinking water this morning. Got a big grocery order too. Look, I'll tell Mrs. Phil you're not feeling good, and you make us some coffee and sandwiches while I'm gone, huh?" His eyes took on a wet glisten; he said, more gently, "You're right, we should eat our first meal in this house alone together. My God, Van, but I'm happy." He almost choked. Then he was gone, boots thumping with happy arrogance, like the first rubber boots of a small boy. She sagged against the dresser and felt tears crawl burning into her eyes.

The next day she thought with grim humor, They never missed the fact that we moved out here with about two wheelbarrow loads of possessions done up in Campbell's Soup cartons. Now they know we're truly derelicts . . . She kicked the nearest carton and went away from it. The way she felt now, the stuff could sit there forever.

They had had meals of a sort yesterday—sandwiches and coffee at noon, and a mess of lobsters for supper. She'd been hungry in spite of herself. Barry did all the talking, used to her silences, and they had both slept as if stupefied. Then Barry was up and gone by daylight in the morning. Windy weather didn't hold up these men, because it was almost always windy out here and their boats were built for it.

Barry was learning the grounds, the currents, the shoals and ledges, before he was given a boat of his own. The chart that he'd been studying the night before was still on the kitchen table. She was drawn to it, but repulsed the temptation and went on prowling around the house, refusing to imagine Barry at work in his new world. She'd met Philip Bennett yesterday, but he was indistinguishable from the several other men who'd been on the wharf. She knew only that they were all bigger than Barry and burnished with the maddening superiority of men on their own ground. She had loathed Barry's eagerness among them and the way he'd used their first names.

Upstairs she stood at a back window, arms folded on

27

the middle sash, and stared hopelessly out at the long rollers crashing in on the barrier beach, whose dike of polished stones had been thrown up higher than the field behind it. The field was tawny with dead grass, and toward the east it ended at a set of white buildings at the foot of a wooded hill. Beyond the side of the hill she saw the eastern horizon, and suddenly the sea turned to a brilliant blue as the sky cleared. The winter-black spruces shone green, the houses were bathed in sunlight, and the dead field burned with an amber light. The dazzle pierced her through, but not with joy. She thought, I *could* get a job, I *could* hold it, and swung excitedly away from the window, only to remember that even now they might be starting to tear down the house.

As she stood there in anguish, someone knocked at the back door. She felt the blows on her flesh as she listened, her fingers laced so hard that they hurt. "Anybody home?" a woman's voice cried outside. The door was opened and the call repeated. Another voice said, "If she isn't in, we can leave these things on the table."

They would come in and see the shameful collection of unpacked cartons. They might make remarks which she would overhear, and then how could she ever live another day on the same island with them?

"Just a minute!" she called in a strong bright tone. She ran her fingers through the thick bang to fluff it up, tucked her shirt more neatly into her jeans. Then she ran downstairs and into the kitchen, her heart beating so fast that she felt out of breath.

"Hello!" A tall black-eyed woman stood smiling at her. Warm authoritative voice, strong handclasp. Vanessa thought, I'm suffocating. "We met yesterday but you were so wretched you hardly saw us," the voice went on. "I'm Joanna Sorensen, Philip's sister, and this is Philip's wife, Liza."

Van tried to smile in response; she was sure the effect was frightful, that she looked like a skull. "Won't you sit down?" she asked. "Come into the sunporch."

Mrs. Philip Bennett was shorter than either her sister-in-law or Van, her straight fair hair done in a low knot on her neck, her face almost classic in its oval serenity until she smiled, when something at once mischievous and passionate sparked in her brown eyes. "This paper is exactly right for this room, Jo," she said. "I refuse to be modest about it. Don't you think we did a good job?" She appealed to Van. "It's the first time I ever did any papering. Of course you've probably done it. I think every woman in Maine has, but I'm a New Yorker."

"Yes, she came down to rusticate and ended up married to a lobsterman. It was good luck for all of *us*, but poor Liza. She didn't know what she'd let herself in for."

"I worked on a fashion magazine, so I was in pretty good fettle," said Liza.

Van smiled politely. She was sweating. "You've got such a gorgeous view over here," Mrs. Sorensen said. "Of course if you didn't like the ocean it would be hellish, but Barry said you were used to the water. You both grew up in Seal Point, didn't you?"

Van nodded with difficulty, her neck felt so stiff. She wondered if Barry had told them she was a state ward. Mrs. Bennett said, "Philip likes Barry so much. He's not only enthusiastic, but he knows the business, and men like that are hard to find."

You're wondering why he was practically a waterfront bum if he knew so much about lobstering, Van thought. But it won't cost you anything to be nice to a couple of tramps while you wait to see if he's a drunk and she's a slut. . . . "I hope you like it out here, Vanessa," Mrs. Sorensen was saying. "Barry says you like being out of doors and you like to read, so you ought to do all right. You can always find somebody to go for a walk with you, and we're forever passing books around."

"And if you like to walk alone," said Mrs. Bennett, "you don't have to worry about bears and moose and stranglers, things like that." They both laughed and she heard her own laughter like an echo, and despised herself for joining in, for letting them think she was flattered and easily won over by their attention.

If they didn't get out soon she was going to fly apart. Their gay complacency was an evil-smelling and deafening fog in the room, so that Joanna Sorensen's words seemed actually obscured by it.

"The sewing circle's over at Hillside this week . . . my brother Owen's place . . . you can see it from your back windows . . . a good chance for you to meet everyone at one whack."

Van pushed her back against the back of her chair and willed her hands not to grip the arms. "I don't go around

29

much," she said. "I don't know if Barry told you that I'm kind of—I mean it's hard for me to meet a lot of people at once. I'd r-rather take my time." The slight stammer was genuine, and humiliating. She blushed, and Joanna Sorensen exclaimed at once, "You take your time, then. That's what we have plenty of, out here." She got up. "You've probably got lots of things to do that we hauled you away from. I must say you look a lot better than you did when you got off the mailboat yesterday. A trip across the bay aboard the *Ella Vye* in an easterly is enough to kill off for good any love you might have for the ocean."

"We brought you some things to help out with your baking while you're getting settled," said Mrs. Philip. "And if there's anything you need and can't find, just holler."

"Thank you very much," Vanessa said grimly, giving up the attempt to smile. She stood watching them go toward the next house. Barry can run around like a grateful mongrel, she thought, but I wasn't included in the deal.

The blonde girl came out as they reached her steps, and all three talked for a few moments, looking out across the harbor and now and then glancing toward her house. They're telling Dandelion-Head how stupid I am. Not a word out of me—not that they gave me the chance, they're so crazy about the sound of their own voices—and my trash still standing in the middle of the floor, and dishes in the sink. They'll probably take turns checking on me to see how I'm taking care of their goddam property.

Half-blind with tears, she pulled the man's raincoat off the hook and from habit picked up the book beside her coffee cup. The wrapped pans were on the dresser, and she wanted to hurl the whole business out over the rocks into the surf. But it was food and Barry could eat it; it would save her that much effort. She went out the back way and ran for the shelter of the point.

CHAPTER SIX

She cut behind the point, along the edge of cranberry bog to the high bank of stones, rockweed, and tide litter called Long Cove. She walked to the far end of the barrier beach, crossed an unused and rocky pasture, and discovered a thick stand of spruces with branches sweeping low to the ground. She lay on a sun-heated ledge there, reading and smoking, or watching the spring clouds move past the spruce tops and the high unhurried circling of gulls against them. When there were no boats hauling nearby she explored the shore. Broken sea-urchin shells and crab bodies littered the flat red ledges where the gulls fed. Damaged lobster traps, barnacled buoys and glass toggles, and wood in all forms—silver-smooth tree trunks, the side of a dory, odd shingles—lay about the rock entangled in masses of rockweed.

She returned again and again. Out here she could maintain a comforting sense of invisibility, and pretend, too, that the others on the island didn't exist. This was simple, because since her arrival she had talked with no one but the two women who had called. The next morning some psychic impulse had made her glance out toward the Campions'—a view which she usually avoided—and Dandelion-Head was coming with a covered plate and a coffeepot. She'd had just time to latch the back door and get upstairs, where she stood without moving and almost without breathing until the knocking stopped. After that, no doubt Dandelion-Head carried her treat over to the house on the other side and spent a happy hour telling her neighbor that Barry's wife was an oddball, and poor Barry, wasn't it a shame how such nice men got caught by such awful women.

One mild pearly day it began to rain while she was out. At first the drops were gentle and infrequent, and she didn't start home, but sat on the big shelves of rock, liking this emptiness smelling of deep water and of old rockweed rotting, and the sea pale and quiet for a change, with a flock of eider ducks talking and splashing a little way off shore. The crows and gulls were now used to her in her black raincoat, and walked near her on their foraging. It rained harder, the drops hissing on the satiny water, and then it rained very hard; she put her book under the raincoat and started back along the beach. It was impossible to run on the ridge of loose stones, and there was no shelter from the rain. The coat was no longer weatherproof, and her feet squelched in wet socks and sneakers. For the first time she thought of the house with some pleasure; it meant warmth and dryness, and no one would come calling in the rain.

Barry was in the kitchen. Expecting him to be out hauling, she stared at him open-mouthed and he stared back, biting at the inside of one cheek. Then she saw beyond him the other man sitting at the kitchen table with a mug of coffee. Rain ran down her nose and the back of her neck, but men never made her feel as nakedly self-conscious as women did. She reached for a towel, and the man smiled at her and pushed back his chair. "I hope you don't mind a couple of scavengers making free with your kitchen while your back's turned."

"Not at all, if you found something to scavenge," she said, drying her face. "I think that was the wettest rain I ever tried to hurry home through but couldn't."

"We never do anything by halves out here."

"So I've noticed." It was foolish, but they both laughed. She remembered him now from the first day, a big man, fair-haired but graying, with a rugged face.

Barry had been standing by in silence. He said in an oddly tight voice, "We came in with engine trouble, and I brought Phil home for a mug-up."

"We found some uncommonly good doughnuts," Bennett said.

"I'm afraid your wife made those," Vanessa answered, and they both laughed again. She peeled off her dripping raincoat and dropped it, and flipped the towel expertly into a turban. Barry leaned down and picked up the raincoat as if it were a loathsome object, and muttered, "You'd better change your clothes before you get cold."

She walked by the two men to the stairs. In a few minutes she heard them go out, and from where she stood drying her hair she saw them going along the boardwalk past the Campions', their yellow oilclothes gaudy in the pigeon colors of the day. Barry walked fast, as if he had a time clock to punch. Bennett was in no hurry, he kept looking around him. She wished she hadn't met him. It put her at a disadvantage, because Barry worked for him and he owned this house. He had a right to come into it, and she could say nothing about it. And never before had she come face to face with anyone for whom Barry had worked.

She was drinking coffee and reading at the kitchen table when Barry came home. He took off his oilclothes in the entry and hung them up, then he came into the kitchen and sat down on the woodbox to take off his rubber boots. "Find the trouble in the engine?" she asked amiably, without looking up from her book.

He didn't speak and she became lost in her story again. His voice came at last as a deadly surprise, a tidy and quiet knife between the shoulder blades. "Have you washed one dish or hung up one thing or wiped off that stove since you came into the house a week ago?"

"Since when have you been so house-proud?"

"Is that what you call it when I'd like to ask a man in for a mug-up and not find the house looking like a mare's nest? My God, I was never so ashamed in my life. Had to scratch some to find a clean cup, and if it hadn't been for his wife's cooking I'd have had nothing to offer him."

She sat back in her chair and studied him. Whether it was the dull light from outside she couldn't tell, but his skin had a grayish tinge and there were harsh shadows around his nose and mouth that were new; at least she hadn't noticed them before. *"Jesus,"* he said softly. "Here's a house better than we've ever had, all done up bright and clean, and you turn the place into a pigsty. Why, Van? Just tell me why. What makes you so goddam perverse?"

"What I do in this house is my own business."

"It's my business too. I'm supporting you, I've made more this week than I ever made in a month before. I got a right not to be shamed in the face and eyes of everybody here. On Water Street they were all trash. This is different."

"What's different about it?" she demanded. "They make more money, but at least on Water Street I didn't have to dodge and hide all the time to keep people's noses out of my life! Did your boss tell you I was a lazy bitch and I'd better keep his house better, or else?"

33

"He never said a word. Nobody's said anything but what's friendly," he protested. "But how long before they catch on to the way you go scooting out around the island in all kinds of weather like the law was after you? How long before they wonder if you've got anything else to wear but those pants and sneakers and that goddam raincoat? So help me, I'll tear that thing up into rags and burn it some day before you're out of bed."

She laughed and turned her back on him. His feet hit the floor behind her and he clutched her shoulder. "When are you going to start acting like a human being instead of a fugitive from a crazy house?"

"Take your hands *off*."

After a minute he did, and sighed heavily. "All right, I know how you hate that. But when you turn your back on me, that's what *I* hate, Van, and I've got a right to hate something, don't I? It don't have to be all on your side."

She pretended to ignore him, but the words on the page were senseless marks. "What do you have to have before you'll do your part out here?" he asked her in misery. "Just tell me, will ye? You can have the handling of the money, send off and get yourself all the clothes you want, magazines, books even——"

She shut her eyes and expelled a long loud breath. "I've done my part. I said I'd come, that's all. Nothing else. If none of the women get in here they won't know what a dirty house I keep. And if you don't bring any more men in for mug-ups, they won't know I don't spend my days cooking the way their perfect slaves do. If I don't go to any of their damned sewing circles and suppers they won't know what I wear. It's as simple as that."

He came around to face her, flushed and wild. "But it's different now! We're living among decent people, we got a chance to be respectable for once!"

"What do you want for dinner?" she asked, looking back at her book.

"I don't want any dinner." He went into the living room and threw himself down on the couch. She knew how he lay with his head buried in his arms. She used to wonder what he was thinking when he lay like this, and would sometimes feel compassion or even guilt, but indifference was better. Besides, there was nothing more to discover about Barry—she knew it all before they'd been married a year.

She was hungry even if he wasn't. She made a thick sandwich with canned corned beef, took more coffee, and carried the food upstairs. She settled herself in bed with a book, and after a while she heard Barry kicking the cartons and swearing, and then he slammed out. When his footsteps had died away, a wonderful velvety silence settled down. The rain had stopped, and there was no wind. The harbor was silvery and still; only the wakes of home-coming boats sent small delicate waves washing against the shores for a little while. Whenever the stillness returned it was with a new profundity.

The house was free of the mocking waves of light, and darkness pooled undisturbed in the corners under the eaves, creeping out into the room like soundless water sliding over flat sands that glimmered faintly in twilight. For the first time since Water Street she was wrapped in the security she had known there. She read, slept, waked in delicious safety to deeper darkness, slept again; woke to know it was really night and she was alone in the bed, alone in the house. She didn't know how she knew that— it was simply one of the facts of which she was certain. Carefully, she didn't rouse herself enough to wonder what time it was or where Barry was, but slipped into dark sleep again.

She awoke from a dream in which she was saying to someone, "I wonder if Lazarus really wanted to be hauled out into life again, blinking and dazed and stared at." She knew in the instant of waking that she was thinking of herself as Lazarus, for she lay blinking and dazed in a room she was positive she had never seen before. The white curtains and the blue-sprigged paper, the scent of cold coffee and stale corned beef so close to her face, the unpleasant constriction of the clothes in which she had slept—they were all alien and hostile. *She* was alien also. Her heart seemed to plunge about sickeningly under her ribs, into her stomach, and up into her throat. Sweat sprang out on her body; she thought she was going to vomit. She got frantically out of bed and saw through the window Western Harbor Point and the breakwater washed bronze and rose with the sunrise. A boat was going out by the breakwater, and the man was putting on his oilclothes, now and then touching the wheel.

It was Bennett's Island out there, and she was Anna. Annie. *Vanessa*. She said it aloud, in a hoarse dry whisper.

35

A door shut downstairs, followed by the unmistakable thumping of rubber boots on hard ground. Barry was going out. She heard his voice exchanging greetings with Terence Campion, who soon appeared on his own wharf, dinner box under his arm, and went down the ladder to his skiff. She crouched at the edge of the bed and watched Campion row out to his mooring, using the quick short strokes of the professional fisherman.

She felt filthy for sleeping in her clothes, and the room smelled of the uneaten food. She flung the bedclothes back over the foot and opened the windows, breathing deeply the cold oceany air. Carrying the tray of food downstairs, she wondered how long she had slept. It had been noon when she'd gone to bed. How could I have slept like that? she asked in frightened awe. How do I know this is the day after yesterday? It could be two days after. This set up the panicky lunging of her heart again until she realized that Barry would have been scared if she'd slept through a day, and wouldn't have left her alone. That would really have been a treat for the neighbors! she thought, trying for humor but not successfully.

She pulled off her clothes and washed herself roughly in cold water direct from the cistern, and rubbed her skin with a coarse towel until it hurt. When she was through she ran upstairs naked and put on clean underwear, jeans, and an unironed shirt of Barry's. She hadn't dried her sneakers yesterday, and didn't own another pair, so she put on thick woolen socks and Barry's moccasins. She brushed her teeth with brutal vigor, wondering how Lazarus's mouth had tasted, then loosed her pony tail and brushed her hair as if the act were a form of mortification. When her scalp was smarting and her eyes watering, she fastened the long mane tightly back, glad of the discomfort for something to anchor her to reality.

She put water on to heat for coffee, and a panful for dishes. While she waited she began setting the kitchen to rights. She couldn't even sit down to drink her coffee, but kept picking up the mug for a swallow and then going on to something else. She finished unpacking the boxes in which she and Barry had rummaged for what they wanted, then untied and unpacked the others. She ran up and down stairs, putting things in what she considered at this moment their proper places. There was Barry's .22 seven-shot rifle, a gift from his father on his twelfth

36

birthday. He hadn't used it, or even had shells for it, for a long time, but he kept it clean and wrapped in an old flannel shirt. She hung it on two pegs in the sitting room that must have held other rifles in the past. She had the few books she'd hung onto during all their moves, their handful of necessary papers which she kept filed inside her *Anthology of British and American Poetry;* a box of oddments including the cheap jewelry given her as presents by foster parents and by Barry, an initialed handkerchief with a lacy edge tatted by Mrs. Bearse, an imitation jade cigarette holder, buttons, an empty perfume bottle she'd had for so long she couldn't remember not having it. The last ghost of scent had gone. She used to think it had belonged to her mother, but now she couldn't remember why she had ever thought so. Still she held on to it. There was also a thick gold watch that Barry treasured because it had belonged to his great-grandfather. It didn't work, and they'd never had the money or the interest to take it to a jeweler and find out why.

In the last carton, wrapped in rough-dried shirts and work pants, were the objects she'd taken from Water Street. She'd found them when they'd moved in, hidden away in a corner of the attic that must have been too dark for the children who'd ransacked the rest of the house. She hadn't shown them to Burrage, for fear he'd insist on giving the relics to the heirs. She knew nothing of the value of such things, but these felt alive and responsive in her hands and she couldn't bear to part with them. Besides, since she had rescued them they were really hers. They comforted her now, as if she'd been able to bring fragments of the house's splendor with her; the green-flowered tureen with a lid, three square little glass sauce dishes that flashed rainbows when she washed them and set them in the sun, a small jug and sugar bowl, lilac-colored, with raised white figures that reminded her of a cameo brooch worn by someone in one of her foster homes. She couldn't remember the person or the house, only the brooch, and how she used to look at the cameo and long to run her finger over the miniature perfection of the profile. The intensity of that longing was remembered now like a flavor or a fragrance. The last treasure was an amber glass dish whose lid made it into a hen on a nest. She arranged them all on a sunny window sill and admired

37

them for a few moments, drinking luke-warm coffee. Then she set to work on the dirty dishes, the grease-filmed teakettle, the two stoves. It came to her as she scoured that Barry would think he had prodded her into this, but she couldn't stop even for that; she was rushed on as if by a fire at her heels. She took the braided rugs out into the light wind and shook them till her arms ached.

"Hi there!" somebody called, and she jumped. The blonde girl laughed and waved from under her clotheslines.

"Hi," Vanessa called back, and hurried into the house. Suddenly she was exhausted, but everything was done, upstairs and down. She was trembling and ravenous. She fried bacon and eggs and heated up two of Mrs. Philip's doughnuts, and carried a tray into the sunporch, where she ate by the windows. She was careful not to drop crumbs on the newly swept floor. As her trembling lessened, she was able to lean back and smoke a cigarette in something like peace.

Outside, the grass between the house and the shore was taking on a green shimmer. Sparrows ran over the rim of old rockweed and chips left on the turf from a winter storm. The changeable harbor seemed curiously empty and lifeless this morning in spite of the skiffs at the moorings and the gulls picking through the fresh wet weed on the ledges. It was as if an invisible tide had gone out with the men and wouldn't return until they did.

The children were in school, and one imagined the women static, transfixed in time until the men came home and gave them breath and significance again.

No wonder Barry's getting above himself, she thought wryly. This is a place for men, and he's drunk with the proposition. A new Barry is emerging and naturally the old Vanessa won't do.

He'd never before harassed her about being a solitary. Now it meant that she was crazy. How many times, in how many ways, had he flung it at her yesterday? She laughed aloud, and then an evil thing happened, choking the laughter off but leaving her with her mouth stretched open in a silent cry, *What if he's right?* The long sleep, the dream of Lazarus and the subtle terror of a small bright room not recognized and a self not known. It had lasted only a moment but it had happened; she couldn't deny it. What if it happened again?

She sprang up to escape, but where was the refuge from what lay in her head, what was implicit in her bones, the color of her eyes, the shape of her hands? As a child she used to wonder who her parents were, until she learned that it was a dangerous and futile sort of indulgence. A few times she had received a picture postcard from far off with a message scribbled in pencil and signed "Mama," telling her that she would see her next Christmas, and to be a good girl. But next Christmas never brought her, or even a card.

"She would have come if she could, Anna," Miss Foster said once. "I'm sure of that."

"Do you know *her?*" She was eight then, and had not learned not to ask questions which adults would not or could not answer.

"No, I don't," the visitor admitted. "We've tried to find her, Anna. Perhaps she won't let us find her because she's afraid. We do know your father is dead. He was a soldier and he died in the war."

"If you don't know my mother, how do you know she really wants to see me?" Anna persisted. "If she likes me so much, why did she leave me with that woman and never come back?"

"When you grow up, Anna, you will know that sometimes people aren't responsible for their actions. They can be sick in their minds as well as their bodies. If your leg is hurt you can't walk well. If your mind is hurt you can't think well."

"Is her mind hurt?"

"I don't know. It might be."

Later, when Anna was at the Bearses' and beginning to be Vanessa in her own mind, after a woman in a book, Miss Foster said—trying to pin her down to some serious thinking about her future—"I hated those postcards that came for you, Anna, because as long as they came, you weren't adoptable. And yet we couldn't trace her by those cards and talk to her about releasing you."

"Who'd ever have adopted me anyway?" the girl scoffed.

"You'd be surprised how many people are drawn to the sort of child you were. Well, that's all in the past now. You're almost grown-up and you can be a good-looking girl if you put your mind on it." Her humorous despair took in the blue jeans and the stripped-back mane of thick ginger-colored hair. "What's more important, you're an intelligent girl with a great many capabilities. You can build a fine life for yourself." She smiled. "I imagine you've given up the idea of being a lobster fisherman. Remember, when you were twelve or so?"

"I'd be one if somebody'd stake me to a dory and traps."

"I think you would, and do well at it too. If you were a boy there'd be some chance of it. But—" She shrugged, faintly regretful. "So you're raking blueberries this summer. That's fine. Toward the end of August we'll see about your clothes for school. Remember, if you get the marks I *know* you can get, there could be a scholarship at a business college for you, and that would be a really wonderful start."

"Yes," said Vanessa stolidly. Miss Foster was almost at the door before Van remembered her manners and unwound her legs from those of her chair and got up. Something bedeviled her. It was something she wanted to ask, yet could not frame the words fast enough, or bravely enough. Before she knew it the instant for asking had gone by, and she hadn't known how to break in later with the crude question, Did you ever find out about my mother? If she isn't dead, is she insane? Is she shut up in Bangor or Augusta?

CHAPTER SEVEN

Thirteen years later, on Bennett's Island, Vanessa leaned her cheek against the cold glass and shut her eyes. What if my mother is, or was, insane? she wondered. Suppose that everything about me, all my ways of being different, all my ways of letting them know I don't give a damn, all my strangenesses that I'm so proud of—suppose everything is a warning that I could go insane too? One great signpost pointing to just one road. Does Barry know? Did his people know? Was that why they went wild when he said he had to marry me?

Then she shook herself like a dog coming out of the

water, realizing Barry never could have kept anything like that to himself. No, he called her crazy because she wasn't like his mother and everybody else's wife. He was proud of her difference until it got in his way, and then he became ashamed and spiteful.

But if he sensed something ... Was there any expert who could look at all the known facts of her life and say, "There walks a sick woman"? Could he prophesy that she would again sleep eighteen hours at a stretch or longer, and wake up not knowing who she was or where?

The pain of a bitten knuckle brought her up sharp. "Oh, damn it!" she said angrily and stamped out into the kitchen and opened the back door. The air was cold and she reached for something to put on, but when her hand grasped the black raincoat her fingers flew apart as if she had touched something foul. She ran upstairs for a light jacket of Barry's she'd just put away.

"I am not insane," she said in a loud measured voice. "I am not eccentric. And I am not afraid of anyone."

Next door the younger child was out alone, squat and sexless in warm clothes and cap. It gave Vanessa a long dispassionate blue stare as she passed. Rather you than your mother, Vanessa thought, walking a little faster. She knew that some day the mother would ambush her, and she felt like breaking into a run now, except that to be seen running would be another bad sign.

As she passed by the third fishhouse, she could see through an open door a man working at a bench. "Good morning!" he called, and she answered hastily, then jumped as from the house opposite there was a sharp rapping on a window. A stout red-faced woman beckoned and smirked at her from between ruffled curtains. "Oh, hello," Vanessa mouthed back, waving and smiling with a sensation of horror as if she'd been caught naked and they wouldn't look away from her.

There was nothing after them for a while but the harbor beach and the marsh. Today she saw things she had been unable to see on her flight from the wharf that day; seine dories newly painted in buff and blue at the edge of the coarse grass, a graveyard of old hulls rotting beside a litle pond, as harmonious with their background as the seine dories. A red-winged blackbird sprang into the air over the pond, flashing scarlet patches. A sandy road led up through the marsh toward a distant rise, away from

41

the sea wall and the school, to where a long gray house and overshadowing barn stood against the dappled southeast sky. The Bennett homestead, of course. Nothing much at the harbor could have escaped that row of windows. Do all the Bennett descendants have to be born in a certain room to make them legitimate? But humor was no help. She felt too much in view of herself—too vulnerable—and hurried till a long shed hid her from the windows.

The beach was empty except for the gulls scavenging over the wet stones, and sparrows running about the litter of dry rockweed on the brow. The marsh gave off its own earthy essence in the strengthening warmth of the day. Standing quiet and alone, suddenly pierced with pleasure by the pale wash of sunlight on curled mossy shingles, she wanted to cry out, Why can't this be enough? Was it a sign of mental derangement that she could repudiate people and find it enough, like the moment on Water Street when she stopped to look at her house?

She forced herself to walk on, trying for the complacency that had borne her along the broken pavements and into the hall to deal with Brig. She pinned her mind to wretched little details: vanilla, cheese, baking powder, paper napkins, dried beans. She tried to see the inside of the refrigerator and the cupboards, but she could not remember what they had been eating the last few days. She passed the other fishhouses, the wharves close together and crowded with rows of new traps and old ones taken up to dry out, giving off the sweetish reek of the rotting vegetation that had grown on the laths in deep water. She heard a door shut, a dog barking, someone calling and a small child answering, a clatter of pails at the well, but no one confronted her, and she got around to the big wharf at last. Mark Bennett's store offered cover, but before she reached the door she heard a strong burst of laughter inside.

She went quickly through the long shed that covered part of the wharf and out into the open. The tide was low, and the lobster car was a long way down. She walked to the end and stood looking out past the end of Brigport toward the horizon.

She had come this far, but she was not sure that she could go into the store and hold her own with those people. Yet if she didn't go in she wouldn't be able to keep reaffirming her sanity to herself. Miserably she walked around the end of the wharf, trying to take deep breaths. One side of the wharf reached close to the static avalanche of yellowish rock that formed Western Harbor Point, and between the wharf spilings and the shaggy base of the point the low tide left a small pool of water that mirrored the sky. Like the lobster car on the other side, it was a long way down. She stood looking at part of herself reflected in silhouette against the luminous pallor overhead. The motion at the outer rim of her vision made her start nervously, and she saw a small boy in denim pants and jacket going down over the massive blocks of yellow ledge with an expression of determination. She responded instantly to his mood. For the moment he was like herself, a solitary, though he wouldn't be one for long. He might have been four years old.

She hoped she could move back out of sight before he should tip back his round dark head and see her up there, his logical enemy, the adult audience who spoils everything. She stepped back cautiously, waited, took another step. He swung his legs over a granite angle, leaned out and looked down, then pushed his seat forward and dropped to the next level. A large gray striped cat appeared out of the spruces above him and made a questioning sound. He said without looking back, "You just mind your own business, Louis."

The cat began to follow him down. He was almost to the wet rockweed now. "Any crabs I find down here are mine, Louis," he said clearly. "And that's my starfish. That big one we saw from the wharf. You remember." Louis joined him on a steep slant down which the boy moved on the seat of his pants and the palms of his hands.

Louis stopped at the bottom of the ledge and considered the thick growth of wet rockweed below. The boy jumped off into it. His sneakers flew out from under him, he cried out in surprise and anger rather than fear—it seemed to Vanessa—and shot toward the water, catching at the slippery weed as he went. Once he caught a good handful and it slowed him slightly; he struggled to right himself, but the strand gave way and this time he pitched headfirst, somersaulted, and hit the water. Louis crouched on his belly, staring and lashing his thick tail. Van waited for the child to rise out of the water, bawling in shocked anger, but he did not. After a moment she saw the two halves of his blue denim bottom showing on the surface.

43

As if in a dream of moving fishlike through a crystal element, she saw that there was a ladder on this side, the rungs too far apart for a small child, which was probably why he'd gone around by the rocks after he'd sighted his starfish. She hoped they were strong enough for an adult, and started down, each foot feeling through the slime for a worm-eaten slat that might give way under her weight. None did, though her moccasins slid on the greasy wood, and the rungs ended far enough above the water so that she had to let go, trusting to land on solid barnacled ledge rather than in mud. The water closed icily around her legs, and she wondered dispassionately if she'd been driven out of the house this morning for the purpose of dying at low tide in quicksand.

She went ankle-deep into mud, but not quicksand. The pool was deeper than it had looked—almost to her waist; and she waded across it, her stomach quivering each time she put her foot down and felt it sink so far and no farther. Her jeans wrapped her legs like sheathings of lead. She reached the boy and picked him up, finding him unexpectedly solid. He didn't move. She dangled him face down over her shoulder and scanned the woods on the point, the wharf, the sky itself. She wanted to shout but she could not. A purple finch sang out loudly from a spruce top, and Louis looked into her eyes with a penetrating green stare whose intelligence mocked her. He padded back and forth along his dry ledge like a tiger in a zoo.

"All right," she said to him. "I'll try, you damn thing. But if you were any good you'd fetch somebody." She laid the boy on his stomach on what seemed a level surface, remembering from God knew where something about turning the face to one side and something else about the tongue. Her hands were wet and dirty, but so was his face. She pried open his teeth and found his tongue where it should be. Then she felt around through the humps of weed for a place where she could plant her knee. Back at Seal Point she'd climbed over rockweed often enough. . . . She found what she was probing for, got one knee securely into the niche, and leaned forward on her stomach, groping for something to grip, while above her head Louis began to purr enthusiastically.

"I can do without a cheer leader," she grunted. If she could heave herself onto the ledge where the cat was, and somehow get hold of the boy and drag him up . . . Louis's

44

head bumped hers ardently. Close to her ear his purr was an asthmatic roar. Half-kneeling, half-lying in the rock-weed, she felt along the edge of his rock and discovered a small depression—enough to press her fingers into—and began to haul herself up.

All she saw of the man were the slacks and loafers jumping from ledge to ledge, and they could have been an hallucination to be ignored in this desperately personal struggle. They were certainly less real than the cat. She got herself up onto the ledge and stretched down her fingers toward the back of the boy's jacket, but the man was already reaching for him. His face was suffused with dark color and rigid as a stone mask. He did not look at her or speak but went back up over the ledges carrying the child.

A woman had come down part way behind him. She put out her hands to the bobbing black head, and then she pulled her gaze away and glanced toward Vanessa. "Are you all right?" she asked in a low voice. In an absolutely white face her eyes looked as green as the cat's, and Vanessa was positive they didn't see her.

"Yes, I'm all right," Vanessa said loudly. The woman turned and ran up after the man. Her fair hair shimmered against the dark boughs before she disappeared among them. The silence returned; if it were not for chilled flesh, soaked clothes, and mud-coated moccasins, the whole incident could have been a fantasy. Nice to have proof that I didn't dream it, she thought. I'm not that far gone.

Louis had followed the woman, and she rather missed him. She felt for her cigarettes but they were soaked. The front of her jacket and shirt were wet where she'd lain in the rockweed. She would have to go home, but she hated to uncoil herself and straighten up where the cold air could reach her. She sat hunched passively together for a while, wondering if it had been a dead child she had held. Unexpectedly she felt a tremor at the idea.

"Good Lord," Mrs. Sorensen said from behind her. "That's gratitude for you. Nobody gave you a thought."

"Why should they?" Vanessa didn't look around. "I was alive, obviously."

"Well, *he* is now. He's mad because he lost his chance at the biggest starfish in the world. Mark is swearing, and Helmi is making coffee as if twenty minutes ago she

45

weren't positive her only child was dead." She came down beside Vanessa, holding out a tweed topcoat. "Here, put this on and come on up to the house."

"I think I'd better go home."

"You can't walk around the harbor in those clothes. And my brother will lug you into the house by force if you don't come." As a shudder seized Vanessa, she said gaily, "You *see?*"

There was no way out, with the woman standing over her like a jailer holding a horsewhip instead of a coat. Vanessa loosened the grip on her knees and shuddered again, not completely from cold. It seemed as if the time lengthened out beyond all reason. She could see it stretching to the breaking point like an elastic, and if Joanna Sorensen hadn't yet made up her mind about Vanessa, this could do it. As if I cared, Vanessa thought wearily. I don't know why I ever did care. If I hadn't, I wouldn't have gone tearing out of the house like Mrs. Bearse's aunt in her change-of-life fits, and walloped myself right into this.

But she was freezing now, and she unfolded herself and stood up, staring sternly under the wharf at the harbor, and held out her arms for the coat. "There," said Joanna. "Come on. I could do with that coffee, couldn't you? Good Lord, if anything ever happened to that child we'd all be sick, but I think Mark and Helmi would die. They waited about twenty years for him." Her hand under Vanessa's elbow was not to be escaped. Relentlessly it guided her along the path up through the spruces to the house. Vanessa considered making a break for it when the path branched off down the hill to the store, but the moment was lost when Mark Bennett opened the door and came out.

The stone mask had been replaced by a smile which took years from him. His black hair was gray at the temples, but his eyes, like his sister's, were lively and young. "I guess I didn't act half-civilized down there," he said. "But he looked dead to me."

"To me too," she said gruffly.

"Just say it," said his sister. "Don't keep her standing here—she's blue as a whetstone."

"I don't know how to say thank you."

"Take her to my room, Jo," Helmi called from the kitchen. "I've put out some things."

Van stepped out of the mud-laden moccasins and Mark

46

took her arm and led her in, saying, "Hadn't she better have a stiff drink first?" Didn't they ever keep their hands to themselves? Her flesh was crawling.

"You let her get out of those clothes," his wife said. The little boy came out of the kitchen in dry clothes, with the cat hanging limp from his arms, and his father said, "This is the lady who hauled you out, you young hell-bender. . . . He wasn't supposed to stop off anywhere. Swore to his mother he'd go straight to the house and get his dump truck and come back to the store. Well, he knows the score now. If he hadn't got his come-uppance by heaving up his guts, I'd have blistered his bottom."

"Oh, stop growling," said Joanna. She took Van upstairs and left her in a white-walled room that looked out across the island to the eastern horizon on one side, and to the north on another. A thick towel and clothes lay on the bed. Showing off what the upper crust wears, she thought resentfully, as she handled the flannel slacks, a woman's shirt in soft fine wool tartan, and the hand-knit socks. The underwear was also much better than her own. She wouldn't have changed except that she was cold, and besides, she didn't know a quick escape route out of the house. Stiff with self-consciousness, as if the furniture were animate and gazing ruthlessly at her poor belongings, she undressed and rubbed her chilly flesh with the towel.

Downstairs she stood in the kitchen doorway and said crisply, "Here's the towel. Thanks for the clothes. I'll send them back later."

"No, you don't." Mark Bennett was in her way, broad and solid. "We've got you and you won't get away if we have to lash you to the mainm'st. Any woman that saves my son's life is stuck with me, by God." His arm around her propelled her into the kitchen. She detested being touched without permission. Even Barry knew better, but none of these people were sensitive enough to feel her disgust. "How about that drink?" Mark was saying.

"No, thanks." She was strangely exhilarated, almost cheerful. She smiled and sat down at the table. Coffee was set before her, sugar and cream thrust at her, a plate of warm coffee bread, butter. She was hungry enough to eat and drink, knowing the gesture would be lost on them if she refused. This kind needed everything spelled out for them, they were so snug and cozy in their arrogance. In a few minutes the impertinent questions would begin, and

47

then by brevity and indifference she might be able to insult them.

She had finished her first cup of coffee when she realized that they hadn't asked her anything except if she was warm enough or wanted more to eat. They talked among themselves of people and events that meant nothing to her, though she dimly remembered hearing Barry say some of the names. Sometimes one of them turned to her and explained a reference, told her who the person was and where he lived. She nodded and said, "Oh?" or "I see."

"Has Gina taken off yet?" Helmi asked. "I haven't seen her for a few days."

"No, but I expect her to start rowing anytime now, if Willy won't give her fare for the mailboat," said Joanna.

"Needs her bottom warmed," growled Mark.

"Mark has one cure for everything," Joanna said to Van. "Gina's our child bride. Her husband works for Steve and as far as Gina's concerned, this is like Death Valley, only not so nice." They laughed at that, and Van smiled. They are so stupid, she thought. The cat leaned against her legs and she reached down and scratched behind his ears. She felt a curious relationship with him, because he had been with her as she struggled up over the ledges. The child played on the floor with his boats and cars. She was glad he was not an effusive brat who would insist on charming her as his father was trying to do.

"They live in the yellow house," Helmi was telling her. "The one you pass on the way here, after the Binnacle. The Eastern End's too lonely for her, Willy says."

"More people to despise up here," said Joanna. "Keeps her toned up."

Somebody rapped at the back door, and Mark shouted, "Don't be so formal! Come in!"

A skinny, sandy young woman put her head in and said, "The store's wide open and nobody's there. Anybody could steal you blind."

"Anybody that hungry around here, they're welcome to it." Mark shoved back his chair. "Hey, Maggie, you met Vanessa? Maggie Dinsmore, Van Barton."

Maggie grinned at Van. She was freckled, and had a gap between two big front teeth. "Hi! Come in when you're out walking around. Ours is the house where the

48

roof's always going up and down. Mark, you got any decent lean pork for beans?"

"Let's go see."

"Coffee, Maggie?" Mrs. Mark asked.

"If I get set down, Lord knows when I'll get up again."

"It's time for me to go," Vanessa said. "I need some things at the store."

Helmi got up and walked to the door with her. Her voice was still low, as it had been on the ledges, but no longer lifeless with dread. "We'll always be grateful to you for being where you were when that happened. And don't stay away. Jo says you like to read, so please, any time you run short come over and help yourself."

"Thank you," Vanessa murmured. In a hall mirror she saw two tall effortlessly elegant women, one in a skirt and cardigan, the other in narrow, impeccably cut slacks. She was suddenly fascinated by this stranger and wanted to look into her face and find a name there, an identity, but sane women do not stop to stare into mirrors as if at ghosts, even if the ghosts are there. When she got out into the air the wind seared her wet forehead. She picked up her moccasins and strode down the path with her bundle of clothes under her arm, while behind her Mark was telling Maggie Dinsmore what had happened.

"Well, I never!" the girl gasped. *"Imagine!* And you know something, I bet that's what my dream meant, only I thought it was one of *my* young ones about due to fall overboard. I ain't been letting them out of the dooryard!" She caught up with Vanessa at the foot of the path. Her freckled bony face was brilliant. "You were *meant* to be there. Something made you go there—you was sent, sure as preachin'. I know about these things."

"Now, Maggie," said Mark, "you be careful about what spirits you haul into this pure atmosphere. You might drag in some bad actors on that beam of yours."

"You laugh, Mark, but you know the truth just the same." She tapped his chest with her finger. "It's all right, I can stand being laughed at. I'm not one of them dead-serious ones. I've seen some that was crazy as coots."

"Mebbe we better drag for that lean pork, my girl." He winked at Vanessa.

"I can't remember what I wanted," she said abruptly. "I'll be back later, or Barry will." As she turned and walked away from them she almost bumped into a young

49

girl who gazed at her from heavily made-up eyes that seemed to fill half a short and pallid face. Her hair was done up high on rollers and wrapped in a scarf.

"Hi," she said indifferently and passed on, swinging her large handbag. She wore an immense hairy cerise sweater and black stretch slacks. She was like an apparition from Water Street, an affirmation that it still existed.

Behind Van Maggie exclaimed, "Hello, Gina! When are you going to stop in and have that cup of coffee with me?"

"Well, here's Merry Sunshine in person," Mark said.

Van walked faster and faster, as if something inside her were going to give way if she didn't get inside her own door as fast as possible. Once she was there she leaned against the entry wall, panting and dry-mouthed. "I can't stay here," she whispered. "I can't. They'll be the death of me."

She remembered the frenzy in which she had cleaned the kitchen this morning, but it seemed like a very long time ago. The sun had moved away from the window sill where she had set her dishes, and they were now ordinary and a little pathetic. She looked down at the clothes she wore; the illusion of elegance set off in the Bennetts' mirror had been as deceptive as the rainbows flashing in the sauce dishes and illuminating the amber glass hen. She dropped her wet clothes and sodden shoes and ran upstairs, where she got out of the borrowed things in shuddering haste, and crawled naked into bed.

CHAPTER EIGHT

Barry didn't get home until late afternoon and by then she was up and dressed, with supper ready, the borrowed underwear washed, all Helmi's things put into a box ready to be returned to her. Barry was proud and excited, gazing at her with merry incredulity, as if she had changed from a toad to a princess. He'd been ashamed of her when he left in the morning; she knew that he had probably hated her. But he had come in to find out at the lobster car that he had a wife whom everyone else admired. He could hardly believe it when Mark said, "That's some woman you've got, Barry."

He repeated it to Vanessa again and again, taking new fire each time from the very sound of it. He told her also what Philip, Charles, and Stephen Bennett had said; what Foss Campion, Matt Fennell, Rob Dinsmore, and Nils Sorensen had said. He reported each significant nod, glance, or turn of phrase that had occurred when the boats gathered at the lobster car.

"You're *in*, Van," he told her in triumph. "Not but they all wanted to be friendly before, but you acted like you didn't think anybody was good enough for you. Now it's different ... they know you're alive, they know you're real."

"Did anybody interview the cat?" she asked him.

He didn't know what she was driving at, but he was pleased because she was talking to him and the house was clean. "That's a damn' good fish hash you turned out. I've never eaten anybody else's fish hash was any good. Where'd you get the pickles?"

"They were in the cupboard." Poor Barry. In these intervals of detachment she knew that cruel things had been done to him. Now he was as giddy with joy as a child at Christmas—not every child, not the child Anna, for instance—but she wished she had never gone out of the house this morning, at least not across the harbor and down onto the wharf, to be drawn into the vortex of people. But the alternative would have been a dead child, and she couldn't honestly say that did not matter to her. She studied the tablecloth, tracing a flower with her finger. "Come on, walk around the harbor with me," Barry said. "I've got a chess game on with Nils Sorensen. You know his wife."

"Spend an evening with *her?*" She laughed aloud and Barry looked hurt.

"I suppose if she ran a whorehouse you'd find her real interesting company. What's the matter with them around here, too goddam respectable?"

He slammed the door when he went out. She stacked the dishes in the sink and took the Aladdin lamp upstairs. It made the room too warm and she opened the windows. There was a low hum of generators as those who had power plants prepared to watch television; it sounded as if

51

the island itself were warming up engines, getting ready to voyage out into the dream-world of stars and black ocean.

Much later, when the Aladdin smoked up and she had to turn it down to let the mantle clear itself of caked soot, she got out of bed to kneel by the window with her head and shoulders out. It was a soft night and sometime earlier the generators had stopped. Now from the cranberry swamp behind the house the peep frogs were singing; she used to hear them as she lay in bed when she was a child and longed to be out in the spring dark. Now there was no one's permission to ask, but now, alas, she knew there was nothing out there for her.

The lights around the harbor went out almost as on a signal, and then she heard Barry coming along the boardwalk, whistling a tune his father used to play on the fiddle for square dances at the Grange Hall. She blew out the lamp so he would think when he came to bed that she was asleep, and lay in the dark trying for ancient magic. *There was this girl, and nobody knew who she was.* . . . But it had become black magic, conjuring up the dreadful awakening and the fear that the madwoman who wrote the postcards might have passed something horrible on to her.

She was almost glad when Barry came upstairs. He was in his stocking feet, and undressed quietly. He could be as stealthy as a cat when he chose. She wondered if he were being considerate, or if he was still too mad with her to want to speak. After he had got cautiously into bed and settled down she said in a normal voice, "Who won the game?"

After a moment's silence he said, "I got one, and Nils got two. He's one of these deep guys. A real thinker."

"That's all he could be, living in that family. He'd never get a chance to be a talker."

Barry ignored that. "Jo was real disappointed because you didn't come. I had to make up a good story about you taking a chill, and then she got worried about you."

"If she comes poking around here tomorrow with a bowl of calf's-foot jelly, I'll tell her the truth," said Van. "What you said earlier, that she's too goddam respectable, among other things."

Barry chuckled as if she'd been witty. He was determined to avoid a fight, still warmed by the praise of her act. "Talk about respectable. Owen came in. *That's* a real wild son of a bitch for you."

"You mean there's somebody in this paradise who raises hell once in a while? All the sweetness and light must drive him to it."

"Oh, he talks respectable enough, and he's a family man. In fact he had one of his kids with him, little girl twelve or so." Barry's voice trailed off, he yawned, and then said, "But you can see it right in his eye. Like something sleeping in a cage."

Barry could still surprise her after all. His words evoked the tiger sprawled behind bars, the gold of his coat dull and the black stripes dusty, the eyes extinguished. As she watched, the cage door swung gently open and the tiger awoke. The eyes came alive in the great mask, and the dusty fur took on the burnish of vitality as the long body stretched out in the leap to freedom. It was as if the tiger had landed here in this room on his huge pads; lying in the dark beside Barry she saw the fiery splendor of the eyes. She quoted aloud,

> *"Tyger! tyger! burning bright*
> *In the forests of the night."*

"Huh?" Barry mumbled. He turned over suddenly and put his arm across her and hugged her. The glory was gone, leaving a deeper blackness than before. There was no glory, never any glory. "Christ, I've been proud of you today," he muttered. "If we ever needed anything to put us in solid with them you've done it, hauling that little tyke out of the drink."

"I wish to God I'd let him drown!" she exclaimed. She rolled over and sat up on the edge of the bed. "Or else never walked around to the wharf at all just in time to be a damn heroine! The last thing I'd ever want is to be in solid with the Bennetts. I *hate* them."

"You hate them for having something." His voice was dry and cold. "Well, we've got a chance to have something for the first time. I can buy this house and a boat. We'll have a place where we belong."

"Not me. I'll never belong here."

"You'll never belong anywhere, then! You've always got it in your head that you're a state kid. You think it sticks out all over you like salt rheum and makes folks shy off like you're contagious? *You're* the one that shies off. They

53

don't know you're a state kid, and even if they did they wouldn't care."

"They're too wrapped up in themselves. It's a wonder they all don't marry each other to keep the bloodlines pure."

"Oh, don't talk so foolish. Are we going to have a little something or not?" His fingers felt along her back, hooked inside the elastic of her pajamas. She sprang away from the touch and stood by the window. "I knew it," he groaned. "What's turned me so damn repulsive all at once? I don't know what I've done to deserve this, but it sure must have been something pretty bad."

He stumbled out of the room, hitting his foot against a chair leg and letting out an outraged howl which she knew expressed more than the pure physical pain in his toes. Gasping and swearing, he felt his way downstairs. She stood by the window a long time, shivering until the tremors were so great she could hardly stand. She knew they were like Barry's howl, that they came from something else besides externals.

She stayed in bed until Barry had gone in the morning. He had never been so quarrelsome on Water Street, but it was a wholly different condition here. If he'd only stop this idiotic insistence on appearances, they'd achieve some sort of peace again. She sat up and watched him leave the harbor in a boat called *Kestrel*. He was steering while Philip Bennett pulled on his oilclothes. Barry had talked to her about the boat with love and lust, not with envy, because at first he couldn't imagine himself ever having the money to possess such a boat, built to order and fitted out with everything to turn lobstering into a gentleman's profession. She'd been repelled by the lack of resentment in his radiant account of how the diesel started at the touch of a button, how he had called the mailboat by the radio-telephone to find out if Phil's new fathometer was aboard, and how the new trap-hauler made hauling so much easier. Now he was beginning to believe that he too could be a gentleman-lobsterman some day. As if they would ever let him. The unrealistic Barry, fattening on hope, angered her more than the unresentful one. She supposed he was happy now as he took *Kestrel* out of the harbor, unless he was allowing thoughts of his wife to spoil his pleasure. If he does he's a fool, she thought.

When *Kestrel* disappeared around the breakwater she

watched other boats leave the harbor in the cloudy sunrise. She wondered which one belonged to Owen Bennett, and as she thought his name she saw the tiger again, free now, the muscles flowing under his coat as he padded through the light and shade in a jungle that proliferated richly within the walls of this house.

The clouds outside were dissolved by a northwest breeze and the sun was strong and warm. She took a sandwich and a book and got away before Dandelion-Head could catch her, or the fat florid object that had rapped and beckoned so horribly yesterday. You don't really have to build a better mousetrap, she thought. You find a child in a puddle and pick him out. Then you lose all your rights as a private person.

Eventually, lulled by the sun's warmth and the soporific swash of water a little way out of sight, she became absorbed in her book. After a time she was aroused by a penetrating chill; she was surrounded by complete shadow, and a freshening wind was blowing through the spruce boughs. It was late and she hadn't known time was passing . . . she hadn't even eaten her sandwich. She saw that she hadn't read much of her book and realized that she must have slept part of the time, and this gave her a small twinge of fright.

She broke up her sandwich for the crows and walked home. When she came into the house, it was well after six, and Barry had been in and gone out again. His dinner box was on the table and his rubber boots stood against the wall. He had cooked some lobsters and eaten a couple; the shells were in the sink. She put two still-warm lobsters on a tray and carried them into the sunporch to eat by the windows, breaking them open with quick professional twists of her hands and getting the meat out in big pink-and-white chunks.

The wind died out as the sun dropped toward the horizon, and the western sky turned a clear lemon-green color that cast a strange light over the grass and trees, and filled the house; it was silence with its own color, or color that carried its own silence—an element in which she could immerse herself, like water. She seemed to be floating in it when the experience was violently ended by three loud knocks at the back door.

At first she refused to go, then she was too angry not to. She ran out to the entry, but the door opened before she reached it and a man stood there, a solid dark shape against the unique light beyond. "Barry home?" he said.

"No, he isn't! And—" *And what?* She stepped back, and as the man came into the kitchen she could see him. "I don't know where he is," she said, out of breath as if she'd been running.

"I'm getting my crew together to stop off the harbor," he said. "It's full of herring. I'm a man short, and Barry could fill in if he's of a mind to."

She heard his words without answering, he didn't repeat them, and the silence between them took on the curious quality of the light that surrounded them. Unsmiling and unspeaking they looked at each other, and her suspense composed of terror and delight was familiar; she knew at once that the tiger was here.

"I'm Owen Bennett," he said finally.

"Yes."

He put his hands in his pockets and leaned against the cupboards. His black eyes didn't move away from her, and she felt that her blouse must be moving with the beat of her heart. She said tonelessly, "I don't know where Barry is."

"And he doesn't ever know where you are, does he?"

"What does that mean?" She tried for insolence. "Is that what they say about me already?"

"I don't know what *they* say." He straightened up and moved toward the door, still watching her. "I only know what I can see for myself. I'll find Barry." He was gone, the door shut hard behind him; she heard his boots hit the two steps and then nothing. It was the worst *nothing* she had ever known. She pulled the door open, and heard herself calling after him, regardless of the Campion house, "What do you mean, what did you see?" But he wasn't there. She ran back through the house to the front door and saw him already halfway back along the boardwalk and already indistinct, so swiftly had the light begun to go.

"Fine evening, ain't it?" Terence Campion called to her, crossing from his wharf to his front dooryard.

"Yes, lovely," she murmured, and went back inside.

She hurried to get to bed **and** to sleep before Barry came in. But it was not possible to sleep. She heard soft sounds from the harbor—an outboard motor running, men's voices, thumps, the rhythm of oars. *He* was out there. What did you mean? she asked him, saying that Barry didn't ever know where I was?

You know what I mean, he answered. Even when he's looking at you across the table or lying in bed beside you, he doesn't know where you are or what you are. Nobody does but me, and I knew it in the first glimpse.

But *how?* she persisted, seeing herself rangy in the jeans and Barry's shirt, with the thick ginger-colored bangs and the hair tightly skinned back; the angular face, the high cheekbones prominent with windburn, the long jaw. Those were externals. He had to see something else. She knotted herself tightly in the bed, knees to chest and arms clasped around them, a sowbug or caterpillar curling up small when its flat rock was overturned and left it defenseless to ruthless fingers or foot.

CHAPTER NINE

She awoke at daybreak, aching from her tense sleep, but hungry and energetic. She got up and looked out at the harbor. She could just make out the start of a line of net floats spilling from an orange dory that nuzzled the rocks below the lawn.

Barry was asleep on the sitting-room couch. She moved quietly around the kitchen, making percolator coffee and oatmeal. Barry liked oatmeal, and she felt an affectionate indulgence toward him this morning. Until now whenever she set the table she had perversely ignored the inexpensive but vivid set of dishes in the cupboard, and used the few mismatched plates and mugs they'd brought with them. This morning she used the matching set. If he should ever come in when they were eating, he would see that she was not slovenly about serving the meals.

Barry came out rubbing his face hard with both hands, squinting against the sunrise shining in over the sink. "I smelled that coffee while I was dreaming, and thought I was in heaven. Hey, what's this?"

"I wish I had some brown sugar for it."

"Never mind, this looks damn good anyway." He start-

57

ed to sit down and she said, "Wash first. You're not living aboard a boat."

"Sure, Marm." He laughed and gave her a slap on the rear as he passed. It was a measure of her new mood that she didn't spring back at him like an enraged cat. He washed noisily, and when he emerged from the towel he looked clear-eyed and young. "It was so late when I got in I didn't want to wake you up so I turned in on the couch. We stopped off the harbor last night."

"You slept in your clothes, I see. I'm glad you took your boots off."

"I almost kept 'em on, scales and all. I was some bushed. But we figger we've got about twelve hundred bushels out there. Owen's not going to call up for the carrier to come after this lot; we'll share it out for bait."

She sat down opposite him with a dish of oatmeal. "Who else went after the herring?"

"Well, Owen's the cap'n. He came over to the store about dusk, trying to raise his crew. That's Phil, and Rob Dinsmore—he's Owen's man anyway—and Charles Bennett's boy Hugo. Well, Hugo was courting over to Brigport, so I got the chance to go." He was jaunty with the prestige of it, but she let that pass for once. So Owen hadn't mentioned coming to the house first. She felt again the visceral excitement that was half-pleasant and half-sickening. Barry's voice faded out as if on a radio and then strengthened again as she tried to listen to him. "We're going to salt down my part in this fishhouse. When I start going by myself I'll do everything, like the gear and boat was my own."

"When do you start by yourself?"

"Next time we go to haul. We're shifting pots today." He was delighted with her attention, and talked and talked as greedily as he swallowed his food. She listened kindly, protecting the mood in which she had awakened.

"Well, I've got to get moving," he said at last. "Any coffee left there I can take?"

"Plenty, and I'll make some sandwiches." She got out a couple of lobsters and opened them. He watched her, tipped back in his chair and smoking. "You know something, Van?" he said diffidently.

"Not much." She gave him a quick smile. "What?"

"There's no reason now why you can't send off to the catalog for some new clothes. Them shirts of mine don't

58

do much for you, and they got some real nice things you'd look good in. Not that you don't look good in almost anything you put on, except that goddam raincoat."

She wrapped sandwiches and put them in his dinner box. "Well, maybe I'll think about it," she humored him. "You haven't got so many shirts that we can divide them, anyway, the way I hate washing and ironing."

He was pleased by her response and rushed on. "And get yourself a couple of dresses besides pants and shirts. You know those kind with the tight top and full skirts?"

She looked over her shoulder at him and saw him grinning, a little red and overheated as if by lascivious thoughts. "I'm not the type," she teased him.

"Sure you are!" he blustered. "You're a woman, ain't ye? They'll be having dances pretty soon and you want something nice to wear. I'll be blasted if I can see how anybody can do a Lady of the Lake in one of them straight-up-and-down nightshirts that looks like a grainbag stitched up."

That was Barry, pushing his luck and talking about dances. She said indifferently, "I'll see."

"Well, anyway, you can do with some new slacks," he said, more subdued. "See if they got some like those of Mrs. Mark's you had on the other day. Pick out something for me too, huh?"

It was crafty of him, but she could forgive him that today, even while knowing how he'd tell the other men that the wife liked to pick out his clothes for him.

When he had gone she took the bedclothes off the couch and hung them out in the yard to air.

"Hi!" It had happened at last. Kathy Campion was coming across the wet grass, her blue eyes sure of welcome. "Look, I'm not pushy—well, maybe I am—but how'll you know you can use my washing machine if I don't tell you?"

Be ordinary, Vanessa warned herself. You need protective coloring. "Thanks," she said in a friendly if not effusive manner. "But so far I've only got a few things to wash, and I'd just as soon do them by hand, the cistern water is so soft."

"Isn't it, though?" Kathy lingered, hugging herself against the chill that raised gooseflesh on her arms. "I haven't had a chance to ask you how you like it out here."

"I like it a lot," said Vanessa. "It's so good to be out of the city with spring coming that I can't seem to stay in the house."

"Oh, I know what you mean!" Her fervent and puppy-ish responses would be wearing. "Most of us feel like that. We couldn't stand living anywhere else. Well, there's one who doesn't, but it might be because she's so young."

Dying for me to ask who, and then we'll move inside for a nice kaffee-klatsch, Vanessa thought, but was surprised when Kathy bubbled on, "Well, if I don't get back, my kids will be fixing their own breakfast, and they'd eat chocolate-coated herring if they could manage it." She ran back in her wet sneakers and Van called after her, "Thank you!" Kathy waved and went in.

Barry would be proud, Van thought wryly. I sound so goddam neighborly and housewifely and every other stupid thing I can think of. . . . But it had been necessary; a great many things had now become necessary.

She started a chowder with the rest of the lobsters, and then sat down with coffee and a cigarette. Instantly, and without any seeming wish on her part, she began reliving last night. She shut her eyes so that she could see him clear against the dark, and felt under her fingers the structure of big nose and jaw and cheekbone; the brown skin would feel burning hot against her cold palms. Suddenly she felt certain that she would one day know these things and more, that there was no escape.

You sound, she told herself cynically, exactly like Maggie Dinsmore. She got up and found the mail-order catalog. It had been so long since she'd bought anything but sneakers and jeans that the vivid pages of styles and colors, the directions on how to make the correct measurements, made her painfully nervous. Still, Barry's remark stayed with her. *Those shirts of mine don't do much for you.* They made her conspicuous, that's all they did for her; they made her a white blackbird among the non-freaks. She had to cease to be someone to whose every habit and gesture they would be acutely sensitive.

Finally, she made a rough selection of clothes to choose from; with a small derisive smile she marked a couple of full-skirted dresses. Then she checked off some men's clothes for Barry to look at.

After that, she walked restlessly around the rooms. She found herself coming back again and again to the front windows, and realized that she was acting like the women she despised, waiting for the men to come in. Oh well, she thought, I'm not all gone yet; at least it's not my own husband I'm looking for. In the afternoon, she went upstairs to change her clothes. Now that she had decided to get something new to wear, she regarded what she had with loathing.

Nothing suited her, and suddenly she became despondent and sank down on the bed in the tumble of clothing. The fiery energy that had driven her all day seemed to have consumed itself. Tears gathered in her eyes, and slid from the outer corners down past her cheekbones to her ears. She didn't know why she was crying. "Except that I'm miserable," she said aloud in a cracked voice. "That's a simple fact, isn't it? Like being black or white or crippled or tubercular."

She heard a boat coming in and bounded off the bed. She dressed fast then, not caring what she put on as long as she could be around the harbor when Barry came home, a woman who walked down on the wharf to greet her husband. Her hair was full of electricity when she brushed it. It flew out from her head, lay in a tough lustrous web across her mouth, and wound itself around her hand and the brush. Finally, she got it gathered up and the elastic on.

When she left the house at last she felt hot and nervous. The youngest child next door was playing in the path and she hurried around him as if he were a rock. There were more boats coming in, the harbor danced with their crossing wakes, and she wondered feverishly which one was Owen Bennett's. Supposing he'd come in, sold his lobsters, and gone home while she'd been struggling with her damned hair?

She saw Mrs. Foss Campion taking in her wash, but got by without being noticed. At the harbor beach she stopped and shaded her eyes, trying to see across the flashing water. An outburst behind her made her jump, and she saw the children spilling across the field from the schoolhouse, exploding into the day like a box of fireworks into which someone had dropped a lighted match. She hurried on, around to the front of Philip Bennett's fishhouse.

Here, hidden among the rows of traps, she sat down on a crate and put her back against the old gray shingles, and shut her eyes. She was out of breath, as if she'd been

61

running for miles. The sun was hot on her lips and eyelids, the shingles warm through her jersey, the worn dry wood of the crate satiny under her palms. She grew calmer.

When she opened her eyes again there were three boats around Mark Bennett's lobster car, and Barry's small agile figure stood on the bow of one. Someone laughed; she was sure it was Owen, though she couldn't sort out the other figures on the car. She walked around to Mark's wharf, and reached it just as Owen Bennett's boat left it.

White Lady IV was the name on her stern. *Bennett's Island*. No *Maine* after it. It could have been a separate country. It's a wonder they don't have their own flag, she thought, venomous with disappointment. . . . He wasn't heading out of the harbor to go around the Eastern End and home, but across to the other wharves. He didn't look back to where she stood against Mark's shed. Idling toward Nils Sorensen's wharf, he took the gaff and pulled the boat in alongside the spilings, made her fast, and went up the ladder onto the wharf and disappeared between the fishhouses.

"Hi, Beautiful!" Barry shouted from the car, raucous with pride and euphoria. "Hey, Rob, you met my wife yet?" Rob Dinsmore, Maggie's husband, was stocky with thick hands and a mild, almost stupid face. "No, but I heard about her," he said in a twanging, upcountry drawl. "I guess everybody knows about her hauling the young one out of the drink. Maggie's talked about nothing else."

The other men, besides Mark, were Philip Bennett and Terence Campion. She answered their greetings with a nod and a faint smile, but since Owen had disappeared she was furious with Barry for being so loud and cocky on the car. The others were laughing at him, she was sure of it.

She went abruptly back up the wharf, but when she reached the path she walked slowly, not knowing what to do next. If she had to give up without seeing him, she'd run off somewhere or go to bed, anything to get through the rest of the day. Then she saw him across the road from Nils' fishhouse. He stopped to speak to a couple of young boys who had a great deal to tell him, then headed up past Philip's toward the Sorensen house.

She walked briskly in the same direction, waving to Maggie on the way. She was a woman out for a call, and no one could think anything different. She passed between two clumps of budding lilacs, and a black-and-white collie

62

came to meet her. His benign eyes reassured her, like a good-luck omen. He walked beside her, and she kept her hand lightly on his neck as she approached the door. As she knocked, the action seemed duplicated within herself in the now-familiar rhythm of delight and terror.

"Well, for goodness' sake!" Joanna pulled her in. "Isn't this nice!"

"You said I could borrow a book," Van said hurriedly. "At least I think it was you."

"It doesn't matter as long as you're here. Come on in and browse."

She knew at once that Owen wasn't in the house. Joanna was alone. She fought to hide her disappointment behind a set smile, and when Joanna turned to lead the way into the sitting room she was desperately tempted to run out. But she could not. She was committed now.

"I was just wishing somebody would drop in for a cup of coffee," Joanna's voice came back to her, "I baked this morning too. You're the victim."

"I'm afraid my feet may be muddy."

"Oh, don't worry about that. Nobody else does. Owen's just tramped through here in rubber boots. Short cut to Charles's, he calls it. Well it is, I suppose, but I'm glad everybody else doesn't think so."

She could make an honest comment here. "I thought Charles lived in the Homestead up the rise."

"He does. But you can go through the woods behind the barn here and across the lower meadow, so it's a little shorter. Well, here are the books. Take as many as you like, and I'll go make some coffee."

Van sat on the edge of a chair and stared blindly at the bookshelves. Out in the kitchen Joanna set out cups and saucers. Van tried to read titles, but bindings and dust jackets were so many abstract designs. She took two finally, without knowing what they said, and when she heard Joanna's approaching footsteps she quickly opened one of the books and pretended to be leafing through it.

"I hope you like that one," Joanna said from behind her. "It's one of my favorites. What's the other one?" Silently Vanessa held it up.

"Now *that* one I'd like to discuss with you. It's the darndest thing I ever read, but I couldn't put it down. Then I couldn't get anyone else to read it and talk about it with me. My daughter gave it to me for my birthday."

Say something, you idiot, Van commanded herself. She nodded toward the photographs on the bookcase. "That youngster?"

Joanna laughed. "That's Linnea and she's only fifteen, in her first year in high school. No, my oldest, Ellen." She went across the room and brought back a good studio portrait of a girl in her early twenties. Van took it in her hands for something to engage her clammy fingers.

"She's good-looking. Better than pretty. I mean, she'll always be good-looking, even when she's eighty. It's the bones."

"That's what I think too. I'm not a bit modest about my kids. Ellen's been through art school and she's teaching outside Boston."

"She seems to have her father's coloring."

"She does, but Nils isn't her father, if that's what you're thinking. Come on out into the sunporch and have some coffee."

"You were married before, then," she ventured.

"Yes, when I was nineteen." She lifted her cup. "Ouch. Been near the fire. I wasn't divorced, I was widowed. Alec was drowned one June and Ellen was born the next January."

A tremor went through Van's hand and she put down her cup. "I'm sorry," she said awkwardly. "It must have been terrible."

"It was," said Joanna. "It was over twenty years ago but I can remember exactly how it felt. I can see Stevie standing there in his wet clothes looking up at me. They'd sent him to tell me, you see, and poor Stevie, he was only sixteen . . . I don't think he's ever forgotten it either. Or Owen," she said absently, lifting her cup again. "Sometimes when I think of Alec it's strange to realize that I'm a woman past forty, but Alec always stays the same, a boy. It shakes me, sometimes. Ellen is as old now as her father was when he died." Matter-of-factly she added, "I saw him. I went straight down there, to the old boat shed by the harbor beach."

"I don't see how anybody survives anything like that," Vanessa said. She wished she were huddled in her room, walled safely away from this.

"I didn't know how I was going to, but I did. And look what people go through in wars. The concentration camps, for instance. It's astonishing what you can stand."

She smiled. "But small things can do a lot of damage. You can make the big effort, be gallant, hold your chin up, and then some tiny thing knocks it all down. You come across a glove he lost one time, a note he made of something he wanted over at Brigport. And to see his violin gathering dust. . . . I'd been married to Nils a good while before I could stand hearing somebody play fiddle tunes that Alec used to play."

"But you got over it."

"Yes, I got over it."

Van shook her head and Joanna said, "What's the matter?"

"I couldn't. I'd want to die too." The words spurted out and she was ashamed.

"You mean if you lost Barry. Well, I hope you never do, but if you did, well, you're not weak." She got up. "Let's have some hot coffee. I don't know why I told you all that. I haven't mentioned it to anyone for years, not since Steve's wife first came here and told me about *her* first husband. He was killed in the Pacific during the war. . . . There must be something about you that draws people out. You don't make small talk, for one thing." As she came back with the coffeepot she said, "You have beautiful hair."

"I'm going to cut it," said Van at once.

"Oh, *why?*"

"At my age a pony tail looks idiotic."

"What does age matter, if you can get away with it? Liza and I were saying the other day that you could. You're tall and you've got a face that can stand that sort of—how would you describe it?"

"Scraped-back look, Barry calls it." They both laughed. She'd cut it tonight, or earlier; she could hardly wait to get home and do it. They were commenting on it. "Besides, it's getting too heavy and hot. Sometimes it makes my head ache."

"I suppose that's the drawback. Look, while I think of it, will you come to our sewing circle on Friday? We have it at night so Laurie can come." Van's expression must have changed in some way, because Joanna said as an explanation, "Owen's wife, you know. She teaches school. I forget you don't know all about the place yet."

Someone who consistently refused to mix was conspicuous. "All right," she said reluctantly, "but I haven't anything to sew."

"I'll give you something to do. We're making things for a fair over at Brigport this summer, and for once we've started early enough."

"Well, I'll do what I can," Van heard herself saying in this fantasy that had become her life. "I'd better go home now and think about supper. I can hardly wait to start in on these books. Thanks for the coffee and conversation." It sounded unnatural and jerky to her, but Joanna didn't appear to notice. She walked with Van to the end of the spruce windbreak and they stood by the lilacs. "It's spring," said Joanna dreamily, touching a fat bud. "These are white. You have some around your house, you know, the purple ones."

"On Water Street I had lilies of the valley." Again she was undone by the sudden arterial spurt of words. "I don't know what's become of them. They're tearing down the house." Her face burned. But Joanna, stroking the bud, said, "Laurie's got a nice big bed of them. She'll give you some, I'm sure."

"That would be nice. . . . Now I have to go."

"I'm glad you came in, and I'll see you Friday if not before."

Van gave her a brief smile and left. She wanted to laugh at the spectacle of herself; each thing she had done, borrowing books, sitting down for coffee, holding a personal conversation, promising to work for a fair, only added to the incredibility. She could feel her mouth twitching with held-back laughter.

"Hi, Mrs. Barton!" the Dinsmore children chirped at her, and she looked solemnly down at them and said, "Lawks a mercy on us, this be none of I."

She laughed at their faces and went on, knowing exactly how the old lady had felt. The little housewifely talk of plants on the end had been the final joke. But was it? Her private picture of the fresh green spears and minute buds crushed into muddy death was oddly confused with the image of the drowned boy.

But she had been diverted in spite of herself, and when she reached home she was less feverish in her activity. It was dark before the men were done with handling the fish, getting it ashore and salting it down in the bait butts. Barry's was the last, and they worked by lantern light in the fishhouse. Her uneasiness returned. The knowledge that Owen was only a few yards away exerted a powerful influence on her. Once she found herself at the front door, holding to the knob, and arguing passionately with herself. There was no reason why a woman shouldn't go across the road to tell the men she had the coffeepot on. But she couldn't make herself open the door. It wasn't to be like this. She had to wait.

Barry came in at last. Herring scales glittered in his eyebrows and on his skin. His boots were spangled with them, and he brought with him the cold deep-sea scent of fresh herring. He had cleaned a dozen large ones, and he wrapped them in wax paper and put them in the refrigerator.

"I've got hot water for you," she told him. "Want to wash up before you eat?"

"I guess so, if I don't fall into the sink." Leaning against the wall he tiredly kicked off his boots. He took off his shirt and went to the sink.

She wasn't hungry, but she told him she had eaten earlier; she sat down opposite him and sewed buttons on his shirts while he ate and listened to news on the radio. It was a perfectly ordinary scene. She imagined a secret onlooker saying, *You see, she's just like any woman.*

"That's a good mess of bait we've got here," Barry said when he'd finished eating. "Give me corned herring instead of brim any time. I just hope Cap'n Owen waits a couple of nights before he wants me to do it again. He never gets tired. Phil kept telling him to take it easy."

"You still think he's a wild one?" She didn't look up from her needle.

"The way he acts proves it. I've seen that kind before." He gave her a wise wink and nod. "He may be married, sure he loves his wife and kids, but he's in his prime yet and he keeps thinking of the old days when he was laying 'em left and right."

He snickered enviously. "He's trying so damn' hard to be good, he's like to kill himself at it. But I like the bastard, I sure do." He yawned till his eyes ran, and headed for the stairs. At the foot he stopped and looked back at her. "That was a good supper, sweetie. Finest kind. Place looks good too. I wanted to let you know I saw it, but I'll be damned if I know how, my eyes are some bleary." He went upstairs. After a few minutes she went and listened, and heard his heavy breathing. She went back to the kitchen, and pulled all the shades, took off her jersey, pinned a towel around her neck, and began to cut her hair.

CHAPTER TEN

Barry was childishly disappointed because she had cut her hair. "What did you do it for?" he demanded, as if asking her why she had committed murder.

"Because I'm too old for a pony tail," she said. "Because it made me stick out like a sore thumb."

"So what?" His eyes were shiny with tears.

"You don't like me to stick out like a sore thumb. You've done nothing but tell me I should be like the rest and not shame you."

"That didn't have anything to do with your hair, for God's sake! I was proud of *that*. Hey, let it grow again, will ye? Come on, Van, let it grow."

"I like it the way it is," she said. "I was getting tired of it." She turned her head back and forth before the kitchen mirror, not complacently but as gravely dubious as a scientist. At that she might have done wrong to cut her hair; he might have been looking at that when he came in the other night. Some men were funny about long hair. Look at Barry now, blowing his nose and sulking. She smiled at his reflection and said, "Can I go to haul with you?"

"You mean it?"

"I certainly do. This is your first day on your own. And I haven't been to haul with you since before we got married." Her eyes held his in the mirror. "Remember that time?"

The resentment went out of him, he wore a grimace of ecstatic anguish. "Ayuh, I remember," he whispered. "Kee-rist!" He moved closer behind her, pressing her body against his, his hands gripping her waist. "I remember. There was nothing ever so perfect before or since."

"Maybe whoever said it's better always to court and never to marry had the right idea."

He didn't want to talk. He was flushed and urgent. "Come on upstairs right now." His hands couldn't stay still, but she was motionless.

"You've got traps to haul."

"But today I'm by myself and I don't have to punch a time clock. . . . *Annie.*" His fingers didn't know whether to creep up or down. He pressed harder against her and pushed his face avidly into her neck.

She felt kindly toward him, not cruel as she said, "Not in the morning. Night is best."

"I might have known! You won't do it at night, you'll have some goddam excuse, pick a fight, say you're too tired or under the weather—I know all about it!"

"Do you want me to go to haul with you or not?" she asked calmly. "I've made a double lunch."

"Oh, to hell with it. Sure, come along, I don't give a damn." He went slamming out of the house. She gathered up extra clothes and the lunchbox. Kathy Campion called to her when she went out, and Van exchanged enthusiastic greetings with her, snug in her frame as a woman going out to haul with her husband on a fine spring day.

The boat was the *Liza Jane,* short, sturdy, and broad. Working on his own for the first time, and able to show off before her, Barry began to cast off his bad mood. He told her the names of coves and ledges and invisible shoals; he pointed out the other boats and named them. He told her where there was always a tide rip to watch, and the spots where the lobsters crawled thickest but where the traps could be completely demolished in a southerly blow. He was almost poetic about the size and number of lobsters he took from the traps. He was nonchalant about hauling in the deep swells that broke high against a rocky wall on the deserted back side of the island. "This is flat-arse calm compared to the way it is sometimes. Of course if the engine stopped all of a sudden we'd likely end up plastered against that cliff."

"But it wouldn't dare stop," she told him. "It belongs to a Bennett."

He grinned. "Some day you'll forget yourself and give 'em a good word. Wow! Look at that old soaker! If he doesn't go the measure I'll break down and bawl." The lobster just fitted, the big claws were plugged, and he was

69

laid reverently in the crate. "In you go, Baby mine, Daddy needs a fifth, and you'll just about see to it." There were two other counters, not as spectacular, and a crowd of little ones. "Run back home, Sport, Sonny, Junior, Peanuts," he called as he tossed them overboard. "See you next year for the Fourth of July!"

They ate lunch anchored to a trap on the southeast side of a high ledge of red rock; the light wind was from the northwest. The sun broke strongly through the thin clouds and it was summer-warm in the lee. Across a brilliant blue sparkle of water the island climbed in a giant fall of black volcanic rock toward the everlasting spruces. There was about its height and solitude a sort of poetic grandeur which, if she remained dispassionate, she could appreciate. It was a good day to be on the water; relaxed by the mild air, food, and the return to a once familiar and beloved element, she was taken unaware by delight and by something at once deeper and sharper. She could understand the Bennetts' pride of place, through she did not like them for it but resented them all the more because their pride was unconscious—not the hard-won arrogance of those who have clawed their way up from nothing.

They went back to hauling. It seemed as if they had been out here for days, and that night would never come. Rob Dinsmore came alongside once, the men talked a few minutes about the day's progress, and then separated. Foss Campion waved when he passed at a little distance. Philip overtook them about five miles away from the island, and asked Barry how he was doing. "I can see you've been bringing him luck," he said to Van.

"I've been having to fight her off," said Barry, "or she'd be hauling the traps and baiting 'em too. She always wanted to be a lobsterman."

"Well, there's no reason why she couldn't have a few traps out when they start coming in from offshore," said Philip. "You could set out eight or ten for her outside the harbor later on. I've got a double-ender hauled up you could use," he said to Van.

"Hear that, Van? Gorry, what more could anybody ask?" Barry's eyes urged her to be nice.

She smiled primly and said in a suitable voice for the wife of the hired help, "Thank you, that would be real nice." The sleek, high-bowed *Kestrel* sprang away from the short round-bottomed *Liza Jane,* which rolled in the wake like a fat sea pigeon. Barry looked after him and shook his head. "Yessir, that's a man," he said reverently. "That's a real man."

Van turned away from him, aching with too much light, aching with everything. Owen was somewhere on these waters. How long would it be?

They went by the Seal Rocks; naturally, since the order had been passed down from Mount Sinai, Vanessa thought. She would have ignored the seals if she could, in order to show her contempt and independence. She hadn't been bought and paid for—she needn't look at anything just because the boss-man told her to. But she had never seen more than one or two seals at a time, hanging about a weir, and she was amused in spite of herself by the sophisticates who remained on the ledges, tails and heads uplifted so that they looked like chunky gravy boats made out of a shiny, mottled, grayish pottery. The more timid seals slid overboard and tumbled in the surf, coming up to gaze at the boat with round eyes. She was leaning over the side, trying to coax one closer with a piece of bread, when she heard another boat coming, but didn't look around. From the corner of her eye she saw the approaching bow, and concentrated on the young seal. You're far more important and more beautiful and everything else than any mere human being, she told him silently. It seemed terribly important for him to respond to her; for him to feel her need of his response. It would be the sort of gift she had never been given and had always longed for without knowing what it was.

Liza Jane rocked gently as the other boat idled alongside. Suddenly and gracefully the seal sank back into the water and disappeared. Pierced with angry grief, she expressed it in a swift swing of her head on a rigid neck, and a wide hostile stare across the boat at the intruder. It was Owen Bennett.

It was as if their two bodies had collided at great speed. She was thrown off balance, the wind bounced out of her lungs. His face was wooden and very dark. He was looking at her hair, and then his eyes came to hers with what appeared to be a deliberately insulting blankness.

"You two met yet?" Barry was fairly prancing. "Owen Bennett—and this is the wife. Naturally, who else?" He snorted. "Couldn't smuggle out any other woman. She wouldn't let me."

She leaned back against the washboard, her shaking hands braced behind her. "Hello," she said calmly.

"Hello." You could almost doubt that the earlier reaction had occurred. Where his brothers' and sister's smiles were warm, his blazed. Oh, and he knows it! she thought. He uses it. Well, if he thinks I'm *that* simple—

What? She couldn't complete it. He and Barry were talking lobstering, the boats rocked lazily together in the wash from the ledges, and she eased the grip of her hands and turned around as if she were watching the seals again, though she saw nothing from her hot eyes. After a moment Owen's engine speeded up and Barry shouted, "Be seeing you, Cap'n!" She didn't turn to watch *White Lady* leave them.

In two days she had established herself as one of the black blackbirds, no albino freak. After this she would have to maintain the illusion, but she didn't doubt herself. There was something else to be done quickly, and she took the initiative, knowing that if she waited for Barry to make a move his fumbling hints and hands could drive her into temper and send him out of the house hurt, raging, and ready to confide in the first good listener.

When she had finished the supper dishes after the day on the water, she went into the sunporch, where he was reading by the last light of the sunset. "Saving oil?" she inquired.

"Huh? Oh." He took a book of safety matches from his shirt pocket and tossed it to her. "Light the Aladdin, will you?"

She didn't move. "I thought I'd go to bed. You still want a lamp lit?"

"Huh?" he said again. Then he understood, and dropped his magazine. "Hell, no. I'll be right along." His voice was uneven. "Soon as I wash up."

Poor Barry, she thought as if she were standing off at a distance from them both. She was determined to make the evening so successful that he would feel like a hero instead of a victim.

It wasn't difficult. Barry wasn't an overwhelming lover, but he was neither awkward nor inept. In spite of herself she responded, and afterwards as they lay together in the dark she remembered the time aboard his boat before they were married. It was the first time and the last time

72

when she had answered him with all her body and mind; when she had believed that it would work. For twelve years she had pitied the children they had been, and yet perhaps they hadn't needed pity then as they needed it now.

Barry slept, his arm across her, his mouth against her shoulder. She lay awake for a long time gazing upward through the dark.

CHAPTER ELEVEN

Now everything was ready. From the dissociation of their lives on Water Street they had changed to something that passed, for outsiders and for Barry, as unity. For him that one night had been the symbol. He wouldn't want another one right away; that would be forcing his luck, and Van's generosity. Besides, working as strenuously as he did, he was almost instantly snuffed out by fatigue as soon as he was warmed and fed. But it had been proved to him that he had never lost Van and so he was happy. Now I am one of the wives, Van thought. I observe the proper ceremonials and rituals. I send away to the catalog, I walk to the store on boat day and have a mail order made out by Helmi; I smile at Mark Bennett's jokes, and listen when other wives talk to me, and sometimes I play a speaking part. And I do housework. God, how I do housework.

But she still sneaked out the back door and ran away to the point or to Long Cove mornings to avoid the moment when Kathy Campion would arrive, coffeepot in one hand and a pan of fresh Finnish coffee bread in the other, for a nice snug getting-acquainted session. She knew she was doomed, that sooner or later Kathy's relentless good humor would illuminate her kitchen, but for now she would fight. The house might belong to the Bennetts, but while she lived in it it was hers, as much as the Water Street house had been hers, and the thought of being cornered in it gave her the old claustrophobic nausea.

She ran away, but she couldn't disappear into a book as

73

she had done. She would wander like a spirit along the shore or through the woods, sitting down long enough to smoke and then restlessly moving on, always wondering what was going on back at the harbor. Barry thought it was a victory for him and the island and the Bennetts that she stayed at home more and kept the place clean; she allowed him that satisfaction.

On a day when Philip and Barry hadn't gone out, but had worked at Philip's fishhouse on new gear, she walked that far in the afternoon and sat on the chopping block in the sun listening to the familiar rhythm of trap nails being driven. From Nils Sorensen's fishhouse came the spasmodic whine of a circular saw as Rob Dinsmore split laths. *White Lady* was tied up at the end of the Sorensen wharf; Nils, Owen, and the island's best mechanic, Matt Fennell, were working on the engine. Vanessa didn't look that way. This was neither the time nor the place for a meeting. She felt an exhilarating steadiness, as if she were pumped full of adrenalin and could manage anything. Mrs. Philip Bennett and a tall gray-eyed woman introduced as Mrs. Steve stopped for a few minutes, and Vanessa talked with them easily, explaining with a smile how familiar this atmosphere was to her, that she had grown up with it, had built trap bottoms and painted buoys, and had even baited up. She knew they thought she was speaking of her own home, and Barry didn't throw in anything to spoil the illusion. He just gave them his charming little-boy grin as he added another new trap to a stack and went inside again, whistling "The Road to the Isles."

Swallow it, all of you, Vanessa thought, letting her eyes slant toward the boat at the next wharf. She wondered if he knew she was there.

Next door the saw whined as it bit through spruce, quieted, attacked again. Steve and Charles Bennett, youngest and oldest of the brothers, stopped at the fishhouse and Barry introduced her with ebullient pride. Charles was solidly built, his hair shot through with gray. He was curtly civil, where Steve had a slow-spoken courtesy and an oddly gentle way. He was thinner than all the rest, and it made him seem peculiarly young, though he was at least forty. She remembered what Joanna had said: *I can see Stevie standing there in his wet clothes looking up at*

74

me. . . . Poor Stevie, he was only sixteen. I don't think he's ever gotten over it. Then she'd added, *Or Owen either.*

If it was something that involved Owen she wanted to know about it; she wanted to know with such greed that she was afraid she was going to blurt out some incoherent and inexcusable question. When the two men went over to the next wharf and aboard the boat, she was relieved. She turned to leave the place, and Barry shouted at her from the fishhouse doorway. The whine of the saw drowned his words and she walked closer.

"I said wait a minute," he said. "We'll be through here in half a tick, and I'll be going home."

"I f-feel sick," she began. "I—" He was looking past her, mouth gaping in shock. Rob Dinsmore had appeared around the corner of the fishhouse; she saw his fish-belly pallor, and the bright red glove he was holding out. He fell on his knees, swaying, and said, "I've cut off my hand."

The glove was dripping. Steady drops splattered on the pebbles. "Phil!" Barry yelped, rushing forward. Philip came out past Van and at once Rob was hidden from her. She stood thinking, *I want to be away from here,* but she wasn't able to move.

"All right, Robbie," Philip was saying. "Just let me get this bleeding stopped, huh? The rope'll do it. Come on, boy, hold on, you haven't lost it yet."

Between them they raised him to his feet, Philip supporting the arm with the injured hand. "Give the others a hail, will you?" he called to Van. "We'll go to my house."

She ran between the buildings and out onto the Sorensen wharf. The men were crowded around the engine down forward; Steve squatted on his heels in the small companionway, looking in. "There's been an accident with the saw," Van called down.

They came swiftly up over the side of the wharf, passing her on both sides. Owen was the last one out. Like the rest he had to thrust his shoulders and head forward to come out, and when he straightened up in the cockpit she was alone on the edge of the wharf. He stared up at her as if she had no right whatever to be there. Then he pulled himself up over the side of the wharf.

"How bad is it?"

"I don't know, but Rob thinks he's cut his hand off."

He shook his head and went after the others. All at

75

once the place had the ringing emptiness that follows on catastrophe. In the Sorensen fishhouse the saw was still quietly running. It was like the one Mr. Bearse had, so she knew how to shut it off. When she came out, Joanna was crossing from the Binnacle to Philip's house with her arm around Maggie Dinsmore. The smaller child stood on the doorstep howling while the dog leaped at her, trying to lick her face.

"Darling, be good, Mama'll be right back," Maggie implored her. The child threw herself down, screaming. Mag's freckled face contorted as she struggled between husband and child. "Oh, dear God—"

"I'll stay with her." Van heard her own voice, cold as if in disgust at all this display of passion.

"Thanks, Van," Jo called to her, and hurried Mag along. Van wished she had gotten away before Rob showed up with his blood splattering on the stones. She strode to the Binnacle doorstep, gathered up the screaming and thrashing child, and carried her inside. The dog bounced officiously around her. There was a rocking chair in the kitchen and she sat down and began to rock, strongly pinning the wiry child against the convulsive arching of its back. She sang the first thing that came into her head, wondering dispassionately why in hell she'd picked that one and where it had been all these years.

Come o'er the stream, Charlie, dear Charlie, brave Charlie,
Come o'er the stream, Charlie, and dine wi' MacLean.
And tho' you be weary, we'll make your heart cheery,
And welcome our Charlie and his royal train.

Her voice was hoarse and low. It went on steadily under the child's gasps and sobs and occasional shrieks. She sang of the red deer, the black steer, the lamb from the bracken and doe from the glen; of the stream in the starlight and the red wine, of the bold Highland men who ranged on the heather with bonnet and feather. Suddenly the child gave up and lay limp, staring up at Van's face. Van didn't return the look. She kept on rocking after she had finished the song and gazed off across the kitchen. The dog lay watching her with pricked ears and shiny eyes, a small chunky red fox.

"Daddy was bleeding awful," the child said in a quavering voice. Her small chest rose with a long breath. "Is he dead?"

"Of course not," said Van. "He cut his hand on the saw. But everybody's helping him. What's your name?"

"Tammie. Mama was scared," she said accusingly.

"Weren't you ever scared? But you got over it, didn't you?"

Tammie thought, then admitted with a sigh, "Ayuh." She reached out wanly toward the dog and said, "Here, Tiger." He sprang joyfully at her fingers. Feet pounded across the doorstep and the older girl burst in, as white under her carroty bangs as her father had been. "She's Diane," murmured Tammie.

"What's happened?" she cried. "The other kids told me—told me—" She couldn't speak, but gulped. Van put out her free hand and took hold of the skinny shoulder, holding the child still.

"Your father cut his hand on the saw. He's not dead. He's next door. Your mother's there too."

"But I saw all the blood, on the stones by the fishhouse and on the road, and on the steps—" She gagged and retched, and vomited past Van's arm onto the floor. "We'll have to tend to Diane," Van said to the younger one, who sat up and slid off her lap. Van washed Diane's pallid face with a cold washcloth and put her into the rocking chair with her mother's sweater around her, then cleaned up the floor with old newspapers the five-year-old brought in from the entry. She put them in the stove and washed her hands. "There," she said. "You should feel better to get rid of all that. What did you have for dinner, for heaven's sake? Now I think we all need a good cup of tea."

"Oh boy!" Tammie, recovered, danced around the kitchen.

"Diane, did you ever have a nosebleed?" Van asked the silent one in the rocker.

"Sometimes," she answered languidly. The dog leaped into her lap and licked at her chin.

"Well, you know what a mess that can make. A little blood goes a long way." Her voice was cold with authority.

"The cups are in the cupboard over the water pails," Diane offered feebly. "Show her, Tammie."

The three were sitting at the table solemnly drinking

their tea when a shadow passed the window, and the dog flew barking at the door. Owen came in. "Hello, Tiger," he said to the dog. "You plan to take my leg off?" He looked across at Van. "They've gone in Phil's boat," he said. "Steve went along, and Jo's holding Maggie's hand. They got the bleeding stopped, but they knew enough to leave the glove just as it was." He dropped into the rocking chair and took out his cigarettes. "Phil's kitchen looks like a—" He glanced at the children's faces. "Well, no call being so fancy with the details. You having a tea party?"

"Yes, we are!" said Tammie. Diane gave him a small smile.

"Mind if I join ye? Don't get up, I know my way around." He made instant coffee in a mug and sat down at the table. "I should've baked a cake and brought it along." The children burst into giggles.

"What's the matter, don't you think I can cook?" he asked them. They sputtered into their cups. He folded his arms on the table and looked at Van. "Would you mind telling me why in hell you cut your hair?"

"I don't think that's any of your business." He lifted one eyebrow and then paid attention to his coffee, watching the motion in the mug as he stirred. The children talked across the table to each other. As he reached for the can of milk she saw with a shock of astonishment that three fingers were gone from his right hand. As if he felt her fascinated eyes he glanced up with a malicious smile. "Yep, today has a kind of nasty familiarity about it. That's my war wound."

"What branch of the service were you in?"

"None. I wasn't fit, old rounder that I was. Nope, this was somebody else's war. I picked up something on the shore to see what it was and it blew up in my hands."

She kept wanting to look back at his hand; it seemed as if she could look nowhere else except with a great effort. The mocking grin stayed around his mouth and his eyes watched her as if for signs of some sort of disintegration. She said very breezily, "What about the children tonight?"

"Oh, they can go over to Kathy. She gave me a hail. How'd you like that, kids?"

"Oh boy," shouted Tammie. Diane said, "What about Tiger?"

"Take him too. You go get your nightdresses now."

"We wear *pajamas*," Diane said primly. "And we better take our toothbrushes." When they'd gone into the bedroom he said in a low tone, "Maggie had a dream last night that meant death, she says. You should have seen her. She's prepared for him to die on the way in."

"Will he?"

"I hope not." His voice followed her as she carried the dishes to the sink. "Do you believe in omens? Are you plagued by dreams?"

"Sometimes," she said indifferently. "Isn't everyone?"

"Have you had any lately?"

"Maybe a halluncination or two."

The children came out, Tammie carrying a grimy plush rabbit, and Diane got a paper bag from under the dresser and stuffed their things into it. They and the dog looked expectantly at the adults.

"Well, I guess we're ready," said Van. Without glancing toward the man at the table she led the way toward the door. She knew as they left the doorstep that he had come out behind them, but she still didn't look around. She wanted to, but she was afraid. That she had been afraid all the time he was in the kitchen with her, she knew by the way she breathed now, out-of-doors and away from him, as if she had been holding her breath for a long time.

CHAPTER TWELVE

The three Bennetts came back the next day. Rob had survived his trip and was in good condition in the hospital, and Maggie was staying with her aunt. "She won't come home," Kathy said. "She still thinks he can die any minute." Van had at last allowed herself to be cornered, as a matter of policy. It wasn't too difficult because Kathy liked to talk, and though she was acutely interested in finding out all she could, she was too polite to ask Van questions beyond the obvious ones. She talked more about Maggie. "I don't think her aunt's any help. She brought Maggie up to believe the way she does. Everything's planned out ahead of time for you, and if you're lucky you get a warning just before something happens. I don't know if I call it lucky or not. Would *you* want to know?"

"Well, it would depend on what I found out," said Van.

"But you can't change anything, according to Maggie, and it's always the bad things you hear about, never anything good that's coming to you, so all you can do is stew around being scared foolish and waiting for the ax to fall." She looked impressed. "That's it, the ax. Like kneeling there waiting and waiting for the headsman to drop it. If they'd been going to execute me in the French Revolution they wouldn't have had to use the guillotine. I'd have died long before I got to it."

Vanessa laughed and got up to leave. "I'll see you at the sewing meeting tonight," Kathy called after her. "Can we walk over together?"

"Why not?" Van said. It was a question to herself as well as an answer to Kathy. It was all an essential part of the fabric. Not that she hadn't already woven a tight, strong bit of goods, first with Mark Bennett's child and now with the Dinsmore two. Tiger bounced and wriggled at sight of her, as Louis the cat rubbed familiarly around her ankles if she went to the store. She was branded as someone safe and ordinary; children and animals liked her, and her quietness was being marked as high quality.

At the sewing circle she met Owen's wife for the first time. She was a youthful-looking woman in her late thirties, with a sturdy body and fine coloring. There was something ingenuous about her, you could see in her the girl she had been, with the firm handclasp and the rosy cheeks, and the burnished hair that curled around her head so becomingly only because it grew that way, and not because she had any knack or patience for fixing hair. She wouldn't consider it as important as her field hockey game or her student council meeting or, later, her class of fifth-graders whom she'd organized into two softball teams.

She wasn't aggressively hearty. If she had been, Vanessa would have liked her better, or at least tolerated her more, because one can always tolerate whatever one can laugh at.

She asked Van to come over and call on her, and Van, basting quilt squares together, said without looking at her, "I'd like to." She knew she would never walk inside his house. How had he ever married this woman? He must have grabbed at her to get away from the family. And she, poor fool, thought it was love. He couldn't have loved her. It ran him down in Van's eyes to imagine him passionate and besotted about the sturdy clear-eyed true-blue captain of the girls' basketball team. No, he'd chosen her deliberately, to run a home for him. Such men always chose women who had neither the courage nor imagination to be anything but virtuous.

There was some talk going on, and out of it Laurie's husky voice said, "Owen's having one of his spells where he can't sleep."

Van ran a needle into her finger and exclaimed. The blood drops welled out. There was a little wave of exclamations, and somebody handed her a clean tissue.

"I'm not very good at sewing," she apologized, "but I'm willing."

"You can knit trapheads," said Philip's wife, "and around here that's a priceless talent."

"I should *say* so!" Mrs. Foss Campion was the stout florid woman who had tapped on the window at Van one day. "I tried to learn when we was first married, but Foss said it took him more time to get out my slipknots than to knit the heads himself."

"I'll tell you one thing," Nora Fennell said, "your husband bragging that you knit all his heads has got my husband looking at me with a hard eye." Everyone laughed; everyone began talking about experiences in learning, or refusing to learn.

"I wonder if Owen knows you knit," Laurie Bennett said to her. "I try to help him but I'm not at all fast, and right now he's trying to get three hundred new traps ready for the water as fast as he can. He lost a lot in that really bad storm in March." Van made three beautiful stitches. Owen's wife said tentatively, "*Would* you knit for him? He'd be glad to pay whatever you ask, and he's in such a hurry."

Yes, he is, Vanessa thought. She said, "I charge four dollars for a ball of nylon. Yes, I'd knit for him."

"What a relief! He's been really worked up about those heads. I think it's why he can't sleep. He gets up and knits at two or three in the morning."

"Owen always did things harder than anyone else," his

81

sister said. Vanessa basted with careful neat stitches, her head bent, trying to keep from smiling.

He came the next afternoon when Barry was around the harbor somewhere. She had been waiting for him with such intensity, waked up at dawn by it, that when she actually saw him coming past Foss Campion's she felt scattered with panic, absolutely blank. He had two children with him and she thought in bitter relief, Well, we couldn't talk anyway. Yet when the children stopped off next door and he came on alone she considered hiding upstairs and not opening the door. In a paralysis of doom she heard him coming and waited for the imperious rap of knuckles; stiffly, with great effort, seeing herself a scarecrow come to life, she went to open the door.

"My wife said you'd knit for me," he said at once. She nodded and stood back. He had three two-pound balls of nylon under one arm, and he put them on the table and took two meshboards out of his hip pocket. "'This one's for the big heads and this for the little ones," he explained, showing her the B and L burned into the ends. The meshboards were polished with use, and warm from contact with his body.

He was so curt that the children could have been safely in the room with them. As he started to give her instructions for the heads, she said, "Wait a minute, I'd better write everything down." She went into the sitting room. But she could find neither pencil nor paper, and she got very hot and her eyes stung. "Oh, damn it," she wailed softly, pawing without sense at magazines, and he called to her, "Never mind, I've got something in my pocket." When she went back to the kitchen he was sitting at the table writing on the back of an envelope. She stood looking at the bulk of his shoulders and the back of his neck, at the way the wiry black hair grew down on it and at a small puckered scar—a white seam against the burnt dark skin. She lit a cigarette after several futile attempts to scratch a match because her hand was infuriatingly unsteady.

"There you are," he said, reading the figures off the paper. "And knit them in sets, will you? Got plenty of needles?"

"Plenty," she said.

"All right, then." He pushed back from the table and the moment was over. She had to reclaim it somehow, her mind dashed wildly about as she'd searched for paper and pencil. "Oh—do you want the rings knit in?"

"No, I'll put them in myself." He looked at her then. "I guess I'll get used to it."

"To what?"

"Your hair." Before she had time to warm to that he was on his way out; then he stopped abruptly halfway through the door and said, "A man's so drove up this time of year he can't think."

"Or sleep either," said Van, marvelously, drunkenly warm now as if wine were running through her veins and flushing her skin.

"How'd you know?" Without waiting for her reply he went on. "I'll have to use up tomorrow afternoon going around the shore in a dory looking for traps of mine gone ashore. This morning I saw three down in Ship Cove."

"I'll bet your youngsters will enjoy going with you."

"I'm not taking them. They'll still be in school."

"Oh." The syllable floated between them, a leaf or a feather borne on light capricious air currents, and they were bemused by watching it sail first toward one, then toward the other. Van said, "I must know Ship Cove by sight but not by name. I've been all over the island, I think."

Like someone asked by a passer-by for directions, he said, "You know the deep cove over past Mark's point on the west side? You can see Fennells' from there. That's Barque Cove. Next is Wood and then comes Ship, the third one. You know the place where the woods rise up steep from the shore, all great old spruces straight as masts?"

She realized how intensely she was staring at him. She nodded. "Yes. It's beautiful down there. You could be a thousand miles away from the world."

But he was already going off the doorstep, not looking back. He met Terence Campion coming from his wharf and stood there talking. The children eddied around them in some foolish, giggling game. Terence looked down with an absent smile once or twice, but she noticed with a queer relief that Owen was like a rock amidst splashing surf, impervious even when his daughter put her arms around his waist and leaned her head in a proprietory manner against his middle. The boy, about ten, and the image of his mother, climbed up his back like a monkey;

Terence, as if noticing the sudden loneliness of the Dinsmore children, rumpled Tammie's head and drew Diane against his leg where she leaned quietly as a cat. But Owen, garlanded and even half-strangled by his children, appeared still separate from them.

When he and they had gone, she went to filling needles with the white nylon twine, and while her hands worked automatically she purposely drove tomorrow from her mind, knowing that if it should rain or blow she would be physically sick. She did not dare examine her feelings closely for fear of reasoning herself out of them; or, like Maggie Dinsmore, being visited by signs and portents.

She set a cuphook in the sill of a sunporch window so she could watch the harbor as she worked. When Barry came home he was grinning with satisfaction, "Knitting for Owen, huh? Well, from now on you'll have all the work you can handle. They use a lot of baitbags out here, too."

"I'm not going to make a thing of it," she warned him. "So don't you go drumming up trade for me. His wife cornered me at their damn sewing circle and I couldn't get away."

"All right, all right." He was good-natured about it, talking on and on about his day's work as he got himself a mug-up. She went on knitting, looking out at the molten boil of the harbor under the wind. The rhythm of the twine pulling taut and the creak of the small rocker were hypnotic, putting her into a familiar state in which her mind moved free in suspension between dream and reality. The difference from her knitting in the past was that these heads belonged to Owen Bennett and that soon they would be handled with careless expertise by those brown hands with the long thumbs which she could see so clearly as they wrote, gestured, lit a cigarette, and held out the meshboards.

CHAPTER THIRTEEN

It did not rain or blow, and almost everybody went out to haul. Toward noon she washed herself carefully and put on a new yellow shirt, called "gold" in the catalog, and new slacks and sneakers. She found a lightweight cotton jacket of Barry's to wear. Her raincoat hung on a hook in the entry, and she hadn't worn it for so long that it had become like something dead; she felt a twinge of revulsion and then guilt when she brushed against it. It had been her companion for a long time, she couldn't remember the exact moment when she had forsaken it.

Outside it was quiet and empty, except for the birds. Older children had gone back to school, and younger ones were having naps. So were some of the women, who had got up at daybreak when their husbands did. She had a thrilling sensation of invisibility as she walked through the village and then across the lower meadow toward the woods.

With the sun almost overhead there was a strange light among the spruces, and the sun's heat brought a resinous scent that spoke of summer. Her feet moved without sound on the thick floor of old red-brown spills and dense moss. She could have been utterly alone on the island, in the world, except for the flock of crossbills that at one time accompanied her, unseen in their progress among the spruce tops but communicative.

She came out beyond the deep rock slash of Barque Cove and went along a rough trail above the black volcanic shore to Wood Cove. Here she sat on a boulder and smoked, watching two boats working close to a ledge that occasionally threw up an explosive burst of spray. She did not allow herself to think of what might or might not lie ahead in Ship Cove, but concentrated on externals: birds, boats, scents, and the long-drawn-out rattle of shingle being dragged out by the light surf.

Then she walked on, climbing up and inching down among the jagged peaks of dark rock. At last she came to

Ship Cove, a gleaming slant of pale sea-smoothed stones and a great jumble of driftwood; she saw the splintered half of a skiff enmeshed in a wiry brown tangle of last year's beach peas. She saw the fresh colors of a buoy in the rockweed, and went down to it. It was Owen's, and the trap was nearby. She set about freeing it, working with all her strength, yanking, skidding, soaking her feet and the bottoms of her slacks. Finally she had the trap cleared and the warp unsnarled, coiled up, and put inside. She looked for another buoy; he'd said three. She found one in a crevice. She had to discard her jacket now; she was warm from her struggles. But at last she had this warp untangled from a water-soaked derelict spruce. In sodden squelching sneakers she was climbing about the rocks looking for the third buoy when all at once Owen was there. She hadn't heard the outboard.

Suddenly lightheaded, she realized that she had hardly believed he would come. Yet he nodded up at her as if he, at least, had never been in any doubt of *her*.

He came to the two freed traps, each with its buoys and coiled warp tucked inside. He stood looking at them, his hands in his pockets, his head canted. Then he grinned. "Your work, by the looks of you."

She saw then the smears of crushed rockweed on her new slacks and shirt, the wet patches, felt the stickiness of sweat on her neck and forehead. She felt ridiculous standing there, mute and dirty. But as if he didn't notice he said, "Come on down and rest from yours labors and have a cigarette." Without watching to see if she obeyed he went up the beach and sat down in the shade. She could have disappeared while his back was turned and she felt the temptation like a great sea trying to knock her off her feet. But it receded, leaving only its roaring in her ears, and she was on her way to Owen. She saw everything with fierce clarity, and even stopped to pick up a piece of glass turned amethyst. When she sat down on the log beside him she held up the glass to her eye and looked at the sea through it.

"Better that way?" Owen asked her.

"A change." She laid the glass on the log between them and took the cigarette he offered her. She had got steady again. She could even lean forward to the match.

"You like change," he said.

"Doesn't everybody?"

86

He picked up the glass and studied her through it. "Gives you a hell of a complexion." They both laughed. Her confidence increased. They smoked without speaking. Behind them the wood was silent except for the small twitterings that came and went. They sat in its shadow, lost in it to anyone out on the water.

"What did you come here today for?" he said suddenly.

"For a walk. I often come down this way." She played with the glass again, watching a gull through it.

"Why just this time? Why not earlier, or later?"

"I came out when I had my work done—oh, all right," she heard herself saying. "*All right*. Why were you so damned explicit about where you were going to be, and when?" She started to get up but he grabbed her forearm and pulled her down again.

"All right, you're here. Sit still. I was explicit, as you call it, because I'm a goddam fool. I went to sleep last night knowing it, and I woke up this morning knowing it. What's your excuse?"

"Curiosity. Did I get the message or wasn't there a message?"

They looked at each other, she steadied by the violence of his outburst against himself. "Oh, there was a message all right, but last night wasn't the first one."

"You said something the night you came looking for Barry to help you shut off the harbor."

"What?"

"That Barry never knew where I was. What did you mean by that?"

"Just that. He never does know, does he? I don't mean right now. I mean even when he's looking at you he doesn't know."

She moved away from him out into the sunshine, sitting on the warm stones with her back to him and began unlacing her soaked sneakers. "That's too deep for me," she said.

"You don't want to admit it, do you? But you give him a hell of a hard time. He praises you up to everybody. My wife this, my wife that. But underneath he's puzzled and sometimes he's scared foolish. He's a nice little guy, but a nervous little guy."

She looked back at him furiously. "How do you know all this? Are you a mind-reader? A psychiatrist? And do you talk this over with all your relatives over a cup of coffee? Got us torn into shreds and shoved under the microscope?"

His hand was on the nape of her neck. "Listen," he said. "I've talked about you to nobody. Understand? What I think is my business. And right now, yours." She shut her eyes. The light grip of his fingers sent a torrent of desire over her like warm water. She could have drowned in it easily, but pride held her up. She fumbled for words.

"B-Barry's all right. He's been unhappy because he never got anywhere. Now he thinks he's in the promised land."

His fingers gently kneaded her neck. He couldn't see if her eyes were shut. "It's not that simple," he said. "He's not a kid. He wants more than money in his pocket and three meals a day."

"I've been married to him for twelve years," she said.

"And you don't know him any more than my wife knows me," he said. He let her go and got up from the log. She sat rigid a few moments, and listened to the grating of stones under his rubber boots as he walked. She wanted to be away from here. She sprang up angrily and went to pick up her jacket, all without looking at him.

"Vanessa," he said. The word transfixed her. It was the first time he had ever said her name. She looked slowly around and saw him standing at the edge of the woods, his face dark and stony in its shadow. "Come here."

"No," she said, but she went. He put his hand and took hers and pulled her up beside him. Then they went into the woods a little way; the bank under the trees was steep, and soft with years of spruce spills. They stopped by a massive, scaly yellow birch and he took her into his arms and kissed her, at first gently and then with a kind of desperate ferocity which she returned, holding him with all her strength, half-smothered, her ribs aching, a taste of blood in her mouth. When he let her go she fell back against the birch trunk, her mouth throbbing.

"There, by God," he said violently. "Let that be the end of it."

He went plunging down the steep slope through the shadowy light toward the pale gleam of the beach. She slid down the trunk until she was sitting, her knees under her chin, and peered through the dark columns of spruces to watch him lug first one trap and then the other down the beach to the dory. He splashed into the water to push the dory off and then its bow disappeared from her vision, and in a moment she heard the outboard start up with a roar and then settle into a steady hum as the dory sped away.

She sat there a little while, listening to the blood beat in her ears. Her jubilation grew and grew. She couldn't help smiling and hugging her knees. Her triumph was more than victory, it was a physical metamorphosis. Her whole body felt remade, turned fluid and translucent, a thing of beauty. She sprang up and ran down the slope, jumped from the bank onto the beach stones, and went home leaping from rock to rock, climbing the steep faces by toe and finger holds when she could have gone around by them, just for the pure pleasure of using this new body. In this way she went up the high red wall of Barque Cove, crawling diagonally over it until the surf was swirling and creaming below her. At the top she lay on her back on the brown turf, out of breath but still transfixed in joy like a fly in amber.

Suddenly it came to her. The Day. This could be it. What she was born for, what she had been moving toward all the days of her life. She'd had to marry Barry, they'd had to live in a miserable crawl from one poor situation to another, so that he would be hanging around the Limerock waterfront at the right moment to meet Philip Bennett. *That* was why the Water Street house had to be sold, she knew now, goose-fleshed with awe; so she'd have nothing to hold her back.

The Day. This was it.

CHAPTER FOURTEEN

She could hardly believe the happiness in which she awoke these mornings. She seemed to be budding like the lilacs, taking on a sheen like the new grass, a warmth like the spring sun. She realized that Barry was basking in it but it didn't matter. She felt splendidly kind toward him and took a special pleasure in getting the meals ready and keeping the house neat. Sometimes she felt almost breathless with excitement when she opened her eyes in th morning, hearing the song sparrow that sang always from the fishhouse roof, because she did not know what the day held. But she was confident of its joyous surprises. This was the way fortunate children woke up, she knew, but she was experiencing it for the first time in her life. When she was alone in the house she hugged herself for her good luck in being born new when she was old enough to appreciate it.

She was glad Owen didn't keep his boat in the harbor, because she would have been wanting to be up early enough to see or at least hear *White Lady* going, and she might not have been able to hide that from Barry. As it was, she never looked for a glimpse of him before mid-afternoon, when he would be in the harbor to sell his lobsters and so she was sustained all day with this warm bubbling current. A glimpse was enough for now. Paradoxically it would not be enough to meet, to nod, and to keep her eyes blank.

"It's going to storm," Barry said one morning.

"Is it?" she said cheerfully. From the window over the sink, if you moved to the right angle, you could see Owen's house against black woods and smoky red sunrise. But if he wasn't in, it didn't exist. The wife and children were everybody else's fantasies, not his, not hers.

"Southwesterly," Barry gloomed. "I hope to God we don't lose those traps out on the Barn Ground. Of course Phil's got five hundred more on the bank, but all those new nylon heads and warps. . . . We could lose in a day as much as I used to make in a year fubbing around." He shoved back his chair. "Oh well, get moving, Barry. This won't buy shoes for the baby nor pay for the ones he's wearing."

She stopped looking out the window and went back to folding his sandwiches in waxed paper. He came up behind her and put his arms around her, and nuzzled the nape of her neck. "Hey, damned if I don't like it after all. Short hair, I mean. Speaking of babies—" He stopped and waited.

For an instant a hideous cold chilled her, and then she thought, I'm free from that now. "Don't rush me, Barry," she murmured.

"But you look so damn' good these days." He pushed

harder against her, his fingers crawled up her ribs. "God, I feel like a young rooster."

"What do they say to the last man out around here?" she asked. He chuckled in her neck. "Same as they say to the one who always wants a nap after dinner. I'd be proud. They'd be some envious now, I can tell ye."

"Well, I don't intend to give you a chance to grin like a Chessy cat this morning. Your lunch is ready, and if it's going to blow you'd better get to work before it gets here."

"You're like all the women, got your eye on the almighty dollar." But she knew how he'd brag when he got to the beach, muttering profanely that the wife wouldn't give him anything this morning, that she'd kicked him out of bed and said, "Get to work, you leechous old bastard." And when someone laughed at that, he'd be set up for the day.

She went to work on her ironing when he had gone, had finished, and was sitting down by the harbor windows with a fresh cup of coffee when there was a soft knock at the back door. The threat of interference clawed at her, and then she remembered she was free now, and got up to answer. At least with that timid knock it couldn't be Kathy, whose signal was as uninhibited as she was.

The child had velvety black eyes, and round cheeks red with embarrassment. Her basket held turfs pierced by the new tips of lily of the valley. "I'm Holly Bennett. Mama sent these. Aunt Jo said you liked them, and we have millions." The little smile was enough like her father's to hit Van in the stomach. And Aunt Jo could mind her own damn business.

"Thank you," said Vanessa. "I'll find something to put them in, so you can take the basket." You did not insult a child, even a fortunate one. "Or will it make you late for school to wait a minute?"

"No, we come early with Mama."

"That's right, she's the teacher." She set the turfs in a cardboard carton in the entry. "It must be strange to go to school to your own mother."

It must be strange to *know* your own mother.

"Well, we're used to it," Holly said. "We're just like all the other kids. We can't call her Mama in school." She was more confident now. "A lot of the kids call her Laurie outside, but they have to call her Mrs. Bennett in school.

91

It seems funny for *us* to say that, so we just don't call her anything." She had a soft chuckle. Turning to hand her the basket, Van was surprised by the resemblance again, and its dull blow. "How old are you?" she asked.

"Twelve." The coaly black hair grew in a drake's tail down her neck. She jumped neatly with both feet together onto the walk. "Cindy Campion's got chicken pox this morning!" she called back. "I bet everybody'll get it now and we'll have some more vacation!"

"I hope so," Van said, marveling that she should sound so ordinary. She went back into the kitchen, feeling a dragging tiredness that slanted into nausea. For four days she'd protected her new splendor, and now it was dying, struck down by a child at the door, a handful of lily of the valley, a black-eyed smile. She looked around the kitchen as if she had never seen it before and didn't know how she'd got into it. Twelve years ago the woman was delivered of his child. Nine months before that they'd conceived it. She couldn't endure the picture and bit at a knuckle until the pain startled her. Twelve years ago she'd married Barry because there was nothing else for her to do. "And he was *here*," she whispered in the empty kitchen. "All the time he was here but I didn't know it. And he married her not knowing about me. Oh, damn, damn, *damn!*" she shouted suddenly. The tears began to run down her face. "Why did it have to be? Why couldn't it just once be for *me?* All those rotten filthy despicable years, and I *knew* there was something else, there had to be, but *where?*"

Her howl hung in the air. She was as startled as if someone else had shrieked. She looked quickly outdoors to see if anyone could have heard, but the mild cloudy morning was empty except for the birds. The boats were all gone. Trembling as if she'd almost been caught committing a crime, she locked back and front doors and tried to restore herself. "No, you are not insane," she said between deep breaths. "Anybody can shriek in frustration. It's the same as swearing. It makes you feel better. You feel better, don't you? *Don't you?*"

She didn't. The wasteland of the lost twelve years surrounded her. She went upstairs and crawled into bed, covering her ears against the insistent song sparrow.

She didn't go to sleep after all, and imperceptibly the sense of shock and outrage died down. The sound of wild geese, like dogs barking in the distance, got her up; it had always excited her. With her head out the window she was lucky enough to see the long V fly low over the island under the thickening clouds. Exhilaration replaced depression; the geese had been like a sign to her. V for Victory, she thought jauntily, and went downstairs to have the coffee that Holly Bennett had interrupted. After all, the twelve years hadn't been a lifetime. She didn't have to dwell on them; she was freed from all that because The Day had come.

By mid-afternoon the wind was blowing hard and boats were beginning to come in ahead of the storm. She went out into the damp blustery air smoky with spray, and odorous with churning rockweed. Children seemed to be everywhere, wild as cats in the wind. Women were out too, skirts whipped in the gusts, and the men were picking up loose gear around their fishhouses. On her way to the store Van met Maggie and Rob Dinsmore; Rob's hand was heavily bandaged. Mag gave Van her happy small-boy grin. "I was just going over to your house. We want you and Barry to come to supper Saturday night. The kids talk about you all the time, after the way you took hold that day."

"Ayuh," Rob said in his slow mild voice. "We're much obliged. That was some doin's that day as near as I can remember."

"He can't remember it all, ain't that funny?" Mag said. "But maybe it's a blessing. *I'll* never forget it," she said militantly. "I might's well be honest, I didn't want to come back! I figgered it was a warning, what with my dreams and all. But Rob he never said a word, just lay there and stared at me like Diane while I carried on."

"To tell you the truth," Rob said, "while she was carrying on so, I was thinking I was all done anyway."

"Then Owen called up. Ain't it strange," Maggie demanded reverently, "that it's the same as what happened to him, only in a different way, and Rob works for him? And he said, 'You tell that man of yours it didn't do me in, and it needn't do him in unless he's so minded. So he's still working for me, and I'll get somebody to help out till he can manage again.'"

"That's Owen for ye," said Rob.

That's Owen, said Vanessa behind her smiling nod. That's pure Bennett doctrine. Grapple them to your heart with hoops of steel or something. A kind word and they worship you for life. They're all like Barry, seeking salvation from bumhood and ready to grovel. *Owen.* The word scalded where it touched.

"I'd better get my shopping done before it rains," she said.

"But what about supper?" Mag put her hand on her arm. Van started to stiffen, but controlled it and kept on smiling.

"Baked beans," Maggie urged. "Barry says he's crazy about 'em."

"Yes, he is. All right," she heard herself saying. "Saturday night." Incredibly she was adding, "It will be nice."

Maggie squeezed her arm with both hands. "Won't it!" Rob smiled gravely. He did look like Diane, his round eyes were ridiculously fringed. She walked away carrying the image with her, as of some odd flowering plant with twin blossoms.

In the store she had to wait until Mark finished telephoning an order for trap stock and nylon twine. The only other Bennett there was Charles, who didn't share the family compulsion to make conversation. Feeling amiable and relaxed, she listened to the thud and slosh of water under the floor, and decided to give Barry one of his favorite suppers tonight; fritters, bacon, and applesauce.

She was almost back to the house before she realized that her side of the harbor looked strange; something was either out of place or intruding. A boat lay where there had been none before—*White Lady*, using the empty mooring that lay beyond Barry's and Willy's smaller boats. She looked as big as a yacht. Van was unreasonably excited to see her there, as if there must be some profoundly significant reason for it. She walked faster, not able to shake the conviction that she was on her way to a meeting with him, though she kept telling herself there was no sense to it and that she was behaving like a love-sick fifteen-year-old.

When she passed Terence Campion's, Kathy came out on the porch. "Hi! I've got one popped out with chicken pox and two to go. They're miserable, poor peanuts."

"What's that doing here?" Van gestured toward *White Lady*.

"Schoolhouse Cove's a mess in a storm like this, so he always brings her around to the harbor."

"Oh. I'm sorry about the kids," she added. "Anything I can do?"

"Just pray for them to break out tonight. So long!" She went back inside. Van felt cheated and forlorn. So it was nothing out of the ordinary after all. But still, if she hadn't stood there being so damned sweet to the Dinsmores and if she hadn't had to wait in the store, she would have seen him when he rowed ashore from the mooring; there was the strange skiff tied up next to Barry's in the lee of the wharf. He might have come into the house, saying he wanted to check on the knitting, using that for an excuse. And she hadn't been there. . . . She was dreadfully tired.

CHAPTER FIFTEEN

Barry brought a lamp into her room and woke her. She surfaced out of a hot, muffling blackness and put her arms over her eyes. "Go away," she said. There were curious sounds in the room with him, rattlings and thumpings. "What's that?" she asked thickly from under her folded arms.

"It's the storm. It's backlashed, coming north now, straight into the harbor like all hell's broke loose. Come on, get up."

"What for? The house washing away?"

"They're coming to watch the boats from here. In case one starts ashore." He tried to pull her arms away from her head, half-laughing, half-exasperated. "Get up, will ye? Make us up a big pot of coffee and some sandwiches. It's only nine o'clock. Owen's coming down and Willy's bringing Gina with him, if they don't get blowed away coming around the harbor. She's scairt to stay alone."

"Over here?" She sat up and glared at him. "What'd you have to invite her for? Why can't they go and watch at Campions'? Terence has to keep an eye out for his boat, doesn't he?"

"For Christ's sake, they got three sick kids over there,

Now are you getting up and acting like a normal human being, or aren't you?"

"You mean I've got a choice?"

The lamp threw his shadow over the slanting ceiling with an impressiveness he never had. "Come on. You don't have to talk to her, you can work on those trap-heads. But if you don't come down it'll look funny."

"Say I'm getting the chicken pox too. No, bubonic plague." Ignoring that remark he said excitedly, "Owen ought to be showing up pretty soon. That boat of his is doing some fancy larruping around on her mooring, and she's some heavy son of a bitch. If she comes down on me and Willy, that's it, period. We're likely all three to come ashore and break up."

"What good does it do to watch?" Seal Point's harbor had been almost completely sheltered and a man could get to his boat very easily in any kind of storm. What did Barry think they could do in this gale?

"We've got a big seine dory with an outboard tied up alongside the wharf here. When you see a boat coming ashore or moving down on another one, the thing is to get a man aboard her to start up the engine and get her on the lee side of a wharf. If the engine starts, that is," he added jauntily. He ran downstairs whistling. Barry never became gloomy or apprehensive about an emergency with boats and salt water; it was the one field in which she could quite objectively admire him.

She sat there a moment looking at the dark doorway, listening to him downstairs. A new gust shook the house and rain beat like hail against the windows. The lamplight flickered and Barry's whistle was drowned out. Then she remembered that Owen was coming, and she was frightened. She didn't know how she could sit in the same room with him and Barry. The cove would be there in the room with them. Everything. She touched the back of her neck, trying to remember if it was the maimed hand that had taken hold of her there.

Finally she got up and into fresh slacks and a clean blouse, brushing her hair but not bothering with lipstick. When she went downstairs Barry was in the darkened sun parlor, flashing his five-cell torch out at the moorings. She measured coffee into a pot and added water. He came out into the kitchen grinning as if it were the start of a party.

"Somebody's buglight on the way. Must be Willy and his child bride."

Gina, shucked out of boots and red rainclothes, wore another of her immense sweaters, lavender this time, with violet stretch pants. For once her hair was out of rollers. She gave Barry a languorous smile and Van an indifferent nod, then sat down at the table and laid out the contents of her handbag. She began to groom herself with the concentration, but not the tidy charm, of a cat. Vanessa, disliking hairbrushes on the table, watched coldly sidewise as she made sandwiches at the dresser. Willy, flushed with happy embarrassment under his acne, talked loudly with Barry about the storm and lobstering. Barry took on a mellow twinkle and called him "son" quite often, though they might have been only ten years apart in age.

Gina's black hair was pushed with the brush into a different kind of tangle from the one she'd come in with; eyelashes were minutely scrutinized, and the long black lines drawn under the eyes were refreshed, the green iridescence on the lids renewed. Two lipsticks were used in a process which for Van had a certain repulsive fascination; they left Gina's mouth much larger than life, so dark and thickly glistening she wondered how the girl could move her mouth to speak. After that powder was fluffed vigorously over the whole ensemble, also dusting the table, which Gina wiped off with a swipe of her arm. She picked up a small gold-colored vial, squeezed it, and scented herself heavily with a fragrance that reminded Van of rotting hyacinths. Everything done, she packed away her equipment, took out her cigarettes, and with a manner ineffably languid and cynical, lit a cigarette and sat gazing into space. If Barry glanced at her, a large smile flashed on with mechanical brightness, and a kind of twitch ran through her body as if by automatic impulse; it happened so often in just the same way, beginning with a toss of the head, a switch of the shoulders, a wriggle of her skinny seat, that each time Van was fascinated all over again. If Willy looked at her, which he did often, and said, "You all right, honey?" she sagged instantly into boredom.

Van suppressed for the time being the desire to scrub the table with hot suds. She sat down across from Gina and began to fill needles with nylon twine. "Have you ever been through a bad storm like this before? Out here, I mean?" she asked. There was the hike of a shoulder toward one ear, a lift of an eyebrow, smoke blown professionally from the nostrils.

"Oh, yeah," Gina said indifferently. "But nothing ever happens."

"Well, that's a help." What would Gina look like scrubbed?

"Would be a help if that goddam boat really did come ashore and smash up."

"Listen to her!" Willy erupted in a bray of nervous laughter. "She's got a sense of humor," he assured Van, but she saw the expression in his eyes. You young fool, she thought, you're Barry all over again, though I wasn't the rotten little trollop you've got.

Gina went on in a dead voice, touching the elaborate mass of hair with pearl-painted nails. "I'd like to see every boat in this harbor smash up tonight. We'd be off here tomorrow with me dancing a jig."

"Kind of hard on the rest of us, aren't you, dear?" Barry asked her. "Some of us like it. Some of us got a living to make, including your husband."

"*Him*." She slanted Willy a glance that turned him dark red, and he forgot to try for a laugh but looked abjectly at his feet. "He could do something else besides being a—" She flickered her thick lashes, and almost smiled. "He could maybe get on a dragger and make damn good pay."

"What would you do, darlin' mine, while he was on a trip?" Barry teased her. Willy's hand lifted from his knee in a small futile gesture of protest.

"Oh, I'd make out," she assured Barry. "I could get a job too. I could wait on tables anywhere."

Not quite anywhere, Van thought. Aloud she said, "If you hate it here so much why don't you go ashore and work anyway?"

The sound might have been a laugh, but looking at the unchanged face one couldn't be sure. Gina blew out more smoke and her eyes became glazed; her mouth dragged down into an expression of sulky idiocy.

"She wouldn't want to live apart from me, Mrs. Barton," Willy explained earnestly. "We married to be together, and even if she don't think much of it, being a city girl, she knows this is where I can make a hell of a good living."

"He makes a hell of a good arse-wiper, too," said Gina.

Barry laughed very loudly and thwacked Willy on the shoulder. The boy smiled feebly. Vanessa decided to scrub the table and then to go back to bed.

"Hey, let's get a card game going here," said Barry, jumping up. "Hey, Van, where's the cards? We've got some, haven't we?"

"In the table drawer," said Van.

The door to the entry swung open and Owen stood there, needing room to get out of his streaming oilclothes. His face was red with rain and wind.

"Hey, Cap'n Owen, you're drowning us!" Willy protested as a wet sleeve swung past him.

"You're likely to be wetter than that before the night's out. Hello, sweetheart. How's the poor man's Cleopatra?"

Gina giggled. "I haven't found Mark Antony yet."

"Everything's all secure out front so far, Admiral," said Barry. "You're just in time for some of the best coffee you ever doused a lip in."

"Here, we can liven it up a dite." Owen set a fifth of whiskey on the table in front of Gina, who giggled again.

"Oh, boy, this'll be the best storm-watching *I* ever did!"

"Gina likes to pretend she's tough and drinks a lot," Willy explained. "She don't really touch it, hardly."

Gina made a raucous sound, and Barry laughed obligingly.

"You pouring, Admiral?" he asked Owen.

"You can do the honors." Owen sat down at the table and began shuffling the cards. They flowed and snapped through his hands so that the missing fingers were not missed, and Willy said in admiration, "Gorry, anybody'd think you used to work in one of them big gambling houses."

"They keep writing to me all the time from Vegas," said Owen.

"Let's see, Gina, Willy says you get just a sniff." Barry gave her a twinkling smile, and she whooped.

"Willy says! Who cares what Willy says? I wanta glow, and when you gotta glow you gotta glow." She rocked with laughter. Barry poured out half a cheese-glass full. Willy, smiling desperately, said, "Make it last, honey.... Tastes better if you sip it real slow, don't it, Barry?"

"I wouldn't know." Barry splashed liquor into another glass. "I'm a gulper myself. Here you be, Willy. Drink her down and join the human race."

Owen went on laying out a game of solitaire. Van stood at one side. She had never felt quite as invisible in her own home, or whatever shelter passed for her own home. She had always been in control. Tonight she was here but not here. Owen hadn't given her even a glance. Gina was blossoming nastily in the presence of the men, and Willy was so concentrated on her that Van wondered why the others couldn't feel the agony of that concentration. Barry had got drunk with the occasion even before the whiskey had been poured. From now on he would become progressively profane and salacious. He might be sorry for Willy, but that wouldn't keep him from entering into a duel of juvenile double-meanings with Gina. He was too stupid to realize that Owen was already bored with them all.

Is it insane to hide in a book from *this?* she thought. If she could move quietly now toward the stairs, they'd never miss her. But as she turned her head hungrily toward the dark corner Barry slammed down his glass and shouted, "Hey, how about getting the grub out? We're about to have us a little poker game. I'm leaving it to Gina to decide whether it'll be draw, stud, or strip."

"When I've had a few more drinks I won't care," said Gina.

"Gorry, here!" He tipped more into her glass. Willy got up, almost knocking over his chair.

"I'll take a look at the boats," he mumbled and went into the other room, cracking one elbow against a door casing on the way. Gina leaned her head against Barry's arm. Her giggle had now become a gurgle.

"Say, when," Barry commanded, and she breathed, "Any time."

"Don't you know I never tamper with married women?"

"Think of all that experience lost to the world." Gina rubbed her face along his sleeve. All that goddam makeup wiping off, Vanessa thought, and me washing by hand.

"Ayuh, ain't it fierce?" said Barry. "But I don't mind you working on me. You might just weaken my good resolutions."

"Here's your cards." Owen slung the pack across the table, and they slithered and spread out. Gathering them up, Barry said, "You playing, Cap'n?"

"I'm not much of a card player." He tilted back in his chair and looked restlessly around the kitchen; his gaze

100

skipped Van, whose face began to burn. Willy came out, blinking and forlorn. He sat down without speaking and stared at his knobby hands.

"Come on, son," Barry said with a benign twinkle. He began to shuffle the cards. Owen swung his chair around till the lamplight came from the side, picked up a magazine, and began to read. Gina maneuvered her chair until she was elbowing the back of Owen's and cozily leaning her head toward his.

Van got out a plate for the sandwiches of canned luncheon meat and relish, put out mugs for the coffee, and sat down to knit from a cuphook screwed into the edge of the dresser. The scene around the table lacerated her nerves, and yet she could not bear to go away from the oblivious black head. . . . He could at least look in my direction once, it's his trapheads ruining my hands. . . . Choosy, is he? The bouquet from that one should be strangling him. I don't think her hair's been washed since she was born. I wish all their damn boats would come ashore at once. Then you'd see some hopping and swearing. And I'd sit here and laugh. I'd laugh myself sick and I'd never stop. That's what Gina said. Sisters under the skin. What a nauseating thought. . . . She drove the needle hard through the loop and gave a vicious pull. A good bit of nylon around the neck and twisted just right would get rid of that giggle. Gigglotomy. And that Willy. He makes me want to puke too. The pair of them.

"Tell me what to do," Gina commanded, waving her cards around in front of Owen's face.

"Well, good God, get 'em off the end of my nose." He turned in his chair, hooked one arm over the back of it, and studied her cards, then touched one. "Play that."

She hunched up a shoulder and moaned, "Ooh, your breath is warm. Makes me feel all funny."

Willy put down his cards, pushed back from the table, and stumbled out through the entry. Barry looked around, and Owen said, "He's sick."

"I better go see," said Barry, getting up.

"Oh, let him heave and get it over with," Gina said gaily. "He's not used to drinking. He's an awful baby. I don't know what I married such a green kid for. I coulda had an older man." She gave Owen an oblique glance from under heavy green eyelids. "I go for older men, you know?"

101

"Is that so?" Owen grinned at her. "I wonder why."

"Experience," she breathed. "They know how to give a girl a good time, you know?"

"Well, it takes two to tango," said Barry, and doubled over the back of his chair in appreciation of his wit. I might join Willy in the back yard and we could vomit together, Van thought. Outside Willy yelled something, and then came crashing in, spattered with rain.

"Hey, they're tearing around Foss's wharf! Looks like a boat's ashore!"

Barry seized his big light and ran into the other room. "Ours are all okay!" he shouted back. Owen was already hauling on his rubber boots and Willy was scrabbling around for his in the entry. Barry got his from behind the stove. Owen moved the fastest. Without stopping for oilpants he took his oiljacket and went out pulling it on. The others slammed out behind him, and when they were gone the kitchen was still full of them; it vibrated with the urgency and confusion of their departure. Gina, who had stared at it all without expression, threw down her cards and said in a flat voice, "Well, how do you like that? And it's not even one of their boats."

"You ought to know how fishermen operate," said Van. She began to clear the table of glasses and the remaining sandwiches, then gathered up the cards.

"Yeah, I know how they operate," said Gina. "These Bennett's Island bastards." Then she giggled. "Hey, that was some poker game. I was doing good, in more ways than one. Boy, I didn't know anybody could have so much fun out here. That Owen's right ready for it, isn't he?"

"Ready for what?" Van asked, neatly squaring the pack.

"*You* know. You been watching him. Well, I suppose he's getting to the age. They start liking 'em younger and younger, kind of works them up more, you know? Now Willy," she went on complacently, "he's always ready. He don't need any working up. It's because he's young," she explained.

I must tell Owen all this, Van thought. He should know that he's just a lecherous old man. She leaned against the sink, shuddering with the attempt to control her laughter, then overcome by it she reached for a towel to wipe her streaming eyes, and then was shaken by new convulsions.

"Hey, what's so funny?" Gina demanded angrily. "*Me?*

Well, let me tell you, your own husband's just as horny, and—*Hey,* are you all right? I mean, are you having high strikes or something." The vicious edge had given way to the shrillness of fright. "Maybe I better go get Barry—" She was halfway to the door.

"No, don't go, I'm all right," Van assured her. Still gasping, she pumped cold cistern water into the basin and splashed it several times over her face. "It's something I can't share, but I wasn't laughing at you," she said through the sloshing. She straightened up and dried her face.

"You scared me," Gina accused her. "I've heard people go off their heads like that and they ended up in Bangor."

Vanessa thought of telling her she'd already been in Bangor for committing a gigglotomy with a carving knife, but it was too much work. She lit a cigarette, supported one elbow in the other hand, and gazed placidly at Gina, who began to fidget. Suddenly her small claw seized the huge handbag and groped for the compact, in whose mirror she gazed at her reflection with the concentration of a scientist cooking up a miracle mixture. Then, as if she had found the reassurance she needed, she put the compact away and said, "It sounds like it's slacking off. I guess I'll go see what they're doing and then go home."

Van watched her getting into her red rainclothes. She was frankly in a hurry now. . . . I suppose it'll be all over the place tomorrow that I acted like a crazy woman, or that I *am* a crazy woman. . . . But it didn't matter any more.

CHAPTER SIXTEEN

She was in bed when Owen came back with Barry to get his oilpants. The rain had stopped and the periods between gusts were long enough so that when she went to the head of the stairs she heard them talking quite clearly. They both sounded subdued, voices slow and interrupted by yawns, but whatever boat had been threatened had been saved. There was a brief discussion about the whiskey, and finally Barry agreed to keep it. *That* was a hard decision, wasn't it, old boy? Van thought. "You'll need it in the morning," Owen told him. Oh, take your patronizing bullshit out of here, Van thought and for God's sake, Barry, don't thank him again.... Then she remembered Gina and she was almost overcome again. It was rich, rich—it paid her for almost everything. What a fool he'd look when she told him, and if she never spoke another word to him beyond that, she'd see that he was told, all right.

She went back to bed, feeling so exhausted that she didn't know when Barry got into bed. He was gone in the morning when she woke up. She rose on one elbow and saw by the slant of the sun it was mid-morning, and a mild one; the song sparrow was going it again, and she was overcome by a crushing homesickness for her bedroom on Water Street. A song sparrow used to sing in one of the old syringa bushes, starting early as March. Funny, she'd forgotten it yesterday morning, when the song sparrow had meant something quite different. Yesterday morning or yesterday year. It had been a long time. She squeezed her eyes shut, and then opened them and got quickly out of bed.

She dressed and, oblivious to her unbrushed hair and unwashed face, went out, taking her raincoat and a book but nothing to eat. When she came to her place inside the edge of the woods, she threw down the raincoat and lay on it and opened the book. But it wasn't the one she'd reached for, a novel borrowed from Joanna. It was her high school poetry anthology. She threw it from her. It hit a tree and fell at the bottom, open, its leaves fluttering. She felt sudden grief and shame, the way she'd felt once when she'd hit a bird with a stone.

She had not allowed herself to consciously remember the incident until this moment, seeing a page flicker as the dying bird's wing had flickered. I committed murder at an early age, she thought now, trying for cynicism, but she ran to the book and picked it up and brushed it off. She had read all the poems so many times that most of them she knew by heart, or knew snatches of.... *Then I saw the Congo, creeping through the black. . . . Whenever Richard Cory went downtown.... When I consider Life and its few years. . . .*

She sat down crosslegged on the warm greening turf

and looked through the pages. It had meant so much and promised so much. It had been precious to her as the empty scent bottle was precious, for what it had once held. She laid her hand on the book and said, "You ought to be burned, like an old flag." She jumped up and carried it down onto the flat rocks, and gathered up handfuls of dried chips and rockweed. In a crevice she started a fire and then fed the book to it, a few pages at a time. She saw familiar words leap and blacken in the flames. The Traveler's horse that nibbled at the forest's ferny floor died, and the Hound of Heaven, and the Wild Swans of Coole; the soldier-poets, the Brownings, Walt Whitman, Robert Frost. Her face began to feel made of stone, as if she couldn't move it if she tried. At the end she ripped the binding apart with strong hands and watched that burn too. The tide was coming, and presently it would lap at the place where the fire had been, the ashes would float, the essence of the words would go out on the cold salt current. Tonight the scent bottle would join the poems.

She walked home in the late afternoon, in a warm light full of fresh bird song; she was hungry and disconsolate, her raincoat too hot for comfort. When she came through the spruces into the yard, Kathy was hanging out some clothes and called over to her, "What a gorgeous day, and my three stuck in with chicken pox. Aren't you lucky!" she said without malice.

Van gave her a wave and a slight smile and went into the house. Barry wasn't there, but he'd been home and cooked bacon and eggs. She was so hungry her stomach hurt, so she fried bacon and eggs for herself. She was still sitting at the table, her chin in her hands, when Barry came home again.

"Hello, stranger," he said jauntily. "Long time no see." The last word ended in an uncertain upward note as he looked around the kitchen. There were no signs of supper, and the dishes from last night and this day were still in the sink. His smile went weak. "You all right?"

"I'm all right."

"Oh." If he had been a more violent man he would have yelled at her, "Christ, are you starting this up again?" Instead he accepted it, with just a furtive glance around and a feeble grin.

"Do you suppose Willy tiptoes around Gina?" she asked abruptly.

He was stacking dishes. "Huh?" he said.

"Never mind."

"You want me to get something at the store for supper?"

"No, I'll fix something." She pushed back from the table and got up in slow motion, as if her heart were scarcely beating. She took the raincoat from another chair, and when he saw that, his eyes widened briefly and she thought he would say something. But instead he walked into the sitting room, and she heard a chair creak and the flutter of magazine pages.

Supper was a conglomerate of left-overs from the refrigerator. She made a pot of coffee to go with it, and Barry ate noisily. Sometimes she suspected him of chewing, gulping, and smacking his lips to annoy her. Finally he tipped back in his chair, pressed his hand against his stomach, and emitted a long rolling belch. "Thank the Lord for that bite, some folks would call it a meal. Hey, they're getting up a dance for Saturday night. Some of the young ones were cleaning up the clubhouse this afternoon. Anybody been around to ask you to help out on the refreshments?"

"I don't know. I was out all day."

"Well, hey, a dance'll be pretty good, won't it?" His eyes twinkled. "Way we've all been drivin 'er around here, it's time we shook out some of the kinks. A couple of Charles Bennett's kids are damn good on the accordion and gee-tar, and young Ralph Percy's a hot fiddler, especially on the square dances. They have cake and coffee during intermission, that's why I was wondering if they'd been around to you. Anyway," he added complacently, "I told 'em you'd make something."

"Well, I won't," she said without raising her voice. "You should've known better than to promise. Now you'll look a fool." She got up and began clearing the table.

"You mean you'll let me down?" he asked.

"Haven't I always? Why is it such a shock?" She ladled water into the dishpan and set the pan on the gas stove to heat. "If you'll get out of the way I'll clean up this kitchen."

"And about time too." He came up glaring, shooting out his jaw. "I wondered how long it would be before you went back to your slutty screwball ways, and now I know. It was too goddam good to be true." He stood in her way, flinging out his hands. "Why couldn't you keep it up? What am I supposed to do? Just tell me, for God's sake, and I'll do it!"

She went on about her work, not bothering to answer or even show by her expression that she heard. Finally, muttering as many obscenities as he could think of, he slammed out.

They didn't speak again that night. The next day she didn't stay home for fear someone would come calling or to ask for a cake. When she went home in the afternoon she laid out clean clothes for Barry, his good pants and shoes, a new white shirt and a cardigan he'd got her to order from the catalog.

Kathy came over and said Terence's aunt was going to sit with the children so she and Terence could go. "She's mellow because Foss's boat was saved the other night," she explained. "You going?"

"I doubt it," said Vanessa, "I never was one for dances."

Kathy looked disappointed. "I'd think by the way you moved that you'd be a good dancer."

She smiled and shook her head. "Two left feet."

Kathy stayed a little while longer, talking about the storm and the rescue of Foss's boat. On her way out she met Barry coming in.

"See if you can't coax Van into coming to the dance! I've been trying to talk her into it, but I can't get anywhere."

He said something which made her laugh, then came in to where Vanessa was. She went on with her knitting while he stood watching her. Then he said, "What crap have you been telling her?"

"Nothing except that I wasn't going to the dance."

"Why aren't you?"

She sighed. "Your clothes are ready. All you have to do is take a bath and change."

"If I go up there alone you know what everybody'll think."

"That I didn't come, that's what they'll think. They'll know damn well I didn't stay home to entertain a lover. And you can have a good time prancing around Gina."

"That's it!" He bounded at her, shaking his finger in her face. "That's it!" he shouted in triumph. "You've got a hair crossways on account of me fooling around with her the other night. I saw your face, you can't fool me. You're jealous of that little tramp."

"I wasn't jealous. I was amused. Afterwards Gina told me she'd made fools of two old men who were both drooling to climb aboard."

"*Old* men?" His voice climbed. "*Me?* And who wants to climb aboard *that?* Hell, no knowing what kind of a dose she's got. And Owen was just raising hell with her, same as I was." He puckered his face into dry virtue. "I thought it might wake Willy up."

"The Willys never wake up. They just get their hearts broken. She's Helen of Troy to him, and he's so grateful when she gives him a kind word that he falls on his face."

"You're probably right, Van," he said eagerly, perching on the window sill. "You know an awful lot about people. I was telling Phil just the other day, I'd trust Van's judgment before I'd trust my own. She knows people, I told him. I dunno whether it's what they call intuition or second sight, or what, but *she—knows—people*. That's all there is to it, I told him."

"And what did he say?"

"Not a word," Barry said. "He just looked at me. Well, what could he say?"

"That's a good question," said Van, and Barry burst into laughter.

"Honest to God, that humor of yours." He leaned toward her and became winningly intimate. "Ah, come on to the dance, Van. You've got something to wear. You'll look like a million dollars. And put on some of that smelly stuff I gave you last Christmas."

She stopped knitting and looked seriously at him. He leaned forward again, his face crinkled and smiling. "No," she said, and he sat back as if he'd just thrust his nose into a thistle.

"All right then, by God I'll go by myself." He kicked her box of filled needles halfway down the sun parlor and went back through the house, kicking things all the way.

"Your hot water is in that kettle on the stove," she called after him. "If you want to eat first, your supper's in the oven." He didn't answer but something crashed. She shrugged and went on knitting.

When he had finally left the house, leaving a pungent wake of something called "Buccaneer" behind him, she leaned back in her chair suddenly exhausted, hands and arms aching, her head light. Conflict with Barry never used to do this to her. She had simply never allowed conflict, it wasn't real to her; her life was lived apart from him and from everybody else. Now that she'd been forced out of that protective world, she felt that she was disintegrating.

The process had gone far enough so that she couldn't get back into the cave or under the rock. She had books to read but to curl up in her bed was an impossibility. She walked around the house hugging her elbows, feeling for the sharp bones as if for reality. She went out the back door and heard the generators throbbing, and next door a lamp was lit in the Campions' kitchen, where Terence's aunt and uncle were watching out for the children. But in spite of this evidence of survivors she couldn't get rid of the sensation of having been left alone on an unanchored planet. Idiot, all planets are unanchored, she ridiculed herself. It's just gravity or magnetism or something that holds them in orbit.

A cold scent of rockweed and sea rose from the shore. The stars grew brighter atop the spruces. The field was filled with shadow, as if the sea were silently flowing into it from Long Cove and Schoolhouse Cove at the same time. No illumination picked out the windows across at Hillside, and in this new freedom she allowed herself to see Owen, not leaning over Gina's shoulder but coming up from the dory among the boulders and squinting at her in the glow of noon.

He had gone to the dance. That was why there were no lights. They'd have the children along too, and he would go home early, in his pretense of being tamed, when the children got sleepy. She ran into the house and got ready without lighting a lamp, dressing in the petticoat and full skirt she had ordered from the catalog when she felt indulgent toward Barry. It was moss green, and fastened around her waist with a wide belt. She wore the gold shirt, and sprayed on a mist of scent from the bottle Barry had given her at Christmas. "That name is French for lily of the valley," he had explained. "I thought maybe you'd like it."

Now the delicate fragrance reminded her of the plants the Bennett child had brought. They were still in the entry. Oh well, I'll stick them in somewhere, she thought as she put on lipstick. Poor little things, it's not their fault.

She had no coat, and had to put on the raincoat; yet she cringed away from the touch of it on her neck and arms and against her calves, as if the garment held the infection of the other personality.

Walking around the harbor, she met nothing but a pair of cats playing. There were no lights up at the Bennett homestead, none in Philip's house. The Dinsmore kitchen was lighted, and Tiger flew hysterically off the doorstep, stopping short when he recognized her.

Once in a while she saw another lighted window, but most places were dark. As she turned into the shrubby lane that led toward the clubhouse, she began to hear accordion music. She didn't know what she would do when she got there, but she kept walking toward the sound.

A thicket of young spruces half-filled the dooryard of the building, screening her in the black coat from the light shining through windows and the open door, and from the men who stood around on the porch. There were more men altogether, inside and out, than Bennett's Island had; a crowd had come from Brigport because the night was so quiet and so fine. She stood unseen in the lane, annoyed, making tight fists in her pockets. She should have been prepared for those who came only to watch and spin cuffers with the other watchers, and those who stood outside when they weren't dancing, to smoke and pass the bottle and dirty jokes around. She heard their feet shuffling and shifting on the porch, and saw them silhouetted against the dull-glowing windows. Someone laughed loudly above the romping rhythm of March and Circle. Dancers flashed by the door like designs in a kaleidoscope; suddenly she saw Barry whirl into view in a set with Joanna, Nils, and Kathy Campion.

While she was watching, the dance finished. Puffing and laughing, people went to their seats, children began to slide on the floor and were called back, and a small stream of men came out the door, lighting cigarettes on the way.

From the front step, a cigarette butt curved through the dark like a small meteor, and just as the accordion and violin began a waltz she realized that someone was coming out to the lane. She thought in ridiculous terror that she might put her arms over her face and thus not be seen, but the man was there too soon. Through the music she

110

heard the words but not the voice. "Who's there?" Before
she could hide her face with her black sleeves he was close
enough to touch her.

"*You*," he said under his breath. "Wait a minute."

He turned and went back across the porch and into the
hall. She felt no longer clammy or constricted as she
watched for him to appear again against the light. His
head almost brushed the top of the doorframe. "Where
you bound for, Cap'n?" someone called after him. "You
got something stashed away to sweeten the evening?"

"For God's sake, don't broadcast it!"

"Hey, Cap'n, you mind if I dance with your wife?" That
was Barry from the doorway.

"You go right ahead. Tell her I trust you both." He
came on quickly, took her by the elbow, and turned her
up the lane, propelling her rapidly without speaking. To be
pushed and controlled like this was new because she had
never allowed it.

They went toward the pale blur of the Fennell house
under the low thick stars. The breath of the spruce woods
lay cold and heavy in the air. Their footsteps slid soft on
the grass as they entered the woods. The blackness was
entire. He put his arm tightly around her waist and they
went forward steadily. She was not able to see where she
was going, and she didn't care. We could be ghosts! she
thought with the joyousness she sometimes felt in dreams
when she floated airily through dark places with no fear
or obstruction.

Her feet were quite soaked and so was the hem of her
skirt, but she was not cold. They began to climb up
through the spruces where there was enough space among
the trees for her to see the stars thin out the black.
Suddenly they came to a clearing that had such an atmosphere of height it could have been on a mountain top.
The dreamlike sensation persisted; this place bore no relationship to any other she had ever known, she knew that
by day it would not exist.

He took his arm away. His shirt was lighter than his
face, but when he moved his head his eyes caught a spark
of light from above. The only sound was their breathing
as they rested from their swift passage away from the
village and up the hill. He moved and a lighter flicked on,
held at eye level, and their faces sprang to life against the
night, burnished and spellbound as if until then they had

111

been spirits and had just now been materialized; as if the radiance sprang from inside them and not from the minute light.

His eyes moved over the roughened frame of her hair, the long throat, the sheen of colors where the black raincoat fell open. "Well," he said, smiling. *"Well."*

"What did you tell her?" It was like being letter-perfect in a part, not having to think.

"I said I had a headache and was going home. I get them when I'm short of sleep. She wasn't surprised. What about Barry?"

"He didn't expect me. I said I wasn't going."

"So that's why he's been goddamming the women to hell all over the place. Then you changed your mind. Why?"

"I went out and saw no lights over at your place."

The lighter clicked shut and they were dematerialized again, in a thicker darkness than before. "If I hadn't come out just then would you have come in?"

"I don't know," she said honestly. "I was losing my courage. If you'd asked me to dance I don't know wh- I'd have done."

He laughed without humor. "I wouldn't have, never fear. Of course if I'd got you in a Liberty waltz——"

"Don't worry, I'd have gone out with a headache then," she assured him. "I couldn't stand to have you touch me with anyone looking on."

"Don't be so damned honest," he said with despairing violence. "As long as you don't admit it, it's not so. I told you the other day there was an end to it."

"But you didn't believe it." Her voice was flat. "Did you? You've been losing sleep enough so your wife doesn't question your headache."

"I don't know what in hell I'm doing with you up here. I don't know what in hell you had to be standing out there for, wearing that whatever it is. That's what I smelled first."

"Lily of the valley," she said.

"I was just going down to take a look at my boat. Then I'd have gone back. I'd be dancing with my wife now, or taking my little girl through Lady of the Lake." She could tell he was making wild, wide gestures in the dark. She stood immobile, her hands clenched in her pockets.

"Go back now," she said. "You can make believe it

never happened. You can start again, coming out to go look at your boat, and I won't be there. I didn't lie in wait for you, whatever you think." She sounded bored and distant, a triumph of achievement because there was a thick beating in her throat that threatened to overcome her voice. She turned her back on him. "The only thing is, I can't find my way out of this place."

"I'll take you back," he said behind her, "when it's time."

CHAPTER SEVENTEEN

On the southeast shores the deep swells rolled in one after another out of the fog and the invisible bell buoy clanged. The wind was wet on this side, soaked the hair, and turned sleeves sodden. But away from the sea the fog was irradiated by the sun, the grass was dry; it was very green now, with the flat blades of blue flag beginning to show in marshy spots, and there were strawberry blossoms in the lee of old stone walls and of boulders. They starred the turf that lay thin and warm on its granite bones in Van's clearing.

"They won't come to anything," Owen said.

"*Long night succeeds thy little day, / O blighted blossom,*" said Vanessa. He rolled over on his stomach to look at her where she sat with her back against a tree.

"What's that from?"

"A man's epitaph on his baby daughter."

His face twisted in distaste. "That's nothing to quote on a day like this. If you ever had a kid, you'd know better. . . ." He stopped short. "I shouldn't have said that. Maybe you do know something about it. I don't know anything about you, you could have been born the day you stepped onto this island as far as I'm concerned."

She arranged bleached sea-urchin shells and blue mussels meticulously on the sparse grass. "I never had a child and I was never pregnant. And I never wanted a child. That verse used to make me cry for a while. I had a kitten in one place I lived, and something happened to it. I found it dead. So when I came across that verse I never thought of human babies, only kittens."

"You could have had other kittens afterwards, couldn't you?"

She shook her head.

"I'll bring you one," he offered. "Holly's cat's got a family. Holly'd be tickled for you to have one."

"There could never be any kitten but that one," she said without expression. "There never will be." It was not strictly true. There had been that kitten, which she had never remembered aloud to anyone and hardly ever to herself, but she would not object to a kitten now; only she didn't want one from his house—it was bad enough to have to accept the lilies of the valley.

"And you and Barry never wanted young ones," he went on.

"Barry did." She gave him a brief smile and then returned to her shells again.

"You afraid to have one? Narrow women have it hard, sometimes."

It was odd that he knew now her narrowness. Her mind wavered into a dark, gold-shot sweetness, then came back to the day and the doomed strawberry blossoms, the weight of the hidden sun on her bare arms. "No, I wasn't afraid," she said. As if he knew she didn't want to talk about Barry here, he rolled over onto his back and lay quiet with his eyes shut. From where she sat she could see his lashes clearly against the red-brown ridges of his cheekbones, and his nose seemed to jut out larger than she'd noticed before. The gray was sprinkled through his hair like very fine silver wires. He was a big man, lying there, arms sprawled, one knee drawn up, the other leg flung wide. He crowded her clearing with its miniature treasure of shells, spruce seedlings, and strawberry blossoms, like Gulliver. As she watched, he brought one forearm up before his face and looked at his watch, then dropped the arm again.

"When does school get out?" she asked him.

"Not yet."

She took that contentedly; she was not yet greedy of the time with him and didn't expect to be. This meeting today was like the one at the dance—fated, yet accidental. Walking along the high barrier ridge of Long Cove, she had not known that he was working at home today instead of visiting among the harbor fishhouses; he had gone up to the house from his workshop in Schoolhouse Cove to get some coffee just at the moment when the mist ˡᵉᵃred enough to show her solitary figure moving against a lilac-blue band of fog. A fresh wave of it blowing across from open sea blotted her out again, but he had already set out from the house to find her.

"Oh—hello," she had said offishly when he confronted her. And he had said, as if accusing her of trespassing, "Do you come here often?"

Now he said, "Any of your folks still living?"

"No."

"Tough."

"Why? Do you think that everyone who isn't part of a clan is unlucky?"

"You trying to pick a fight with me?... Was your father a lobsterman?" The maimed hand lay on the grass, a two-inch spruce stood in the curve of his thumb. She wanted so much to take his hand that she had to press back against the tree trunk and gaze sternly at the sky as she answered him.

"No, he was a soldier. Infantry," she invented. "He made a career of it. He was killed in an accident in the war games in Louisiana one year. That finished my mother off. She was delicate to begin with." She saw them taking flesh before her eyes with each word she said. First Sergeant, her father, rather like Burt Lancaster in *From Here to Eternity*. "My mother's lungs were never good," she went on. "She should never have had me. They warned her about childbirth." She saw the mother, slender, sadly smiling at the little girl she had risked her life for. *The blessed damozel leaned out / From the gold bar of Heaven*.

Owen turned his head on the grass to look toward her.

"I'm sorry as hell," he said gruffly. "Sorry for them, sorry for you. You must have had it damned lonely." Her pride of invention gave way to chagrin; she felt squeamish and prickly. His compassion was real, but she had taken him in, and she wished he had known from the first that she was lying and had called her a liar. It was all she could do to keep from getting up and running away, but that would make her look crazy.

"But it explains something," he was saying, and she said quickly, "What?"

115

"You marrying Barry. I've never been able to figure it out. But if you were left alone, it must have been plain hell." He sat up and lit a cigarette. "Barry's a decent chap. He's friendly, willing, hard-working. But he's not your type. You're like an osprey married to a robin. And you know it. You've been beating your wings against the walls of that birdhouse ever since. It's just God's wonder you haven't beaten him to death in the process."

"What about *you?*" she jeered at him. "What's *your* excuse? Lonely, with all your brothers and your sister and your in-laws? Or did you think you ought to choose a good healthy no-nonsense girl to raise your kids and keep your house and never raise any storms while you had your fun on the outside?"

He was as angry as she was. "Laurie's all right. You don't know anything about her."

"So I shouldn't breathe her name, is that it? Well, I know as much about her as you do about Barry."

I've done it, I've killed it, she thought with dreadful calm. This is really the end. Suddenly before her smarting eyes his face broke up into slashes and creases of laughter. "Oh, good God! I apologize, I take all the blame, I started it!"

He crawled over to her on hands and knees and put his face close to hers. "You know what your eyes do when you're mad? Change color, I swear it. I can't tell whether they're green or yellow or no color at all. How do you do it?" He was managing me, she thought frigidly. The famous Bennett charm. The famous *Owen* Bennett charm. Cap'n Owen, he's Jesus's little brother, didn't you know? Or the devil's. She would not be won, her face went to stone as it did when she burned the book of poetry, and he knelt by her with his hands on her shoulders, waited, then shook her a little. "Is anybody there?" he asked. "Or have you gone away?" Still smiling, his eyes fixed on her intentionally glazed ones, he ground his fingers into her shoulders until she winced. "You're still there," he said. "What are you thinking or don't you think at all when you look like that?"

"Why'd Laurie send me plants the other day?" she blurted.

"Did you put them in, or give 'em a heave over the bank?"

"I put them in. It's not their fault."

116

"What isn't? Oh, don't answer. I thought we weren't going to talk about Laurie and Barry. No, she sent them because you like lily of the valley. You told my sister so."

"What else do they pass on about me? Do they all think poor Barry's a song bird in a hawk's clutches?"

He let her go and sprawled back again, propped on one elbow, fishing in a shirt pocket for cigarettes. He held the package out to her and she shook her head. "Let's see what I've heard," he said, his eyes in slits. "Oh, nasty things. Turn your stomach. . . . What do you think they think?"

Proudly she turned her face away. He said, "You're too self-centered. They've got other things to notice beside you. When they do think about you, they like you. You know how to be a lobsterman's wife," he said sardonically. "At least as far as the women can see. So they approve. That suit you?"

"You'd have to say that," she grumbled. "You're related to most of them." But she was satisfied that all her work had paid off. She had presented an image to them, and they believed what they saw.

"Five minutes more," he said. He put his hand on the nape of her neck and caressed it. She shivered and at the same time resented the action and her own reaction. It was the casually affectionate gesture one gave to a dog, and she tried not to lean back against his hand.

Neither spoke. Suddenly, well before the five minutes were up, he took his hand away and got up.

There was nothing said about meeting again, there was no guarantee that there would be anything more than this, but she did not allow herself to concede that in a week from now it might already be in the past. Nor would she dream forward to other meetings. The Day had imposed its discipline since she was twelve; she glided from one moment to the next, fluid as water and yet rigidly controlled, her only indulgence to wonder if he thought about her at all when she was out of his sight. She would not conjecture what she was to him. For *her,* he was the true north toward which her needle had always pointed. Their coming-together was inexorable, but even to herself she used no words of love or tenderness, for none had passed between them even that night on top of the hill in the woods.

She wanted to see if she could find that place, but it

117

would mean going by the Fennells', and Nora Fennell would think it queer if she tramped through the dooryard without stopping in. Besides, she had a half-superstitious fancy that she'd never be able to find the place, that it had existed only on that night.

Meanwhile she knit his trapheads, and did not allow herself to imagine that he might come unexpectedly to the door and say he'd come for the finished heads; in reality it would be because he wanted to look at her again. Such fantasies could make you sick, spread a veil between you and reality. I'll look for you when I see you coming, she told him silently, watching *White Lady* ride into the harbor on towering seas; Steve Bennett's *Philippa* rolled deep on one side, and Nils Sorensen came in behind, easing his boat when she slid downhill on the smoking green slopes. Charles rounded the breakwater after them, sinking out of sight in the trough. There were other fishermen, but when the family came close on each other's wakes it was like watching an armada.

"Arrogant bastards," she said aloud over the traphead twine, but without the earlier venom. They weren't all that invincible. She'd gotten under the hide of one of them.

CHAPTER EIGHTEEN

On Saturday night they went to the Dinsmores' for baked beans and homemade brown bread. Rob's round mild face was flushed and smiling perpetually with shyness and pleasure. Mag was excited, flashing between stove and table like a goldfish in its globe. Barry was easy with them, and they felt perfectly at ease with him; he was one of Rob's kind, the well-meaning but inadequate kind who could never be his own man. Whenever he attempted it, he would attract disasters to him as a magnet attracts iron filings. Watching the two of them tonight, expanding in each other's company, intensely absorbed in lobstering talk, she thought, This is the only way they feel safe. In

Philip's shadow, in Owen's. Even the shadows are stronger than they are.

Maggie was leaning against the dresser watching her with a smiling glance as she watched the men. "Isn't that the limit?" she said. "They never get tired talking about boats and how somebody did on the Coombe Spot, and how fast they got away from a breaker when it broke under them."

"Did you ever hear how long a couple of lobstermen can keep going on different ways to knit a traphead?"

"All I can say is, their wives have to be born to it or else they'd go crazy." Mag handed a wooden bowl of salad to Diane. "Be careful, sweetie. Here, Tammie, you can carry the fork and spoon. . . . Though I have to say Liza does real well, coming from away and all. And my lands, the people she met when she worked on that magazine! Movie stars and duchesses and everything." She was incandescent with awe. "And here she is on Bennett's, just as natural as you please. Gina, now——" She cocked her head at the children, then pursed her lips and chose her words with caution. "Well, it's hard for her, being so young. Lonesome, you know. City girl. She thinks Willy ought to've learned the whole trade in six months so they can go back to the mainland and make a fortune."

Barry heard that and laughed. "Lordie, he's not out of the primer class yet." He pulled Tammie gently to him and onto his knee. Tiger came bristling out from under the stove, and Barry said, "I just want to heft her, boy. I got no little girls of my own and my lap's being wasted." The child ducked her chin in her bashful pleasure. Barry reached out and drew Diane to his side. "Now I've got two. You going to give 'em to me, Rob?"

"I dunno. I'd have to study on that. Times when I'd part with 'em gladly, but then who'd get my slippers for me and stand my boots beside the stove?"

"Tiger could," suggested Diane and buried her giggles in Barry's shoulder.

"He just loves young ones," Mag murmured to Van. "Well, you do too," she added with humorous defiance, "and don't say you don't, the way you handled these two when Rob hurt his hand." She sighed, shook her head, and then sang out, "I'm about to take the beans out of the oven!"

It was no effort for Vanessa to be pleasant tonight. She

felt so detached and objective these days, as if she floated a little to one side and slightly above the rest. She realized that Rob was bashful about being at the table with her. He wasn't going to enjoy his food, and his good hand fumbled with the silver as if he'd never held a fork before. It amused her to put herself out to get him over his nervousness.

"When I was a kid this was always my favorite meal of the week," she said to him. "I'd come up from the shore all smelly with bait where I'd been helping to bag up, and so hungry I could hardly stand to get washed, but I couldn't come to the table till I'd got the herring out of my ears."

"*You* used to bag up?" Rob laughed incredulously.

"I certainly did. Oh, I drowned out the smell of the beans and johnnycake when I came into the kitchen."

"That's the truth, Rob," Barry said proudly. Across the table his eyes brimmed with appreciation of her conduct. "Y gorry, I thought she was coming to our wedding in dungarees and rubber boots, but they hogtied her and sewed her into a dress."

Rob looked at her, shook his head, and then began to eat with good appetite. "I be damned. I thought you'd been a teacher or a nurse, or something like that."

"He's making it sound good, Van," said Mag mischievously. "When he first laid eyes on you, he came home and told me you looked like one of them artists down on Monhegan."

"*You're* making it sound bad, woman," Rob protested. "Like I thought artists were immoral or something."

"Well, maybe I am," said Van. "How do you know?" Everyone laughed.

Before the children went to bed they wanted a song. Maggie was embarrassed, but pleased when they urged her. Diane brought out a guitar and Mag stopped her blushing and grimacing and began to tune it, her face sharp with concentration, her small square hands competent.

"*Now.*" She struck a chord and looked into the girls' faces. "One tune apiece and that's all. Folks weren't invited to a concert, you know. Diane?"

"Bendemeer Stream." She ran over and climbed into her father's lap and laid her head against his chest. Maggie's voice was a surprise, low but unexpectedly strong and

120

true. Van felt a start of genuine pleasure and then exasperation; she was always disturbed by the sentimentality aroused so easily by certain voices singing certain words. She knew Barry would be blinking back tears, and what bothered her was the fact that she too could be moved; it was something absolutely false, it was like taking a lot of drinks and becoming lustful so that any man would do. Maggie was a nice simple young woman who could play the guitar and sing nice simple words, and the fact she happened to have a voice with which to give the words poignance was no more to her credit than the fact that children have silky hair and velvet skins. It was all a matter of glands.

She finished, and in the silence Diane said with infinite longing, "I wish I could hear a nightingale sometime."

Barry blew his nose and lit a cigarette. Tammie said, "Well, *I* want 'Whistle.' "

"I hope that song doesn't give you any ideas for when you grow up," her mother told her.

"I like the funny words."

"My father was Scotch," Maggie said to Van. "I know a lot of old songs and the kids love the sound of 'em even when they don't understand." She began to trot her foot and sing. The pressure was relieved and Van enjoyed the song and Tammie's delight in it until suddenly the words took on a piercing significance.

> *At kirk or at market where e'er ye meet me,*
> *Gang by me as though that you cared no flie;*
> *But steal me a blink o' your bonnie blacke'e,*
> *Yet look as if ye were no looking at me.*

There was more, but Van didn't hear it. She sat looking blindly at her hands in her lap until the last words rang gaily into her head. *O whistle and I'll come to you, my lad.*

"And now you two go to bed," said Maggie. "And dinna ye lallygag ... or something ... or I'll give ye a blink of my bonny mouse-colored e'en, and that won't be all." Laughing at her, the little girls took the flashlight she handed them, and went out to the toilet. Tiger went ahead, growling militantly in case.

There was no need for Van to say anything about the singing beyond a conventional remark. Barry could fill in

121

all the gaps, praising and marveling, while Rob was complacent. Mag, getting the children off to bed, apparently was too busy to listen.

"Where'd you ever learn to sing like that?" Barry asked her when she came back to the kitchen.

"I didn't *learn*. I could always sing. Father taught me the guitar chords." She grinned. "Then my aunt had me singing hymns at her seances, but not with Father's permission. Of course *I* felt as important as all-out. The medium—she was this fat lady who worked in the fish factory where my aunt did—she said she never could get off into a real good trance without me singing 'There is a Happy Land' or 'Love Lifted Me.' "

"Was she real?" Barry sat forward.

"Of course she was," said Maggie. "And she had this control named Jenkins. He put her in touch with the folks that had gone to Summerland." She smiled at him. "That's what we call it. Isn't that nice? There was one man—I can't tell you his name, my aunt swore me to secrecy and even now I couldn't break my oath, but he was *real* important in Limerock—well, he was always coming to Ida to get in touch with his mother. My, it was pathetic, the way he'd be. Like a little boy. He kept saying, 'Mama? Is that you, Mama?' " She wiped her eyes with the back of her hand. "Wasn't that something now, a grown-up man, president of a bank, and him so lost and helpless?"

"He warn't all that lost," said Rob. "If he got to be president of a bank."

"Well, he never got married," said Mag.

Mama? Is that you, Mama? Nightmare touched Van lightly again, but she drove it away. Hundreds of thousands had asked that question besides the banker, besides the child waking up in the night probing the dark with eyes and ears because she dreamed someone had spoken to her. I must have been very small, she thought, or else when I dreamed I forgot what I knew in the daytime.

"Ayuh, but what did she say to *him?*" Barry persisted. "You hear her, with your own ears?"

"Of course I did. She called him 'Sonny' and told him not to worry, how beautiful it was there and someday they'd be together ... And oh yes, sometimes she told him about handling different deals at the bank."

Rob said solemnly, "I wouldn't ever keep any money in

that bank. Don't seem hardly reliable. I mean, how did you know if the old lady was a real financial expert?"

"Oh *you.*" For a moment they were still, gazing into each other's eyes, then as if a signal were passed between them color flashed into her freckled cheeks and Rob's amiable witless grin took on a new dimension. It was only for a moment, and then he leaned back and took out his pipe.

Mag hung up her apron. "Anybody feel like a game of Sixty-three?"

"Sure, sure!" cried Barry, snapping his fingers at a prancing Tiger. "I was just saying to Van the other day, 'We haven't had a good game of Sixty-three for a hell of a long time.' Didn't I, Van?" His eyes beamed loving kindness at her, he was as much carried away by the characters they were playing as she was by The Day.

Later, walking home by Terence Campion's, she heard peep frogs from the marshy spot on the edge of Long Cove, and she wished she could keep on walking straight by the house, and have the frogs and the May night to herself. But they went inside, and while she was lighting the lamp Barry came up behind her and put his arms around her, gently squeezing her breasts. "You were some handsome tonight. They winked and blinked at sight of you. Never knew what you looked like dressed up." He nuzzled into her neck. "I'd forgotten too. God, I was hardly able to keep my mind on the cards all evening. Didn't you see me squirming?"

She wanted to go quietly to bed without hurting or being hurt. She stood still in his embrace. "It was a nice evening, Barry. And now I'm tired."

"Too tired to talk?" His hands slid and slid.

"Yes. *Don't.*" She tried not to snap or sound annoyed.

"But honey, I haven't had you in a skirt for so damn long."

"Barry, please." She went over the rim of patience and put his hands violently away from her. Across the kitchen from him, watching him so he couldn't surprise her, she said with an effort at calm, "I'm too tired for anything, and that's final."

He did not look hurt. He shrugged. "Okay." He kicked off his moccasins and went upstairs. She took off her

123

blouse and washed her face and brushed her teeth, then read for a while at the kitchen table.

She was brought back by the lamp dimming; the oil in the clear glass base was almost gone. She turned it out and felt her way silently upstairs and undressed in the dark. She looked forward to tomorrow, in which anything could happen, and she put this day efficiently out of mind as if crossing it off a calendar. It was gone, it would never have to be endured again. She slid quietly into her side of the bed, and began to think of a way to get her own room. Barry was willing to put up with almost anything, but the thought of separate rooms or even separate beds could send him into a tantrum. As if she'd disappear if she wasn't where he could hear her breathing, and then what would he be? Alone, and therefore nothing. . . . Barry was terrified of solitude. It was almost as if he believed he existed only in other people's eyes. He could sleep soundly beside her, only occasionally furious because she repulsed him, and still draw something even from her indifferent or contemptuous denials.

She stretched and sighed. Instantly Barry said, "Van."

"Did I wake you up?" She imitated a good yawn. " 'Night."

"I've been waiting for you. I thought to God you'd never get through reading." His voice was quiet but unblurred; he had never sounded more awake. "I thought you were too tired for anything."

"You know I have to read before I go to sleep. It settles my mind."

"You mean you wanted me to conk out before you got up here."

"Have it your own way." She yawned again and turned over facing the window.

"Listen," he said. "I'm not going to touch you, goddammit. I just want to talk to you. Now will you do me the favor of listening like I was a human being?"

"I'm listening." It occurred to her that if they ever could talk reasonably, she might be able to mention a room of her own without his going to pieces. "Go ahead, Barry," she encouraged him.

"Well, when we came out here I said this was a place where we could put down roots and belong, didn't I? And I said that we could even start thinking about kids of our own. Well, I've been thinking about that right along. And after tonight, seeing those little girls of Rob's, I made up my mind to——" he was beginning to lose his momentum—"to say something about it." Belligerence rushed in. "I want a kid of ours more than I want anything else."

"More than staying here? More than owning your own boat and your own house?"

"That goes along with it. It's because I've got more than a chance being my own man that I'm talking about a kid. And I figger we'd better get started on it right away because sometimes it takes quite a while."

"Oh, does it?" she murmured. She'd made a mistake by reading so long. He'd been lying up here rehearsing the whole thing over and over.

"You like kids, Van," he said eagerly. "And you'd be a damn good mother. Any baby of yours would be smarter than all these others put together."

"Even smarter than Bennett babies?"

He laughed, put at ease by her, and felt for her hand. "You said it. And I don't care whether we have a boy or a girl. Maybe we could have both. You and I know what it is to be a loner." He squeezed her hand. "Will you start thinking about it, Van? Right off?"

"I've thought about it," she lied. "Barry, if you wanted babies you should have married somebody else."

"Jesus, I married you because I thought we *were* going to have one!"

"And when you found out it wasn't so, you should have walked out on me and gone back home. You could have four or five of your own by now."

"I didn't want to walk out on you! Baby or not, I wanted *you!*" He was outraged. "Go home and eat crow? You think I'd do that, after the way they treated me? And you?" he added belatedly. "I didn't want anybody else. I still don't. Aw, listen, Van, don't say *no* right off, promise me you'll think about it. I know I've never made enough to take care of a family but I'm making enough now and I'll keep making more."

"That's not the reason. That was never the reason." That, at least, was the truth. "Barry, it won't do any good for me to think about it, because thinking'll never get me over being scared." Now she was lying, but with genius, because at once he was anxious and solicitous.

"I sh'd think almost every woman is scared, but they get over it when the time comes, and they forget it. You

125

ever notice that, Van? I guess having the baby is worth everything. And you don't have to suffer when you have it, Van. They can put you right out."

"Thank you, dear aunt Barry." They both laughed. Barry put his arm around her; he had never before been allowed to comfort or encourage her in anything. Well, at least I'm giving him some pleasure now, she thought wryly. "Listen, Barry, there's something I never told you. The reason I'm scared isn't the pain. I could stand that. But I could die having a baby. Or the baby could. Or both of us."

"But that never happens now! How many people did you ever know died that way?"

"My mother did," she said.

"How do you know? You don't know anything about your mother!"

"I do now." She saw the scene rolling out vividly before her, a color movie projected on the ceiling. "I didn't tell you before because I didn't want to think of it. But one day about two years ago I met Miss Foster in Limerock. It was right in front of the People's Bank building."

She was wearing that wine suede jacket Barry'd gone into debt for one Christmas, and black slacks. Miss Foster was wearing that blue suit she always used to wear when she came to Mrs. Bearse's, with different gloves and blouses. No, don't be silly, she wouldn't still be wearing it ten years later, and she'd look older too. And her hair would be gray but still curly. "I never realized Miss Foster was such a pretty woman," she said aloud. "I don't suppose I really saw her as a human being at all, back in those days."

"What did she say about your mother?" Barry persisted. People went back and forth through the bank doors behind them, the doors kept flashing in the sun. Cars streamed by. "She invited me into Scott's for a cup of coffee," said Van, shifting the scenes and instantly conceiving a ferocious hunger for a warm honey-dipped yeast doughnut. "I had a raised doughnut," she told Barry dreamily. "I wish I had a good recipe for them."

"For God's sake get on with it!" He threw back the covers and sat on the edge of the bed, scrabbling around for cigarettes.

"I remember the doughnut, because afterward when I felt sick I blamed it on the doughnut, but that wasn't

126

really it. She told me—she told me—" She faltered as the scene became jerky and out of focus. Would Miss Foster lead up to it or come straight out with the facts?

"She said, 'You know how you always wanted to know about your mother.' I didn't know what was coming. I didn't know what I wanted to hear. I mean, I knew I wasn't suddenly going to be presented with a perfect mother. But with *what?*"

Barry thought the huskiness in her voice was due to emotion. "You want a cigarette?" he offered kindly.

"No, I'll hurry and get it over with." She was actually making herself a little sick living the scene; the smell of fresh doughnuts was now nauseating. "I won't go into all the details. But just by sheer coincidence, a case-worker found out about my mother when she was investigating another case. It's so crazy I could hardly believe it, but Miss Foster wouldn't have told me if she wasn't sure. She said she checked and double-checked." She cleared her throat. "I—I wasn't abandoned by my mother, Barry. She died having me. She was too narrow, you see. There wasn't enough room for the baby, if you can imagine me being a baby—to come down—through—out, whatever the right word is. They started a Caesarian, but she'd been hemorrhaging, and so——" The last word floated. Trapped in her own spell, she saw torrents of blood. "This friend of hers—so-called—took me. They don't think she made any attempt to get in touch with my father. . . ." Her voice sank. "They weren't married, and he wasn't a soldier, he was a Coast Guardsman, and he'd been sent somewhere else. But maybe if he'd known he'd have come for me. . . . This woman, *she* was the one who abandoned me. She left me with someone for a day, she said, and never came back. That's how the state got me."

"What a rotten deal," Barry groaned. "My Jesus, poor little tyke." He rolled her back into bed and put his arms around her, not offended this time by her stiffness. "Poor baby. What kind of a bitch was she, anyway?"

"She must have had a conscience of a sort," she said dryly. "That's how this case-worker found out." It was a relief to leave the bloody operating room for the slattern slopping tea and pouring out her guilt to the case-worker, one of those fresh-faced young college girls. "She'd gone there to see about the grandchildren," she said, watching the new scene. "The bitch had a bunch of them, none of them legal, and each of 'em with a different father. She wanted the state to take them over. So she started talking about me, as if she'd planned the whole thing, you know, done the best thing for me. . . . She'd named me after my mother. Anna Howard. So when the girl went back to the office she asked Miss Foster about that name."

Barry hauled her close to him, all comfort now and no sliding hands. She was surprised to be so cold; the story had been almost too good, her mouth had been trembling there at the end. "Poor little Anna Howard," he said. "But now you know. . . . I mean, it makes a difference, doesn't it, knowing your mother didn't drop you somewhere and skin off and leave you?"

Her trembling increased to a shudder. Mouth locked shut she rolled out of Barry's arms and out of bed and felt her way downstairs in the dark, hearing him call after her as she concentrated on not vomiting on the stairs. She accomplished it in the wash basin, and was lying over the dresser shivering, waiting for the next spasm, when Barry came down and lit a lamp.

He looked at the basin and whistled. "You almost puked your guts out!" he said in awe. "That *did* upset you, didn't it?" He walked around barefooted in his shorts and undershirt, putting the teakettle on the gas stove to heat, shaking his head and making reverent comments that made Van want to shout at him to keep quiet. She thought she had never been so nastily cold in her life, her pajamas glued to her with sweat, her hair damp.

"Will you take that basin out to the toilet and dump it?" she finally asked him, on her dizzy way to the sitting-room couch. He pulled on pants and shoes and went out, and when he came back he asked her if she wanted a cup of tea.

"It might start everything up again," she said between chattering teeth. She burrowed into the blankets. "I'll stay here the rest of the night, I guess. I'm scared of what'll happen if I move."

He brought her another blanket, and a hot water bottle wrapped in a towel. She thanked him, beginning to float now in reaction, the heat from the water bottle spreading deliciously into her stomach. He went out to the kitchen and made a cup of cocoa for himself. She lay there listening to the faint clinkings, and the rattle of a magazine page. He was enjoying his tenderness and concern; he would tell about it tomorrow, though not the reason for the attack, and he would exaggerate her helplessness and dependence on him, adding details that would surely infuriate her if she knew them. Oh well, he has to have something, she thought, and it would be quite a long time before he talked babies again.

She marveled at her own reaction to her lies. It was as if she had lived it through, been both the mother dying of exhaustion and the child fighting to be born; and she had been the winner in the ghastly duel but knew also what it was to die in defeat. It could have been that way, she thought, and maybe I know it in my subconscious, maybe I was living it all again. But if that woman exists, that bitch who never wrote to my father, I should have known it. If I ever passed anywhere near her in Limerock the truth should have clanged and battered in my ears. I want to kill her. She stole my father from me. Why didn't she throw me into the harbor one night and be done with it? No, she stole. . . . Vanessa fell asleep on the word, crying silently, while Barry was still drinking cocoa and reading out in the kitchen.

CHAPTER NINETEEN

It had been a week since the time in the clearing; she had promised herself then not to try to make things happen, and she had kept her equilibrium marvelously well, except when the little surprises almost knocked her off balance. The sound of his name on somebody else's lips; a family joke referred to by Joanna at the sewing circle and laughed at by Laurie, something that concerned Owen; the sight of him unexpectedly at mail time, when he was supposed to be out hauling. That was the worst of the surprises. Past the other women's ears and shoulders he had glanced at her and no more. *But steal me a blink of your bonny black e'e*, and this wasn't even a blink. In its indifference it wiped out everything. He stood with his arm around his brother Steve's wife, and called Gina Elizabeth Taylor, which she took—not surprisingly—as a compliment. Conceited bastard! Van raged, gazing blindly at her grocery list, then thought, I'm probably the only bona-fide one hundred per cent pure bastard in this room. . . . It was assuaging, as if she'd yelled a dirty word aloud, shocked them all into silence, and swaggered out.

Then she was ashamed and angry, and had to work hard to keep from hurrying away. Crazy behavior even in your thoughts was unforgivable. With a sense of bitterly won victory she felt the heat subside in her, the heartbeat slow, her vision grow clear so that she could make sense of her grocery list. Owen left in a few minutes, and the last tightness loosened in Van's chest.

She walked home with Kathy in the razor-sharp azure light of a northwest day, cold in the wind that blew the tops like smoke off the crests of the harbor, June-hot in the lee. She laughed and talked with Kathy, hearing herself with a sort of despairing wonder that she should do so well. It was a triumph, but of what and for what?

The two younger children, over their chicken pox, played in the old skiff hauled up in the grass. School was out, and Cindy, the oldest, and the Dinsmore girls were hurrying away to their playhouse in the woods on the point, carrying their dolls and paper carryall bags, and a brand-new orange crate. "Oh, to be that age again," Van said to Kathy, like a proper young woman. She walked across the bright grass toward her own back door. The lilies of the valley were growing. At first she had hoped they would die, but now she saw a stubborn poetry in their existence. Crows flew up jeering from the yard, whereupon the small birds came back.

The gulls went circling, circling high over Long Cove. She stood on the doorstep and watched them. She heard a sound from inside the house and was half-decided to go then over to the beach rather than listen to Barry. I'm like the kids, she thought wryly, I want to rush to my playhouse and make new rooms out of mussel shells.

But she went in anyway, to get a drink of water, and Owen was standing by the table, holding a mug of coffee.

She jumped violently. "Where's Barry?" she said.

"Spinning cuffers around the shore somewhere. You can move away from the door. I didn't come with intent to rape." He took a drink from the mug. "How many heads you got ready?"

"Enough for a hundred traps."

"I'll take them. Got anything to go with this coffee or don't you cook?"

"There's some cookies in that can, since you're so good at helping yourself. I'll get the heads." She went around the other side of the table and he didn't move, but as she entered the sitting room she heard the mug set down on the table and he came along beside her and put an arm around her ribs, clamping tight.

"What's the idea of looking at me with those yellow eyes as if you hated my guts?"

"What's the idea of looking at me as if I was a common tramp, and making yourself at home in my kitchen? With Barry's favorite mug, too."

He began to laugh and both hands squeezed tighter over her ribs as if he were trying to crush them in. "I don't know why I'm laughing, because God knows it's not funny. I couldn't stand to look at you straight in the eye today for fear of showing it."

She was so glad she began to laugh too, but proudly, so as not to show her relief. "I thought seeing me with all the others you were ashamed, you wanted to show me I was nothing to you unless it was something contemptible. I suppose that's what I am, beside them."

"Shut up. *Shut up.*" He shook her. "Somebody'll come ramming in here any minute. Listen. Steve and his family are going to Vinalhaven for the weekend. Tomorrow afternoon I'll be down at his place. I want you to come down there. Make it around three, and come down along the shore. If you meet any kids prowling around, you're bird-watching. That covers everything around here but hauling somebody else's pots."

She released herself and walked into the sun parlor and began lifting the bundles of heads off the wall.

"You want me to pay you as you go along or when you're all through?" he asked.

"When I'm all through." She laid the lustrous knotted festoons over his outstretched arm, counting to herself in whispers, very busy and seeing nothing else. He stood looking at her. Looking was too weak a word; his eyes left a track of heat wherever they touched.

"Two lots of fifty big heads in each," she murmured. "Four lots of fifty side heads each. That's it. . . . It's nice twine," she said, turning away and arranging the filled needles that lay on the window sill. "It holds a good tight

131

knot." She saw Barry rowing in to his wharf with quick short strokes, his cap pushed boyishly back. He pulled abreast of Terence Campion, and they were calling back and forth and laughing. Owen said heavily, "Well, I'll get out before Peter Pan nails me." She listened to him without turning around. He slammed doors behind him. When he didn't appear by the end of the house, she realized he must have gone back the way he'd come, across the field behind the houses. There was a finality about his disappearance, like death.

She had not told him she'd come, she'd shown him nothing but insolence and indifference. She linked her fingers and crushed them against one another, pressing the palms together until her wrists ached. How could I, how could I? she mourned. I love him.

She jumped as if she'd been caught saying the words aloud. Saying them even to herself, the shock was as great. *Love.* How ridiculous! I don't love. I'm incapable of love, she thought haughtily.

In the morning the warming-up of engines competed with the dawn chorus of birds. Barry was set up with new importance; Philip and his wife were goin to Vinalhaven with Steve, and Barry was going to use *Kestrel* to haul some deep water traps a long way off shore.

He wanted her to fix a lunch and go with him. She refused by pretending she had an intestinal upset and wanted to stay close to the house, so that he went off thinking she'd really wanted to go and felt bad to lose the chance. For him that was almost as good as having her along.

It would have been nice far out there today, she thought, but not with Barry in Philip's boat. She did not let her thoughts move toward how it would be with Owen. She didn't even let them go toward the afternoon. In fact, no time existed except now, and the ghost of time— yesterday afternoon and the sound of departure.

The north wind began to blow when the tide turned and put an edge of cold on the day. When she walked along Long Cove the surf was splashing noisily, shifting the stones, swirling with debris and rotten rockweed, while on the land side the field and cranberry marsh were green, and red-winged blackbirds whistled.

Brigport lay across a mile of wind-whitened water. Like

yesterday, this day had a blue light that wounded the eye and slashed one cheek with cold while the other took the sun. When she passed the faint track she had made to her place among the spruces, she continued over wide shelves of pinkish granite against which the surf broke, sometimes splashing her face with salt. The spruces here were draped with moss, holding tenaciously to their shallow footing except where four or five had gone down together and turned up their roots to the sky and the sea.

The land climbed upward, and it seemed as if this rough-scalloped shore would go on forever, until she saw a path steeply ascending among the juniper and bay to her right, followed it, and came out above Stephen Bennett's place.

The whole place seemed absolutely deserted, dazzling and unreal in its emptiness. Though she hadn't allowed herself to anticipate anything, she thought at once that she'd been deceived and made a fool of. She shut her eyes against the blazing light, and slowly swallowed the pain in her throat; when she opened her eyes again Owen was coming toward her up a winding track from the house. A long-haired dog ran ahead of him.

After her forlorn anger, she felt an almost unbearable happiness. She wanted to run to him, but held herself here by gripping an old fence post. The dog reached her first, his tail going in circles like a wringer handle. She kept looking at him instead of at Owen, until Owen took her hand and said softly, "What's the matter?" He smiled. "Argo wants to know what the matter is, too."

The dog's eyes moved from one face to the other. Vanessa put her free hand on his head and said, "Is this another of your nephews? He's got the Bennett coloring."

Owen laughed. "He's got a better disposition than most of us. Stays home and minds his own business. Of course he might turn out to be a real old rake if there was an attractive bitch on the island." Argo waved his tail. Owen tightened his grip on Van's hand. "Come on."

He took her across the lawn past the house and onto a path through the field. With the dog leading, she walked ahead of Owen toward the rising ground to the east. He didn't speak and she wondered if he had asked her to meet him so he could tell her the adventure was over. Probably he never let his adventures go very far. There might have been a look about her, an intensity, that

133

warned him off. Oh well, who wants me? she thought jauntily. It was like the old joke, *If she ain't good enough for her own kinfolk she ain't good enough for us.*

She turned abruptly, as if to run, and collided with him. She had one glimpse of his face before he took her into his arms. For herself, she could hardly stand; the very force of her weakness terrified her, she was no longer herself, proud and whole in isolation, and she felt a dreadful pang like bereavement even while she clung to him. They had never before met like this, she had never felt like this, even lying under the trees the night of the dance. They held each other like survivors on a raft, afraid to look at what lay around them, knowing only that each represented life to the other.

After a few moments they broke apart. Shaking, she sat down on a ledge. He stood looking away from her, down through a narrow opening in the fresh young green growth, his hands in his pockets. The set of his shoulders, and the back of his neck and head, made her eyes swim with tears and this too was something new and appalling. The dog lay on the warm turf, his head on his paws. He seemed to think it was good of them to keep him company. Owen turned around and came and stood over her. "Why in *hell*," he said, "did Phil have to pick Barry out of all the men in Limerock?"

"I almost didn't come," she said. "It was only because I didn't have anywhere else to go. They were going to tear down the house."

He ran his hands through his hair as if the alternative were to seize her by the throat. "But why, *why?* I was safe out here. There was never anyone except for that woman over at Brigport one summer. . . ." He sat down beside her, his elbows on his knees and head in his hands. "I sized you up all right. First look. It takes one to know one, they say. I went home and fought it out with myself. Well, all right. I've been damn steady for seventeen years. They never thought I could do it. So what's the harm? You know the score, I know it, we're both the roving kind and with a hide like tanned leather. Only I haven't been roving." He turned his face sidewise, showing a one-sided grin, half-sneer. "Like Argo I could stay home and mind my own business as long as there weren't any distractions."

"You mean I'm the attractive bitch?" Her voice was croaky. "Thank you."

"You know I don't mean that, goddammit. But dogs have a better arrangement than people. They don't go trying to make it anything different from what it is. What I thought it was between you and me. Where we should have left it."

She tried to think of something devastating to say, to salvage herself. She could always do it to Barry. She could not now. She kept wanting to cry.

The dog got up and came to them, concerned. She touched his warm coat, more to steady her hand and dry its clamminess than to reassure the dog. Looking into Argo's face she said, "I haven't been roving either. Maybe if I had been I'd be better off now."

"You could have stopped this."

"So could you, but neither of us did." She felt better again. "But there is absolutely nothing to prevent us from stopping here and now. I can get up and walk home, and you can get up and go home, and we'll never meet again by the bonny bonny banks of Loch Lomond."

"All right." His smile was deadly. He stood up. "Agreed. Here and now."

She matched his smile. "As it said in my school poetry book,

You to the left and I to the right,
For the ways of men must sever;
And it well may be for a day and a night,
And it well may be————."

She didn't know which of them made the first move. She had to step near enough for him to take her by the nape of the neck and clamp a hand over her mouth. She stared at him over it, knowing that neither of them had intended to win or lose. Everything was in that wildly silent exchange; the survivors on the raft had seen the sharks.

When he took his hand away she said faintly— *"Forever.* That was the last word. I know a lot more good quotations."

"I'm sure you do," he said. They began climbing the slope among the trees. It was very warm out of the wind, though she could hear surf booming and swashing, and the wind in the spruces higher up the slope made another kind of surf. At the top of the rise the bay lay before them, the gaudy blue of a child's water-color painting of an ocean. It all but hurt the eyes.

Van looked down and saw the powerful pattern of incoming seas, rearing together in leisurely but deadly conflict, subsiding into separate whirlpools, pouring back out over weedy humps of ledge; then the slow building up for a return assault. She stared down at it, feeling as if either she or the rock under her feet were moving. Suddenly Owen pulled her roughly away, back among the trees. She saw then two boats coming home in company from the direction of Matinicus Rock on the southeast horizon.

"Could they see us?" she said.

"They're too far away yet to know who it is. Sit down."

"It's funny," she said. "I never thought anything until now about being seen."

"It's because everything's changed now." He lit a cigarette for her. "We think it sticks out all over us."

"Until I saw those boats I thought we were on some other island where nobody else had ever been but us."

He nodded. "It's what's scared the hell out of me. Losing track. Forgetting who I am."

"Or remembering. I don't know where that piece of wisdom came from, but maybe the way we've been—the way we *are*—the rest of the time is false. I feel different from any other way I've ever felt in my life, but it seems exactly right." She watched to see if he knew what she meant, and went on. "For instance, I've never talked like this in my life. I haven't had the words or the inclination. And now I don't even feel self-conscious."

His eyebrows went up. "Never to Barry?"

"We weren't going to mention them. Tell me how you feel different." She took the flawed hand between her own.

"Mostly I beat my brains out wondering why this had to happen to me, at my age. It makes me sick with the kind of guts-ache I could do without. It keeps me awake nights and it makes me growl at my kids." He got up, not seeming to notice how he'd pulled his hand away from her as if from a pocket, and went and stood in the opening, looking out at the bay. The dog went with him. She imagined the three of them on an island alone, a far island, one of those blue clouds lying lightly on the sea as if they were not made of earth and granite. She had never wanted a dog, but now Argo belonged in the picture because he was in it today. She enjoyed watching the man and dog together, and if the man were full of bewildered anger and self-reproach as he stood there, he would soon forget them. The thing was that she was causing the ferment and yet she was stronger than it and could supersede it. She got up and went up behind him and put her arms around his waist, rested her cheek against his back.

He said irritably, without looking around, "Don't you feel anything about Barry? Can you look him straight in the eye when you go home to him from me?"

"I'm nicer to him these days than I ever was," she said candidly. "Maybe because I'm glad to be alive. It's easy to be kind to him, for once. Usually it's easier to be mean. He invites it."

"Jesus, you're cold-blooded." He unclasped her hands and turned around to face her. "I can't make you out. I can't make *me* out, going down to bottom like this about you. I swear it's not just because you're a good—"

"Lay?" she suggested.

"That's not the right word but I'll be damned if I know what it is. As far as that goes you're what every man dreams of having but never gets. But it's more than that. And what in hell is it?" He scowled at her. "What are you, what do you think behind those yellow eyes?"

"If I told you," she said, "you'd be shocked." She walked away from him, superbly sure of being followed. "But I can tell you that I've known all my life about you. I didn't know what you'd look like, where you'd be, I didn't even think of The Day in terms like ..." She laughed, and sat down on the turf, and put her arm around Argo's neck.

Owen stood over her, an inquisitioner. "What day?"

"With a capital D. It's been the continuity of my life. Not Christmas, not Thanksgiving or July Fourth, those were everybody else's days. I had my own." She was suddenly assailed again by that icy bereavement. Telling these things was like dripping out blood. "You were it. The birthday of my life, I suppose."

He knelt down beside her and took her chin hard in his hand. "Maybe this is part of it. You don't think like anybody else, let alone move like them. I dunno. . . . I

137

don't get it about Barry. You're married to him, and you're absolutely free of him. And he worships you. He never stops talking, he's so proud of you."

"It's easy for Barry to worship. He worships the Bennetts, for instance. And he talks about them so much that I could have strangled him, but all I could do was despise him for crawling."

He let go of her, sat back and took out his cigarettes. Watching his closed expression she wondered if she had repelled him. There was no help for that; if he suffered one way in this business, she suffered in another. She wanted to shriek at him, Can't you see that to talk about myself like this is destroying me, shred by shred, but I have to do it for *you?*

"Why'd you every marry him?" he asked finally.

"You asked me that before. Why'd you ever marry Laurie?"

He put the cigarettes back in his shirt pocket. "Well, there's always one way to shut your mouth."

CHAPTER TWENTY

To stop in at Liza Bennett's was a test of some sort; doing it of her own accord, instead of being trapped into it, gave it a chance of success. *We think it sticks out all over us,* Owen had said, and that was the challenge. She considered that Liza, because of her background, was more astute about people than the islanders. To Vanessa their classifications were laughably simple; islanders, non-islanders. All quirks of behavior could be explained according to this specification.

Oh, some of them are all right, she thought carelessly. It's a profession of its own, being a Bennett or a Bennett's Islander. Sometimes, in the store or at the sewing circle, there were tiny instances, so short that one almost doubted that they'd happened, when she was startled by a recognition that her own attitudes, viewpoints, and vision were not absolutely unique. Sometimes signals flashed a

readable code that showed the relationship, however tenu-
ous, between her and them.

She thought cynically, Well, we're all women. We have
the same component parts, it's how we use them that's
different. . . . The sparks of acknowledgment always made
her uneasy, as if she were in danger of losing her national-
ity; her country had been swallowed up so many years
before that she didn't recollect ever having been in it. She
used to read about displaced persons with a dry hard rage;
she knew she had suffered nothing in contrast to them,
and yet she felt that if she had any kin in the world it was
those people, and she did not want to become like anyone
else.

It was all right to pretend, in fact it was necessary. But
one must never fall into one's own trap. She remembered
this as she talked with Liza Bennett about books. She
admired her own fluency very much. Liza named off
authors and books, and when she came to one Van hadn't
read she jumped up eagerly to find it in the bookcase. "His
style is so peculiar, the first few pages are likely to put you
off. But he's worth persistence." She came back, carrying
four books. "You should have all four at once, but be sure
to read them in order. And you'll want to keep referring
back."

"I've no education, you know," Vanessa warned her.
"I've just worked my way stack by stack through the
Limerock Public Library."

"But that's education! Listen, I know people with de-
grees who read only the bare minimum in college and
haven't opened a book yet. You could give them an inferi-
ority complex as far as being well-read goes."

Vanessa gave her what she hoped was a modest smile
and drank her coffee with real enjoyment. She'd got Barry's breakfast and fixed his dinner box before sunrise, and
then had walked across the island to the accompaniment
of the dawn chorus of birds and engines in the cold sweet
air; she had hunched among the rocks at this end of
Schoolhouse Cove and watched *White Lady* move out
from the wharf at the other end of the cove.

From this distance Owen was an anonymous figure in
oilskins, but she had kept her eyes on him till they
blurred, and then the red globe of the sun rising up over
Windward Point had blinded her, and blotted the boat and
the man out of existence. She heard the engine speed up

and, blinking her eyes against the purple blobs left by the sun, she saw the boat vanish behind one of the gull nesting islets.

Then she had crossed the Homestead meadow and gone into the woods, and tried to find the place where she a Owen had gone from the dance. But though she sa where the land rose, she found no signs of a track. Wherever she went the way seemed to be barred by blowdowns or thick new growth. She was soaked by cold dew, and the sun had not yet struck down into the woods to warm them. At last she followed a path that went through the orchard of ancient trees around which the spruce forest had grown up in a high wall. The trees were beginning to bud and were full of wood warblers that hushed as she passed, and then began again. The path ended at an iron gate between cement posts, and beyond lay the small cemetery.

She had no morbid thoughts about this, though it occurred to her as she stood looking at the stones that Maggie Dinsmore would have been in a fever of foreboding about finding no path in the woods but one which led to a cemetery.

Her walk had ended up at Liza's, with coffee, brioche, and Laurence Durrell. She couldn't help admiring the variety of her morning so far, as if it were a particularly complicated piece of needlework she'd created. Now she had established herself in Liza's mind as a passionate reader, and she'd keep that picture intact if it meant borrowing, reading, and discussing every book on Liza's shelves. Once at a sewing session Liza had said of someone, "Well, at least he *reads*."

Steve Bennett's wife came in and Vanessa got up, collecting the books. "Oh, don't go," Philippa exclaimed. "We never have a chance to talk."

"I'm not much of a talker," said Vanessa.

"Don't worry, you won't get much chance," Liza said. "Sit down for a few minutes. At least for one cigarette. Here, have some more coffee."

This was the difficult part; she wanted to rush out, but to leave the two behind meant they'd compare notes. Between them she was trapped. She laid the books back on the table and sat down.

"There," Philippa said, smiling. Listening to her voice as she and Liza talked, Vanessa tried to channel her discomfort into observation. The Bennetts went in for wholesome women, it appeared—especially schoolteachers—who had a sense of humor and who never spent long nights in tantrums or nightmares or the unmoving, undreaming sleep that was worse than the other two. . . . She sipped her coffee, lids downcast, and saw against them the blazing blue of the bay and Owen's shoulders. The smell of coffee was overlaid with the orangey pungence of crushed ground pine. She wanted to laugh, thinking how shattered these two would be if they had the slightest idea of what sat at this table with them.

"Well, have you heard anything about Gina?" Liza said.

"No, but there's a new chapter." Philippa glanced at Van. "We should fill you in on this. Otherwise you'll hear all sorts of versions. And I want to talk about it so I'll stop thinking of Willy's face."

Van composed herself into a suitable attitude for listening. Philippa went on. "Gina went to Vinalhaven with us, you know. She was going to stay with an aunt, buy some clothes, and go to the movies. Willy wanted her to go, in fact he asked us to take her, to give her a little change. And Gina was bored all the way except when she talked to Steve." She burst out laughing. "She had on false eyelashes. It was all she could do to lift the weight, so it gave this sort of slumbrous effect whenever she looked at Steve. He said afterward it made him nervous."

"Poor Gina," said Liza. "There's something pathetic about her."

Philippa gave her a sidewise look. "Is there? . . . Well, the aunt met her—looking pretty apprehensive, I might add—and Steve told them what time to meet us on Sunday afternoon, and that was that. And on Sunday afternoon, no Gina, but the aunt, now frantic. Gina had run away to Limerock on the Saturday afternoon boat."

"With somebody?" asked Van.

"No, she just went. Apparently the sight of the city across the bay was just too much for our street sparrow. The aunt had been running up enormous telephone bills calling everybody she could think of, but nobody had seen so much as one of those foolish eyelashes."

"In the old days," Liza said, "Gina's just the type who'd disappear into the white slave traffic. You know, you meet a motherly woman with a concealed hypodermic, and you wake up in Buenos Aires, the toy of Latin lechers."

141

"I don't know," said Van. "They might make her take a bath first, and she'd prefer death to dishonor."

Liza laughed, but Philippa looked depressed. "According to Steve's low language she's probably shacking up with somebody, if those false eyelashes haven't worn her out by now. No, it's Willy who's the tragedy. He was down at the Eastern End to meet us when we came home last night. His smile practically lit up the dusk."

"I take it back," said Liza. "Gina isn't pathetic. She did something. She *acted*. You know something had to happen there, Philippa, the thing's been mulling too long. I'm sorry for Willy, but maybe this is the best thing in the long run."

"Willy was desperate, making excuses for her. She must have had a toothache, he said. In fact she'd been complaining of one, poor kid, but she was brave. He kept telling us that. I didn't know whether to cry for him or shake him."

Kick him, thought Van, and you still wouldn't get any reaction. I know, I've got one. Sometimes he gets mad, but it's like a fly buzzing on a window.

"So this morning," said Philippa, *"he's* gone. He saw Nils on the shore, asked him to tell Steve when he saw him, and went in on the mailboat."

"For good?" Van asked.

Philippa shrugged. "If Gina wants it, that's what it'll be. So it won't be the best thing for Willy, Liza, because he'll be making nowhere near the money he makes here, with that insatiable little monster wanting more and more. Good God!" she burst out angrily, "what kind of eyesight do these boys have that turns these grubby little wretches into Helens of Troy?"

"It's a matter of chemistry, dear," said Liza briskly. "And I've seen more than one bright attractive girl losing her head completely over something from under a rock. What *you'd* pick out for them they wouldn't give a second look. They rush into disaster like lemmings."

"Oh I know that. But I feel for Willy, and for Steve too, to be practical. Willy's got the makings of a good lobsterman, and Steve's got him trained to where he doesn't have to stand over him all the time. He says Willy has a real instinct for it. He's being charitable about the whole thing—you know Steve—but he knows darn well that if Gina tells Willy not to come back, Willy won't."

Vanessa gathered the books and stood up. "I've got to be going. Thanks for the coffee and conversation and the books."

Philippa said, "Do you think we're being pretty ruthless about Gina? Me, particularly? Liza has qualms of pity for her, by spells."

"Not pity so much as guilt," said Liza. "We don't know a lot about her background, but we can imagine it, can't we? None of us knows what we'd be under the same circumstances. The sight of her wandering around in those hideous sweaters and rollers, and that bored curl of the lip you get when you speak to her, can spoil the landscape for me, I admit it. But she jabs my conscience."

"But why?" Vanessa asked bluntly. "You can't do anything for her. You couldn't even be a friend to her. She looks down on everybody." How well I know, she thought.

"She *pretends* to look down on everybody," said Liza. Vanessa felt a small stinging surprise. "I think we all remind her of teachers or welfare workers or church visitors, everybody who's tried to corral her in the past. She's suspicious as a cat gone wild. So she calls us squares, or whatever the word is now, and sneers, all because she's not like us. And I know what that sounds like!" Liza defended herself. "Smug—conceited—insular—"

Van sat down again. "What makes you think she wants to be like you?"

"I didn't say like *me,* I said like *us.* She thinks we're on the inside and she's outside and never can get in. If we try to bring her in, what passes for pride with her digs in with all its claws."

"Maybe she likes it on the outside," said Van. "Maybe she does really despise you, for not knowing what she knows, for never having to claw your way up instead of being brought up." Stop, stop, she warned herself. They are watching you. Next they will be thinking about you. "Of course I don't know," she said with a shrug. "We're just theorizing, aren't we?"

"I'm inclined to go along with you," said Philippa. She turned her coffee cup slowly in the saucer, gazing into it as if for a fortune. "Gina could very well feel superior to us because she thinks we've been sheltered and protected all our lives and have never known any hard knocks. Well, we can't do anything for her and she's gone. And I'm

143

afraid Willy's gone too. I don't like to think of what'll become of him."

"Willy's as far beyond help as Gina is," said Van, getting up. "It isn't as if he'd ever be anything, with or without her."

"Only a good lobsterman," said Philippa gloomily. "If he'd come back, he could live with us. He did before he married Gina. He's really a nice boy, Van."

"But he'll only pick up another Gina," she pointed out.

"This time I go along with Van," Liza said. "Willy's a born masochist. Steve had better put an ad in the Limerock *Patriot* and see what he gets."

"He's thinking of trying an educated chimpanzee," said Philippa, and they all laughed. Van left after that, richly amused by their gullibility. *We. Us.* One thing with claws had got at least partway inside; and they hadn't guessed. The only thing that could possibly disturb her this morning was that they surmised what creatures existed out there and sometimes thought about them.

CHAPTER TWENTY-ONE

Barry went out after supper, but came back soon, walking fast. "Herring," he said tersely, pulling on his rubber boots. "Sounds like the harbor's full. We'll have to get set before the moon rises." He gathered his oilskins from the entry. "Owen's got Jamie Sorensen and Charles's boy. He wants me along."

"So they all come when he whistles," she remarked.

"Huh?" He was burrowing through a drawer, trying to match up cotton gloves. "Oh hell, I've got some new ones in the fishhouse. Hey, make a pot of coffee by and by, huh?"

"No," she said tranquilly, walking away from him with her finger marking her place in her book. "It's no emergency tonight. I'm not having a bunch tramping through here. I'm going to bed early and I want to sleep."

"Okay, *okay!*" He gave her a revengeful look and went out, slamming doors. Next to having her make a call with him, he wanted to lead noisily into his own house, shouting at the men to sit down, calling her "woman" and quite possibly whacking her on the rear.

Left alone, she couldn't settle down to read after all. *Alexandria* called for something different from this. She blew out the lamp and went outside. The power plants throbbed gently around the harbor. Using both hands and feet she climbed among the pale-gleaming chunks and slabs of rock that rose along the harbor side of the point. After a while a band of spruces muffled the sound of generators. She sat high above the harbor, and the village lights seemed very far away. Suddenly she was homesick for the old, different isolation, for the tough-walled privacy in which she had moved, wanting no one to breach it, not even herself. She bowed her head heavily onto her knees.

Then she heard a soft thump and a stir of the water below her. She knew at once it was the seine dory from which the net had been set out across the harbor mouth, and now the men in her would make her fast to some special spruce, and then would be picked up by another dory. She wondered if it were the two boys down there, or if one of the men were Owen, and her heart seemed to get out of rhythm, as if even his unseen presence could cause the muscles to jump or contract.

To calm herself she imagined how the herring appeared to the silent men, a silver cloud rushing through the black water, shooting off single arrows of light. A pocket of net would be formed off the running twine, and the herring should be driven inside and securely enclosed before the moon rose and distracted them. Then silence wouldn't matter. But for now it was a time not only for silence and sure movements, but for instinct and intuition.

As the night blackened she watched the phosphorescence around everything that moved, the light splashings of white fire around the stern of the dory as glowing ripples broke; the luminous string of netcorks stretching away across the harbor. Out there a mysterious repeating pattern was the motion around a moving dory and softly dipping oars.

An outboard motor started up all at once, and the speeding boat was picked out of the dark by the shimmering curl of the bow wave and the bubbling light of the wake. She circled, then slowed, and bits of voices sounded above the idling rhythm. Suddenly the outboard exploded into full life; the water flashed high along the dory's side as she shot forward into a long wide turn. There was a faint, small cry above that ripping and snarling. From somewhere a searchlight went on, swept the harbor, and picked up the dory. There was no one aboard. Frantically the light searched the water and the dory kept swinging through the beam in drunken circles.

Philip Bennett's front door opened and people stood against the light. Someone ran out onto Terence Campion's wharf with a flashlight. Van saw all this as objectively as she listened to the shouts and cries. She thought, Owen was in that dory. Now he isn't. That's it. That's all there is to it.

She got up and began to make her way carefully down over the rocks, keeping her face turned away from the harbor and her hand over the ear on that side, though nothing could keep out the hideous racket of the outboard motor. She wanted to be in bed, pretending to be asleep, when Barry came home to tell her. He would wake her up, but she could act dazed, and keep her arms over her face.

She had just reached the corner of the house when the outboard suddenly stopped, leaving a yell in the pounding silence. ". . . Over here!"

She felt her way around the house and in at the back door. She went upstairs and into her room and began to undress in the dark, her back to the window. They must have found the body, she thought calmly. They'll be using artificial respiration by now, but it won't help. It'll be like when that boy Alec died. They'll work hard on him for a long time.

She got into bed, arranging herself carefully, flat and straight. She folded her hands on her stomach and looked at the ceiling. It had to be this way, she thought. Just when I came to The Day.

Voices outside, Kathy's high and clear over the men's. Feet tramping on the wharf. Barry was coming home. He was telling Terence and Kathy how it happened. Kathy made a funny sound, like laughter; it would be the hysterical bursting into tears. I wonder if someone's already gone to the true-blue manager of the girls' varsity basketball team, Van thought.

Downstairs the back door crashed open. "Van!" Barry

shouted. "Wake up! Come down here!" She didn't answer and he said loudly, "Take a chair. I'll go up."

"Don't wake her if she's sleeping that hard."

"Let her sleep through *this?*" He laughed wildly. *Laughed.* She got out of bed and began to dress. Her hands were cold and shaking. That wasn't Owen's voice that answered him, it was one of the other Bennetts. That wasn't Owen, she repeated it deliberately. That wasn't Owen. Barry is laughing because he's hysterical. He and Kathy and maybe the 4-H girl. I am simply going down there to shut him up and send this other man home.

She ran down the stairs and into the kitchen. "Here she is!" cried Barry with drunken delight. He was taking off his shirt. Owen stood by the sink ladling water into the teakettle. In her dazzled sight he seemed to give off all the blaze of light in the room, rather than the lamplight glancing off white and yellow paint. He gave her a serious sidewise glance, then put the cover on the teakettle and set it on the gas stove.

"I fell overboard!" Barry kept laughing. "Right smack out over the stern of that dory and I gave the handle a twist when I went, so she revved up to top speed and started going in those goddam circles! Kee-rist! *'Swim!'* they kept yelling at me. *'Swim, you bastard!'* So I swam, oilclothes, boots and all, and they could see me! They said I looked like a seal with all that damn fire in the water—" His chattering teeth stopped him, but he kept on laughing.

"Go change your clothes," Vanessa said. "Here." She took a couple of bath towels out of the chest drawer. "Rub down hard."

He grabbed the towels and started for the stairs. "You tell her about it, Owen. I'll never forget the way that propeller sounded under water . . . and all I could think of was to get out of the way before it caught me. . . . *'Swim, you bastard!'* they kept yelling at me." Laughing like a drunk, he went up the stairs, stumbling in the dark and swearing happily to himself. "Hey, Van, that water wasn't a bit cold! Dunno but I'll get me some water wings and go in with the kids!"

"The unsinkable Mr. Barton," said Owen. "He scared the guts out of us and came up grinning."

"How'd he happen to fall overboard?" she measured instant coffee into mugs.

"Oh, he was standing up when he gave that starting

147

handle a twist without meaning to. Got a little flourishy with those twenty horses, I'd say." He sat down at the table and folded his arms on it. His voice sounded heavy and there were deep creases in his face.

"It sounds like Barry," she said dryly. "Being flourishy and nearly killing himself. And coming up grinning."

"Has he got any hard liquor in the house? He can use it and so can I."

"It was probably worse on you than it was on him." She took out the bottle.

Watching between bottle neck and glass, he said, "And you never knew a thing about it. Sound asleep."

"No, I was out there." Their voices were colorless. "I heard the engine start up, and the shouts. I saw the dory going in circles and nobody aboard. I thought you were the one who drowned." She went past him to the gas stove where the kettle was now boiling, and he reached out and took hold of her wrist. She half turned toward him and looked into his face.

"Don't," she murmured. "Look, for half an hour you were dead. I'd had long enough to *know* it, don't you see? Now you're alive, and it's so—well, I can't even feel overjoyed. I'm afraid to."

He nodded. "How would you feel if we hadn't got Barry?"

"Poor Barry," she said, and turned away from him to the stove. He let go her wrist. Upstairs Barry was singing in a false baritone, "Rocked in the Cradle of the Deep." "I'd have to leave the island," she said. "Philip would want this house for another man."

"Is that all Barry means to you?" Owen asked as she poured boiling water into the mugs.

"At the moment, yes. Though if I saw him lying dead I might feel something different. I don't know."

He pushed back violently in the chair. "You'd have done better to go to work instead of marrying him."

"Do housework for somebody with Miss Foster still checking up on me?"

"Who was she?"

"My case-worker," she said dryly. "I was a state ward. I had no parents. I was found under a cabbage leaf."

"So that really happens, does it?" His wintry look softened. "How come you didn't turn into a white butterfly?"

"Wrong kind of caterpillar." Suddenly they were both smiling; the danger, if there had been danger, was gone. "I don't advertise it," she told him. "Some people think if you were a state ward you must have been a girl gangster, or a teen-age harlot. I didn't mean to tell you."

"I'm glad you did. I like to think I have a few rights. But don't worry, it's nobody's business."

Barry came running downstairs like a boy and into the kitchen rubbing his hands. "Nothing like a night swim to give a man an appetite. *And* a thirst!" He poured out a drink. "You having one, honey?"

"In twelve years it must have dawned on you that I don't drink," she told him. He blinked at her as if the lamplight were too bright.

"Look at her, Cap'n Owen," he said, waving his glass. "Ain't she some good-looking tonight? Cripes, I dunno but what I might have a beauty on my hands after all."

"Sit down and have some hot coffee. You'll be going straight up through the ceiling in a minute."

"No, but look at her," Barry insisted. "Just look at her and tell me if I don't have a damn fine wife."

Solemnly Owen regarded her across the table. After a moment he said, "Very handsome, I'd say. Drink your coffee and then you'd better go to bed. We won't need you again tonight."

"Ayuh, but—" Barry was up again, hurt.

"Four tomorrow morning we'll take the fish out, and if you're not on deck I'll be around to haul you out of bed."

Barry sagged back into his chair, grinning happily. "Good-night," Owen said to Vanessa. "Oh, his boots are out by the doorstep. They ought to come in and dry out tonight. His oilskins are in the fishhouse."

"I'll get the boots now." She followed him out through the entry and onto the doorstep. She could see him in the glow of lamplight from the window over the sink as he picked up the boots.

"You know," he said just above a whisper, "I thought out there, what if Barry didn't come up alive."

"But there's still Laurie and your kids," she added cruelly.

As if he hadn't heard her he said, "I *thought* it, but I was about to go in after him when he surfaced by the net corks. Drowning one man in my lifetime is enough."

"Who was that?" Barry was making a clattering in the kitchen and she hardly heard her own question.

In the ghostly light of the rising moon his upturned face had black hollows for eyes, like a painting of Oedipus she'd seen once. "My sister's husband," he said. "Because I was drunk. The more you know me the worse I look. What about tomorrow?"

She was trying to place one reality over another and she got a double-exposure that couldn't be sorted out. "What about tomorrow?" she repeated.

"If I get a chance when I come in from hauling I'll come to the place." He tipped his head toward the dark of Long Cove.

"All right." She blinked in a sudden attack of fatigue, and in that instant he disappeared. Except for the faint hollow thud of his boots going away around the house, he might never have been there at all.

Borne down by a weariness that made her whole body feel soggy and spongy, she went back into the house. Barry was having reactions too, yawning till his eyes ran with tears. "Go on up to bed," she told him. "Are you having chills? You want a hot-water bottle?"

"Kee-rist, I never felt a thing from it," he bragged. "I never even had time to be scared. It was the other three got shook up enough to puke, and Hugo did, I guess." Gasping in the middle of his laughter with a convulsive yawn, he went stumbling upstairs. Van dropped his wet clothes in the tub in the entry, and stood his boots up behind the stove. She washed the cups and the glasses and wiped off the stove. Then she blew out the lamp and listened at the foot of the stairs. Barry was snoring, like a man knocked out with a drug. She lay down on the sitting-room couch, pulling over her the wool afghan some Bennett woman had knitted. She was too tired to be happily relieved that she could sleep alone. She knew that when she shut her eyes her head would begin to spin and her sodden body go tumbling over and over into the pit that awaited her for such special occasions as these. She forced her eyelids to stay up for a while, staring through the sitting-room doorway at the pallid shapes of the sun-porch windows. When she did fall asleep it was all at once. She had only an instant to protest the dizzying fall and it was over.

CHAPTER TWENTY-TWO

He didn't make it that day. After a while, moving along the edge of the woods like an Indian scout, she came to where she could look across the pasture, and saw him with the children by one of the big barn doors. At once she was explosively angry and jealous and wanted to do something outrageous, like whistling loudly on two fingers to start the children running off to find out who it was in the woods, while he roared after them to come back, and then had a hard time explaining his bad temper. But she knew she wouldn't do it; the thought of his rage with her froze up the will to do violence, and she went sadly away from there. At least he was alive.

That night Barry asked her to go over to the Dinsmores' while he played cribbage with Rob, and to his delighted surprise she went. The fact was, she couldn't tolerate being alone in the house and hoping against all common sense that Owen would come to her. She could no longer forget herself in reading.

She took along socks to darn, and sat with Maggie in the small sitting room while the men played cribbage in the kitchen. "I thought you were awful different," Maggie said with her boyish bashful grin, "when I first laid eyes on you. But you aren't. I mean, here you are, doing things just like everybody else. My, that's a beautiful darn. Did your mother make you learn to patch and darn when you were real young?"

"No, she wasn't much with her hands," said Van. "Another woman taught me this." It had been Mrs. Bearse.

It was a way to use up a few hours. They went slowly enough, but they'd have stood still if she hadn't put herself out. Mag's pleasure in her company, and Barry's beams and winks were what she had to pay.

That night Barry wanted to make love to her. It had been a long time and he promised her he would take no chances. Besides, she felt a little guilty because he had been so compassionate about the story of her birth. The

151

guilt surprised her, but it was undeniably there. Of course the lie had given Barry a chance to be sorry for her, which he enjoyed, but his pity was genuine just the same, and he had put it—for the time being—above his ambition to father a child.

For a long time she hadn't been much of a participant, and she wondered if Barry felt cheated when he remembered how she had once been with him. But he had never said so. Perhaps he thought that was the way some women were and that only whores were different. When he slept, she lay awake in the dark and remembered how the tiger had been evoked in this room, and she wondered about the love-making of tigers.

In the morning after Barry had gone she took her breakfast into the sun parlor, and saw that the new batch of trapheads no longer hung on the wall. Owen had come that night after all, while they were at the Dinsmores'.

That afternoon she walked the curve of Schoolhouse Point, down by the water. At the far end, where the land hooked steeply into the tall granite prow of Windward Point, *White Lady* was tied up in the L of the wharf. The workshop and baithouse seemed to grow out of the almost vertical bank above.

She climbed up over exposed ledges and walked between stacks of new traps, headed with her work, and then onto the broad steep ramp of planks laid from the wharf to the fishhouse door. Until now the action of the water splashing among rocks and around the wharf spilings had drowned out any other sound. But now she heard a hammer, and for the first time admitted that she had hoped he would be there. Until now she had kept up the fiction that this was simply a walk and that Owen was certainly around the harbor somewhere or at home.

She found herself out of breath, not from exertion, and stopped between the open door and a window. Inside someone came noisily down a flight of steps, and a young boy's voice said, "Hey, Dad, can I have this bailing scoop I found upstairs?"

"I thought you had a bailer for the dory, the one you made out of a Clorox jug." The hammer went on. Heading traps. She knew the rhythm.

"Ayuh, but this is a real one. I mean, it's wood, and you made it, didn't you?"

"Yep. You can have it." That he was lifting the trap off the bench now, she could tell by the way he spoke. "I'll have to take a look up there. Every time you go up you come down with something different. You're likely to show up with buried treasure next."

There was a little-boy giggle, and then Holly's composed voice. "Maybe you should look round, Daddy. I bet pirates have been coming ashore here on dark nights and stowing stuff away."

"Pirates," the boy scoffed. "They don't have them now."

"How do you know? Have you looked in the sea chest lately? There could be a body in there." She paused. The hammer tapped precisely. "Dismembered," Holly added. "That means—"

"I know what it means," the boy snarled.

"I was reading," his sister continued, "where these kids kept finding all these brown-paper packages in this dump, and what do you suppose they turned out to be?"

"A bunch of girls who couldn't keep their mouths shut," said Owen.

"No, it was just one girl, in hunks."

"I bet her name was Holly too," said the boy bravely, "and her brother did it."

"In self-defense," said Owen. "That's enough. You may not find yourself in hunks, my girl, but you could find yourself in durance vile, as the feller says, and with nothing to read. Rich, you go out and get yourself a mouthful of fresh air. And start gathering up a pile of loose ballast for those new traps."

It was too late to get away without being seen. Vanessa and the boy confronted one another. He looked like his mother, round-headed and rosy-cheeked, with blue eyes slightly uptilted at the outer corners; they saw her with surprise and then a brightly curious friendliness. "Hi, Mrs. Barton! Hey, Dad!" He looked back into the dim workshop shot through with sunlight. At the bench, his hand on a trap, Owen half-turned toward her and froze. The little girl was knitting baitbags by the two small front windows, she too gazed over her shoulder, motionless with surprise. Then the boy shot on past Van and down toward the wharf, and the two inside came alive.

"Afternoon." Owen half-growled it and turned back to

153

the work bench. Holly said with pleasure, "Hello, Mrs. Barton."

"I guess I'm trespassing," said Van. "I was out for a walk and I kept on going. I didn't know anyone was here." She stayed in the doorway, blushing foolishly. She felt the aura of his displeasure across the room. Motion overhead attracted her and she looked up at the light ripples that flowed constantly across the ceiling reflecting from the sunny waters of the cove.

"Isn't that pretty?" asked Holly. "I wish our house was where I could have those reflections in my room."

"You'll have to move down here," said Van.

"I wish I could." She gave her father a quick little scowl, ridiculously like his. "Won't you come in?" she asked politely. "There's a nice view from these windows."

Damn you, she said to Owen's broad shoulders, It's your fault. "I'd like to see it," she said to Holly. She had to walk past Owen and the bench and he didn't look around, though out of the corner of her eye she saw his fingers fitting the small white net she had woven. Holly had her baitbag hook in a scarred window sill, and a little armless rocker. She kept on knitting, with brisk decisive movements and a preoccupied face, and Van knew she was expected to be impressed.

"You make a good strong knot," she said.

"Thank you," said Holly primly, as if it were bad manners to show pleasure at being praised. "I make all Daddy's baitbags. He pays me."

"That's good. I wouldn't want to see him take advantage of you just because you're in the family," Van said, and Holly gave her an upward glance, black eyes narrowing with held-back laughter. It was so unexpectedly and unfairly Owen's gesture that her belly went hollow, as if the black head had crashed into it. Her hands trembled in her pockets. She took them out and braced the fingers on the middle sash of a window. "Yes, it's quite a view," she said. "You really should move down here, Holly."

"You ought to be here in a storm!" Holly exulted. "Once Rich and I came down here to watch the surf in the cove, and it began to blow so hard we thought the roof of the shop was coming off—oh, you should have felt the whole place shake and shudder—so we started back, and the combers were crashing in both sides of the point so the air was full of spray. We really got scared. We

154

were afraid the wind would blow us overboard so we crawled on our stomachs. Then Daddy came out to meet us and grabbed us both— Well, not *really* by the scruff of the necks," she said gently with a glance at him, "but I thought he was going to. He was so mad he could have done I don't know what. He thought all the time we were out playing in the barn, till he looked out the window and saw us crawling along the point. You see, it was a hurricane, and we didn't know it." She added with some pride, "You should have heard Daddy *swear!*"

Vanessa shook her head, as if she were beyond words. She saw him in the sheeting rain, grasping his two children, swearing at them out of his agony of love and terror.

Down on the beach below Rich scrambled about on the shifting stones, gathering flat rocks for loose ballast and carrying them by the armful up to the place where the wharf met the bank. Inside, one trap was set out of the way, another lifted to the bench. Holly knit a few meshes, but she was clearly disturbed by her father's silence. After a moment she observed, "Sometimes my father is very quiet."

Owen spoke in an ordinary tone. "Holly, run on back to the house and tell your mother to put the coffeepot on. Mrs. Barton's coming up." Holly dropped her baitbag needle to dangle from the half-finished bag, and gave Van a conspirator's grin on her way out.

"And take Rich along with you," Owen called after her. "He's lugged enough rocks for one day."

"Okay, Daddy." Outside the door she shouted between her cupped hands. "Rich-ard!"

"Her lungs are as powerful as her manners are," said her father. Outside there was a shouted argument which ended when Owen put his head around the door and said, "Pipe down. And scatter."

When they'd gone up by the door, he went on working for a few minutes, and Vanessa finished the row on Holly's baitbag. Then he left the shop and went up the way the children had gone, was out of sight for a moment, and returned. She knew he was standing by the bench watching her. Without looking around she said, "I don't have any intention of visiting your wife, and you know it."

"How should I know? Around here women don't call on

155

a married man in his fishhouse unless they're on the way to call on his wife."

"I didn't have any intentions of visiting you," she said stiffly.

"Bullshit. You saw the boat tied up here when you started around the cove, didn't you?"

"Yes, but you could have been at the house or down at the harbor." She dropped the needle and baitbag and stood up. "Why in hell am I explaining anything to you? I've never been in the habit of explaining my actions to anyone."

"That's obvious." He leaned back against the bench and folded his arms. "And you've never felt any responsibilities to anyone, have you? Oh, in one way I don't blame you. Nobody felt much of a duty toward you except the state and that makes for damn cold mothering. But you married Barry on your own hook, and you must have been glad he was there for you to marry, but you don't feel any responsibility toward him, do you?"

"I was insane to tell you anything about myself."

"I knew already about you and Barry. I told you that." She threw back her head in forced laughter. "You're a prize. You were quick enough to move in, but every time we meet I get a lecture on my marital duties. Why don't you ask when I went to bed with him last?"

"When did you?" he asked coldly. She walked by him toward the door. His arm went across the opening and held her back.

"Where are you going?"

"To my responsibilities. For good. It'll be a relief to feel like an honest housekeeper after being made to feel like a prostitute who dared to breathe the same air as your children did."

"Don't be such a goddam fool." He held her upper arms to her sides. She couldn't move, she wouldn't have been able to even if the touch had been easier. "How do you think I felt when I looked up and saw you in the doorway?" he said softly. "With them here? It was an ax smashing down through my skull, like slicing an apple in two."

"Schizophrenia, in other words." She tried to laugh.

"Call it anything. But it told me something I don't like. Scared the hell out of me, and that's a feeble way to say it." He pulled her to him and put his face against her hair.

"Oh, Christ," he muttered. Held so tight she couldn't move to embrace him, she felt the pressure of his hands increase until tears of pain came into her eyes. "I love you," he said. "I love you. Now will you get the hell out of here?" He turned her around and walked her to the door. She resisted, trying to squirm free and face him, but he was too strong. Frustration turned her frantic, the open doorway could have represented the edge of a cliff, and when she stepped through she would disintegrate; but she was saved from whatever shameful form it would take by a war-whoop from the path above.

She was released at once, and staggered against the doorframe. Holly burst in screaming and wrapped her arms around her father's waist and swung behind him, shrilling, "Save me, save me! He wants my long black tresses!" Richard pounded behind her, beating his hand against his mouth and whooping; Van's brain seemed to dance loose inside her head with the noise. She went blindly down the wharf. Behind her Holly gasped, "Mama isn't home. She left a note that she's gone to Aunt Jo's."

"That's all right then," said Owen. "Mrs. Barton can't stay anyway."

"Good-by, Mrs. Barton!" the children called after her, gaily hysterical. She waved without speaking. Walking across the stones where Richard had been gathering ballast, the sun in her eyes, she saw the long curve of the cove that had to be traversed before she would be anywhere near shelter. Then there was the path across the marsh to the harbor, where there would be faces, and then around the shore more faces, all before she could get up into her room and bed. The terror of not making it became the chief thing now. She felt so delicately put together that a word could shatter her and she would go to pieces in front of everyone.

Now she was walking on the wet sand studded with boulders, and deliberately she sat down on one and took out her cigarettes. But don't forget, she said, you aren't insane. You've been all through that. You made up your mind one day that you wouldn't be. You're going to be proof that it can be held back. . . . Look. There is the shop up there on the bank. Think what colors you would use if you were an artist. Those mossy shingles. I hope they never reshingle it. There is the wharf below, and the boat. *White Lady Four*. Was the first *White Lady* named after someone? You don't know anything about him; that may be where the real abyss lies.

She was beginning to feel calmer, and very tired. Up there he is heading traps and the children are talking to him. *Sometimes my father is very quiet.* She blew out smoke and looked around her. A flock of little sea birds ran along the lacy edge of water swirling over the sand. They made small, fine, busy noises.

He said *I love you* as if it were torn from him in some kind of bloody torture. Disemboweling or the living heart ripped out, or the Vikings' red eagle. A man felt this way about her, and it was a man whose touch took from her every defense. Many women wait their whole lives for this and it never happens, she thought, but when he said it he was putting me out the door. Over the cliff. Into the abyss. Off the world.

Sh saw him coming toward her, walking among the boulders, a big man in rubber boots, no fat under the jeans and faded flannel shirt, long bones and hard brown flesh that was burnt darker wherever the weather touched it; his face a squarish black-browed mask scowling against the sun-glare, his bare head casting off frosty glints at certain angles, as a rock held to the light shows the glimmer of mica.

He sat down on a rock near her and appeared to be watching the seabirds. She watched them too, saying, "Where are the children?"

"Holly's knitting and Rich is painting his new scoop."

"I should think they'd have chased you."

"I told them not to . . . Vanessa."

Her name tricked her into looking at him. He was filling his pipe, and the motions were incongruously peaceful. "I'm going into Limerock on the mailboat tomorrow. I have to see my lawyer about an income-tax snarl."

"When will you be back?" She made a tic-tac-toe tern in the wet sand with a stick.

"Next boat."

"Saturday to Tuesday makes a long weekend." She felt too empty to even miss him.

"I'm tired of this, Van," he said quietly. "Grabbing a minute here and there, watching the time, never having time enough. It's like being locked up in a place where you can't sit, stand, or lie down, or breathe either."

158

"So you're through," she murmured, watching the stick make x's.

"Didn't you *hear* me?" he asked. "I said I was going to Limerock tomorrow."

Carefully she made an O. "Hooray. I win. I think." She didn't watch him go, but sat there and contemplated her pattern for a moment and then got up and went back along the beach.

CHAPTER TWENTY-THREE

At suppertime she winced suddenly and put down her fork. Barry broke off an account of a suspenseful afternoon spent looking for a leak in Philip's boat. "What's the matter?"

"I don't know. I bit down on a tooth and it feels as high as a mountain."

His face puckered in sympathy. "It's not ulcerating, is it? This is one hell of a place for a toothache."

"Anywhere is one hell of a place for a toothache, but at least it's good weather, and the mailboat's running."

"You'd better go in tomorrow before it gets a chance to grab aholt."

"But I'd have to stay till Tuesday," she objected, "and I hate Limerock. And where would I stay? Not in a hotel!"

"What's the matter with a hotel?" He was being affectionately reasonable with a petulant young bride. "You know how to behave, and if you need more clothes, get some. Take a good handful of money with you. You can go to the movies twice, because they change the show on Sunday. And hey! Why don't you buy yourself a good batch of books? You could have a hell of a time in the bookstore looking around. Get some you've always wanted, poetry and that highbrow stuff you read."

He was captivated by the idea of buying books. She could hear him telling the other men, You know where the wife'll head for first, soon as she gets that tooth taken care of? The bookstore! Yep! I have to beat her over the head to get clothes. Nope, books is what she wants. Well, better books than gin, I always say.

"Well. . . ." Van resumed eating, cautiously. "I'll see how it is in the morning. I'll put cold compresses on it tonight and take aspirin. Maybe I can head it off."

He said sternly, "I don't want you to take chances. I was going to take you up to Sorensens' tonight. I got a chess game on with Nils, but it's kind of raw so you better stay put."

"I think so too," she agreed, as if otherwise she would have gone willingly with him. It pleased him. He left whistling, and she went upstairs to look over her clothes.

Excitement woke her early, and she took her clothes downstairs and dressed while the teakettle heated. It wasn't daylight yet, but she could tell by the clear sky, still faintly starred, that it was going to be a fine day. She was high-spirited with anticipation, and felt jolly and kind toward everyone; she wished there was time to bake a lot of sweet stuff for Barry, and go through all the womanly preparations and bustle that wives were supposed to make when they left home for a few days.

When Barry came down in his sock feet she gave him a wan one-sided smile. "Acting up, is it?" he asked.

"That's what got me up. It's calmed down some since I've been on my feet." She sighed. "I guess I'd better go, all right. But I don't want to stay at a hotel, they're too expensive and fancy, and we haven't even got a decent suitcase between us." She put her hand to her cheek. "So I thought I'd get a room somewhere. There's some rooming houses a lot of the island people go to, Kathy was telling me about it once. They'll let you make yourself some tea in the kitchen, or heat up some soup."

"That'll be a good idea, if he pulls out the tooth and you don't feel like moving around much afterward. I'm damn glad you aren't a bleeder, or I'd have to go along with you."

"I'm glad too," Van told him. "You have to stay here and make some money to pay for this business." This touched him and he patted her hand.

"Jo and Nils said get Dr. Northrup, and say they sent you. He'll fit you in."

"I will," she promised. It was a relief when Barry took his dinner box and left. His concern for her tooth kept

160

him from kissing her with the ardor which always sprang up in him when she was amenable.

She dressed in her new slacks and jacket for the trip, at the last moment recklessly deciding on the old raincoat. It meant nothing to her now but something to keep out the wind and keep off smuts from the diesel smoke. The woman who had worn it as a portable womb was still back in that kitchen on Water Street, frozen forever in the moment of hearing that the house was to be torn down. She felt a stab of something like compunction or guilt, but she was saved from it by Kathy.

"You going off on the boat?"

"No, by broom—it's the only way to travel," said Van.

Kathy laughed. "Cleaner too, since Link changed engines. Hey, isn't this sudden?"

"Sudden as a toothache."

Kathy winced. "Ouch! Is it awful? Look, I've got some pills that'll make you sleep all the way."

"I've got it knocked down with aspirin. If I took anything else I could fly without a broom. Any errands you want done?"

"I can't think of anything right now. So long, and have a good time." She grinned. "I mean, I hope you get fixed up so you can have some fun. The nice, safe, moral fun allowable for us good wives."

Van laughed at her. It was so easy to laugh this morning that she enjoyed hearing herself.

"Know what?" said Kathy. "I'll miss you something awful."

"Why? I'm not much of a neighbor."

"Oh yes, you are. I don't care if you don't run in. I like knowing you're around." She wriggled her shoulders self-consciously. "Oh heck, maybe I just like having a captive audience. Well, that's all." She flipped her hand and went out.

Van stood looking at the empty doorway, reflecting with mild wonder that no one had ever before said she would be missed. She shrugged uneasily. . . . It would probably be part of the neighborly pattern, of being a black blackbird, to bring the children something from the five and ten. She wrote it down, then with a resigned sigh added the Dinsmore children.

The shore was quiet again when she walked around to the wharf with her raincoat and suitcase. The mail had been given out, the women had bought fresh vegetables, meat, and milk, and now most of them and the children were at home having early lunch after early breakfast.

All this time she had not consciously anticipated meeting Owen, but as she approached the wharf, she received a sudden revelation, that it was all a vicious joke and he wasn't going anywhere.

As she came out by the store at the head of the wharf, she heard men's voices inside, but not his. I could say I'd lost my nerve, she thought. But the prospect of spending the weekend at home, fighting her sick disappointment with Barry fussing over her, was not to be considered. She thought frantically that she wouldn't be scared now of sleeping eighteen hours at a stretch or even twenty-four, if she could only accomplish it.

"Hello, Mrs. Barton!" Owen's boy Richard came out of the store, holding young Mark by the hand. "Are you going to Limerock too?"

Holly came out behind him and said loftily, "She must be going, unless she brings a suitcase to carry her mail in." She gave Van a suitably genteel smile. "Hello, Mrs. Barton. You'll have a lovely change across."

When Laurie appeared after the children, Van felt like breaking into witless laughter. Laurie's wide forehead wrinkled gently with concern. "You don't look as if you felt very well."

"I don't," said Vanessa hoarsely. "It's a tooth. I don't want to go ashore and I don't want to stay here with it, so the only alternative is to jump overboard halfway across the bay. Only I hate cold water."

The children appreciated that. "Well, at least it's not rough," Laurie said. "You can sit quiet. Have you got anything to take?"

Holding her lips stiffly together as if her whole face were sensitive, Van nodded. "Well, you'll be glad you had it taken care of," Laurie comforted her. "Has anybody called your dentist for you?"

"I think Barry did," Van lied. She put her hand against her cheek. "I'll go aboard, I guess."

"And get a good seat," said Holly. "That bench across the stern is nice, but if you don't get onto it here there's always a pile of people going in from Brigport, and they grab it."

162

"I'll carry your bag," Richard offered. "Holly, you take Mark."

Inside the store male voices burst into laughter, and this time she heard Owen's. "That must have been a good one," she murmured to Laurie above her rising joy.

"I think they were saving it till the children and I got out." They walked down through the long shed that smelled of damp, and salty hogsheads. "The engineer feels it's his duty to bring out all the latest. We're so isolated out here."

"Dad says Cliff don't talk fit to eat," said Richard wistfully. "He must know an awful lot of real nasty words." The two women exchanged smiles.

Out in the full sunshine, the gray striped cat sprawled on the top crate of a high stack and blinked tourmaline eyes. "There's Louis," young Mark said suddenly to Van, as if to recall what lay between them.

"So I see." She caressed the broad blunt head, arousing a rusty purr. She kept wanting to laugh. It was getting a little frightening. She heard herself trying to explain it to some impersonal faceless observer. . . . Escorted by his whole family . . . blessings and sympathy and advice and children's faces. It's so insane. This time it's the situation that's insane, not me. . . . Good God, I still don't know if he's going or not.

"Nobody else going but me?" she asked brightly, looking around at the empty wharf.

"Owen is," said Laurie. "Mark, you must let Holly hold your hand or you'll have to go back to the store. . . . I was going to say he'd look out for you, but I don't know what he could do about a toothache, do you?"

"Maybe he could take her mind off it," Holly said. "He tells good stories about when he was young. I wish I'd lived then."

"So do I," Richard brooded. *"Boy!"*

"Here they come!" young Mark cried suddenly. He broke loose from Holly, and rushed to his father, but Owen caught him and lifted him up, struggling and flailing. Holding the boy above his head he looked around, laughing. The look passed over Van.

"What you scared of?" he teased the child. "Afraid a fish hawk'll come and grab ye?"

"I ain't scared, I'm mad!" the child exploded.

Van sat alone on the stern bench as far as Brigport,

163

feeling the rather pleasant sense of separation from everything but the moment which comes to one traveling by water. At Brigport the boat had to maneuver through a long harbor full of moorings, and tied up alongside a big lobster car anchored in the lee of a breakwater. Here dripping crates of lobsters were hoisted aboard and lowered into the hold, and she saw Owen, pipe in mouth, helping to steer the crates toward the opening in the deck. There was a good deal of laughter between the men on the boat and those on the car. Everyone looked pleased with himself, as if the May sunshine were restoring the virtue the long winter had stolen.

As the boat headed for the main dock, Owen came aft and sat down beside her. "How's the tooth?"

"Not dead but sleeping," she said.

"You staying with somebody, or in a room?"

"In a room, if I can get one."

"I'll go up to the store now and call," Owen offered. "Likely to be a crowd in town this weekend, and Marshall's is a great place for the Swan's Islanders and Vinalhaveners."

"Well, if it won't put you out too much, maybe—"

"I need tobacco anyway." He was gone up the iron ladder against the stonework, shouldering his way through the small crowd; she saw the flash of his smile sometimes, and heard his voice genial and joking. He slapped a man on the shoulder and they walked away together. The Brigport passengers began to come aboard, three large women who looked all of a kind and gave her polite smiles as they settled themselves on the bench, and then a young girl heavily pregnant and harassed by a wiry two-year-old wearing harness and leash. The engineer took this one under his arm and growled, "You keep quiet or I'll tan your hide," at which the child went into a state of trance while he was handed down into the captain's arms. Then the engineer went back up the ladder, and guided the girl's foot to the first rung, then the other foot, and came down the ladder just a few rungs below her. He half-lifted her across the gap between dock and deck.

"Thanks, Cliff," she panted. "I was some nervous when I saw how low the tide was."

"Don't thank *me*. Just don't have it on this trip. We ain't none of us got our midwife papers."

164

"Don't discourage her, Cliff," said the captain. "We might put Cap'n Bennett here in charge."

"Well, now," said Owen from the top of the wharf, "that's something I haven't tried yet. I did think we could save some money that way once, but my wife didn't have much confidence in me."

The girl came aft, towed by the speedy child. The bench was full, and Vanessa got up. "I can get a couple of camp stools from the cabin," the girl said.

"Suit yourself," Van said. "But I like to move around, when it's calm enough."

"I used to like to go all over the boat before I got so loaded down," the girl said without resentment.

Van moved away between the rail and the cabin, and went forward. The engineer disappeared down his hatch, a couple of boys on the wharf cast off the lines, and the boat backed away and out into the harbor. Van walked around the forward hatch and sat on the side of it nearest the bow. Owen came and stood with his back against the mast. "I got you the last room she had," he said. "And I talked her into it. She was saving it in case somebody or other showed up from Isle au Haut this afternoon."

Van had to put her head back to look at him. "Thank you," she said.

He made some small repudiating gesture with his hands, and his lower lip thrust out in a way she hadn't noticed before. He didn't look into her face but around him at the outer shores of Brigport gliding by, and then at a cloud of gulls rising from a green islet on the other side. After a few moments he left her. She heard a door slam and a burst of masculine greetings and amusement, and knew he'd gone into the pilot house; while he had been out here with her they had been under the eye of the captain, steering from his tall stool and half-leaning out the open window, and two men who'd come aboard at Brigport.

She pulled up her knees and laid her head forward on them. The steady motion and swash of water rushing by the side half-lulled her into that state of separateness again. The unborn child does nothing but wait to be born, she thought, and he doesn't even know he's waiting. This is the birthday of my life. . . . *Long night succeeds thy little day*. . . . *I've reached the land of corn and wine, Beulah Land, sweet Beulah Land* . . .

"You all right?" It was repeated, louder and nearer. She

lifted her head, blinking unfocused eyes that watered at the radiance of the sky. Owen was sitting on the hatch cover beside her. "You can get seasick like that. Tooth acting up?"

"You know damn well," she said carefully, like a drunk, "that I've got no toothache."

"Well, don't advertise it. Everybody's sorry as hell for you right now. Cliff wanted to bring you coffee, but I saved you from that."

"Thanks, I guess." She looked blurrily around her, running her hands through her hair and then rubbing her palms hard over her jawbones. "We're almost in! I must have gone to sleep after all."

"That's why I stirred you up." He began filling his pipe and she sat with her arms folded on her knees and watched the way ahead. As the boat cut across the harbor traffic and the city grew clear at the base of the blue-violet hills, she could place the trees of Water Street as a long bank of green beyond the roof of the sardine factory. Seen from out here, everything carried an illusion of cleanliness and grace in the warm shimmer of spring, as if Water Street looked as it used to look long before her time. The house is down by now, she told herself. They may have already started the new building. But there was no conviction in her; she saw in her mind the sun on the iridescent roof slates, and the air was full of the scent of lilies of the valley.

She pulled her gaze away from that side of the harbor and concentrated on the big ferry landing on the opposite curve. She realized then that Owen had gone again, and she was alone when the mailboat docked.

The three stout women were met by a stout man whose quips and uninhibited whacks on any handy rear turned them into jellies of mirth. They offered the pregnant girl a lift. Laughter floated from the car windows as it left the slip. There was one taxi, and Van took it, not looking back to see where Owen was. He was helping to get the lobster crates out, and had given her an impersonal nod as she passed him, as if he hardly knew her.

In a room under the eaves of the mustard-colored Victorian house, she washed her face and hands in water from a tall flowered jug, and then went out, still in slacks. Limerock was no longer the serene, embowered city seen from the bay. She was glad to get into the comparative

166

quiet of a booth at the back of the Crow's Nest. She had just sat down when Owen came in.

"Link dropped me off at the corner of Sea Street, and there you were, just going in the door. How's that for timing? I was trying to figure out a way to reach you without getting Eva Marshall all hawsed up. . . . What do you want to eat? Better make it dinner, you look some ganted up." He grinned at the waitress. "We'll have some of those scallops, if they're fresh."

"Of course they're fresh," she said severely, then gave in and smiled back. It took years off her. She had once been pretty and full of a kittenlike smartness and life, and Owen's smile had reminded her of it. When she had gone, Van said, "How do you plan on explaining this? Somebody you know could walk in that door in the next five minutes."

"My wife and your husband aren't going to bust a gut because we happened to meet in a restaurant and eat together."

"You think you have everything under control, don't you?"

"I have."

Amused, fairly content, Vanessa ate. The food was hot and good. There was no conversation until they sat back with their coffee and cigarettes. "I called up my lawyer," he said. "We can't see the revenooers till Monday morning."

"What have you been doing, cheating?"

"Nope. But they think so. Now what I want you to do," he said matter-of-factly, "is to be ready with your dunnage when a taxi calls for you about five o'clock. He'll know where to take you." By expression or tone he gave nothing away to the couple in the booth across the way. Van sipped her coffee and looked past him as if she hardly heard him and didn't care. Yet she almost felt she should cover her throat in case the heavy beating in it showed. "You can tell Eva Marshall," he said, "if anybody shows up from Isle au Haut they can have that room tonight and tomorrow night."

Swallowing didn't ease anything. Watching the people passing by the windows she said, "All right."

The waitress was with them again. "We've got nice fresh custard pie today. It's real good." Her voice and eyes implored Owen to let her feed him with custard pie.

167

"Darlin' mine, I've got no room for it." He patted his middle. "Look, no pot yet. My wife's some proud of that and you wouldn't want to contribute to my downfall, would you?" She gave Van a sidewise look, then closed up her face and wrote the slip.

CHAPTER TWENTY-FOUR

He left her outside the restaurant and she walked along for a block, finding her way by instinct among the other walkers. She certainly didn't see them. Suddenly she returned to reality like an awakened sleepwalker and stood staring into a shop window, trying to orient herself. Beyond the ghostly flicker and sweep of reflections, there were women's clothes, and suddenly she felt that the poverty of her wardrobe was shameful. She couldn't go anywhere with Owen like this, in slacks. She stood examining the clothes, trying to concentrate on details and colors, while sweat prickled between her shoulder blades. Miss Foster used to take her shopping for clothes, and once they had gone in here, simply because Van had kept looking back at a dress in the window. Van had never allowed herself to show any interest or preference in clothes; no matter how hard the woman tried to give her a choice, Van always stood stiff, unpliable, armored against the humiliation of being on charity. The dress had taken her unawares; standing here now, she could remember the taste of her longing for it. She had been about fourteen, tall but still flat-chested, and unable to force herself to show pleasure once it was on her with its soft pleats, and cool green-and-white pattern of leaves and blossoms. Woodenly she stood before her reflection while Miss Foster and the clerk admired and exclaimed, trying to make a dent in her. She thought, Well, I have the dress now, and so what? It didn't really belong to her; it belonged to the other kind of fourteen-year-old, the kind with families. The taste of longing turned sour enough to make her sick. She hardly ever wore the dress after that, unless Mrs. Bearse asked her to wear it to church.

168

Whatever became of it? In any case, the store had changed hands several times in sixteen years, so there was no chance of meeting the saleswoman again. And now there was a point to choosing clothes. She was ironically amused to find herself wanting, just like anybody, to look nice; or at least nice enough so that Owen wouldn't be ashamed of her. The line *It is the birthday of my life* popped irrepressibly into her head and she thought, Good God, how sentimental can you get?

She went into the shop and chose, with an efficiency that pleased her, a beige tweed topcoat, moss-green skirt and sweater, a matching plaid jacket, a two-piece dress in apricot silk shantung. "You have taste," the man told her. "Not many would dare those colors—not many could wear them." She accepted his praise with composure, knowing he was right, confident that he couldn't guess she had never bought a dress for herself except by catalog. "Do you need anything else?" he asked her. She bought some stockings, accepting his advice on the shade. She handled for a few minutes a wide bracelet set with topazlike chunks.

"It matches your eyes," he said without flattery.

She gave him a slight smile, shook her head, and handed it back.

"Too bad," he said. "Well, come in again."

"I shall." The transaction set some sort of seal upon the day. She walked briskly back to the rooming house and told Mrs. Marshall that she'd met a friend who wanted her to spend the weekend, and she wouldn't want the room again till Monday. Naturally she'd pay for using it today to wash up and change her clothes in.

"Oh, don't talk so foolish," said Mrs. Marshall. "What's a few towels?" She was buoyant in her relief, because a cousin had shown up from Isle au Haut, just as she'd expected.

Van put on the skirt, and the shirt that belonged to the dress. Her loafers were old, but she hadn't worn them much and they were of good quality; with her long narrow foot her shoes had to be expensive. She packed away her slacks and sneakers, wrapped the full skirt of the new dress in tissue paper and packed that also.

She remembered how she had felt wearing Helmi's clothes that day, how she had looked in the mirror at an elegant stranger. The stranger had returned again, a woman reflected in glass as if caught in time for an instant on her way from one life to another. The only link with the past was the old raincoat thrown over a chair behind her. She could see Mrs. Marshall moving around in the kitchen at the back of the passage when she went downstairs with the raincoat over her arm. "Could I leave this coat some-place over the weekend?" she asked. "It's nothing much. I only wear it on the mailboat to keep my clothes clean."

When she got into the taxi she felt at once an upsurge of gay anticipation reinforced with relief. The driver was middle-aged and incurious. He looked like a fisherman, and said with a down-east accent, "Real pretty weekend for a trip."

"Yes." They were heading north, through the quiet residential streets with broad lawns and shade trees.

"Likely a weather-breeder though," he said. "It'll rain on Monday."

"It always does," she said.

He laughed. "It does, at that."

This was a part of the city she had always avoided, but now she looked out at it with the excitement and curiosity of a traveler in a foreign country, enchanted by the shapes of trees in their translucent leaves and the brightness of children's hair flying out in the wind. When her eye could be ravished by that, she knew that she no longer resented all children who had not been abandoned; she had at last been given something to make up for it. I give you permission, she said grandly to the children, to be happy. Then she almost laughed aloud at herself.

They left the city and drove a little way into the coun-try, and turned in at an expensive motel. She knew of it, it was one of Limerock's glories. The restaurant had a quiet elegance among its landscaped lawns and borders, and the cabins were set on natural terraces under the spruces. For this first really good May weekend the parking lot was already full of out-of-state cars, and as the taxi circled it Van's euphoria began to shred. They stopped at a discreet cabin carrying the sign of a car-hire agency. Owen and another man stood talking like old friends, and as she looked out at them from the taxi Owen was as unknown, as meaningless to her, as the pink, short, balding man who was telling him a story with great wild gestures that made Owen grin and dodge. In this foreign place, in those different clothes, he was no one she knew, and her head began at once to ache in a queer way.

The driver had opened the door and was setting her bag out. She sat still; her eyes on the man in the tawny tweed coat and brown slacks. He was laughing, his pipe in his hand; she and her taxi were invisible to him. Her head wanted to split. "I'll go back," she said to the driver, but he hadn't heard her, and she was frightened to think she mightn't have spoken aloud. Smiling kindly, he was saying, "It's all paid for, and a good tip beside." He reached in his hand as if to help her out. Did she look sick? At last she stood on the crushed stone drive, the new coat over her arm.

"Here she is!" Owen was there, between her and the sun, taking her coat and picking up her bag. "Are you all right?" he asked sharply, bending his head to look into her face.

"I think I was just about to get carsick."

"You should have told him you'd rather ride in front. You want a drink before we start out?"

She shook her head. "No, let's just get going."

"The car's over here." She followed him, blinking like a child fighting to keep from bursting into howls of despair among strangers. The other man gave her a nod and a bashful smile. "How d'you do? Well, it's been nice talking to you, sir," he said to Owen. "You've got my card, now remember it, if you ever need anything in the way of marine valves."

"I shall." They shook hands warmly. She was in the front seat of the car, her things put in the back, and doors were slamming shut. They were circling out onto the road. Owen did not speak and she didn't look at him but stared through the windshield at the road which appeared like a steel-blue band flattening before them. The whole scene lay in a dazzling haze. The sense of being in a foreign country now became nightmarish.

Suddenly the car swung off the macadam and onto a dirt road between stone walls, into the low rustling shade of maples. They pulled off onto a wide verge, and some black-and-white cattle stood regarding them solemnly over the wall.

"Now what in hell's the matter?" said Owen. She looked sidewise under her lashes at his hands resting on the wheel. "You act like some sixteen-year-old kid, never been touched, going out on a dare and scared foolish. You think we'll be caught—checked up on somehow—is that it?"

"No, no! I'm like this," she began uncertainly. Another little piece of herself was going. But you couldn't just sit here, stupid and shaking. "I—I freeze. Or melt. Or dissolve. I don't know what." Vanessa was going away from her down Water Street. "I lift way up and it's wonderful. Anything can do it. It used to be my lilies of the valley. Or my house. The way the light fell on it in certain ways, you could see how it used to be when it was alive. . . ." It was a long street and at the far end there was a tall free woman in a blowing black raincoat, with books under her arm. She wanted to call her back before she disappeared, but instead she went on saying, "Then something happens just as suddenly to make me go the other way. Down. And it's like dying, only at least when you're dying you don't think so much. I'm talking in bunches." She clasped her hands to keep from putting one against her mouth.

Owen turned sidewise and put his arm along the seat behind her. "You know what you sound like?" he said.

"A lunatic." He would drive her back now, but it would be too late; with every wretched laboring word she had driven Vanessa away.

"No. A Bennett." He began to laugh. His arm dropped around her and pulled her up to him. He spoke against her temple. "A goddam Bennett. Up one minute and down the next. Only when a Bennett is down there's hell to pay. We make sure everybody knows it, by God."

"No one else knows how I am," she said bleakly, stiff as a dummy against his shoulder. "I've never talked about myself to anyone."

"And it's sticking in your throat now. Well, I'm not anyone, am I? You'd better make damn sure I'm not." She felt the laughter in his chest rather than heard it. "Your hair smells good. And hey, what's this?" His fingers fumbled at the collar of the silk shirt, gently brushing her skin. "I haven't had a chance yet to tell you how handsome you looked getting out of that taxi." He rested his hand lightly across her throat so that it beat under his fingers. "We never have enough time," he said. "That's what this is for, remember?"

"I remember." She was coming to life again, she rejoiced at the tiny yet specific spark of warmth deep within her. She relaxed against him and sighed. Everything, even the solemnly chewing cows, began to intensify in beauty and significance. Owen took her chin in his hand and turned her face up to his, and kissed her. Then he started the car and backed out onto the road.

They stopped at a place where the cabins were built on the side of a hill between spruce woods and a rocky shore; he had been there before on his way to Canada with one of his brothers to buy a boat. She expected to be stiff and lumpish in the enforced intimacy of their small quarters. It occurred to her as she stood in the small bathroom washing her face and putting on fresh lipstick that Owen might suddenly be attacked by conscience; she dreaded going to eat at the log-cabin restaurant across the road for fear of seeing children there that would remind him of his own. She herself felt nothing. Barry was less consequential than some of her dreams had been. Limerock and even Bennett's island might have ceased to exist the instant she turned her back on them.

She put on the apricot silk shirt again and went out into the bedroom. Owen stood looking out into the spring dusk. But he turned quickly and he was smiling. "There are times," he said across the room, "when I think what a hell of a thing to happen to me when I'm fifty. Then I think, what a hell of a thing if it hadn't happened at all."

"If we'd missed each other somehow," she said. "If they hadn't made me go to Bennett's by taking the house. If it had been to some other island." The cool words wavered. "I always believed in The Day, and now I know it almost mightn't have happened. For all of my life to be so sure of The Day I could live by it, and then to know there was nothing sure about it. It makes me sick."

He crossed the room quickly and took her by the shoulders. "We're here. It did happen. Nothing can change it. Tell me more about The Day."

"I'll tell you later," she said, suddenly drunk with the desire to tell him everything so there would be no one last thing he didn't know about her.

In the morning sunrise woke them. She liked the way he awoke, all at once. "There's one thing I appreciate about the Bennetts," she told him. "Their vitality."

"That all?"

"Well, they produced you. Otherwise—"

173

"Otherwise what?"

"You really don't know how your family strikes people, do you?"

"I didn't expect to bring 'em along on this trip," he said dryly. "This is my life, my business, nobody else's. . . . You didn't tell me last night about The Day."

Hearing the words in his voice gave them a shocking familiarity. "Oh, I just meant the day we'd meet, that's all," she hedged.

"You didn't say it like that. You said it was something you knew about and I didn't."

"All I meant was that I knew I'd have to be in love once before I die. It was owed to me."

"It's owed to everybody," he said, "but how many get it? How many walk through their days just half-living, and go to their graves never knowing what it's like?"

"What is it like?" she asked him.

"You tell me," he said.

"It's like having everything come true at once, knowing it's all true, even the silliest songs they bleat out over the radio, twanging those guitars. And the hardest poems to understand, and the way writers tie themselves up in knots trying to put it into books. It's all there, the most foolish things and the most tragic things, but so much more that nobody else can tell you, no matter how many words they know or how well they can put them together." They were silent, touching yet curiously detached, watching the light run across the ceiling. "I suppose that with each person it's something different. It makes some feel noble, and some feel sick, and some anxious, and some walk on air. You can blow hot and cold, you have pains in your stomach—nobody ever put that in a poem—you're scared witless one minute and think you can do anything the next." He didn't answer and she said abruptly, "I'm talking too much. I sound like a nut."

"I like to hear you talk," he said. "Which way do you feel, out of all those?"

"All of them," she said. "What about you?"

"All of them. I get that pain in the gut sometimes when you take me by surprise. When I come face to face with you in the store. And when—" He stopped so abruptly that the silence was like an alarm bell clanging in the room. Then he turned over onto his side and propped his head up on his hand, looking into her face. "There's something you didn't mention. Age. There's no such thing as an old lover or a young lover. There's just a lover."

"It's true, isn't it?" she said. "You are or you aren't." What was he going to say when he stopped himself? She didn't dare ask him.

He said, "What are you thinking? You're staring at me like a cat. Eyes the same color as one, and never a blink."

"Maybe I'm not thinking. Maybe I'm more like a cat than you realize."

He ducked his head and gave her a brief hard kiss, then rolled away from her and out of bed. "Maybe you are. Come on, let's go to breakfast."

CHAPTER TWENTY-FIVE

"Where are we going?" she asked him when they drove out.

"To do what I've always wanted to do. Poke off down all the little side roads to the gunkholes. We'll come back tonight." He didn't mention Monday, and as long as neither did, it wasn't there. For their purposes Sunday was as long as a week, a month. The day danced like the rainbow light from a swinging prism. The roads were empty this early, and they saw deer in a field, a fox running, late geese going over. They drove down winding roads into small villages, and had coffee and doughnuts in a shack on a wharf. Owen talked with a man who'd had to be towed in. "Serves me right for hauling on Sunday. The wife'll laugh her fool head off. *She's* in church." His eyes picked up Van's with amused courtesy, as if bowing to all wives.

Van smiled back at him with the kind of modest pride a wife would show. Owen asked him how the spring lobstering was up here, and she took her mug of coffee and went to read a bulletin board by the door. There were shaggy kittens for the asking, a dory for sale and a second-hand gas stove. Someone filed saws and sharpened scythes. There was a snapshot of a thirty-six-foot boat to be seen in Mackerel Gut, and a girl named Proserpine Bartlett wanted baby-sitting jobs. "What do they call her for short?" Vanessa asked the large woman behind the counter.

"Prossie," said the woman.

"What was it she ate?" said Van. "Not a persimmon—no, a pomegranate. So afterward she had to spend part of each year down there with him."

The woman looked puzzled, then gave her a sort of all-purpose smile, polite and not understanding. "Prossie's named for her grandmother," she said. "She was Prosserpine Bartlett too, and they called *her* Piney."

"It's a nice name," said Vanessa, and turned back to reading the notices. Owen's arm came over her shoulder and his finger rested on an unobtrusive card that read in neat but even printing, "Island for sale. Twenty-five acres, seven-room house, deep-dug well never known to go dry, wharf and fishouse, deep-water anchorage. Right of way from black road to shore. Inquire at house, Jessup's Cove."

"Here's a place to go," Owen said. Over his shoulder he said to the men, "How do you get to Jessup's Cove?"

"You island-buying?" asked one of the men gruffly. His eyes flickered rapidly from Owen to Vanessa and back again. Owen grinned.

"We're islanders to begin with. From out in the mouth of Penobscot Bay. Nope, we're tourists this weekend."

"Oh." There was a change in the man, not seen but realized, as if his red granite features had begun to give off warmth as ledges do at noon. He gave Owen some directions, and they all said good-by like old friends.

The dirt road led out of the spruce woods to the rim of this eastern bay, in which the islands lay blue-black on a polished morning sea. The great calm glitter filled the eye, and at the same time the noise of birds and counterpoint of distant church bells filled the ear. They waited for a few moments at the top of the rise, not speaking, just looking and listening. Then Owen drove slowly down toward the one house and the large barn. Cats sunned in the barn doorway and barn swallows went in and out over their heads. Tree swallows soared and squabbled over the houses set on poles wound with chicken wire to discourage cats and squirrels. The fields had been mown in the fall and now were as tidy as green carpets surrounding the house. They fell away to the shore, to the gray-shingled fishhouse with its hanging rows of orange-and-black buoys, and the wharf.

After the car stopped, it was as if the world had been reduced to this one spot. Vanessa sat without moving; to shift a foot would be to shatter the illusion. But Owen got out of the car and went toward the back door, and nothing happened, except that two of the barn swallows knew him for a stranger and flew down at his head. She dared to breathe more deeply and got out of the car. Gulls sunned on the fishouse ridgepole in the summer-warm peace. Among the new leaves of the orchard a robin began to sing over and over; a small salt wind lifted the hair on Van's forehead and was gone.

A raw-boned woman came into the sun and pointed out the island that was for sale. There was a dory and outboard rig tied off the wharf that they could use. "My husband and I started housekeeping out there," she said. "His folks lived here then. We raised our family out there too. The young ones came in and stayed with Gramp when they went to school. I always figgered we'd live out there till we was too old to manage all the lugging, and we'd be alone like we was at first. But then Tom took this stroke." She said it dryly, without self-pity. Her wintry eyes took in Owen. "He was a big one like you, but yellow-haired. He'd be like morning beside you, and you night."

"You're all alone here then," said Owen.

"Oh no. Tom's here. But he's shrunk so, and he can't get out of bed without me to help him. . . . No, this is the best place for us. The young ones put in the bathroom and the telephone and they keep an eye on us." Her laugh was short and harsh. "Ayuh. I guess my island days are over. Well, you can't be a gull forever."

"No," Owen said. "Not unless you're born a gull."

The woman turned on Van a fierce penetrating gaze that was like a gull's. "You watch his blood pressure, if he won't do it. Gramp was hauling traps at eighty-five, and building traps for Tom when he was ninety. But Tom took after his mother. Them big handsome folks with the fine complexion." She shook her head as if in irritation. "Well, the outboard should go all right, one of my grandsons had it out yesterday, but if she don't, likely you can row, and you'll have a fair wind back."

Vanessa spoke, to her own surprise. "Could you sell us something to take along to eat and drink?" Owen grinned at her. "Good thinking. How about it, Mrs. Jessup? Bread and butter, something like that?"

"I got some good store cheese, plenty of sardines and crackers too," she said. "That's what the young ones take with 'em when they go off there. And I can give you a thermos of coffee or tea."

"It all sounds perfect," said Vanessa. "And we'll have coffee."

"I'll keep the sugar and milk separate from the coffee." Mrs. Jessup went into the house. They looked at each other and smiled.

"I'm glad you didn't tell her this was the next best thing to her island," Vanessa said. "She knows better and she'd have told you."

"She's like you. Doesn't want any buttering-up."

"Maybe that's a compliment." She leaned down to pat a cat that leaned against her legs. "She's mad with Tom for having a stroke. How is your blood pressure, by the way?"

"Stow that," he said, as offended as if she'd questioned his virility. She laughed and went back to the car to change into sneakers. Owen didn't follow her, but wandered toward the barn. Bennetts never have high blood pressure, she mocked him silently with a tinge of the old hostility. She was not concerned; she never wasted thought on physical defects, and if she had ever developed a chronic condition that demanded time and attention, she would have been more irritated by the inconvenience than worried.

The way out to Jessup's Island was a broad glittering avenue that flowed spaciously among smaller islands, some little more than nesting ledges. The morning was clean, brilliant, and empty; lobster buoys spangled the water, but it was Sunday and no one was working.

Jessup's Island was a high island of woods and fields. The wharf and fishhouse were in a sheltered cove facing back toward the mainland, but the house stood on a rise with its front door facing open sea. It was a low house with a steep pitched roof and clapboards dark with weathering; it seemed as natural as gray rock rising out of the flowered turf. They left the lunch basket on the shady back doorstep, and went exploring. Since yesterday Owen had been one stranger after another to her, and now he was still another, eager to explore, missing nothing, impressed by things she wouldn't have seen: the construction of the wharf, a hand-made iron bolt set into a rock to tie skiffs to, the stone walls enclosing an alder-grown pasture, a bank solid with clamshell, the antiquity of the workshop, and fishhouse. She followed him contentedly. She could almost see the light about them both.

The house was roughly furnished. Apparently the grandchildren sometimes used it, sleeping on cots in the bedrooms under the steep eaves, cooking on the black range in the kitchen or roasting their frankfurters and marshmallows in the parlor fireplace. Sunlight lay across wide floor boards once painted pumpkin yellow. There was a clean dry scent in the house, a serene silence of which the falling sunshine seemed the visible manifestation. The bare windows held water and sky, a white cove, three spruces on a point, a wave of tall grass about to break into a surf of daisies. In the kitchen an old square table was drawn up to two windows facing seaward; they held infinity. Early in the spring someone had picked pussy willows and put them in a mayonnaise jar on the table, and there was a litter of purple mussel shells, small bits of driftwood, and colored stones. A branch holding a bird's nest was tacked against a wall. There was in the house a queer fusing of the ages; the past was not distant here but present, and *now* overlay it in a transparent glaze.

"I don't want to sound like Maggie," she said, "but it feels as if we've stepped back two hundred years in time." Then she waited to see if he would look disgusted with her, but instead he nodded.

"We have," he said. "And I like it. Jesus, I like it. It's another world." He hugged her to him and kissed her. "Poor old house," he said, still holding her. "I'll bet when Tom left it was the first time it had been empty in a good many years."

"The grandchildren must love it, though." She put her arms around him. She had never felt so unself-conscious with him before. "They'll hate her for selling this to rich summer people."

"Their folks are probably telling her to do it, and she's so damned scared of being a burden she'll sell it," said Owen. They stood holding each other and looking around the room. "She'll put the money in the bank and then they'll inherit it and build over their kitchens."

"All electric," said Van, "with those up-high ovens. And

get a color TV. The kids can watch that instead of coming out here to sleep on the island."

"Sure. Who wants to catch cunners off the rocks, anyway? Come on, let's get out of here, or all the ghosts of the old folks'll be on the prod."

The breeze was springing up. Light surf broke over the long scalloping terraces of rock that ran down to the sea. They ate on a shelf here, their backs against a convenient rise, the wind putting an edge on the heat.

"I don't know when anything ever tasted so good," Van said.

"It's been a long time for me too," he said somberly.

"It's been all my life, and I'm not saying that for pity. Owen, this is our first real meal together, because I don't count that one in the restaurant yesterday, and for me it's like the first meal ever."

He grinned at her. "What's that stuff about a jug of wine and a loaf of bread?"

" 'And thou beside me in the wilderness,' " she said. "I love you. I'm saying it out loud. I love you." She leaned back and called to a hovering and hopeful gull. "Did you hear that? I love him!"

The gull made a small cynical sound, and they both laughed. "Are you going to move over or am I?" asked Owen.

"Let's both." They settled back again against the rock, his arm around her, and drank their coffee. Then they threw scraps to the gulls, talking to the birds and naming them as Barry liked to do; she could hardly recognize herself in this soft foolish mood. "Newborn," she said.

"Who is?"

"I am."

"You're a damn long baby. Your mother must've had a hell of a hard time. Like giving birth to a rocking chair."

"And I had all my clothes on too. That wasn't easy."

He took her face in his hands and turned it toward him. "Mine," he said. "Never anybody else's."

"Too bad I can't say the same about you."

"Maybe you can." He let go of her abruptly and got up. "Well, I'm off to answer a call of nature, to be real delicate about it."

"I think I'll take a walk too." She watched him start around the shore and then got up and went in the opposite

180

direction. *Maybe you can, maybe you can.* But Laurie? ... After a while she cut up through the bay bushes and juniper and went toward the house. Poor old house, she repeated Owen's words, recalling the odd tenderness in them; she wondered if the summer people who would inevitably buy the island would keep the old house or tear it down, displacing its familiar spirits, and build something all glass walls and redwood decks. She was surprised at the depth of her animosity toward the unknown. The house, the rock-walled well, and all the other works of the early Jessups, should mean nothing to her, who had no history. It must be because she had come here with Owen and for today it was theirs.

"Ours," she said aloud. "Yours too," she said to an alarmed sparrow.

A little distance behind the house, alders had been allowed to grow, and she walked into their leafy and sibilant shade. It was a place for birds. They flashed and called all about her, chipped and scolded. The ground sank down toward a mossy place where new young ferns sprang up and the ground was wet. From the sun-speckled shade, blue caught her eye; she went to it and found a wonder, a river of violets following the course of a narrow brook. When she leaned forward she could see them going far away among the alder trunks. She felt like crying out with delight; she had seen violets growing wild before, she had picked them for May baskets in one of her homes, but this was different. *"Ours,"* she said again. She turned and hurried out of the alder swamp, to find Owen and bring him here.

When she came into the field behind the house she realized suddenly that the sun had moved a long way since this morning; it was as if a hand had spread deliberately over the source of light for a moment and the sudden gloom stopped her, then she wouldn't acknowledge it but hurried on.

He had come back to the place where they'd eaten, and lay on his back, his arms folded under his head and his eyes shut. She stood looking down at him, sure that he wasn't asleep, waiting for the twitch of nostril or eyelid. It didn't come.

She felt giddy and mischievous with love. *"Beware! Beware!"* she intoned. She began to prowl around him.

Weave a circle round him thrice,
And close your eyes with holy dread,
For he on honey-dew hath fed,
And drunk the milk of Paradise.

A hand closed on her ankle and pulled. She collapsed across him, yelping with surprise, laughing like a drunk. She was seized and held against his chest, her wrists gripped in one of his hands, his face close to hers and leering ferociously. "How about a little rape, honey-bunch?"

"I'll bet that's your line with all the girls."

"Sure. That's why they're so mad about me. I'm direct." He sat up and let go of her. "I'd like to make love to you here and now—maybe up in the field where it's a little softer—but that would be the signal for everybody within ten miles to go out for a Sunday afternoon sail and they'd all head for Jessup's island."

"We have tonight," she said, smiling at him. "Let's take another walk, because I have something to show you, and then eat some more."

"You know something?"

"What?"

"I like your voice. And I like the way you move. I watched you come down through the field. Quick and swinging, with your head up. You always lead with your chin, don't ye?"

"For you, yes," she said. She was almost speechless with happiness. She wanted to tell him the things she liked about him, but she was too shy. Finally she said in a tight croaky voice, "I love you. I'll save the catalog till I know you better."

CHAPTER TWENTY-SIX

They left at sundown. The breeze had died, and when they walked up from the wharf, slow with reluctance and tiredness, the house was lighted up and there were two more cars in the yard. "Family's come in for Sunday night supper with Ma and Pa," said Owen. "Likely telling her to run the price up five thousand dollars more."

"I won't go to the door," said Van, unwilling to end the day with Mrs. Jessup's relatives. Owen was better able to brush people off; her adjustment was too new and too fine. "But tell her from me that that lunch was the best meal I've ever had."

"She'll think I'm some damn poor provider."

She waited in the car for what seemed a long time. The dusk made her eyes heavy, and she was almost asleep by the time he came. "I had to meet Tom," he said, "and two of the sons were there. Digging their graves with their teeth, from the looks. She better tell them to watch *their* blood pressure. Tom's a sorry-looking old party. And all of them but her trying to sell me the island, you'd think they were so poor they didn't have a pot to pee in or a window to throw it out of." He had the car backed around and headed down the tunnel of spruces; the lights picked up bright eyes at the side of the road. "I told them I was a lobsterman and it cast a strange silence over the audience. A proper pea-soup fog. But she came out to the door with me and said, 'I don't care what the rest of 'em think, I'd rather sell it to a lobsterman so there'll be traps piled on that wharf again and an honest stink of bait around the fishhouse.' "

Van said, "She's a gull after all. She'll be full of fight till something brings her down."

"Ayuh, I like her. I told her we'll come again, even if the island is sold."

We'll come again. It had the comfort of a magic phrase. It conjured up a security which lasted, even in her sleep, until she awoke the next morning.

It was very early, and rain drummed on the roof and ran down the windows with a deathly monotony. She opened her eyes to the gray pallor in the room, shut them quickly again, and curled deeper against Owen's back. But it was too late. She was awake, and the night was over. Sometime during that night they had been transported from one country to another, from light to dark, from serenity to squalor. Even the room had changed from last night's warm cave to the poor shelter of refugees; it seemed as if the rain were falling inside it.

Tears fall in my heart as rain falls upon the town. Or was it, *Rain falls upon the town as tears fall in my heart?*

183

Each time she said it to herself, the phrase grew in pathos until she was on the verge of crying. It wasn't fair, to be shown all this and let that be the end of it. Why did I have to meet him, she demanded of a faceless jury, if I couldn't keep him? And I can't ever go back to what I was, I took off all my shell for him, peeled it away layer by layer, and now I have nothing to protect me. No, I've been like a drunk, dancing and singing and giving myself to men, and now it's the next day, and I haven't even got pride left, or what passed for pride with me. I haven't got *him*. The strong legs and shoulders and the brown skin, and the feel of his hair under my hand, his lower lip, the way he looks at me sidewise and lets me run on as if I were his child. And then the times when there is no age between us, because he's right, there is no special age for loving, there are just lovers.

She put her hand to the curving hollow between throat and shoulder where his head had been. Suddenly a sob broke from her, and she put her wrist against her mouth and bit it frantically to use up the passion of grief, but he had already been waked. He turned over to her and gathered her against him.

"What is it?" he kept whispering, with little hard squeezes of his arms. "What is it?"

"I don't want to go back." She was ashamed for admitting it and humiliated by crying. "That's all. You weren't supposed to know." She tried to get away, but couldn't. "I was just going to get it over with before breakfast. All nice and tidy." She couldn't stop crying, or escape either.

"I don't want to go back again either. Good Christ!" he groaned. "When we left that island yesterday it was like going back to the police or the guillotine. I wanted to stow you in that car and keep driving eastward."

She held her breath, listening. Close by her face his flesh was wet from her tears, and she touched it delicately with the tip of her tongue. "I keep trying to figure it out." He spoke heavily like a man exhausted. "Is it because I'm at the age when a man makes a goddam fool of himself? Because I've had to behave for seventeen years or so, for lack of opportunities? If I've been losing sleep like a green kid and breaking into a sweat at sight of you—" He began kissing her forehead and wet eyelids. "If the first time we were together it was like the first time in my life for me with anyone—well, how much of it was because I wanted

184

it to be that way? Because I wanted, at my age, to be in love—guts, feathers, and all? Well, maybe that's it. But you don't come up for air, shake yourself like a dog, and go home and forget all about it." He forced her face upward till he could look into it. "I don't want to go home and forget it. I don't want to go home. I don't want to give you up. I'm not going to."

She felt shaken, literally, out of breath and sense. "The family—"

"They don't run my business. I can live without them, I have before. I walked away once and was gone for seven years."

"Where were you? What did you do?"

"We'll save that for later. We'll have the rest of our lives." The words made her shudder with an almost sickening emotion and he tightened his grip.

"But you came back," she said against his cheek. "You were drawn back to the island and the family. You'll always be drawn."

"I went back," he said harshly, "because I didn't have anywhere else to go."

They were quiet for a few minutes, then she said with diffidence, "What about your own family?"

"I've been thinking about them. And this is how bad it is with me, how deep you've gotten into my bones. I want the rest of my life with you. It's like wanting air to breathe or water to drink. I have to have it to survive. It's no sense cursing because we've wasted so much time. We're going to grab what's left. . . . My kids—" He broke off, then started again. "Joss is finishing high school. The other two'll grow up soon and be off on their own. I love them, but I can't wait."

"Laurie?" she asked timidly.

"She'll do all right. She doesn't figure on falling apart for anything. She can stay there in the house on the island. The whole thing can be hers except my boat and gear. . . . I told Mrs. Jessup last night she'd hear from me inside two weeks, one way or the other."

"I'll give you children," she promised, wanting to give him more than she could touch or embrace or imagine. There was nothing great enough for a gift. He didn't answer, just lay back and gazed at the ceiling, holding her in one arm. The grayness paled in the room and the rain fell steadily on the roof. Van was not yet able to rejoice,

185

there had been too much all at once. Then she remembered there must be more.

"I have to tell you something," she said. "If it makes any difference I want to know now." He turned his head toward her, his eyes questioning. "That story I told you about myself was a lie. It's true that I was a state ward, but the other yarn, about my mother and father, I made that up out of whole cloth as I went along. I don't know who my parents were. Chances are I'm somebody's mistake that was left on a doorstep somewhere. I've got no one that I know of."

"You have someone now."

She went on quickly before the words could break her down. "When I was small I used to get a postcard signed Mama now and then. But the welfare people couldn't ever trace her. My case-worker told me, when I was older, that my mother probably hadn't deserted me because she wanted to; she might have been scared or sick. She explained to me very nicely about people being sick in their minds. It was supposed to keep me from thinking I'd been coldly rejected, or something. What it did was make me wonder about once a week if she was in a padded cell somewhere and I was heading that way myself."

"Poor kid," he murmured, stroking her hair back from her forehead. "Jesus, what people do to young ones and never turn a hair. But it's gone by now. You don't need anybody but me."

They lay there in silence and slept again, but the sleep was shallow and fidgety from their exhaustion.

They hardly spoke on the way back to Limerock. The land that had been a haze of green gold when they had driven through it on Saturday was now sodden in the rain. When they reached the motor lodge the rain had given way to a chilly fog. After Owen turned the car in to the agency, he called Limerock for a taxi. They went across to the restaurant and had coffee. The few other people in the warmly lit room were mostly salesmen talking business over breakfast.

Owen sat with his elbows on the table, shoulders hunched and head sunk forward. She drank her coffee quickly, though it was very hot, and poured more. Suddenly he looked up at her and smiled.

"I don't know if I told you how much I like that color on you. What do you call it? The shirt."

"Apricot." She was ridiculously pleased, and had to keep from touching it like the preening women she despised.

He nodded amiably and she knew he had scarcely heard her. It was as if his declaration had driven a wall between them; until now he had been centered in whatever he saw their relation to be, but now he was distracted and absorbed by all that had to be done. She was actually second to the new concerns. She felt a brush of cold, which angered her because she should have been feeling warmth and joy. She put her hand across the table and touched his, the one with the fingers gone.

"How soon will you let her know?" she asked. His head jerked up, a sort of wild astonishment flashed youthfully across his face. "The woman who owns the island," she added, and he sat back.

"Oh. Next week."

"You thought I meant Laurie."

"What if I did? She's on my mind."

"Naturally," she said coldly. "I won't tell Barry until you've talked to her."

His nod was more of a chopping jab with his chin. He drank his coffee fast. "More?" she asked him.

"No, I think the cab's here."

She would have liked to sink into a trance state at will, and never open her eyes or think until she was back on Bennett's Island. She did the best she could on the way to Limerock, but the trick she used to have, of veiling her consciousness against her surroundings, had been lost somewhere. Owen sat in his corner, head turned away toward the fog outside. His disfigured hand lay on his knee and she wanted to take it, in some hope of establishing contact with yesterday, but she couldn't do it.

He got out at the north end of Main Street, and paid the driver. "I'll see you later," he said to Van. Where, when, she wanted to ask, but didn't. At the Marshall house she had to walk around a happy cluster of island women just setting out to shop, discussing where to meet for lunch and what the movie would be tonight. They included her in their innocent gaiety, nodding and smiling; one cried heartily, "You come in from somewhere in this fog?"

"Must have come by gull," another said, and they all laughed, their excitement and pleasure embracing her. She

187

forced a smile and said, "Oh no, I came Saturday. I've been somewhere else for the weekend, that's all."

"Oh!" They were reassured. "I didn't think anybody in his right mind would set out for the main this morning," one said. She watched them go under the dripping elms toward Main Street, and thought, This time yesterday . . . Then she went inside, and from the kitchen at the end of the long hall she heard Mrs. Marshall's ringing tone, and went toward it. An elderly woman rocking and knitting by the stove smiled. " 'Morning! Eva, you've a visitor." Mrs. Marshall turned from peeling a turnip at the dresser.

"Hello there! Your room's ready. My cousin, she got off to Boston on the eight o'clock bus this morning. You have a good weekend?"

"Too good," said Van. "I'm tired. We islanders can't stand this fast pace." They were amused by that and she was cynically proud of herself. There was a time when she would not make an effort; now that she was obliged to, in order to keep from being conspicuous, she had discovered unknown talents in herself. They were carrying on the joke now, and she smiled, only half-hearing, and went up to her room.

When she shut the door behind her, depression swamped her. Everything about the weekend was a dream, Owen an illusion that had passed through her unconsciousness. She would never see him again, never dream him again. She sank down onto the bed, staring about the room in quiet horror, as if she didn't know how she'd got there.

But the room was indisputably real and she was in it. Tomorrow would inexorably come, and the return to Bennett's. No illusions here. "How can I?" she heard herself whispering. "I *can't*." Yet she would go back because she had nowhere else to go.

She took off her outside clothes and lay down on the bed, pulling the extra blanket over her. Outside on the gables there was a constant conversation of sparrows. From Main Street the sound of traffic was like the rote on the outer shores of the island. Make it Jessup's Island, she thought as if she were praying. I'm on Jessup's Island, in the fog. . . . She slept.

CHAPTER TWENTY-SEVEN

When she woke up she felt refreshed and hungry. She dressed and went out into the foggy streets to the Crow's Nest. She was used to her new clothes now and enjoyed the feel of them; since Saturday she had learned that if anyone looked twice at her it was because she had a sort of distinction. *I like the way you walk,* Owen's voice companioned her.

A waitress handed her a menu and began laying her place. "Thank you," Van said, and looked up at Brenda. Her first thought was that she hadn't realized how many wrinkles Brenda's thin skin had, or how sharp and strong her nose was.

"For Gawd's sake!" Brenda whispered reverently. "If *this* ain't some surprise! I thought you'd dropped off the edge of the world. And don't you look some *fancy!* No wonder I didn't know you when you came in."

"I know I was pretty messy, but I didn't think I was that bad."

"You know what I mean. You look like a million dollars! How does anybody get that way out on that hunk of rocks?"

"You'd be surprised at what it's like, Brenda," said Van. "Electricity, gas, television. And that's not all." She smiled. "Not anywhere near all."

"Well, there's money. I can tell by the sight of you. . . . I'll be back." She went on to another booth. Her rows of yellow curls looked like the wig on a cheap doll. Van recognized her alien emotion as pity. What was a life with no wildness in it, only the small gnawing resentments against employers, aching feet, the loneliness of rented rooms, the nights washed out with beer and television and movies?

Brenda came back. "How's Barry?"

"Walking high, wide, and handsome."

"I'll bet." She smiled reminiscently. "He was always cocky, even without a cent in his pocket. . . . What are you having?"

189

"The special. I'm starved." From a weekend of love, Brenda. A man is leaving his wife for me, what do you think of that? And he's not a bum. If you'd been on duty Saturday afternoon you'd have seen him.

Brenda was back with a tray. "Coffee now or later?"

"Later. Where are you living now?"

"Same place."

Her heart seemed to twitch. "Didn't they tear it down?"

"There's some hitch, I guess. Different parties can't come to an agreement, so in the meantime the house stands there."

"But who's in charge?"

"I am," said Brenda with a satisfied smile. "I've got your place. My Gawd, it feels as big as the Community Building."

Cheated again, Van thought. She tried to keep the instant antagonism out of her voice. "Mooney?"

"Still in the front parlor. But he'll be moving out soon. He's given some girl a diamond."

"What about Brig?"

"He's in Bangor. Exposed himself in the bus station one night. Not that he had anything to scare anybody with, but—" She scribbled on her check pad. "Anyway, they decided he needed to be taken care of. I cleaned up his room good with Lysol, and papered it. Let it to a girl who works in here. She's not on now. . . . You having dessert?"

"No, just coffee. I wish you could have a cup with me."

"I do too, but that's life." She went to relieve the cashier. When Van paid, they had a few minutes more to talk, but there was nothing else to say, at least for Van. "Oh, I cleaned up a couple more rooms and let them," Brenda said. "The other front room downstairs, and the side room upstairs, the one with the bay window. I got some second-hand furniture and scrubbed the places up, and now I get fifteen dollars a week for them, from respectable people."

"Good for you," Van told her, freed at last. It was one word which had done it; *respectable*. Light and air had been let in, the hours of brooding silence washed away, the caverns of dream destroyed. It was no longer hers.

Three men approached the desk, and Van turned to go. "And I've got a couple of boys cleaning up the yard,"

Brenda told her hurriedly. "It'll be real nice this summer, without that jungle." Even the lilies of the valley must be gone. "Come down and see me, Van," Brenda called. Van waved and smiled without answering, and left.

The sensation of freedom stayed with her. She walked slowly along Main Street, looking in the windows at flowers, furniture, sporting goods, jewelry, clothing, shoes, finally at books. For Barry to tell her to buy books was one of the greatest gestures he could make. But she had her own ideas of fairness, and since she had spent more on her clothes than she'd intended, she wouldn't buy books. It was enough of a present to walk into the shop where she had never been before, and say nonchalantly, "I'm just looking around." No one called her a deceiver or an impostor. She was alone with the books except for an elderly man ruminating happily among the nonfiction. She fingered a few bindings, unable to concentrate at first on anything inside until the fire died down and she was able to read the first page of a novel.

She was drawn into the story; it wasn't until someone brushed against her and apologized, that she was jolted back. She didn't like being so close to strangers, but her pride was too strong for her to rush out like an eccentric solitary. *Which I no longer am*, she told herself with sarcasm. She moved on to the paperback racks and remembering guiltily the funeral pyre of the old high school volume, picked out an anthology of poems, and a book containing two stories by Joseph Conrad.

There was a men's shop next door, and she saw a blue sleeveless cablestitch pullover in the window. Philip Bennett had one which Barry admired the way he admired all Bennett possessions. She went in and bought one for him, and a matching shirt in woven plaid cotton.

In the five and ten she bought things for the Campion and Dinsmore children. It was mid-afternoon now. At the corner where she would turn off, she stopped and looked anxiously up and down Main Street, promising herself that if she saw him in the crowd she wouldn't wait to speak to him. She thought she spotted him standing outside a shop window full of musical instruments, and she remembered his saying that Holly wanted a guitar. She waited for him to turn his head; he had a way of doing it that always roused in her a reaction both tender and sensual. But when he did, it was a stranger with a red weathered face

191

and a huge beak of a nose. She felt the cruel disappointment of a child who has been deceived, and she wondered how she could ever have taken this man, even turned away from her, for Owen. The incident shook her own opinion of herself, as if she'd discovered a flaw in her love. She walked fast up the side street toward her room.

When she was halfway up the stairs, Mrs. Marshall called from below. "Mrs. Barton, somebody called and left a number."

The number meant nothing to her. She had never known anyone to call in Limerock. She called now because Mrs. Marshall expected her to. Owen answered.

"H-hello," she stammered, sitting down. In the kitchen Mrs. Marshall and the elderly lady moved leisurely about. She stared at them with fascination, listening to Owen's voice by telephone for the first time.

"Listen," he said, "I can't meet you anywhere today. I planned on it, but I've run into somebody I can't shake."

She couldn't think of anything to say.

"Are you all right?" he demanded.

"Yes. But this is a busy place, and I shouldn't hang onto the phone for too long."

"I get it. Eva's close by and God knows who else. But are you all right? I mean, you aren't too hawsed up because I can't meet you, are you? Not scared or worried, anything like that?"

His concern melted her. She wanted to say so then and there, to murmur I love you through this magical means of communication and send sentimental and idiotic fancies floating along the wires. "I'm fine," she said. "Why wouldn't I be? I've got every reason in the world for it."

"So have I. What are you doing tonight? Going to a movie?"

"I've got a good book. I may stay in and read."

"I'll be thinking of you. Have breakfast with me tomorrow morning. Be at the Crow's Nest at six-thirty and I'll stroll in and be neighborly."

She laughed at that, wanting eagerly to reassure him. Barry's tenderness annoyed her, Owen's turned her weak and desperately yearning. "All right. Thanks for calling. I hope the measles are better in the morning." Mrs. Marshall was tiptoeing through the hall with an apologetic grimace. "Good-by."

She hung up and said, "Well, I didn't really feel like going there for supper tonight anyway."

"Young ones got measles?"

"Yes, and I've never had them."

CHAPTER TWENTY-EIGHT

She paid Mrs. Marshall that night, and when she came downstairs in the morning, in slacks and raincoat for the boat, the sleeping house had the curious anticipatory hush that came with this time of day. Outside, the city was still given over to birds and the scents of damp lawns and early blossoms. Gulls planed over the elms where it was already full day, and their urgent cries suddenly set off some excitement in Van, like a summons. She hurried.

In the restaurant there was the smell of coffee and the early morning look of waitresses, some cheerful, some yawning, being kidded by men on stools at the counter. Van went to a booth where she could look up at the hotel's mansard roof in sunshine and the pigeons preening and courting.

"*Good* morning!" There was a warm aroused burst of laughter from the girls. Vanessa sat quietly, looking at her cup, but she felt a fierce pride.

"Well, here's a face from home!" Owen came toward her. "You going out today? You must be. That's the only reason for getting up early in this goddam place."

"Yes, I'm going out. It looks like a good trip, too."

"Oh, it'll be finest kind. Mind if I join ye, or do you like to sulk over your breakfast and try to get up enough courage to face the day?"

She nodded at the bench opposite, and he slid in behind the table. A waitress came to them, a girl with a towering hairdo that made Vanessa think of Gina. "Sweetheart, what do you keep up there?" Owen asked her. "Your virtue?" Her make-up cracked into a youthful grin and she could do nothing better than jab her pencil at him and exclaim, "Oh, *you!*"

When she left he said, "What did you do last night?"

193

"Went to bed and read *The Secret Sharer*."

"Appropriate title for right now. Good story?"

"I don't know if it's good or not. I kept on reading, anyway. I think I got what he was getting at. The *feel* of it."

His breakfast came and he said to the girl, "You're a dear girl. When you grow up I'll come and claim you as my own."

"I'll put that down in my date book." Unexpectedly a tide of color rushed up her throat and into her face. Smiling broadly, she turned and hurried away.

"Dazzling females before breakfast, even," said Vanessa. "Is that your form of wake-up exercises?"

"After last night I have to do something to prove that I'm alive." He shuddered. "Drank too much, smoked too much, playing poker with a bunch of pirates. They were out to take the old man."

"And did they?"

"Let's say I held my own."

"Spoken with true modesty." They smiled at each other. He lifted his coffee cup toward her as if in a toast. But they said nothing else about themselves. The talk was desultory.

When they finished and went out, he said, "How about walking down to the boat?" She nodded, and he took the bags and went back along the block to where two taxis were parked, and put the bags in one of them.

They turned down toward the harbor. In the street there was thin but constant traffic to and from the waterfront businesses, but they were the only walkers, along with occasional pigeons, sparrows, and cats.

"I wanted to talk to you," he said, his public manner abruptly gone. "When we get back, it'll be pure hell for us, but nobody's going to know it. Agreed?"

"Of course." She gave him a sidewise glance of mild surprise. "Did you think I was going to yell the truth at Barry the minute I got off the boat?"

"Christ, no," he said irritably. "But I don't think we ought to try to see each other right off. It'll be hard to act halfway normal before or after. I know. I'll do pretty well if I stay away from you."

She looked straight ahead. The street shimmered oddly in the blaze of the climbing sun. "For how long?"

"Till I tell her. And I'll know when the time is right for that."

"Right for which of you?" They stopped at a place where the street passed by an inlet of quiet water occupied by paddling gulls, and stood by a rough rail looking down. You can see their feet move, she thought. "It's never going to be right for *her*," she said coldly. "You'll keep putting it off."

"I'm not thinking of when it's right for her. Good God, Van, I'm not even thinking of you when you come right down to it. I'm concentrating on *me*. It's my survival. It's come to that. I've got to live out a little of my own life, not somebody else's *as* somebody else, or die trying."

The rawness got through to her, she saw it in his face. Out here on this public place she was shaken enough to want to take hold of him, to comfort him, as if that were the only way to comfort herself. No, not comfort. If ever a man were less in need of comfort—no, he would do it. He had come to that point.

"Barry's another reason why I don't want us to say anything until we're ready to walk out, clip and clean. The minute you tell Barry anything he'll be off to tell the whole thing to Father Philip."

"And then the family'll be on your neck. I know. You'll never survive that," she said.

"No, not the family then, just Phil." They began walking again. "He'll think it's his duty, and looking at it from his viewpoint, it will be. But I don't figure on justifying myself to anyone, chewing it over, getting put on the defensive, argued with, reasoned with, appealed to—"

"You're furious already," she told him. "Why? Do you really feel, underneath, that they could break you down?"

"No! But once anybody gets hold of it, it's public property—*we're* public property—the whole goddam shooting match is handled, fingerprinted, breathed on—do you want that?" He didn't give her a chance to answer. "Or wouldn't you give a hoot? You'd be showing 'em all, wouldn't you? Good enough for the arrogant bastards."

"I don't want to fight with you, Owen," she said gently. "You've got the hardest thing to do, and I want you to do it the way you want to. When it's all over, there'll be the island. Maybe we'll be there when the strawberries are ripe."

He stopped on the sidewalk. *"You,"* he half-growled. "I

could take hold of you now, and to hell with the world. How do you know how to do it?, Swear back at me, be sarcastic, and I can almost convince myself I don't even like you, there's no love involved, just me out dragging my wing for one good illegal diddle when I've got the chance dropped in my lap. Then you pull the other on me, that voice, that look, straight past the noise and the bluff, and you say, I know what he is, and what scares him, and what makes him want to howl like a lunatic, and what eats at him till he's ready to run. You see all that and the rest and you say, So be it, I love the bastard anyway. It's in your eyes. So then I could go to hell for you."

"You may yet," she said. "But I'll be with you. It will be easy. Because you know me the way you say I know you. I never wanted anybody to, until you. Now I'm committed. It's as simple as that."

His eyes glistened, and his hand moved toward her, then back and into his pocket as a panel truck rattled down toward them. "You're damn right we'll be there when the strawberries are ripe," he said. The truck went by and somebody touched the horn. "Link and the mail," he growled without looking around. The taxi that had their bags followed, carrying passengers. They began to walk again, silently agreeing not even to brush a sleeve.

"The world is too much with us," Vanessa said drily.

"Late and soon,

"Getting and spending, we lay waste our powers," said Owen. "I told you we had one teacher for five years out there who was crazy about poetry. That one had a real racy line in it."

"The sea that bares her bosom to the moon," said Van. They both laughed, and this carried them for quite some distance.

"She was a great old girl, Minnie Lufkin," said Owen. "She pounded the stuff into our stubborn heads, and what we couldn't understand then we still remember. It's like money in the bank, I told my kids the other day. Rich was grousing about having eight lines to memorize, and I gave 'em a few rousing stanzas of *Marco Bozzaris.* The old man surprised them. Surprised himself too."

My kids. A new silence surrounded them for the rest of the way.

At the wharf Owen joined the engineer and a truck driver in loading bundles of trap stock into the hold. The

196

captain and the man from the bottled-gas company were rolling a dozen hundred-pound cylinders across the deck. A couple of boys were trundling cases of canned goods and crates of vegetables down the slip. Gulls squawked and wheeled over the glistening roofs of the seafood factory opposite. A faint cloud-layer was beginning to dull the early morning gold of the sun.

Vanessa didn't sit with the other passengers on the bench, but leaned against the cabin on the side facing out across the harbor, and smoked. Once she heard Owen laugh and felt her face tighten as if it were hardening clay. Tears were squeezed into her eyes. Withdrawal symptoms—she tried to ridicule herself. But she knew that if he came around the pilot house in this instant she would not be able to hide this awful defenselessness, no matter who else saw. She tried to summon up a vision of Jessup's Island, herself and Owen walking over the rocks, but she could not evoke it and in a moment of terror she thought a section of her memory had given way, like a piece of land weakened by surf. She stood rigid against the pilot house with her eyes shut.

Someone drawled at her elbow, "Well, I'd say that was some real old jumbo economy size hangover. You want something for it?"

She stared blurrily and at first without recognition into the small grotesque mask with the Egyptian eyes under a dense black fringe. The fringe was new.

"Hello, Gina," Van said. The spinning slowed. "No, it's not a hangover. Are you going out to the island?"

"Yah." Gina slumped against the side of the pilot house. "Back to Alcatraz. I've got no choice because I've got no money, and neither has Wandering Willy. He's down forrard, trying to sleep. . . ." She gave Van a sly sidewise grin. "I suppose you heard I took all his money when I skipped. I should've got on the first bus for New York or Miami, even." She stared out at the harbor and after a moment said, "I wouldn't be here now. I'd never be here again." There was a tremble in her voice. "But no, damn fool, I had to go on one big kick. Willy's been chasing me around trying to get me to come home. *Home.*" She lifted one shoulder in contempt. "I was onto something good. A guy off one of their trawlers." She nodded her head toward Universal Seafoods. "Money to burn when he come ashore, and no woman. When he was

197

like that I coulda talked him into anything." Her eyes became liquidly bright, she gave Van an eager excited smile that was incongruously childish through the make-up. "He always wanted to get on one of them tuna boats out on the West Coast, so I was working on him about that. California, you know, Hollywood and all that. *Disneyland.*" She said it in a hushed tone. "Jeest, I could just see me, out in all that sunshine. And I look real good in a bikini," she added complacently. "You have to be skinny. Some men like skinny girls. I dunno if it makes them think of boys or not." She giggled. "Got a spare cigarette on you?"

Van handed her a package. At least this ghastly visitation was giving her a chance to come to her senses. Gina lit a cigarette and inhaled deeply, then blew smoke through her nostrils. The boat was backing away from the wharf and a damp breeze was beginning to blow. The harbor wrinkled under a silvery diffusion of sunlight. "Yep, I had something going for me," Gina said regretfully. "He was just crazy for it. Then Willy ran us down in Chuck's room at the Avalon. My God, I never knew him to be so savage! A wild man! He was pounding on the door and yelling, and we was—well, you know—" She leered coyly at Van. "So we didn't answer, but he knew we were there, all right. He'd been listening. So he kicked in the door, and by then the man who runs the Avalon was up there, and I dunno who else, and there *I* was, bollicky bare-arse." She giggled. "My, their eyes popped! And Chuck was trying to get into his pants and Willy was yelling he'd murder him. You'd think he had three pair of arms the way they were swinging around there." Her voice had never sounded so alive. "Some nut called the police, so we all ended up in the police station. I had my clothes on by then, but that fresh cop, Wallace Winslow, wouldn't give me a chance to put my makeup on."

"You must have felt naked," said Vanessa.

Gina said suspiciously, "Huh? Well, anyway, we spent the night in jail, and poor Willy he like to heaved up his whole insides he was so upset. The sheriff had to call in a doctor for him. And Chuck, *he's* moaning for fear he'll lose his next trip out. I was the only one who looked half alive the next morning when the three of us were rampsed into court. Honest to Gawd, I thought I'd die laughing at the sight of them two."

The bow had begun to dip into deepening swells and spray splashed over the rail. Under a dimming sun the water took on the dull gleam of pewter. Van leaned her shoulder against the wall and gazed ahead past Gina, who said resentfully, "And they never even spoke to *me*. Jeest, I warn't the one who made the mess, it was that Willy. . . . Anyway, we got our choice of fine or jail. Well, Chuck paid his and walked out without a blink at me, and Willy didn't have a cent on him. So the goddam numbnuts told the judge he could still have his job out *there*"—she twisted her mouth—"if he got right back to it, but he'd lose it if he went to jail. Stammered and swallowed and blinked away, and the judge said all right, but we had to be out of Limerock *today* and can't show up again without reporting to the goddam probation officer. And you should of heard him read *me* the Riot Act!" she said indignantly. "You'd think I was some old two-bit whore or something. And then ship me off out here at the end of it."

"Would you rather have gone to jail?" Van asked.

"Damn right, and get it over with. Then I'd get my bus fare somehow and I'd be gone." She looked into Van's face and said belligerently, "I'm going anyway, soon's I can get some cash together. Wouldn't you, if you was me?"

"If I were you," said Van, "that's exactly what I'd do." You little imbecile, she thought dispassionately. In six months you'll be strangled by one of your pick-ups who won't be an honest draggerman everybody in town knows, or you'll be half-dead from liquor or drugs or syphilis. You've got neither brain nor imagination, just a colossal conceit that would let you walk right into a sewer and think you smelled roses.

"You know what?" Gina said innocently. "You look as if you didn't want much to go back either. And I always thought you liked it."

"That's not what I was thinking." She was bored and tired, she felt as if the monotonous drawl had been going on forever. She straightened up to walk away. Owen and the engineer were spreading a tarpaulin over some bags of cement piled on the forward hatch. If she went near, she and Owen might catch each other's eye, even have a few innocent words. But some impulse or compulsion niggled at her. She tried to ignore it, but said at last, reluctantly,

"I said if I were you that's what I'd do. That's if I really were you, Gina, with your way of thinking. But being me, I'd always want to be sure there was an escape hatch."

"Meaning?" The girl screwed her face up into a grimace of suspicion. I don't know why I bother to say it, Van thought, she'd be no loss to the world, only to Willy, and he's nothing either.

"Meaning your bus fare home, kept in a safe place. Meaning some kind of a job. Meaning a little common sense about the people you drink with." She shrugged and walked between Gina and the railing. "Oh forget it," she said. "You've probably got more sense than I credit you with."

"Well, that's a hell of a thing to say!" Gina bawled after her. Van didn't look back. Up forward the men had secured the tarpaulin and had disappeared, probably into the fo'c'sle where they would attempt to cheer up Willy. The *Ella Vye* was heading out now between the breakwater and Owl's Head. Ahead lay some twenty wet miles with a freshening easterly wind and deepening seas. Dry lobster crates had been stacked along one rail. She moved one so she could sit with her back against the pilot house and her feet braced against the rail. She turned up her raincoat collar, tied her scarf around her head, pushed her hands deep into her sleeves, and sank back into herself for the hours ahead.

CHAPTER TWENTY-NINE

Owen emerged from the fo'c'sle at Brigport and went ashore. He hadn't come back by the time the Brigport freight was unloaded, and a Brigport man shouted to Link that he'd gone home with one of his brothers. She knew then that she had been hoping he'd have something to say between Brigport and Bennett's. She felt no anger, only a dull loneliness.

As the boat rolled down in the erratic tide-rip off Tenpound, Willy emerged from the forward companionway, bleached and blinking, and stared vacantly around him, his mouth open. When he saw Vanessa he reacted slowly, then gave her an uncertain smile. He began jumbling through his pockets and she held out her cigarettes. He blushed and said, "Thanks. I guess I came without any." As he handed them back she saw that his jacket sleeves were too short, and there was something unexpectedly moving and childish about the bony wrist; she was irritated by her reaction and said, "Did you have a good time on your vacation ashore?"

"Sure did," he answered. "Finest kind. But I'm glad to be getting back to work. Running out of money for one thing." His laugh died at birth. He inhaled hard and stared at the water heaving and hissing past the rail. She could see his Adam's apple working. Suddenly he turned his head toward her and said rapidly, "Gina's glad to be getting back too. It did her good to be ashore for awhile, that's why I told her to go ahead. She's too young not to have fun going to movies and like that. She's so young, you know what she gets a kick out of? Having a cup of coffee and a hamburger after the second show and watching the people come and go. Would you believe it?" He didn't wait. "That's the way she is. But she's had enough to do her for awhile. We had one john-rogers bang-up weekend, movies and bowling, and pizzas till they come out of our ears, and yesterday I borrowed a feller's car and we drove to Portland. She likes to go round in them big stores up there. Got herself a new pair of them skin-tight pants she looks so good in, and a blouse thing, looks like leopard skin."

"It sounds wonderful," Van said.

"It is," he assured her. "She looks like a movie star in it." Suddenly he lost himself in a long blind stare at Long Cove. The whistle sounded and he went down toward the stern without a glance at Vanessa, who no longer existed for him.

There was no sign of Owen at the wharf, no men at all in fact except Mark; everyone else was out, and school was in session, so that only women and small children met the boat. Having felt so far from the island in all respects, she was surprised to be welcomed with enthusiasm. They liked her, but why? She refused with thanks three invitations to come in and warm up with a cup of coffee, answered numerous inquiries about her tooth, and said she hadn't gotten to the movies. Kathy was excited to see her, saying that it felt like years since Saturday, but Van had a chance to go home alone because the mail wasn't out yet. When she left the wharf they were all greeting Gina with a kind of determined enthusiasm.

Barry hadn't washed dishes all weekend, but she made coffee for herself. For a long time she sat at the kitchen table looking at nothing, hardly thinking. Orientation was the hardest thing. Back to playing neighbor again, and wife, and she'd forgotten the lines and would probably go dumb at the first crisis. She could not even see herself attempting it; the fact that she'd been doing it very well for some time now meant nothing. Any minute Kathy would be bounding in at the door with glad cries, and she would not be able to think how to look or respond. This got her up out of the chair and she went hastily upstairs. She drew the shades and pulled off her clothes and went to bed. Instantly she felt calmer in this pale dusk, with the soft shush of the wind blowing past the screen, and the sounds of birds and engines unseen taking on the strange, almost mystic significance given them by distance and invisibility. She began to feel weightless; on the edge of consciousness she drifted to the room where she had lived with Owen. She remembered how they had slept together, touching in some way all night long, and how often she had waked in joyful awareness to be sure he was there—to listen to his breathing, to smell his flesh, to make out his profile in the very first light, to be warmed through by the heat of his body as if she had never in her life been warm before.

Then the room became transferred to the old house on the island with such validity that she knew if she opened her eyes she would see the steep-pitched roof over her, and the bare beams dark with their age, the shreds of ancient bark still clinging. In a gale the house put together with wooden pegs would creak like a ship at sea. The thought filled her with a kind of ecstasy. Tears ran out of the sides of her eyes from under her lids, trickling toward her ears. They were entirely appropriate. A few times in her life she had cried from grief or anger, never from happiness. But then it had been always the life of somebody else. The Day had turned out to be a birth.

When she woke up, the boats were starting to come in. She washed and dressed, and unpacked the presents. She

202

left Barry's on the kitchen table and went next door to give the Campion children theirs. Kathy was almost as rapturous over the surprise as they were. Terence, just in, gave her a slow smile and said, "It was real good of you to think of them." She couldn't help being pleased by their pleasure in the small inexpensive things, and she kept sardonically ridiculing herself for falling into the trap of sentimentality. And worse, she thought. You'll be getting to like the sound of thanks. Next thing you'll be keeping a cookie jar full for all the little paws.

"So Gina's back," Kathy said. "Willy called up Sunday night and wanted to know if they could come."

That would be from the jail. "I suppose they'd run out of money," said Kathy. "Didn't Willy look ghastly? If I know that Gina, she'll be off again as soon as she can get a fistful. Willy ought to have Steve take care of his earnings for him, send a check to the bank for him every so often and just give him enough cash for cigarettes and groceries. I think I'll suggest it."

"I think you'll keep your mouth shut," said Terence.

"But I can make Willy listen to me and they'd be a lot better off."

"Fools rush in, as the feller says. It's none of your business."

"That Terence is a whited sepulchre," said Kathy. "Everybody thinks I run *him*. Gosh, I'm glad you're back, Van."

Liza wasn't in sight and nobody was home at the Dinsmores', not even Tiger. Relieved, Van left the gifts on the kitchen table, and went on to the store. It was one of the afternoons when everyone seemed to have dropped from sight and she was glad of that. She wasn't ready for them yet. Mark was busy on the car with the men coming in, and Helmi waited on her, but was not relentlessly conversational about it. There was a lot to be said for Finns.

When Barry came home she had cleaned up the kitchen and was making spaghetti sauce. He stood in the doorway, shaking his head and grinning wordlessly at her. "There's something for you there on the table," she said.

"There's something for me by the stove." He advanced on her, still incandescent, and she turned her head away quickly, studying the slowly bubbling mixture in the pan. He came up behind her and wrapped his arms around her

203

and murmured into her neck, "You sure look good to me. *Feel* good too. What a feel."

"Don't," she said. "I'm under the weather."

"Oh hell!" He took his hand away, but kept on hugging her and moving amorously against her. "Find something like this waiting for me and I can't touch it." He stood still. "Hey, it hasn't been a month yet."

"What do you do, Granny, keep count?" she jeered at him. "It's early. Maybe it was the change of pace, maybe it was what the dentist gave me for the infection, how do I know?"

He let her go, blew hard, and went over to the table. "All right. But it won't be the same a couple of days from now. Nothing like coming in the door and seeing you there and rushing you right upstairs."

"Cheer up. I mightn't have felt like being rushed."

"That's right, you'd probably be damn cussid about it," he said amiably. "And that stairway's too narrow for me to lug up a kicking, swearing, struggling female." They both laughed. He began opening the packages. "Hey, what about that tooth, anyway? You had it out?"

"No, he wanted to clear up the infection first. I'm taking some kind of antibiotic."

"So what if that whams you again in the middle of the night?" he asked belligerently.

"It won't. The infection might not be anything to do with the tooth anyway," she lied. "It could be something in my system that just chose that place to break out in."

"I never heard of anything like that before."

"Neither did I, but that's what the man said."

He whistled, and she looked around. He was holding up the shirt. "Wow! They'll have to have another dance right off, or I'll go hold one all by myself!"

She said impulsively, "You've always liked nice clothes and there's no reason why you shouldn't have a lot of them now." Suddenly she wanted him to have closets full, to be as trim and dapper as a jockey on holiday when he went to the dances and to Brigport. Now he'd come to the sweater. "How'd you know how much I wanted one of these?"

"I only had to eat and drink that one of Philip's for about a week after you first laid eyes on it."

He laughed. "Ayuh, something like that gets me. I dunno why. I was always like that. Bad as a girl, my

204

mother used to say. Something new always set me up. Didn't seem as if there was anything couldn't be cured with a new shirt, new pair of shoes."

Anything? She hoped so. She began to break spaghetti into boiling water and Barry made himself a mugful of instant coffee and sat down at the table. "You see Cap'n Owen over there anywhere?"

"Those pills must have made me dopey. I didn't move around town much except to do my errands on Monday. But he came into the restaurant this morning when I was having breakfast, and sat down with me."

"I'll bet he was lugging one son of a bitch of a hangover," said Barry with envious admiration.

"Well, he wasn't, and he ate a big breakfast and had the waitress in a state of giggling idiocy."

"He would. Well, if he stayed sober all weekend he must have gone to visit his youngster, the one that's in high school somewhere over to the west'ard."

She contrived to look bored. "I wonder how long Gina and Willy will last this time," she said. "Not that I give a damn. It's just idle curiosity."

"Oh, they'll stick together about five minutes. Everybody thinks Steve's some foolish to take 'em back."

"It's a wonder he dares to go against family opinion. The way they all hang together, you'd think they couldn't function apart. Seems like a lot of roosters crowded onto one dunghill."

"Why should any of 'em go anywhere else?" he asked seriously. "That's not to say any one of those fellas wouldn't do all right wherever he went. They've got the golden touch, you could say. But this is their own place here. They've always been here, always will."

"As it was in the beginning," she said. "So it is and ever shall be. World without end."

He missed the sarcasm and said with innocent fervor, "That's right. They'll always be here unless something wipes them out."

"But nothing could possibly exterminate the Bennetts. It wouldn't dare."

He grinned at her, teasing. "Glad you're getting the right attitude. . . . Spaghetti's about to fizz over." She leaped to turn down the gas. Barry fingered his sweater, his face absorbed and serene.

He'll be all right here, she thought. Such complete

admiration, along with a capacity for hard work, couldn't be dispensed with. He was appreciated out here, and she was honestly glad that someone appreciated Barry so much. He deserved it.

CHAPTER THIRTY

The next sewing meeting was at the Sorensens'. Barry walked around the harbor with Van and Kathy, and went in to play cribbage with Rob Dinsmore. Maggie came out, shoving the children ahead of her. "They've got something to say to you," she told Van, who tried to compose her face into the right expression without feeling like a fool. One child recited rapidly, "Thank you for the sewing kit," and the other chanted, "Thank you for the modeling clay, I already made Tiger."

"She'll show you tomorrow," said Mag. "He's baking on the back of the stove. And Diane's making doll's patchwork. All right, you young ones go in and no works when your father tells you it's bedtime." They rushed in, Tammie crying, "Mr. Barton, look on the stove and see Tiger!"

"They were some pleased," Maggie told Van. "You taking the time to choose something for them."

Van leaned down to pat Tiger, thankful for the diversion. Liza Bennett came down her front steps and called over to them, and they joined her.

Van was preoccupied, but not unhappy. The very fact that she hadn't seen Owen since she'd come home had taken on a positive significance; it meant something was happening, advancing. The break could come in a week. . . . In the golden evening Liza's and Kathy's voices were pleasant. The boys shouted in the field behind them, Joanna's dog came toward them. Joanna and two women were walking along the border of perennials beside the house. She saw and assimilated all, moving in a luminous objectivity as if across a broad canvas peopled with figures that meant nothing to her beyond their beauty at this moment; the dog's eyes, the strong line of Joanna's throat as she turned her head, the light in Kathy's yellow hair.

Possibly a week from now they will all know, she thought; the people here will remember this moment and think, When she was coming through the gate she was loved with this great love, she was going to do this unforgivable but great thing.

"It's a shame to go inside," Liza said.

Joanna was saying, "Nils's grandmother planted these peonies. They'll be red. And her columbines are all over the place."

Then some others came out of the house and through the greetings and joking Laurie Bennett's husky, youthful voice said behind Van's shoulder, "Did the lilies of the valley live?"

"Oh yes," said Van, turning her head just slightly. "And they've got buds on them."

"I wish you'd come over and see what else you'd like. We've a lot of things to spare. Come over after school tomorrow and have a cup of tea with me, and then we'll look at the plants."

She had to look at her then, it would seem odd if she didn't. "I can't promise," she said, "but I'll come if it's possible. It depends on Barry."

"I know, I know," said Laurie. "They like you there when they come in. I'm sure I don't know what they think you can be up to if you're *not* there. Certainly not down-street spending all their money, or carrying on passionate love affairs in somebody's fishhouse. But if *they* want to go chasing off somewhere—show that man of mine a school of herring and I think he'd chase it from here to New-foundland and never give me a thought."

"Is he talking about going seining again?" somebody said.

"He talks about it every year, but he can't get a crew together except from the boys, and they've got the energy but not the experience."

"Jamie and Hugo are dying to go," said Joanna.

"Well, don't worry," said Laurie. "I don't think the Pied Piper will be piping them away this year. He's not talking so much about it now, for some reason."

The last gold had gone, and all at once the air was dulled and chilled. The women went inside to begin their sewing.

The conversation rolled on as they worked, the easy talk of women who are used to being strung together like

207

beads on the string of their common circumstances. Vanessa realized that imperceptibly she had come to see past the good-humored arrogance they had represented at first. They could not be otherwise than they were, living on the island like this, and with no dedicated troublemaker among them. They'd had wars enough in the past on Bennett's, and could have them again, perhaps, when another generation succeeded the veterans.

It was so clear to her, like so many things; now that she was about to leave, her vision was at once quick and penetrating, and she was turning it on the slightest detail, like one discovering the minute elegance of a blossoming weed through the small end of the binoculars.

Liza had just asked Van if she'd had a hard time with her tooth when the dog barked outside, a door slammed, and Owen appeared in the sitting-room doorway. He put one hand up on the jamb and pushed his cap back with the other, narrowing his eyes against the sudden light.

"Evening, ladies," he said, smiling.

"You brought your fancywork with you?" Nora Fennell called.

"Come on out with me, darlin' mine, and I'll show you some real fancywork."

"Oops, I asked for that," said Nora.

"You should know by this time," said his wife.

"Where in time's your old man?" he asked Joanna. "That hellion of yours is over to Brigport girling, but I'm damn sure that's not where Nils is."

"I don't know. You tried all your brothers? Maybe he's gone down to the Eastern End."

"I didn't meet him on the way up," said Steve's wife.

"Well, I want to stop off the harbor. Lot of herring puddling out there. I've got Barry, but Rob can't go yet, and that kid of yours, Mateel, has gone to Brigport too, and Philip and Mark are glued to that chessboard like they were getting messages from Mars through it." He turned to go out and Joanna said, "Nils may be out in his place in the woodhouse, reading. Go and look."

"Thanks." He went out through the other door of the long sun parlor.

"What did I tell you about herring?" Laurie said. In the lamplight she was rosy and calm. Van turned her new vision on her; resentment had gone, she was only curious about what Laurie thought of her husband, if she ever felt that she had snared some wild wonderful beast in a fine, strangling net and had trained him to sit on a stool. Her easy voice and small smile really said, *He snarls and lashes his tail, but that's all it amounts to. And he's a lot happier than he would be having to forage around out in the jungle.* She never feels sorry for him, Vanessa thought, because she's so inexorably right . . . she thinks. This is the way it should be. It was all right to be attracted to his wildness in the first place, but a kitchen's no place for a tiger. She's not intelligent enough to be coldblooded about it. Just by *being* she has done it, and she's so sure of it that it's never occurred to her that something still lives within him to which she should never turn her back.

How had she drawn him to her? Van would probably never know. Owen never wanted to discuss her, and when they had left they would leave everything behind and never talk about it again.

"Don't you think so, Van?" someone said to her.

"About what?" she said. They laughed. "She's with us but not of us," said Mrs. Steve, "or should it be the other way around? We're talking about whether we should have a supper at the clubhouse for the Fourth of July. Of course we don't have to decide tonight."

"Oh. Well, I'll do what anybody asks me to do." I won't be here, she thought. "And if I don't go out back pretty soon, I'll be sorry." She got up and put her work in her chair.

"It's out past the woodhouse," said Joanna. "Wait, I'll give you a flashlight."

"Thanks." She didn't need to go, she just wanted to get out for a few moments. At the thought of going away with Owen she had been suddenly unable to bear the pressure of other people. She didn't put on her light as she went out along the wooden walk between dark masses of lilacs. At the end there were two steps down into the yard, and she sat on one and lit a cigarette. There was no light in the small woodhouse, and she could see the shape of the barn roof against the stars, and beyond that the sawtooth line of the woods. A smell of earth, green grass, spruce, the barn, came to her. The quiet was so extreme that she thought she could hear her heart beating in it, faster and faster, and it was as if—sitting here on this strange doorstep in the silent dark—she had suddenly come to consciousness, wondering, Who am I, what is my business here?

Then she heard footsteps on the soft earth and thought, In another minute I'll know something, but what? ... An animal came out of the dark and thrust a cold nose into her face, gave her hand a lick. Then Owen was there. He took her hand and led her across the yard and into the barn. The dog went sniffing and snuffling in corners, invisible, his toenails tapping on the boards. "How'd you know I was still out here?" Owen asked.

"I didn't. I just had to get out for a minute. It was close in there."

"I've been standing out here waiting for you."

"Where's Nils? And what about the herring?"

"I dunno where he is, and to hell with the herring. I only came up here because you were here. My God, it's a long time since last weekend. And I don't dare touch you now. Out here in the dark, all alone. . . . It's that bad."

"I know," she said. "At night I miss you so. Now that I know what it's like. Did last weekend really happen?" she laughed shakily.

He fumbled gently for her face, pushing back her hair and laying his hand along her cheek and jaw. All the time the invisible dog was noisily busy with his mousing. "Listen," Owen said, "I told you we wouldn't see each other but we've got to."

"What's wrong?" She pressed her face into his hand, shutting her eyes.

"What's *wrong*, for—" The violence shot out like a fountain of blood from an artery, and then was shut off. He said with exaggerated calm, "I've got to see you every day. Maybe only to speak to, just to get a look and know you're still there." He stroked her face. "I'm off the deep end, all right. Everything's just out of whack, off balance, askew—however you want to call it—till I see you." He laughed, a sound without pleasure, expressing a defeated incredulity. *"Me.* Oh Jesus."

"Don't." Shaken, she put her hand over his mouth and felt his lips move against her palm. "When are you going to tell her?"

"As soon as I get things straightened out. I've been going through papers, making plans for the kids, and so forth. I want everything clear, so we can just up and go, no chance to chew things over. . . . Look, can you come to

210

the place over by Long Cove tomorrow? I'm going out in the morning, but I won't haul through."

"I'll wait there all afternoon," she promised. The dog sneezed loudly, twice. They jumped, and then laughed. From the house somebody called across the dark yard. "Van, are you all right? You haven't fallen down, have you?"

"Go on," Owen whispered. "I'll wait here."

She went to the pale opening and called, "I'm all right." She switched on her light to show her the way underfoot, and walked toward the house. The dog caught up with her and bounded ahead. On the wooden walk Joanna was a silhouette against the lighted door behind her. "It was so quiet out and smelled so nice," Van said. "I stopped to smoke a cigarette, and listen to your friend here mousing in the barn."

"I don't know what he'd do if he caught one," said Joanna. "Nils isn't in the woodhouse, I see. I wonder what Owen's doing about his herring."

They went back into the house.

CHAPTER THIRTY-ONE

Kathy came over in the morning to ask her to go greening with her and Maggie. "Nope," said Van. "I don't like dandelion greens and neither does Barry."

"You don't know what you're missing."

"I don't mind missing it, but I'll pick strawberries with you," Van promised, thinking, I'll pick them on my own island.

At noon she took a book and walked along Long Cove toward the place. It was an almost windless hour; heat bounced up from the beach rocks and the field shimmered in green light. The sea had taken on the vibrant, almost artificial turquoise that means an easterly. As she walked along the high barrier of the beach, she imagined herself walking on Jessup's Island, absolutely alone on it except for the birds, eiders and sea-pigeons paddling in the shallows, and the medricks screaming and diving. There would be look-out places to which she would come and stand and look for Owen. When she saw *White Lady* at last coming up through the Thoroughfare she would hurry back to the house to start his meal, then be down at the landing to meet him. Later she would paint buoys for him while he built new pots and headed them with the trap-heads she had made. There would be no one else and they would need no one else. Sometimes they'd go ashore; maybe instead of having a car to drive to the nearest town they'd go by boat, up or down the coast a bit. They might sometimes go to a dance. She hadn't ever cared about dances, but she would like to go with Owen. It would be different to go with a lover. Now she wanted to do all sorts of things she had never allowed herself to desire. It was like having a second chance to grow up, to have youth again with the richness of maturity. All lovers should be past thirty, she thought. They're the only ones who know what it's all about. I must tell Owen that.

At the place she lay in the shade and read at random in the paperback poetry anthology she had bought in Limerock. Some of the poets were new to her. She struggled with the involutions of Gerard Manley Hopkins and John Donne, muttering lines aloud until suddenly their meaning became as lucid as the day. When at last she was tired of it, a long time had gone by. The sun had moved across the sky, and boats were coming up Long Cove; she got up and looked out through the trees and saw Nils Sorensen's boat by Tenpound, Foss Campion's a little way behind him, both boats attended by a lifting, falling cloud of gulls. She thought guiltily that Owen could be in and she hadn't even heard *White Lady*. He could come upon her at any time. She lay back and looked at the sky through the spruce branches and saw a fish hawk sailing in great circles far above the gulls . .

When she woke up, dazed and cold, it was late. She sat with her head in her hands, like a drunk on a curbstone, and tried to clear it; she was heavy with despair as if something—light, joy—had been stolen from her while she slept. Owen wouldn't come now. By the sun it was supper-time for most people.

Suddenly she heard yelping laughter and the thud of running feet. She pulled herself tight together, stopped breathing as if that would make her invisible. In another moment the boys burst through the trees, Richard and one of his dark-eyed cousins. A small startled grunt came from Richard and then both boys froze into statues.

She said hoarsely, "Hello." At once they grinned and came farther into the clearing.

"Is this your place?" Richard asked her.

"You might call it that. I've never found anyone else here."

"We've got a place further up in the woods," he said.

"Got a brush camp there," the other boy offered in the husky voice of some young boys. His nose and the tops of his round dusky-red cheeks were sprinkled with freckles; his eyes looked black and were thickly lashed. He looked more Owen's son than Richard did. He said proudly, "It's the best one we ever made. The rain won't go through it. We slept in it one night."

"They wouldn't let us cook our breakfast up there," said Richard discontentedly. He took out a knife and began chipping away at a tree.

"That's not spruce gum, it's pitch," said his cousin. "And besides, if it was gum, it's hers."

Richard gave her an embarrassed grin and put his knife away. "I should think you'd be baiting up for your father right now," she said to him.

"He didn't come home today. He went to Limerock. Come on, Pete."

She couldn't let them go, she flung words after them like a lasso to draw them back. "But this isn't boat day."

"He went in his own boat," said Richard. "All of a sudden. He called Uncle Steve on the radio and said he was starting in right then and he'd be out tomorrow, and to tell my mother." He shrugged. "Maybe he had a toothache like the time you went."

"Let's hope it didn't hurt as much," she said. They agreed, said so long, and went back the way they had come. She sat there until the branches had stopped moving behind them, and their voices mingled with those of the excited medricks. She was certain that Owen had gone in to call Mrs. Jessup about the island. He could have decided all at once that now was the time. It meant they would be off here by the end of the week. It meant that a week from now they would be sleeping on the island. Her stomach seemed to turn over. Coming out from between the trees into the full white fire of blazing afternoon sea and sky, having to walk with lowered head and feeling the fantastic light dancing across her forehead and crown, she thought of the children, but dismissed them resentfully. They've got their mother and their home and a flock of relatives to be sorry for them. They can spare me their father. I've got nothing but him.

Nothing was everything. The frugal world in which she'd existed had been filled up for her with a wild and prodigal sweetness, everything had become real.

"Wonder why Cap'n Owen took off for the main," Barry said at supper time. He snickered. "Might be he suddenly got to feeling kinky so he went looking for some tail."

"The way you talk sometimes," Vanessa said on a manufactured yawn, "anybody'd think you had but one thought only."

"What man doesn't, if he's a man? And you know what I told you about Owen. When a feller who's lived the life he has gets to pushing fifty, he gets desperate."

"The voice of experience," she said.

"I've seen plenty of 'em, sister." He gave her a wink and a nod. "These guys that go to get a fifth or a package of cigarettes and never come home again. Or they start going out every night, if they're where they can, gone foolish about some little slut like Gina. Not that Cap'n Owen's *that* gormless. There's some pretty good-looking skin lying around loose over at Brigport," he said authoritatively. "Older but better. Like they say about wine."

She got up and began to clear the table. A week from now, she thought. We could have the table by the windows that look out to sea.

CHAPTER THIRTY-TWO

She didn't know he was back the next day until she went around the harbor at boat time, and Joanna asked Philippa about him. "Oh, he's back this morning," Mrs. Steve said. "I saw the boat in the cove when I came up by, but no sign of him."

Mark, unlocking mail sacks behind the window, said, "I

214

suppose you women'll chew that over till you find out what he went for. God, a man don't stand a chance around here." The mailboat captain laughed appreciatively.

"Sure, we're nosy," said Joanna. "What's the point in not being so? Think what you miss. Look at Van's expression. I'll bet she's thinking, Thank God I'm a loner."

They all laughed. Nora Fennell said, "Well, I'd kind of like having a bunch of brothers and sisters."

"Me too," said Maggie. "My kids miss having a raft of aunts and uncles."

"Well, personally, I like being in a large family," said Liza. "Of course there might come a time when you'd like to keep something to yourself, and I think I could manage that."

"Philip being as close-mouthed as Nils," Joanna agreed. "Oh, well, it'll probably turn out that Owen suddenly wanted something he forgot to pick up last week. He always used to be that way."

"Or he had a toothache," suggested Van, solemn-faced; she was possessed with an almost irrepressible excitement, and there was an exquisite pleasure in adding to it. They agreed it could be a tooth, and Mark said, "Well, if the cabinet's got that over with, maybe they can get onto something a dite less pressing, like Vietnam."

"All right for you, Mark," said Philippa. "Sometimes when you want us all to rally round and hold your hand we'll be coldly indifferent."

Vanessa went quickly back around the shore and took the road to Schoolhouse Cove. From the brow she could look across the broad blue basin where a long line of eider ducks splashed, washed, talked, and visited.

White Lady was tied up inside the wharf at Windward Point. Van was about to go down over the rocks and along the beach when a burst of sound from the schoolhouse startled her. The children were rushing out into the warm bright day, older ones already equipped with gloves, ball, and bat, younger ones running toward the tumbled sea wall, scattering through the beach peas and down over the rolling stones. Laurie came out last and stood on the doorstep, shading her eyes. It was too late to escape from the skyline; in a moment she saw Van, and waved. Van waved back and then walked slowly toward the Bennett

215

meadow, as if that was the way she had intended to go all the time.

She was disappointed, but not acutely. It meant waiting only a little longer. She walked on, taking the path that crossed the lower meadow toward the woods. Up beside the house Mrs. Charles was taking down sheets that billowed and shone like sails.

She came at last to the cove where she had first met Owen. Today it was full of glitter and motion. He'd never have been able to land a dory in the surf. The sound of it among the rocks filled the air, and the fine light was faintly dimmed by the salt mist flung off from it; the cool acrid scent alternated in her nostrils with the warm resinous aura of the spruces. A thrush picked tranquilly in fresh, gleaming rows of rockweed. A bright red plastic container swashed in the surf and beyond it a black-and-white buoy. Automatically she went for the buoy; the thrush flew, its alarm like a note plucked from a guitar string, and some little birds running at the edge of the water ran further, half-lifting their wings as they sped. She looked at the name and number on the buoy. *J. Allston.* There were Allstons at Seal Point. She held the buoy in both hands and looked out across the flashing water toward the mist-hidden mainland, conjuring up the Allstons, stocky red-headed men running to fat, and wondering if J. Allston was Joe, who once cornered her in the woods behind the school and tried to show her his private parts. She'd been terrified behind her disdainful manner, and now she realized he'd been quite as terrified; he probably had worried for weeks before he realized she hadn't told Mrs. Bearse. Anyway, he'd been very careful not to even glance in her direction ever again.

Smiling, she turned to go up the steep beach, and saw Owen standing in the shade at the edge of the woods. She stopped as if seeing an apparition; a blink of her eyes and he wouldn't be there. It was an illusion of light and shade. But he was still there and she laughed, dropped the buoy, and ran, frustrated by the slope and the stones sliding under her feet. He didn't come to meet her but stood with his hands in his pockets watching her. Laughing still, she reached him and slid her arms under his and around his ribs, squeezing, leaning her head back to see his face.

"I've never been in love before you," she said, "and it's made me over."

216

His face didn't change. He took his hands out of his pockets, wrapped her in his arms and with one hand pressed her face into his shoulder. She tried to move her head under that heavy hand until her mouth was against his neck. "I love you," she said. She could feel a pulse beating under her lips. "I love you." He didn't answer. They stood tightly holding for a minute. Then he took her by the shoulders and held her off from him. His hands burned hot through her blouse. She had never seen his face so stolid, and it looked darker than usual.

"What's the matter?" she asked him. "Has she sold the island? We can go somewhere else, then."

"Who?" he asked, his forehead creasing.

"Mrs. Jessup! Didn't you go to call her and s-start buying the island?"

"Christ, no," he said, letting go of her. "Sit down." He waved at the uprooted tree and she sat down on it, a visceral apprehension beginning to stir in her. He sat down beside her and began fussing with his pipe. Then he swore softly, snapped the pipe in two, and threw the pieces down the beach.

"It's all off," he said. "We're not going anywhere. It's finished." The words didn't really reach her, they sounded outside her ears somewhere. He kept his eyes on hers, and she didn't know them like this, yet there was something familiar about their cold denial.

"It's a rotten joke," she said.

"It's no joke, Van. I'm not leaving her." He said it with patience.

"She's talked you out of it. She's weakened you—" Hold back, hold back, be just as quiet, don't shriek. "She's brought the children into it, maybe she's even told them—"

"No. I haven't told her anything. I've just made up my mind."

"But you promised. You said we'd pick strawberries there." It sounded whining and childish; she was ashamed, and gave him a quick grin. "Let's talk, if you've got nervous about it. That's the trouble, we need to see and touch each other to get bolstered up."

His face didn't change. He heard her out, then looked down at the restless dazzling water. "It's not that," he said tiredly. "I wish it was that simple. But there's no way to say it but to say it. I had the damnedest feeling in my chest and arm yesterday and it scared the hell out of me. So I

217

stopped hauling and headed for the mainland and a doctor. . . . Well, it wasn't a heart attack, but it was a warning. I could have one any time and it could kill me."

"I don't believe it," she said. "That's all these doctors talk about, all the time. Heart, heart, heart, if it's not cancer. Trying to scare people to death."

"It wasn't the doctor that scared me. It was what I felt on the way in. Something I *knew*."

She remembered the strong beat of the pulse in his neck under her mouth and said loudly, "Well, this is something *I* know. You aren't going to die for a long time, and not like that." The sound of her voice reassured her, drove away a tremor that kept trying to possess her throat and lips. Already she was beginning to feel better. She moved closer to him and put her arms around him; it was like embracing a tree. He seemed totally absorbed in something else. "Owen," she said, "you were scared by something you'd never felt before. And the doctor warned you. Well, maybe you should stop smoking, get more rest, take life a little easier, but everybody should. Owen, it'll be so peaceful there on the island, just us. You needn't run any thousand traps there and you'd still have enough for Laurie and the children, because you and I won't need much—just being alone with each other, that's all we need . . . please, Owen. . . ." She tried to kiss his cheek but it was hard to reach. She said in a different tone, coldly, "What's the matter? Did you think God was striking you down?"

He shook her off him then as if she were an old oil jacket and looked at her. "No. And you're wrong on something else too. I *have* felt this before. A long time ago I passed out with it in the bottom of a dory, when we were out in the harbor trying to get a boat before she went on the rocks. I couldn't get into the war because something didn't sound right in there." He tapped his chest. "But then I married and cut out the liquor and settled down, and never thought about it again." His sincerity shook her, as it always could. The visceral fear was back; in another moment she'd be disgustingly sick one way or another.

"But what I said still goes," she pleaded. "You might never have that—that big one. You've still got your life and it's our life now, Owen. You know what you told me.

218

All the things. You know what I told you. That doesn't change."

"No, the truth doesn't change," he said heavily. "It's just the way of looking at it that changes."

If she didn't question that he might not say it again. She talked fast, winningly, pouring all her passion into it. "Something could happen to *me* that I don't know about! Or maybe there's a bad accident waiting for us. But whatever it is, six months or a year or ten years, we'd have it together, and—and—I don't know about you, but for me it would make up for all the rest of my life. It would *be* my life. The whole. Because up till now I never had any, you see. It's been like a long waiting to be born."

His face softened and he put an arm around her and hugged her to him. "I know all that. I've been thinking about it. But I can't do anything different. It's like being struck by lightning. I thought you'd done that to me, blasted my existence to pieces, but yesterday I knew it had been waiting for just the right minute to plough me under. . . . Whatever it is."

"Fate," she mocked him. "Or the hand of God. You do believe it, don't you? God's punishing you for adultery. Thou shalt not commit adultery, and you've done it so you shall die. That's what you really believe. Never mind everything else you've gone without. You'll go without it for the rest of your life—if you can call it a life—if God will stop being mad with you. You've already made your bargain, haven't you? Without consulting me first, because I don't count. The other woman, the floozy, never counts."

He held her tight with one hand and clamped the other over her mouth. She fought him wildly, but she had to give up at last and huddled on the log trying to keep from crying.

"I don't believe in God," he said. "At least not in a God that's watching everything you do and knowing everything you think and chalking it up against you." This reasonable thoughtful way of speaking was worst of all, because it was so unlike him. Since she had last seen him he had become this stranger, and she put her hand against her mouth and bit at the thumb mound in an effort to hold back a drowning wave of desolation. "If I thought that," he was saying, "I wouldn't worry much because there's a lot worse bunch of sinners than me to take up his atten-

219

tion. No, what I've come up against is *me*. The plain fact is, aside from all the rotten jokes about it being the best way to go, if I die in any woman's arms it's got to be Laurie's."

She stiffened as if shot or stabbed, and he held her tighter. "I owe it to her," he said. "Well, no, not the plain fact of dying in her bed, that's a hell of a thing to do to any woman."

"A week ago you didn't owe her anything," she said bitterly. "Not the rest of your life. She'd had seventeen years of it. She got you in the first place. She couldn't ever have expected anything so good. She couldn't have believed her own luck. How'd she manage it, anyway? How could you settle for a pink-cheeked kid? Or were you just looking for a way to straighten out your misspent life? Making bargains with God again? Oh, I forgot. You don't believe in God. It's conscience. Or honor. What did you say it was?"

"I didn't say," he said. "Van, I've got enough hell of my own making without you badgering me." This sounded, though only faintly, like the Owen she knew. He wasn't completely committed, then.

"I'm sorry," she said, "I won't interrupt again." Let him talk, he needs to talk. He will talk the belated guilty conscience right out of existence if you can listen long enough.

"You asked how she managed to get me. How could I settle for a pink-cheeked kid. Maybe because she was a pink-cheeked kid, and I was in a foul frame of mind, at home while my brothers and Nils fought the war for me. She came out here fresh from the egg, all downy and bright-eyed. It was her first school. She didn't look much older than Richard does now." His smile was cynical and intolerable. "Maybe I should call her a new lamb, not a day-old chick. Because if ever lamb was led to the slaughter, that one was. She never had a chance."

"Did you rape her?" she asked coldly.

"All but. By the time it happened I'd convinced her that was what she wanted, and she wanted it because it would be some great act of faith in me. . . . Oh, I don't remember all the bastardly foolishness I should have been lynched for. I guess I don't want to remember it. . . ." He went abruptly quiet and distant, and she was jealous of his thoughts and tried to take his arm. He went on. "I remember she cried because she didn't think she was too good at it but she hoped she'd be better. . . . So I dried her tears and walked her back to the Fennells', where she was boarding, and that was that. . . . Good God, when I think now she wasn't much older than my girl in high school . . ."

"You married her." She tried to sound calm and objective. "Did she come to you crying that she'd missed, or did she go to Joanna? Joanna's a great one for taking things in hand. Or did she go home and tell her mother and they put the law on you?"

"None of those things. I didn't go near her after that night, and sure, Jo had plenty to say about me leading her on. . . . Jo and I have squared off and sworn at each other all our lives, probably always will. And Laurie got a little pale in the cheeks but she never said a word or took down that chin of hers." Van twisted inwardly, tried to listen, bit again at the base of her thumb as if blood would be some magic restorative. "What happened," said Owen, "was what you'd call the hand of God." He held up his own maimed one. "This. I remember thinking that I might have the kind of blood that wouldn't clot, I never saw anything pour out so fast before they got the tourniquet on. Remember Rob that day when he did it with the saw? And I knew she was carrying my kid and it ought to have a name so she wouldn't go home in disgrace." He shrugged. "Took us a hell of a long time to cross the bay, and all I wanted to do was stay alive till we got to Limerock so I could marry her. Well, I did, there in the hospital, and then I passed out. When I woke up I was goddam surprised to be still alive, and it was fine for about five minutes. Then I remembered. I didn't love her, I didn't want her. And I had nobody to blame but myself."

"You've paid for it," she said passionately. "You gave her seventeen years, a good life, a lot of reason to be proud."

"And I never once told her I loved her. All that I've said to you in a few weeks, all that I've felt about you—what you've done to me—how it's been when we're together—it's never been that way once in the seventeen years with her."

"Oh darling," she murmured, nuzzling into his throat. "For me it's been thirty years, ever since I was born . . ."

"And she's not stupid," he said as if he hadn't heard

221

her. "She knows I've never said it. She's never asked me why. I guess she doesn't want to hear me lie, or tell the truth either. . . . There's a part of Laurie I don't know, the part where she thinks and wonders. Maybe she has some feelings about those seventeen years that would surprise me. I don't know. I don't ask her, and she never troubles me with it."

She cried eagerly, "Then it'll be easier for her when you go, less brutal than if you'd put on a big act all these years. She might even be relieved. She'll still have her place here, and the name, and the children, and—"

He was shaking his head. "Vanessa, I'm not going. It's on account of the way it's been with her and me. I told you I owed it to her."

"I know what you told me. But it's a queer thing to me, how you can owe her your death when a week ago you didn't owe her your life."

"Damn it, I can't make you see it, but it's all clear to me. I've done enough to her without doing this!" he shouted. "Good God, doesn't that make sense, or don't you have any human feelings at all?"

She said quietly, "Yes, I have human feelings but mostly they concern me. Compared to me, Laurie's been rich. And even with you leaving, your kids are like royalty compared to what I was as a child, and what I had. Or *didn't* have, because it was mostly that. Everything I have now is made up or borrowed, even my name. Loving you is the first thing I ever had of my own and now it turns out that was just borrowed too. . . . But I won't give it back." Her voice was rising. She put her hands around her throat to squeeze it back. The words came out half-strangled. *"I won't give it back."*

"What are you doing?" He pulled her hands away from her throat and stared into her face in fury; it was like the confrontation between murderer and victim. Then he let her go and she crumpled back against the log.

"What do you care now what I do?" she cried. "I'm out of it now. I'm something gone by, it's over and you'll go safely home—"

"Is that what you think?" His eyes had a queer shine to them and she saw for the first time a faint twitching in one eyelid. "That it's nothing to me? I can forget it! Oh, my God," he groaned, "I want you so much that when I turn my back on you it's like canceling out my whole life,

222

saying it was a failure, a big nothing, fifty years of bullshit that's fouled every thing I've touched, and all I can pray for is for that big one to come down on me like a sledge hammer next week. Maybe that way my kids will escape something, I dunno."

"The big one won't come," she said. "You'll wait and wait but it won't come, and the years will be wasted. And what will become of me?" She smiled at him. "I may go insane, like my mother. Maybe that's what did it." She burst out laughing at his expression. "Now you're glad to get rid of me, aren't you? Any old excuse so you won't be stuck with a crazy woman."

He slapped her lightly but enough to startle her into silence. "Shut up. You don't know if she was insane or not, and even if she died in a straitjacket that wouldn't make any difference to you and me."

"No, what makes the difference is that you never told your wife you loved her. So at this late date you're going to start. Too bad Mother's Day is past, you could have got her breakfast in bed."

He put his head in his hands and said, "Shut up, shut up, shut up. Or go home."

She stood up, looking down at his black head and the nape on which her hand had lain so often. What will become of me? she had asked, and she knew already; she was turning into a skeleton as she stood there, flesh burning off into the sun and the wind but the passion and resentment still fiery in the bones, never consuming them so that for always, even in her grave, the little torturing flames would lick and lick.

"I have no home but where you are," she said in a low voice. "I came home to you, don't you understand?" He didn't move or answer. She went across the thick muffling forest floor and down onto the beach, blinking in the flashes of light. The cove was choked with a heaving mass of rockweed, driftwood, odd buoys, and green bottles that clinked against the rocks. Each time the water withdrew a little, there was a loud rattling of the beach stones. She went down the steep, careful about her footing, her eyes fixed as if she were a tightwire walker. She walked into the water and at the edge of the surf it didn't feel cold, having to get through her socks and slacks first. It pulled at the stones under her feet, then surged in again with a great strength around her knees, at once pushing and dragging. When she stepped again it seemed as if the land dropped sharply away from her, but her foot struck something solid. A plank bumped against her, and rockweed caught her legs in a bronzy swirl. She kept her eyes narrowed against the seething and smoky silver outside, braced herself as the water struck at her thighs and rocked her. Then the force below the surface withdrew with a great pull, and her footing was being sucked out from under her soles. A peeled pulpwood stick nudged her and she staggered backward and went down; for an instant she saw level with her eyes another sea rolling into the cove, cresting toward her with deliberate speed. Then she was tumbling backward, the cold surprising in her ears and strangling in her nostrils, and she tried to think, This is what you want, don't fight, don't hold your breath. But when the oncoming sea broke over her head, and she felt herself dragged and tumbled and saw the red light against her eyelids, and her flailing hand found nothing but smooth cold stones that came away in her grasp, there was no reason in her.

The planks and pulpwood sticks were knocking her around and she fought them, shot rightside up and was blinded by the world. She let her breath go at last, took in a cold and nauseating mouthful of sea water, and began to fight again at whatever new thing wouldn't let her alone. Something struck her on the side of her jaw. She felt no pain, and barely the impact, but had no time to think about it.

She sat with her head between her knees and threw up salt water. The sun was hot on her back through the wet jersey. She lifted her head slightly and turned it and saw Owen's feet. He had put on his moccasins again but his pants steamed gently in the heat. They're probably made of drip-dry cotton, she thought foolishly. They'll be dry before he gets home. She turned back to contemplation of the rocks between her raised knees. There was a stiffening soreness along one side of her face.

Nobody spoke. Through the swash of water she heard the plinking alarm note of the thrush.

"What were you trying to do?" Owen spoke from over her head. "Kill us both off quick?"

She hadn't drowned but she felt as soggy and exhausted as if she were speaking from the bottom of the sea. "I don't know what I was trying to do. Stop thinking, I guess. I'm sorry. That you saw me, I mean. Another minute and I'd have let my breath go, and that would be it. . . . That thrush wishes we would go away."

He made some sound and dropped down beside her, took her into his arms and rocked her against his chest, his face in her soaked hair. "Oh God," he said in a low voice. "Listen to me, if I thought there was anything to pray to, I'd be crawling on my hands and knees begging. If there was a devil I could sell my soul to, I would. Just to be there again on that Sunday and have the chance to choose not to come back here, and *not come*."

She tried to struggle up to look at him, saying, "We could go back tomorrow. Today! We could just go, and pretend nothing happened in between." She tried to get her hands free to take his head between them, thinking that if they kissed it would work, but he wouldn't let her. He got up and pulled her up, but held her off.

"Now go on," he said. "We'll get over this. I think we will. You've got guts, more than I have. It'll be like what they tell alcholics—live one hour at a time."

She wrenched herself from his hands, hurling herself away from him in savage repudiation. She ran up over the rocks in her squelching sneakers, and kept on running without looking back.

CHAPTER THIRTY-THREE

Someone spoke to her. She jumped and her surroundings suddenly leaped at her from all sides; she was menaced by something arched head-high at her, red-scaled; she blinked and it became a fluke of the big anchor sunk in the marsh where the road came out at the harbor beach. "I said, what happened to you?" said Philip Bennett. Big in his oilclothes, he was tying his skiff at the head of the beach. He straightened up, his smile changing. "Are you all right?"

"I was trying to salvage a buoy and fell in." All at once

her teeth began to chatter. She looked wildly along the beach. He was the only man in sight. "Is B-B-Barry in?"

He kept coming past the graveyard of old hulls. "No, I got a warp in my wheel and had to jog home. Come on along to the house, my wife will have the coffeepot on. We'll put the brandy to you too."

He made a gesture toward her, as if to take her arm, and she backed off, trying to laugh and wondering if she looked like a wild woman. "N-no thanks, I'll g-get right into b-bed and that'll w-warm me up in no t-time."

She turned and fled along the boardwalk. She *was* cold. It was in her spine, in her stomach. It was a cold at once nauseating and empty. It surrounded her so that everything outside looked the same and yet was not the same. The anchor had reared up before her, Philip Bennett had been a threatening apparition, Helen Campion, calling to her from the clothesline, wore a leering fright-mask. Kathy's youngest, sitting by a sandpile with his trucks, was like a ventriloquist's dummy propped up there. When his head suddenly turned and he stared toward her with round blue eyes, she felt pure horror. With a final effort she flung herself toward her own house; if Kathy should stop her she might disintegrate, she felt like it now, ready to shatter like ice. And she was as cold, as cold.

Upstairs she pulled off her clothes, an agonizingly long business with her fingertips gone dead white and numb, and wrapped herself in blankets. She lay down, pulling herself into a tightly knotted bundle. She couldn't tell if the cold was a physical phenomenon; she wanted it to be the beginning of some swift lethal pneumonia. For the moment it kept her from thinking.

No sounds reached her inside the cocoon of blankets but the thudding of her own blood in her ears, like footsteps that never retreated or advanced. When finally the voice broke through to her she had the feeling that it had been calling for quite some time. "Are you all right, Van?" It came from the foot of the stairs. It was Kathy. "Shall I come up?"

"No!' She sat up in terror, then modified her shout with a gust of comradely laughter. "For heaven's sake *don't*. The place looks as if it was suddenly called for and couldn't go."

Kathy's echoing laughter floated up; she was relieved but still doubtful. "I saw you run by. You looked sick or

scared, and there are no bears or mad rapists in the woods
. . . at least not that I know of."

"I was frozen. I tried to get a buoy in the rockweed
over in Ship Cove and I slid overboard and got soaked."

"Oh, my *gosh!* You could have *drowned!*"

That, my girl, was the idea. "It wasn't deep enough, I
wasn't ever in danger."

"Well, want me to make some coffee or bring over
another hot-water bottle or something?"

"Thanks, but I'm warm now. I rolled up in blankets and
went to sleep."

"I suppose I woke you up. That's the story of my life.
Old Fumblefoot. Well, having done my bad deed for the
day I'll go home and stick pins in my child, or something."

"Don't feel bad. I'm glad you came over. It was time
for me to get going again. If I sleep too long in the
daytime I feel rotten."

"Oh, you're just being too darn nice," said Kathy, more
cheerfully. "So long." Her footsteps bounced through the
house and the back door shut. From outside she was
heard to shout, "Johnny Campion! What have you got in
your mouth?"

It was early afternoon, not a week since this morning.
She put on pajamas, and neatly remade her bed. She took
her damp clothes downstairs and put them in the plastic
laundry basket in the entry. She did not want to go out of
the house at all, even to her place, which was now tainted
for her because Owen had met her there. There was
nowhere on the island where she could go. It was as if she
feared the sky itself. She found herself walking through
the rooms, her hands twisting and wringing each other, saying, "What am I going to do? What am I going to
do?" She had no sleeping tablets. Barry's rifle hung on the
sitting-room wall, but there were no shells for it.

The sight of the half-finished traphead hanging from the
hook was as terrible as seeing Owen himself in the embrace of his wife. He would handle that traphead with the
hands that would never again handle her. She stood staring at the lustrous twine, and suddenly thought lighthead-
edly that nothing had happened. It was all a nightmare.
Even talking to Philip and Kathy had been part of it—one
of those dreams so vivid that they become a valid part of
human experience. She had dreamed the whole scene

227

with Owen because unconsciously she was afraid of something happening to keep them apart. That's it! she thought with the joyous recognition one feels when someone dead appears alive in a dream and one cries, *But he's back, he's here, he wasn't dead after all!*

Now she straightened up and smiled very steadily, as if the smile could wipe out the existence of the wet clothes in the laundry basket. Owen would be back sometime today with news of the island. . . . She had only to wait. . . . The boats were coming in. Two were crossing the harbor now, but neither was *White Lady*. She averted her mind hastily from the image of *White Lady* tied up in Schoolhouse Cove, and from the sounds of children spilling out of the schoolhouse, but it was too late. It was all there. So must it be to have committed a murder and to have come away trying to pretend to oneself that you hadn't done it, while all the time you know the body was where you had left it, but that you'd brought it with you too, if you just happened to look down or behind you. A murder was done today. . . . She saw Barry's boat come bounding past the breakwater, racing young Jamie Sorensen. They're *happy!* She thought in outrage.

She went upstairs and pulled the shades and got into bed.

Barry came tiptoeing up in his sock feet, squinting across the half-light of the room, then coming in when he saw her eyes were open. "You all right? Phil told me what happened, then Kathy did."

"I lost the buoy I was trying for, too. Well, no great loss without some small gain. I've given the island a real treat today."

"Ayuh, out here it don't take much," said Barry. "But they were all worried for fear you could have drowned. You take a chill, or hurt you any?"

"Both," she answered. "I'm starting to get warm now, I guess, but I feel pretty tired. I guess it shook me up some. And I banged my elbow on a rock. I don't think I'll be able to knit right off, so will you do something about that twine and stuff down in the sun parlor?"

"You mean Cap'n Owen's knitting?" He sat down on the end of the cot and lit a cigarette. "Oh hell, I might's well finish that up. No sense letting the money go out of the family."

"Suit yourself."

She shut her eyes and turned her head away. After a moment he said, "Well, you want something to eat?"

"No. Can you find yourself something?"

"Oh sure, I'll make out all right and then I'll catch a kink on the couch. We're stopping off the harbor again tonight."

He went downstairs. Presently she heard the radio, with some vocal group singing an unrecognizable distortion of an old popular song. She slept, heavily as she used to sleep, heard nothing of Barry's comings and goings, and woke late the next morning. The feeling was familiar, even to the lurch of terror when she wondered if she had slept over a day. She went downstairs in her bare feet, her head heavy and dizzy, and looked at herself in Barry's shaving mirror. Her hair was tangled from the salt water and sleep, but aside from a tendency to stare she looked well enough. She washed her face and hands in cold water, and heated the coffee Barry had left.

Yesterday's wildness was gone. This was the first day after the death, when you begin to live without him. You think, *Yesterday at this time*—and then stop yourself. You mustn't ever think that, or you'll go crazy again. *Crazy.* That was a dirty word. One of those you didn't look at, you pretended it wasn't there, like the body thrust under the bed or into the car trunk.

"Behave yourself, Anna," she said loudly and sternly. She took a swallow of scalding coffee to emphasize the command, and burned her tongue and lips. She was standing with her back against the sink; the tide was high so that the sun flashed off the water and light reflected into the house. Watching it she suddenly felt a wild upsurge of life. Owen wasn't dead, nothing was dead; all that had passed between them was words, and words meant nothing. She could kill with her own hands the doctor who'd talked to Owen. How did he dare to destroy lives like that, how could anyone be allowed such power? How did he know Owen could die at any moment? He wasn't God or whatever-it-was.

Revived by hope, she didn't know how she could have been so defeated. She began planning at once to see Owen; it seemed as if she could feel a strong communication flowing between them, telling her that today when he woke to the strong pumping of his heart and the warmth and soundness of his body he had been ashamed of that drop into superstitious terror. When they met, their eyes would confirm what they already knew, even if they didn't have a chance to speak.

This afternoon he would be around to help with the herring, as he had done before. Until then she had to keep busy. She decided to do a washing, so she could leave Barry with plenty of clean clothes when she went. She'd do some baking too. Good wives were always baking up a lot of stuff ahead of time when they went home on a visit or to the hospital have a baby. She wondered what he would tell people at first, before it burst out of the tight Bennett circle that Owen had left his wife and gone with Barry's. She wondered if he'd get a housekeeper; these women were always available when needed, widows or divorced women, or some who called themselves "Mrs." to explain the children they brought with them. Oh, Barry would have a housekeeper all right, and she'd spoil him because he was so appreciative. I hope he gets a young one, she thought. I wish him well. In a burst of rich sentiment that seemed to curl up from her very stomach she thought, I want him to be happy, if I'm going to be.

She had the washing done and hung out by midafternoon. Kathy had taken the children after school to dig dandelion greens, and there was an agreeable sense of isolation around the place. Van took a cup of coffee and went out on the wharf to watch the boats come in. The air had the peculiar stillness that foretells an east wind, when each sound rings with great purity and every object is etched in light. It suited her mood.

She realized after a while that everyone else but Owen had come in. Or else he had sold his lobsters before she came out onto the wharf and had taken the boat home; at this moment he could be walking across the field behind the houses, on his way to her, though everyone else would think it was to help salt herring.

Barry, rowing stern first from his mooring, saw her on the wharf and shouted, "Hi, Beautiful!", then looked around to see if Terence Campion, up on the bow of his boat, heard this husbandly salute. "You got up, I see," he said as his skiff came into the ladder. "You were laid out flat and cold as a flounder this morning."

"I don't know what got into me," she said.

"Well, you look real flourishing now." He came up the

230

ladder wearing his version of lecherous anticipation. "Makes a man have ideas. I had 'em this morning. You might of woke up surprised."

"I'm dangerous when aroused."

"I'd take my chances. . . . Well, I'm going up to the house and get a mug-up before we start lugging herring."

"Is Owen helping, like last time?" She tried to sound indifferently polite.

"Nope. He didn't have to last time, just took a whim. . . . He ain't in yet, anyway. I dunno what's keeping him. You coming?"

"In a minute." Barry went, whistling "The Road to the Isles."

She detested and feared the fear, she wanted to wince away from it before it could reach her. It was too late. There was the picture of a boat drifting with no one at the wheel, the light wind and the tide nudging the boat on; she saw it rocking slightly and moving with little swift forward surges. It would travel down past the Rock, and the Coast Guard boys in blue shirts and dungarees would launch a boat and go out aboard. Maybe even at this instant Mark Bennett was hearing the news by telephone, either that Owen had disappeared from his boat or was lying on the platform, dead.

"Well, it was what he wanted," she said aloud in a scraped, tearless voice.

At that moment *White Lady* came into view around the eastern point with a stack of wet traps on the stern. Owen stood with one hand on the wheel, the other in his pocket, his pipe in his mouth. He had an air of solid repose. He was alive.

She pressed her hands tightly together, squeezing her mouth between the fingertips to keep it quiet and in control. That was how close to the surface the savage was; for an instant she'd *believed*. If you ever do go crazy, she said to herself, you'll have only yourself to blame.

She got up and went down the ladder into Barry's skiff and began to row out into the harbor with easy strokes. The water slid away from the oarblades like oil. "Out for a little exercise?" Terence Campion called to her when she passed his mooring.

"I should do this every day."

"You ought to have a little skiff of your own. That one

231

rows like a woodbox. I don't know where she came from."

She held the skiff in one place for a moment and said, "Maybe they knocked her together out of a couple of sardine boxes."

"Now that just may be," he said solemnly. He disappeared into the cuddy. She rowed on among the boats that loomed up around her like large amiable beasts, sometimes stirring slightly but never with menace. But before she reached the other wharf *White Lady* was purring out of the harbor. Owen didn't look toward the skiff, only the lustrous ripples caused by the wake reached it and made it rock gently up and down. She shipped the oars and sat watching *White Lady* go past Eastern Harbor Point so quietly that the wash on the rocks drowned out the engine. When the boat was out of sight Van rowed out around the end of the breakwater. She wouldn't allow herself to be disappointed at not meeting Owen. She felt that he had seen her, and communication had been established. She rowed on beyond the breakwater, along the high shores over the glassy shallows where the bronze-green weed floated until she was abreast of Barque Cove, today an aquamarine mirror for ducks. Then she started back, thinking, Anyone could row all around Jessup's Island in a few hours. I would like a little dory like the one we went out there in. Maybe she would sell it to us. We'll have a dog like Argo and he can go with me. We'll be very self-contained and peaceful, the way I am now. The way I will be forever.

CHAPTER THIRTY-FOUR

In the morning she was positive that she would see Owen today. She ironed Barry's shirts, mended socks, went over her own clothes; she couldn't sit down after that, but washed the sun parlor windows inside and out, and while she was working on the outside Kathy called that she'd just taken some Finnish coffee bread out of the

232

oven. Van was suddenly very hungry—her stomach growled with hunger.

Maggie Dinsmore was there, and the table was half-covered with patchwork squares. "Ain't this nice, though!" Mag cried. "We don't get together often enough. Don't have the time. We'd ought to make time."

"People are always saying, What do you find to do out on that island?" said Kathy. "Well, I'm busier than a three-legged cat with fleas. There's the butter, Van. Can you reach it?"

"Make a long arm for it, as my father used to say," said Mag. Van let them talk. If she smiled now and then it was enough, and it was easy to smile; she felt recklessly gay.

Out of the talk about quilt patterns, dandelion greens, Finnish ways of cooking herring, husbands' choices of food, children's idiosyncrasies, birds, this morning's news, emerged one fact that slashed the high wire under her feet. "Went in real early," Maggie was saying. "The kids are staying with Joanna for the weekend. My, I dunno when those two been off alone anywhere. Of course it's not really alone, getting up to Waterville to see Joss at her school. . . . It's not going on a trip like honeymooners." She sat back laughing like a mischievous child. "Rob told Owen it was real dangerous staying in those fancy motels. Likely to make a baby."

"That Rob," said Kathy. "He's like Terence, never know what these mild quiet ones will come out with. Just the same," she added, "I plan to have a second family when this batch gets grown up some. I think it keeps you young."

"Barry says you folks'll be starting on a family pretty soon," Maggie said kindly to Van. "Anything definite yet?"

"Nothing to be sure of," said Van. Her voice seemed to come from somewhere else in the room. She got up. "Well, as much as I'd like to sit here, I've got to get back to my windows or I'll lose my momentum. That bread is wonderful, Kathy. So long, Maggie." It was a small gem of a performance. She even spoke to the children in the sandpile as she went past them, and called Tiger by name when he pranced furrily at her. She went into the house, up to her room, and into bed.

Barry stood over her, talking in a hushed voice. "What's

233

the matter? You sick? Anything to do with you going overboard the other day and it's just catching up with ye?"

"No," she said to the wall. "And don't talk as if you're standing over a coffin. I'm not dead yet."

"You got a kink? Kathy told me you were up and down that ladder scrubbing windows. Easy to put your sacred lilac out that way." He snorted with amusement, and she knew that he'd say next. "As old Ed Bushnell used to call it."

She sighed without sound and pulled her knees up closer to her belly, shutting her eyes against the obstreperous apple-blossoms on the wall paper. "Sick headache?" Barry pursued. "Bilious?"

"It's too simple for you to understand, I suppose," she said into the tight-closed dark. "I'd just like to be left alone."

He said with triumph, "You got a hair crosswise, that's it. Somebody said something. Now what?" He was sternly and yet indulgently amused. It was a new tone for Barry. He was a man who now made more in a day than he'd ever made in a week. He was a Bennett's Island lobsterman. He might not be a Bennett, but he walked in their boot tracks and knew them by their first names. He stood over his wife making protective, slightly bored, husbandly sounds in a pleasant room in a house for which he was paying the rent. She remembered, while his voice came dimly to her as if the dark were beginning to fill her ears, her early fancy that all meaning departed from this place when the men were away from it. She had become a part of the nonsignificance, the nothingness, and Barry had taken on new flesh and blood.

He was no longer talking. He had gone away. He used to leave her like this in the double bed on Water Street. No, not quite like this; he was whistling now, outdoors. He had such an engrossing life apart from her that he would not think of her again until he came back into the house, unless someone mentioned her to him, and why should they?

Later he offered her supper. She refused it. It was an unspeakably long night, and somewhere in it the foghorn at the Rock began to blow. She saw the fog, a wall moving imperceptibly closer, a wall you could put your hand into and through, and still a wall for all that.

234

The window filled with gray muffling light. Birds began to sing, but no engines sounded.

No one came near her that day. There was no way of telling time as the fog light stayed the same, if you could call it light. It was merely the absence of darkness. She slept and woke, haunted by a line. *And dreaming through the twilight that doth not rise nor set.* . . . Something about forgetting. It was not a day for hauling, and Barry came in at noontime, whistling again. "You up?" he called up the stairs to her, and then when she didn't answer he called in a more subdued voice, "You asleep?" She still didn't answer and he went back to the kitchen.

He made his own dinner and listened to the radio while he ate, and then went out again. Presently she heard the hammer from the fishhouse. She could tell when he finished building one trap bottom and started another. She got up and started downstairs, and was genuinely frightened when she became dizzy and thought she was falling forward. If she broke anything, not enough to die of, she'd be at everyone's mercy; she wouldn't be able to keep them away from her, they'd come through the wall, pitying, comforting, *touching* . . . and triumphant. Now we have got her down we will be nice to her and she can't do a thing about it.

The thought got her up and out into the kitchen. "I suppose I should eat," she said aloud. "Because they won't let you starve to death." No, if you wanted to die without interference the best way was to make it quick and violent. But she'd been unable to drown herself.

She buttered a slice of bread and made a cup of tea and took the food upstairs, where she ate sitting crosslegged on the bed. If only Barry had some shells for his rifle, she could manage it, but she couldn't buy bullets without calling attention to herself.

There was almost a full bottle of aspirin downstairs. If you took it down on Sou'west Point, by the time they found you you'd be good and dead, or close to it. They'd handle you then, but you wouldn't care. . . . Suddenly she rolled over on the bed in a gulping huddle, weeping without shame or caution in an almost voluptuous surrender. She passed from that into new sleep, heavy and dreamless, and woke to a clear red sunset light. Barry was talking downstairs. He seemed to have been talking forever.

"She's been sleeping most of the day. Tonight I went up and took a look, and she was out like a light. But she gets these spells. Always has and always will, I figger." He was blithely authoritative, shrugging off somebody's officiousness with the expert's nonchalance.

"You sure she doesn't need a doctor?" Kathy said. "Dr. Torrey can fly out and land in Owen's field."

"Nope. She'll sleep it off and be fine. You see, Kathy"— he became earnestly instructive—"she's what you might call highstrung. She has these kind of cycles, see? Well, you're a woman, you understand," he said modestly. "Lordie, on Water Street, she had spells when she wouldn't speak for a week, and I just waited on her when she wanted something, brought her little things to tempt her appetite, kind of, and never fussed at her."

You're the goddammedest liar that ever feet hung on and was called a man, Van thought.

"You're awfully sympathetic, Barry," Kathy told him. "A lot of men wouldn't know what to do when a woman feels that way."

"Well, it's easy for me," said Barry. "You see, she's my wife. And I love her. It's as simple as that, Kathy. I love her."

Oh shit, Van thought.

"And it doesn't matter what," said Barry. "I understand her and I'll always be right here when she needs me. And I can darn a sock and dump a slop pail and cook a meal of vittles as good as any woman." He chuckled at that. Kathy's laugh was preoccupied.

"I'll bet you can, but don't turn your nose up at this lobster chowder. Put the bowl in the refrigerator and it'll do you for dinner tomorrow. And put this loaf of bread in your breadbox."

"I thank you kindly. Terence is a damn lucky son of a sea cook."

Kathy laughed again and said, "I'll bob in tomorrow and see if there's anything I can do. It's sewing circle tonight, and it's cleared off so nice. I wish Van felt better."

"She will, tomorrow." He went out with Kathy.

Yes, she will, thought Vanessa. Tomorrow the aspirin. And I'll be doing Barry the biggest favor anyone did him. For the rest of his life he'll be the brave, sensitive man who waited hand and foot on a nutty wife.

Outside, men's voices called back and forth across the dooryard. "Some pretty out now, ain't it?"

"Ayeh, but it'll come off to blow like a man, wait and see."

Barry didn't come back in. Comfortably insulated from all pain, her past and her future cut off so that she was weightless, she thought of the morning; smiled; and slept.

CHAPTER THIRTY-FIVE

"Wake up, will ye? Hey, wake up!" Barry was shaking her, slapping her, dragging at her. "Christ, woman, the island's on fire! Come *on!*" She stood naked and shivering in the cold room. A queer light-and-shadow play danced on the shade. He pulled it up and fire filled the window, until she realized it was halfway around the harbor, and the water was reflecting the flames.

"Get dressed," Barry commanded. "Where's your clothes?" He threw things at her. The sight of the fire had cleared her head. She began to dress, saying, "Go pack up your clothes. It's a good thing we haven't got much. Where is it, anyway?"

"Willy's place, and with this wind the whole place can go!" He slammed into the other room. She spread a blanket on the floor and began piling her books and clothes onto it.

"Anyway, the boats are safe!" she called to him. She looked out and saw little figures running around the fire. It seemed as if she could hear the roar even through the closed window, though she knew it was really the wind blowing in the spruces and the run on the shore. The night was illuminated in red-gold; sparks showed through the sky like the trains of meteors.

"You all right?" Barry charged in again. "I'll take this stuff downstairs and out on the wharf, then I have to go over and help. They're wetting down every building they can, but Kee-rist, if it gets into the woods—"

"Why don't we just drop things out the side window?"

She took out the adjustable screen. "I'll do it, and you go and help."

"You're sure you're all right?"

"I'm fine. Go on now."

"Kathy's out on their wharf with the kids. You can stay with her." He ran down the stairs. She pushed things out the window facing the point, where they'd fall free of the sun-parlor roof. Then she went downstairs and gathered her own dishes from the window shelf, and the tin box from the desk in the sitting room. As an afterthought she took down Barry's rifle from the wall. The rest of Owen's twine was in the sun parlor, with the heads Barry had been knitting. She left it all there. She wondered remotely if the fire would make a clean sweep of the island over to Hillside.

Working sure-footedly, sometimes in the dark and sometimes in the light from the fire, she gathered up the laundry basket and some cardboard cartons, and packed into them the things she had thrown out from upstairs. As she knelt by the side of the house, the wind was surprisingly mild in spite of its strength, and here it smelled of spruce and growing grass. The stars were very bright. Tranquilly she stowed things away, wrapping the amber hen and the other dishes in shirts and underwear. When everything was done she went down onto the Campion wharf. Kathy and the children sat on blankets against the side of the fishhouse, the smaller children huddled under her arms like chicks under a hen's wings. Van sat down beside Cindy and took out her cigarettes.

"How's everybody?" she asked.

"Good now," said Kathy. "We were all pretty scared at first, but now that Daddy's over there he'll save the day. The state provided us with those pumps last year."

"What time is it, anyway?" Van asked. "I was asleep when Barry dragged me out of bed."

"It's a little past midnight. I was reading in bed. Johnny wanted a drink, and that's when I saw it, out his window. I got Terence up without any wild screeching, thank goodness, and he took off. Looks as if either Willy or Gina was smoking in bed and fell asleep and dropped a cigarette."

"I'm never going to smoke," said Cindy sternly.

"Excuse me, Madam," said Vanessa, throwing her cigarette overboard. Cindy giggled.

"Of course that house is old and it's tinder-dry. And Cindy, don't you go to school tomorrow and yelp that I said somebody was smoking in bed. It mightn't have been that at all."

"We mightn't have a school," said Cindy. "We mightn't have a house. We might have to take to the boats."

The middle child sniffled loudly. "And we might have to whale the tar out of Cindy," said Kathy. "Why can't you be one of the silent Campions, like your father?"

"How was the meeting?" Van asked. From here you couldn't tell if the fire was working out in back, spreading across toward the Sorensens', or up toward the Percy and Webster houses and thence into the woods that almost enfolded the Fennell house. She neither hoped nor despaired; she felt indifferent as to the course of the fire.

"Oh, it was good, it always is because they're a good bunch. Not a lot of backbiting going on, but fun in our simple way. We missed you." Van didn't comment, and Kathy went on. "Oh, and you know what? Maggie brought Gina along! Nobody knows how she managed it. And she can *knit!* She made a pair of baby's mittens tonight. Never said a word all evening, just knit away like mad. Everybody praised her and she never cracked a smile. She was probably embarrassed."

Or thought she'd burst out laughing, Van reflected. If anybody knits, she's saved. Or sews patchwork with a neat stitch, or nows how to turn a heel. Or reads. It shows she's One of Us. What a nasty fate, to be One of Us, whoever Us turns out to be, I just hope Gina doesn't get to like being praised for knitting baby mittens. No, I don't hope. I don't care.

"Gee, I wonder what Tammie and Diane are doing," said Cindy.

"And Tiger," said the six-year-old boy. "Is he burned up?"

"Of course not!" Cindy cried angrily. "They wouldn't let him be!"

"They're probably all over at Uncle Mark's," said Kathy. "Or even at Uncle Owen's. They've got plenty of extra beds at Hillside." She said to Van, "I guess they had a lovely weekend, from what Laurie said. She was just like a kid, telling about it. She didn't look old enough to have a girl in high school." She didn't need Van to answer, but went back to talking about the meeting. Van could reassure herself that time was passing only by tipping back her head and seeing that Orion had moved. The house across the harbor became a skeleton bathed in gold, and then only the central chimney and a few uprights remained black in the midst of glory.

"I think they've got it," Kathy said, rather quietly for her. "Kept it in one place . . . so far, anyway."

"Somebody's coming," Cindy said. They heard feet running on the boardwalk.

"That's not Terence," said Kathy. "I don't know what would ever make him run. The last trumpet, maybe." The two women sat listening to the drumming footsteps. Van tensed in spite of herself. Then Richard bounded among them and sprawled against a pile of traps, panting dramatically.

"Everybody's all right," he gasped. "They told me to say that the first thing. And—and—"

"Sit down before you die," Kathy said.

"I'm all right too. They said . . . Barry and Terence said . . . for you to—" He hauled in a whooping breath. "Go to bed. They're gonna take turns standing watch the rest of the night. All the men. Aunt Liza and Aunt Jo have got gallons of coffee. My gorry, is this *fun!*" He left at the full gallop.

"Gee, I wish I could go over there," Cindy said. "If it's so much fun."

"You're going to bed, and I'll bet Richard'll be in his bed shortly, too. Come on." Johnny was sleeping and she hoisted him up so that he hung over her shoulder. "Davey, take Van's hand so you won't walk off the edge of the wharf, you're so groggy. Cindy, be careful now. I'll make cocoa for us when we go in."

"Oh, boy!"

"Have some with us, Van," said Kathy.

"No, thanks. I'd better get in all my belongings that I threw out the windows."

Kathy laughed. "All our gear is on the front porch."

"Good night," Van said, letting go Davey's hand at the front steps. A drowsy chorus followed her. She went in and put the teakettle on, then brought in the things and piled them all in the sitting room. Barry had eaten up Kathy's lobster chowder but had left some meatloaf. She made herself a thick sandwich of it and some coffee, and found something to read. She read the first page over and over, eating and drinking steadily.

At half-past two Barry came in, half-swaggering, half-staggering. "You still up, Beautiful?" He leaned against the dresser to get his boots off, scraping one heel over the toe of the other. His words slurred as if he were drunk. He had washed, but he was still sooty in places. "Got any more of that coffee and grub?"

"Sit down, I'll fix something," she said. He sagged into a chair.

"God, I was scared shitless, and I wasn't the only one. Well, the wind's dropping down now, and we'll be getting the dew too. They sent Terence and me home, there's enough of 'em that live around there...." He yawned enormously. "Well, that little bitch really did it up brown tonight. She roasted the goose up proper, she did." He was much amused. "The goose that laid the golden egg. It's now a gone goose. Get it?"

"What little bitch?" She set food before him.

"Gina!" He slapped his palm down on the table. "She did it! Told everybody she did it. Set it on purpose with papers and kerosene, and bawled like a teething kid because it didn't take half the island in a clean sweep."

She sat down opposite him. "Where is she now?"

"Jo and Willy pinned her down after a while. She's up at Sorensens,' in bed, knocked out with about three rum toddies. They didn't have anything else to give her. Kee-rist, she was some wild, running around while we were passing buckets and pumping away, and screeching, 'I did it!' Poor Willy. He was really crying, and no mistake. He kept saying 'She don't mean it, she's sick.' Anybody could take time to say a word, said sure, she was just upset."

"She must hate being in a Bennett house," Van said.

"She ought to, after trying to burn 'em out. Her conscience ought to be giving her conniptions, if she's got one, which I doubt."

"Her big gesture collapsed, and everybody else wins out after all," said Vanessa dreamily.

"What the hell, you sound sorry for her!" He was outraged.

"Somebody ought to."

"Well, sure, if you want to figger she's off her head. But

241

in that case she ought to be locked up. How about another sandwich?"

She made it for him, and then went up to bed.

CHAPTER THIRTY-SIX

Kathy came over as soon as the children went to school. For once her blue eyes were somber. "She might have burned us all out!"

"Maybe that's what she intended to do."

"She couldn't have thought it would go as far as it did! I mean, nobody sets fires to destroy property and maybe lives unless they're crazy or drunk. . . . Or crazy-drunk, and I've seen some of that," she admitted. "Only my father used to throw his ax at anybody that got in his way, not set the house afire. No, she must have been good and mad, and started the fire to scare Willy, and she expected him to put it right out, but something happened. It got away from them."

Van shrugged. "You could be right. What difference does it make? She's made her point."

"That she's a vicious little brat?"

"Oh, it's simple," said Van. "She doesn't like where she is. Maybe Willy'll be fired now, because of having such an unpredictable and dangerous wife."

Kathy was pale. "Whatever it is, she gave me nightmares. I woke up hollering and Terence was trying to shut me up. . . . She must be wishing for a knothole to crawl into this morning. She must be some ashamed of herself, with everybody being so nice and making believe she was just hysterical with fear when she was screeching around last night."

There was no point in saying that Gina probably felt more destructive, if anything. Kathy went home soon, and Van walked round and round through the rooms. Her body felt too strong and full of life for her to go back to bed. It was as if Owen had brought her to the full peak of existence, and then had deserted her with all this strength and spirit moiling in her. She had a sense of precarious-

242

ness, of being so delicately poised that a breath could topple her, but from where and into *what?*

She walked around the harbor to get some food. It was a warm quiet day, cloudy yet luminous. There was no rote, and the birds seemed very loud. Dandelions spattered the well field, and blazed a strong yellow around the black ruins of the burned house with its naked chimney. The charred smell was strong, half-sweet in the still air.

At the store all the talk was of the fire. "If she really did it, she needs her bottom warmed," said Helen Campion indignantly.

"Needs her neck wrung," growled Mark.

"Lord, I was some scared last night," Nora Fennell said. "That was before I found out what she was saying. Then I was mad as well as scared, but Matt said she was most likely thinking of some cigarette she didn't put out, and was scared witless, only he didn't say witless."

"Could have been that," Helen Campion agreed. "But being careless with your smoking is as bad as setting fires deliberate. How is she this morning?"

"Still in bed and very quiet," said Joanna. "I'd say she has a hangover from all that liquor we poured into her last night. Don't you think the state ought to provide us with tranquilizers as well as Indian pumps?"

"The only way to tranquilize that one is with a gun," said Mark, "and Willy'll come to it one day, believe me. Those little fellas take it and take it, and then they explode."

"I hope not," said Nora. "She's not worth prison."

"Poor Willy," Joanna murmured. "He was in a state last night. He kept telling me she didn't know what she was saying."

Van took her mail and groceries and went out, but Joanna caught up with her. "Come on up for a cup of coffee."

"I can't," said Van. "I've got so far behind on my work the house looks like what Barry's aunt used to call a 'lapidated whorehouse.' "

Joanna laughed. "You mean you have girls lying around over there wearing long black stockings and nothing else?"

"I don't know what I'm likely to find when I start digging. They could have materialized off the covers of Barry's magazines."

"Well, be sure to let us all know. We need some sort of

happy change around here." She looked up at the charred ruins. Her face was older this morning than Van had ever seen it, drained of its usual color and vitality. Owen's had been like that down in Ship Cove.

An uneasy silence hung between them until Joanna exclaimed with pleasure and relief, "Oh, here come the kids!"

They were coming along past the harbor beach, Laurie with them, all carrying extra sweaters and jackets. "The Brigport school's invited them over," said Joanna. "They'll go on the mailboat, and then a couple of men will bring them back late this afternoon. Lord, it's nice to think of children at a time like this. Though Gina was one not too long ago," she added cynically. "I keep trying to imagine her a baby, but I can't help thinking she must have been born looking exactly the same, make-up and all, only very small."

The children's noise filled the air like the swallows' chatter. "Don't you wish you were going too?" Laurie asked the women.

"I wish," said Joanna fervently, "that I were going with you and that I were ten years old."

This was acclaimed by the children as great wit. With a little commiserating smile Laurie steered her group toward the wharf. Van was freed from the apathy of the moment.

"Well, I'd better get back to my messy kitchen," she said.

"And the girls," Joanna added, but the effort was obvious.

When Van came to the harbor beach she saw a small figure drooping on the stern of one of the big seine dories at the edge of the marsh. At first she thought it was a child who couldn't go with the others, and then she recognized Gina.

"Hello," she said. "I thought you were in bed."

"I got away while she was out."

"Who?" asked Vanessa perversely.

"Lady Bitchybones. So *kind*. Like she was hiding the straitjacket behind her back." Gina spat into the marsh grass. There was something peculiar about her today, and suddenly Vanessa knew why; she hadn't any make-up. She must have lost her enormous handbag in the fire, along with those great fuzzy sweaters. That must have been a worse blow than losing Willy would have been, Van thought. She sat on the gunnel of the dory and held out her cigarettes to Gina, who took one greedily.

"Why'd you do it?" Van asked her.

"So they'd fire Willy," said Gina candidly. "You know Steve? He's kept Willy on in spite of me. Believe me, I've done plenty to bollix things up. First I wouldn't live at the Eastern End, so they gave Willy a house up here. Then I'd keep Willy up half the night drinking, and trying to pick fights with him, so he'd be so groggy the next morning he couldn't get started to work. But that didn't work because Steve Bennett is next to Jesus, and when he crooks a finger my Willy runs, even if he falls flat on his face. Then he'll crawl on his hands and knees. . . . Then I run off, and I knew Willy'd run after me. And we end up here. But now I've burned up the house and everything in it, and it could have burned off the whole island."

Her small face was transfigured; without the eye make-up her eyes showed a clear brilliant green-blue, as innocent in their joy as Cindy's or Tammie's. "This they can't forgive!"

Van sat looking at her. In herself she felt an enervating dissatisfaction and shame. "If they took you seriously on this you could go to jail," she said. "But at least you've got the guts to grapple with something you hate, and do violence to change it."

"Ayuh," said Gina complacently. "I was born fighting."

"What if you have to go away, but Willy can stay?"

"He won't stay. He's crazier about me than ever. He thinks I need him." She hooted. Van stood up, not knowing if the queasiness she felt was directed at Gina or herself. "I've got work to do," she said.

"They've sucked you in, haven't they?"

Van stopped. "What do you mean by that?"

"I remember you when you first came here!" She was raucous as a crow. "Now look at you. Bird-watching and patchwork. You even dress like them. You could be one of the Bennett women."

Van left her, walking fast, and Gina kept laughing at her all the way across the beach until suddenly the sound stopped. But Van didn't look back to see why.

She washed dishes and cleaned house. Barry came in early and she had a cup of tea with him, not because she wanted it but because her stomach felt hollow. Barry ate a

245

large wedge of Kathy's bread with the inelegant enthusiasm of a growing boy, gulping food down so he could talk between mouthfuls. Van listened to him because she had no world of her own to be lost in. It used to be easy once, over on Water Street, to wander away. But no more.

He was talking about shifting traps, of the habits of lobsters; discussing his work, he was at his most attractive. She nodded from time to time and sipped her tea. Then he went on to talk around the shore. He loved that as much as lobstering. It was a rich part of his life; the visits from fishhouse to fishhouse, the knot of advice-givers huddled over an ailing engine, the arguments in the store, or the quiet unexpected conversation with one man during which something might be said which he would repeat to Vanessa with wonder and awe, giving it some great, almost prophetic significance.

Elbows on the table, she laced her fingers across her forehead and under their shade she stared at the tablecloth. On Jessup's Island the old square table stood by the windows looking seaward. She battled with her anguish, sitting silent, her face shaded by her hands.

"Another chance," Barry was saying. "Can you beat it? Steve Bennett's either a simpleton or a saint. Willy must have talked a blue streak to convince him that little turd-heels would behave herself. . . . Huh?"

"I didn't say anything," she murmured.

"They're all some disgusted, by Judas, I can tell ye. Phil set his jaw some hard when Mark told him. Cap'n Charles looks black as hell. Nobody's heard from Owen yet, but I'll bet he'll go through the sound barrier with a roar that'll break all the windows on Brigport." He laughed merrily. "Rob and Matt ain't going to take it very kindly, I can tell ye, and the rest who was in the path of it last night. . . . Course, they've got to go back to the other house at the Eastern End, there's no house up here for 'em." He went to the dresser and sliced another portion off the loaf. "Dunno how Mrs. Steve'll fancy Gina switching her backside around the dooryard down there, but according to Willy she's real sorry, and she got so scared she's likely to be afraid even to scratch a match again."

She thought of Gina perched on the dory, jeering and exultant. They might as well kill her and be done with it, she thought. They've done the unforgivable. They've forgiven.

"You have to hand it to these Bennetts," Barry said. "They're not only decent, they're *fine* people. The salt of the earth. The rest of 'em don't like Steve being so easy, but it's his decision, so they'll be some nice to Gina. The women'll go call, and give her stuff for the house, and keep on asking her to the sewing circle." He gave her a bright earnest look. "I want you to go and call, Annie. It's the way we do things out here."

"Is it?" she said to the table. "I'll tell you; I'll go when they need somebody to help lay one of them out."

"What in hell does *that* mean?"

"It means that's what all this being forgiven and given another chance by the salt of the earth will lead to. He'll kill her or she'll kill him, and that little fire last night will seem pretty small potatoes alongside it."

He shook his head sadly at her. "You got an awful bitter tongue, Annie. Don't you know that's an awful bad unhealthy way to be?"

"Don't call me Annie. I'm not Annie."

"Have it your own way, dear." He smiled at her. "But try to hold back those words. Don't even think them. Trouble with you is, you never met up with these kind of people before. They're *big*. Nothing mean and petty about 'em, they think big and they act big. Take Cap'n Owen, now. He'll swear like a pirate about this, and call 'em everything he can put tongue to, but he'll be good to 'em. Wait and see."

She heard her voice coming out of the center of the hurricane's eye; she saw the eye, large and yellowish-gray, filling one wall, and her voice came from the pupil as if from a speaker. "Maybe he'll take an interest in Gina, give her a new interest in life, so she'll be contented out here."

"Now look, now look!" He was half-laughing, half-angry. "I called him a wild one, but he's a family man now, and he's not chasing after anything, not that cheap little piece for sure, and not after anything else."

"Maybe he isn't *now*, at this minute," she said, "but you and your holy family! Blessed are the Bennetts and those that suck up to them. You make me laugh, you're such a bloody fool about them." She got up. She could still see the eye. It occurred to her that it was her own eye. "You wouldn't believe that one of them came whoring into this kitchen after me, would you?"

He didn't move. He sat with bread in one hand and mug in the other, his stare a shiny metallic blue. "I warned you about that tongue of yours," he said after a moment. "That's a goddam filthy way to talk, lying like that. What if somebody heard you?"

"I want somebody to hear me." she said. "You." She held onto the back of her chair and went on talking at him. "I'm not lying. A Bennett came whoring after me and I went whoring after him. Simple. One and one makes two."

He stood up. His tan had turned putty-colored, and his lips so pale he didn't seem to have any. He leaned across the table toward her. "You're lying, goddam it to hell. You're back in your old crazy ways, only this is worse, because you didn't bother to lie then. You're trying to turn me against 'em because you know I'm happy here." His eyes flooded. "Damn you, admit you're lying!"

"I am not lying," she said carefully. "The man was Owen, but don't worry, we never did anything in this house. It was always outside somewhere. Thank God his wife's the schoolteacher."

He fell back into the chair rather than sat. His hands were trembling. "You're lying, aren't ye? You're fed up here. This going to bed and staying, I should've known. That's it, isn't it?"

"No, that isn't it. I'm not lying, I told you. He walked in while you were out of the house, and he didn't have to say what he came for. He made it clear enough."

"And you went with him?" His mouth shook.

"Not then. Remember the dance? Remember he left early?"

He was nodding in a kind of palsy. She said, "I've never been able to find the place in the woods where we went. . . . Remember the toothache I had?"

He leaped up, the chair fell backward, and he lunged across the table, knocking over the mugs. "Shut up, shut up! I don't want to hear any more! I don't believe it anyway!" He was half-sobbing. "Jesus, why do you—you've *been* with him? More than once?"

"More than once."

"And I have to beg for it. All this time it's like you're doing me a favor, but *he* walks in and—the bastard—" He went off into a long frantic stream of profanity in a cracked and breathless voice. She stood against the refrigerator, watching and listening in awe at what she had done. He pounded his fists on the table and went on swearing. Suddenly he dropped back into his chair and said lucidly, but in a voice thickened as if with long weeping, "When I married you they said you'd destroy me. And they been waiting for it. Well, by God, I'll do a little destroying of my own so I won't go down alone."

"Are you going to kill me?" she asked as if merely interested.

"No," he said. "I'm going to kill the whoremaster who came in and busted up my home. It wasn't much of a home, but it was getting to be better. No, I ain't killing you. I figger you don't know right from wrong the way you should, never having a mother and all. But he's a Bennett! He's got no call to bust in and steal another man's woman."

"He didn't lug me off and rape me."

"It's the same thing. He come in and dazzled you. He's one of the big Bennetts. Big in every way, huh?" He leered. "Worth laying down for? Better than little old Barry? Well, we'll see who's better now."

He went into the sitting room and she heard him lift the rifle down. "You've got no shells," she called.

"Who said so?" He came out carrying it and laid it on the table between them. His face was now very red. "You don't know everything about me." He started for the stairs, then came back and picked up the rifle, giving her a crafty smile. "I'd better take good care of my old friend here. You're likely to heave her overboard while my back's turned. Don't want me to shoot your fancy man, do ye?"

"He's not my fancy man," she said wearily. "It's over. I only told you so you'd know they were people, not gods. The way you worship them turns my stomach."

"Ayuh? Well, my stomach's turned now."

"So much that you'd kill somebody and go to Thomaston for life?"

"It'll be easier than living in the same world with you and him, knowing he's touched you and you liked it. You're *my* wife! When you told me I had to marry you I was glad and proud. Even when I found out there wasn't any kid, I figgered, well, I had you, and never mind what the rest of 'em said. And sure, I know you didn't want me to touch you, plenty of times, but one thing I could always brag about when somebody give me a sad story about his wife getting it somewhere else—I was sure of you. You had class. Now it turns out you just couldn't find anybody you thought was good enough for you. Till you met up with the Bennetts."

He ran up the stairs and she heard him slamming around in his room. Then there was quiet, and she heard the tiny clicking sounds that went with filling the clip, sliding it into the rifle, and jacking a shell into the chamber. All at once the whole business became real; it was entirely possible that he would do what he set out to do.

She slid out the back door just as he came down the stairs again, and dived like a seal through the alders. Where was Kathy all this time? If she saw Barry with the gun, looking as he did, she'd forget about Gina soon enough, and the whole thing would be out. She shut her eyes for a moment, until Barry shouted "Hey!" from somewhere behind her. Then she ran again, finding the track among the thin growth of spruces, remembering thankfully that Laurie and the schoolchildren were at Brigport.

Out in the field the path was a pale streak diagonally crossing toward the barn at Hillside. If Helen Campion should look out her pantry window now she'll have a shock, she thought. The rites of spring on Bennett's Island. Sacred fires last night and human sacrifice today. She kept running and Barry ran behind her, shouting. She didn't get any of the words as they came in fragments like showers of pebbles flung hard.

At the corner of the barn her aching lungs and burning throat stopped her. She waited for him there, leaning against the old shingles. The day was gray but over-warm, and she wanted to lie down in the lush cool grass and never get up again.

"Trying to warn him, huh?" Barry said.

"I don't want him, I told you. And neither of us is worth your going to prison for. Barry, I'm sorry," she said tiredly. "I'm sorry for all the bad ways I've been to you. Let's go home."

"You still don't get it, do ye?" he asked with patronizing patience. "He's touched you. He's had you. I'm going to kill him."

"You're not a killer, Barry."

"You don't know what I am," he told her with that smile, and she was forced to agree. The only thing to do was to try to keep ahead of him; if Owen wasn't in the house, he'd be at the fishhouse, and if he was on his way around to the harbor in his boat Barry might work off his insanity before he could run Owen down. The thought that he might work it off on her was a refreshing one. She was so tired, she could ask for nothing better than oblivion, short and sweet, in the back of the head. To fall into the thick grass and stay.

She began to walk around the barn. They didn't have cows now, but chickens scattered away from her with an exasperated clucking. Two large cats watched, unstartled, from the open barn door. Against the woods a large vegetable garden had been started, and all along the back of the long white house there were early daffodils and tulips. The yard lay in silence except for the talk of the chickens as Barry, coming behind her, dispersed them again.

She had never been here. This was where he was father and husband, the stranger. She stood staring at the white clapboards, trying to think. She had not seen him face to face since the day at Ship Cove, and now her mouth dried not only with fear but with an anticipation that had nothing to do with Barry and the gun, or anything else that had happened this afternoon. Barry came up beside her and said breathily, "He can't lay you when he's dead."

Without looking at him, still staring at the house, she said, "Barry, it was hardly anything. It would never happen again. It wasn't anything we'd want to keep going." But she knew that the words were wrong, the "we" lacerated him deeply.

"Owen!" he bawled at the house. "Come out here!"

She wanted to cry, "No, stay in!" but she couldn't raise her voice. Could she turn to Barry now, cry, abase herself, hug his knees, beg him to drop the gun? Would the granting of this give him enough self-esteem to last his lifetime? There was no time to find out. Owen appeared at the screen door of the ell. He had a glass in his hand.

"Well, well," he said, coming out. He squinted at Barry and the rifle. Then he swallowed something he had in his hand, drank from the glass and set it down on the doorstep, and came across the grass to them.

"I'm going to kill you, Cap'n Owen," Barry said. He had begun to tremble as if with chills.

"What for?"

"You know. She told me."

"That so?" He lifted an eyebrow toward Van. "Chatterbox, isn't she? Go home, Barry. You like it here, you make money. I'm not worth half a life in state prison, and neither is she. She'd still be out and you'd be in. So who wins?"

"But you wouldn't be walking this earth, you fornicating son of a bitch. I'd wake up laughing at that every day. Prison'd be worth it. And she could think how you looked lying dead, and how *she* really did it because she told me." His laughter cracked. "And I wouldn't believe her at first! I kept begging, pleading with her to say she was lying. I never thought a Bennett would do anything like that, see?" He shifted the gun around, cradling it in his arm, and released the safety.

"You forget something, son," said Owen. "I've not admitted anything yet. She could be lying in her teeth."

Van could feel the waves of uncertainty that stopped Barry, and the passion of his longing to believe she had lied. She looked past the men, on by the syringa and lilacs past the corner of the house, down the road toward the schoolhouse. The yard was empty, and the flag hung limp from the pole under a heavy sky.

"They're coming back," she lied. Both men looked quickly that way. She grabbed the rifle barrel and thrust it up. Barry resisted at once, and the gun fired, the shot going toward the roof of the house. A gull flapped away from the chimney with an offended squawk. As Van and Barry struggled with the rifle between them, their faces close together in a deadly intimacy, she thought how strange his looked, contorted into a sort of frozen leer. Neither spoke. He was stronger, and suddenly he wrenched the rifle away from her; but as he did so, Owen reached them and swept her away with one arm. He knocked Barry down, the rifle flew out of his hands, and he collapsed in the grass, over on his side and unconscious. Owen picked up the rifle, took out the clip, and put it in his pocket.

Vanessa walked away around the far corner of the house, facing the sea. She wished she could keep on going, out over the end of Windward Point, but instead she had to lean against the clapboards and concentrate on not vomiting. Owen came up behind her.

"Why did you tell him?" he asked very quietly.

252

"Why do you think? He worships you all, he goes on and on. And I—I can't get away!" She was going to blubber without shame, she thought. "I tried to get him to shoot *me*. He wouldn't. Nothing works."

He took her by the shoulders and turned her to him, holding her off and looking into her face, not angrily but with a deep-seamed tiredness that she couldn't bear as well as she could have endured rage. "I don't want you to die," he said. "You're young. No matter what you think, you've got a life."

"I had a life for a few weeks. You were it. Oh, damn my nose." He let go with one hand and pulled out a handkerchief. She grabbed it fiercely and mopped her eyes and blew her nose. "He's right. All he says about the Bennetts. . . . I mean about you. There couldn't be anyone else after you. I've had my life and it's over, it ends the way I got it, with nothing." She sounded as tired as he looked, she couldn't have screamed or raged because there was nothing left to do with it. "I didn't tell him anything about us. The island up there, and about—" She had no words. "Oh, about anything *real*. I made him think it was just something cheap and fly-by-night. He was going on about how perfect you all were. I had to shut him up somehow. And now he thinks I'm a tramp, but I don't care."

They both leaned wearily against the house. The eastern sea was a solid gray mass, but somewhere Jessup's Island floated in a globe of summertime; the birds would eat the field strawberries as they ripened. Suddenly a gasping cry was wrung from her. "I don't want *you* to die! I thought at first if I couldn't have you I didn't want her to have you either, but she can have you if you'll just stay alive. I can't stand to think of you dead."

"Nor I you," he said. "So don't do it."

"I won't," she promised. She put her hand on his face. "And you be careful. Don't go getting reckless and trying to speed things up."

He lowered his head quickly and made a muffled sound in his throat. She felt his mouth against her fingers and then, as if they had both heard the shuffling footsteps in the grass, they were standing apart when Barry came unsteadily around the corner. He looked at them from watery, bloodshot eyes, supporting himself with a hand against the wall.

"Are you ready to go home?" she asked him in a flat tone.

"*You!*—the both of ye—" He began to swear again, and Owen cut that off.

"Look," he said. "Nobody but us three has to know what went on here this afternoon. Sure, it's hell, but it's not the first time it's happened to anybody and it's not the last, and folks manage to survive. You can go home, and tomorrow we'll act like it never happened. Ten years from now you'll be sure it never happened. You'll have a kid or two in the school and a big boat in the harbor, and today'll be a bad dream."

"You mean if I crawl on my knees to you like that poor fool Willy and apologize for myself and my slut of a wife, I can stay?"

"Philip's the only one who can fire you." She had never known him to be so quiet. She remembered that he had swallowed something as he came out to them, and she wondered if he were feeling those warning sensations in his chest and arm; if this afternoon killed him, her promise wouldn't be binding any more. She stood apart from the men and stared at that thick motionless sea. "Your wife's not a slut and don't ever call her that again where I can hear you. . . . You don't owe any apologies. It's the other way around. *I* apologize. That suit ye? Now, by God, the both of you put for home, and the next time I think I see a good thing, I'll make damn' sure she knows how to keep her mouth shut."

"Ayuh, you didn't make much a fetch of it this time, Cap'n Owen. Didn't show much sense." There was a tremor in his blurred voice; he was beginning to weaken, to be won again. She knew it with neither relief nor disgust, only exhaustion. In time he would forgive her; it would come all the more quickly because a Bennett was involved. "Well, I'll get my shooting iron and go home," said Barry. "But by Jesus nobody'll knock it out of my hand the next time. I'll lay in the bushes and pick the pimp off when he goes by, whoever he is. You hear that, Annie?"

She didn't answer. "She's right, she ain't worth going to Thomaston for," he said almost jauntily. "But I married her, and if I hadn't got kicked out of my own home for it, I'd never have ended up out here. And I figger on staying, even if I have to lock her in when I go to haul."

Neither spoke. She thought, He thinks we're standing here humbly before him, ashamed and foolish. Well, I suppose it's owed him. She began to walk away, out around Barry and across the yard toward the barn. Under the low cloud ceiling there was a magnified beat of engines coming up Long Cove, and children's voices raised above them.

She knew without looking around that Barry was following her, and she wondered if Owen were standing by the house watching them go, or if he had already gone inside or down toward his workshop. The desire to look back almost overcame her, but she kept on around the barn and found the path across the field.

One thing she knew; she was more tired than she had ever been in her life, but in all this it had not once occurred to her that her mind might fly apart. I'll never go insane, she thought. Even if I wanted to, even if it was the only way out, it would never happen, and it was never about to happen. Whatever became of my mother doesn't touch me. She left me because she was scared or silly, maybe a mean little imbecile like Gina or a sweet and trusting one, and she was wiped out years ago like a kitten crossing a highway. A child who never lived to be as old as her daughter was now.

Suddenly Van's stomach sucked in on a great shuddering breath, but she quickly expelled the air and forced herself to breathe more naturally. At last I'm free, she thought with either grief or irony, she didn't know which.

As she crossed the yard, Barry came through the break in the alders behind her. She pretended to feel the dish towels hung on the line, and he went on into the house. She was alone for this few minutes. She, Anna Howard. *You're young, you have a life,* he had told her, and she had answered, *I had a life and you were it.* They were both right. The agony of the truth struck her again so that she almost staggered, and agony at once took on forever the texture of a linen dish towel, natural-colored, edged in blue.

Then as a gay burst of voices sounded on the boardwalk beyond the Campions', she unpinned the towels and began to fold them with neat housewifely motions. It was a curious thing, she reflected, that in all the disguises The Day had taken she had never guessed until now what its true face would be.

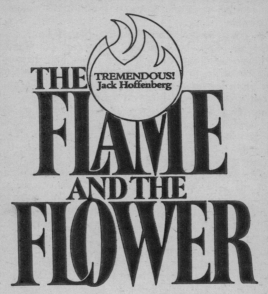
THE FLAME AND THE FLOWER

TREMENDOUS!
Jack Hoffenberg

KATHLEEN E. WOODIWISS

J122 $1.50

THE TRULY MAGNIFICENT
ROMANTIC NOVEL WHICH
ALREADY HAS OVER 600,000
COPIES IN PRINT!